CHAMPIONS OF NOWHERE

a

MIKEHALLOWSEVE

publication

A NOTE ON THE FORGOTTEN COUNTIES

In the southeastern corner of the state
of Oklahoma, strange phenomena and
supernatural occurences take place
unbeknownst to the wider world.
What follows is my attempt to record
those events, one tale at a time.

THE FORGOTTEN COUNTIES

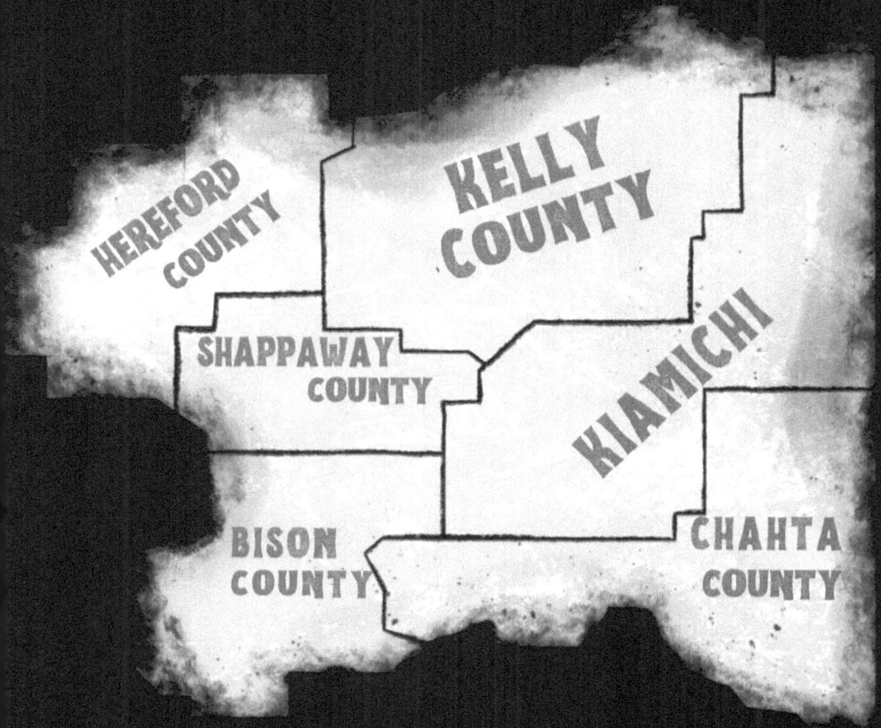

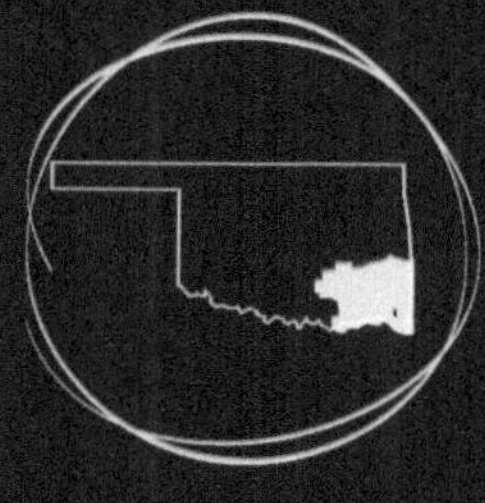

CHAMPIONS OF NOWHERE

A TALE FROM THE FORGOTTEN COUNTIES

Michael Hallows

For those in the middle of nowhere

CONTENTS

2003-2004 NOWHERE DEVILS ROSTER

Kelvin Harris

Logan Tramer

Alex Spruce

Doug Mooreland

Marshal Lovegood

Tim Springer

Mikey Spruce

Sam Turner

Dylan Lovegood

Jack Ward

ONE

THE KITCHEN WELL

1

A LEG WASN'T SUPPOSED to bend like that. After setting one of the best screens of his basketball career, Logan Tramer watched Kelvin float through the air, like he had a hundred times before, and land on one leg, which decided to not support his weight tonight. But he didn't roll an ankle like one might expect. His leg folded backward, bone jutting out below his calf muscle and pointing toward the guilty party. It was a hell of a screen.

A leg isn't supposed to bend like that. It was the first thought Logan had, followed by, *It's over.* The season. Kelvin's basketball career. All of it.

It was Senior Night, the final regular season game for the Nowhere Devils. Logan had no delusions of playing organized basketball after this and had been quite aware of all the "last" moments of his senior year: last Homecoming game, last midseason Red Dirt Tournament, last run at the title which had eluded them the previous three seasons.

But tonight was a first.

Kelvin had fallen awkwardly plenty of times before and

always popped back up. No doubt most of the crowd was expecting that tonight, readying a sigh of relief, like they had the previous times he had fallen. But this was different, and the crowd sensed it. They collectively forgot how to breathe in a humming silence.

Most everyone on the court had been watching the ball's trajectory to the hoop or positioning themselves for a rebound. One of the two referees, history teacher Larry Tune, had seen the injury. He blew his whistle and kept blowing it like he had forgotten he was doing so.

An hour ago, the four seniors on the team had been standing next to their parents, taking pictures. Logan had handed his mom, Janice Horn, a rose and kissed her on the cheek. She wore a scarlet floral dress tonight to match the school colors, but Logan overheard someone from the crowd say she was trying to win herself a new husband.

Tim Springer was also there with a single parent. He had put an arm around his father, Red Springer, who was about twenty years older than everyone else's parents. Alex Spruce stood between his mom and dad, Joanna and Rob Spruce, the latter of whom looked much less athletic these days than when he had been the best player on the 1979 Nowhere Devils, who made it to the Area finals, one win short of the STATE TOURNA-MENT. Kelvin was between his parents, Wendall and Belinda Harris, a few inches taller than both. Neither of them had played sports.

Logan couldn't be sure if Kelvin's parents had seen the injury or not. Either way, they rushed to the court as soon as their son fell. Logan was at his best friend's side before anyone. He crouched on both knees and took Kelvin's hand. He squeezed it and peered down at the leg. It lay limp, turned the wrong direction, toes glued to the court while his other leg spasmed uncontrollably.

"Don't touch it," Logan said when Kelvin grasped at his knee, dragging his fingers closer to the lower-leg injury. "Don't even look at it."

"I'm done, I'm done," Kelvin repeated.

"You're gonna be fine," Logan lied.

The coaches and Kelvin's parents soon huddled around the star player like they were starting a prayer circle. Others made their way to the court. There were no athletic trainers in Class B basketball, no medical professionals to gape at the injury. The coaches had some basic CPR training, but the most they could do in this scenario was instruct everyone to keep their distance.

Logan's sister, Emily, dropped to Kelvin's other side. The two had been dating for six weeks and seemed in love enough for Logan to feel like he didn't belong beside Kelvin, holding his hand, like he was interrupting the end of a Shakespearean tragedy. But he had been there first, and Kelvin wasn't loosening his grip.

Emily dabbed at her eyes to keep her tears from smearing her makeup. Logan didn't judge her for it. You had to control what you could. It wasn't like they would be able to magically heal the leg. The more Logan stared at it, the less his mind could make sense of it until eventually, the sight broke his mind. Suddenly, the leg looked like it belonged that way, like this was fate.

2

It took the ambulance nearly an hour to get to the gym from Holdendecker. Apparently, Friday the 13th in February of 2004 had been a busy one: An elderly woman at Hurst Manor passed away; someone dragging Main Street had hit a guy on a bike, who was headed home from his shift at Subway; and a man at the Choctaw Nation's income-based complex was stabbed when he broke into a house, thinking the tenant—his cousin—was at the Nowhere game, but his cousin had stayed home with a cold.

By the time the ambulance arrived at the packed gym in the country community of Nowhere, everyone was arguing. Every parent's Sunday best, which they had worn for Senior Night, was disheveled. Roses had been left behind on the bleachers or trampled on the court.

After the first fifteen minutes, when they learned it would be a while before an ambulance arrived, the refs called the game for Nowhere because they were up twenty with two minutes left. No one left the gym. Some gawked, some cried, and most split into two camps. Even fans from the opposing team, the Mutton Rams, had entered the debate.

Some, including Kelvin's father, Wendall, wanted to carry Kelvin out of there and rush him to the hospital. Not the Holdendecker hospital—their lone doctor was a loon—but the one in Arrow, a college town about forty-five minutes away. The other half, which included Coach Park and Coach Reed—who were rumored to be having an affair—as well as Kelvin's mother, Belinda, wanted to stay put.

The debate between Kelvin's parents was the most awkward part about it. Their vitriol seemed too intimate for the setting. They argued like two people on the verge of divorce, even though the Harrises were Jehovah's Witnesses and divorce would never be on the table. It was simply the fact the two had never encountered this level of stress.

They could handle coyotes going after their chickens or a cow having a difficult calf birth. But here, they were helpless, their son, idle, in the worst moment of his young life. It was no wonder Wendall wanted to transport him to Arrow himself; he hated seeing his son like that. It was also understandable why Belinda didn't want to move him. Her boy appeared so frail, like if they lifted him, his broken leg would remain glued to the floor, tearing away the flesh from his bones in a horrific self-amputation.

Kelvin seemed unaware his parents were fighting or of anyone else who had courageously entered the debate. He muttered to himself. A towel was spread across his face, like he was about to be waterboarded. Logan listened intently but couldn't make out what he was saying.

His teammates squatted close by. Marshal put an arm around Emily, consoling her, while Alex and Doug held their faces in their hands and leaned by the crooked leg. Tim cracked jokes with the underclassmen nearby, putting them at ease. Logan doubted the young players had ever seen anything like this.

You haven't either, he reminded himself. Logan didn't want to look at the leg anymore. It only made him feel guiltier. He had already taken a moment to apologize to Kelvin.

Before Emily had slid down on his other side, Logan squeezed Kelvin's hand and whispered, "I'm sorry, man. Yo. I'm sorry."

Kelvin had said nothing. He hadn't even acted like he heard Logan's apology. It wasn't until after the moment that Logan realized he had put certain expectations on it. He was disappointed Kelvin didn't look at him and say, "It's all right, man. You didn't do anything wrong."

Even if it wasn't true, it would have felt good to be let off the hook. Instead, Kelvin wasn't even on this planet right now. His adrenaline had not only numbed him to the pain of a shin snapped in two but had sent him away to a land where it was only his face soaring beneath a sweaty hand towel.

Logan wished he could float away too.

3

On Valentine's Day, Logan went to work at Wheelman's Drive Up in Holdendecker. He was the only one of his teammates who held a steady job during the season. Tim had had a job there freshman year, before Logan had even moved to Nowhere, but he hadn't lasted more than a month.

Coach Park didn't like his starting center insisting on working during the season, but for Logan, Wheelman's was a reprieve. Without it, he wasn't sure how he would handle the pressure of being the number one ranked team. Before Kelvin's injury, the expectations for this season had been the highest ever for any school in any sport in Shappaway County.

Logan had moved to Nowhere the second semester of his freshman year and had immediately done two things: He joined the basketball team—and spent most of that half-year on the bench as the backup center—and he got a job at Wheelman's Drive Up. Both had remained important to him, but in the twenty-four hours since Kelvin's injury, his misery had propelled basketball into the only thing that mattered. He could barely focus on his work.

The area between his ribs, where the defender's elbow had jammed Logan when he set the screen, freeing up Kelvin, still ached. There was a dull throb in his kneecap too. When the defender knocked knees with him, it had sent an immediate jolt up his body, but Logan hadn't flinched. Wincing could make the referee blow their whistle if they were an asshole.

Logan didn't know who the second ref was, but Mr. Tune was *definitely* an asshole. He remained rooted, giving Mr. Tune no reason to call a moving screen. The defender wrestled around him but was too late.

Logan's screens and Kelvin's shots had a symbiotic relationship. How many times had he freed up the star player this season?

The pick-and-roll was Nowhere's best offense. Logan was better at setting screens than anything else, even rebounding, because despite being the strongest and tallest guy on the court, he was clumsy, and his hands were slippery. Of all the great skills Kelvin had, his most impressive was getting the ball to Logan in the perfect spot, where he could clasp his baseball mitts around it without turning it over.

But screens? By this year, Logan had perfected the art. Still, this particular screen had been the best of the best.

And now, he wished he *had* flinched. The ref might have called an offensive foul, and Kelvin would have never left his feet. Logan wondered if there were other dimensions where it had played out differently or if this was all that was ever destined to occur. He skewed toward the latter, not because he was a realist, but because of his aunt, Jocelyn Horn.

Logan hadn't given her any thought until this morning when he woke up. Her team, the Green River Lady Bullfrogs, had been the 1990 Class B Girls State Champions.

A flash of her basketball photo came to mind. It was the only way he envisioned his aunt: his age, down on one knee in her uniform, the ball palmed against the court, a cocky smile that still managed to make you like her. He wondered if he pictured the image because she had been in his dream, but he had no memory of dreaming. Logan was surprised he had slept at all.

Like every Saturday, he stood over the grill. Those nights were just as busy as Half-Price Burger Night on Wednesdays. He filled the entirety of the hot surface with frozen patties and the occasional chicken breast and listened to them sizzle. Grease caked his face, and heat seeped through his pores. He wore a hand towel around his neck with which to wipe the sweat from his nose before it dripped onto the patties. Logan flipped the burger meat but never pressed down with the spatula—the juicier, the better.

Will Roebuck rapidly prepped the fixings on the buns, but their shift manager, Larry Unders, hopped in there when he thought Will wasn't fast enough.

"I've got it, asshole," Will would say, and Larry would respond, "If this is getting it, I'd hate to see how you handle your pecker when you got to take a leak."

Will relented at the dress station and tossed buns through the rolling toaster. He begrudgingly marveled at Larry's speed at doctoring the bottom bun with mayonnaise or mustard, then tossing on lettuce, tomato, onion, and pickle. Unlike Burger Night, there were plenty of coney orders and chicken dinners, so they scheduled Melinda to man the hotdog station and Bird on the fryer station.

An extra carhop stayed at the answering station. Because she had no Valentine's Day plans, it was Jessica Fromm, another senior from Nowhere. Logan was quite aware of her presence. He glanced at the way she leaned lazily on the station, her breasts pressed against the machine, covering the bottom row of buttons—which was all right because no one ordered from the bottom row. She pressed the side button when folks were ready to order from their stall and spoke into a headset too big for her head. She yawned between orders and rubbed her rheumy eyes, obviously tired from all the fighting with her ex, Holdendecker's best player, senior Tom Bomber. He was good but no Kelvin, and Holdendecker was a .500 team in Class 2A, not the juggernaut Nowhere were in Class B. *Until now...*

"Hell of a Senior Night," Bird said from beside the fryer during a rare lull.

"That good?" Melinda asked.

"Are you kidding?"

"What? You know I never watch the games."

"You got your priorities wrong, then."

"You mean raising my four kids should come second to basketball?"

"Hey, I got two kids of my own, and I make it to the games."

"That's because it's two kids you never see."

"Ain't my fault their mom's a bitch."

Melinda grabbed a warm hotdog from the rolling grill and threw it at Bird. It smacked him in the chest, leaving a footlong grease stain. There had been a bit of a "will they, won't they" between Melinda and Bird since he had moved to the night shift, and it often involved food being thrown around the kitchen.

"What the hell?" he said.

"Never call the mother of your children a bitch."

"You don't know her, Mel."

"And you don't know what it's like to push a bowling bowl out your vagina."

"Don't put pictures in my head, sexy."

"Can we focus on these orders?" Larry gave the dress station back to Will and rounded the corner to bag food at the "Order Up" station which was next to the answering station, dividing the front half, where the carhops handled drinks and ice cream orders and taking food to cars, and the kitchen. "Y'all better not mess up my time." Larry had the best stats of any shift manager.

"Oh shit." Bird rushed to throw an order of mozzarella sticks he hadn't seen come in into the fryer.

Usually, whoever worked the answering station would holler out sides, like mozzarella sticks, but Jessica did the bare minimum, still leaning, still depressed.

"I still don't know what happened on Senior Night," Melinda said.

"Kelvin got hurt," Logan replied.

"Belinda's boy?"

Bird guffawed. "*'Belinda's boy?'* You know Kelvin's the best player in the state, right?"

"I changed that boy's diapers back in the day."

"Well, he probably could have used a change of underwear last night," Will said. "He broke his fucking leg. It was gnarly."

Logan flipped the patties. The grease popped, snipping at his skin and leaving little red marks.

"I ain't never seen anything like it," Bird said. "Almost upchucked my nachos."

"So much for that championship, huh, Tramer?" Will smirked but didn't make eye contact, which was his cowardly shit-talking way.

Logan wished he had. He might have slapped his coworker across the face with the spatula.

Will Roebuck was one of the few guys in Nowhere who didn't play basketball or go to Vo-Tech. Everyone else was involved in one or the other—or if you were Tim Springer, you did both. Will worked long shifts every Saturday and Sunday and as many weeknights as he could. He had a lot of money to blow on Xbox games and his decked-out Camaro.

Logan remained apathetic toward Will most of the time but outright hated him when Will started talking shit.

The two had hung out a few times. Logan and some of his teammates would go to *Halo* LAN parties at Will's house. And once, they watched one of Will's dad's DVDs—a porn parody of *Lord of the Rings* called *Lord of the G-String*. Not before nor since had Logan watched a porno with someone.

The two of them had laughed while they watched it— surprisingly, the plot followed *The Fellowship of the Ring* closely—but Logan could feel himself growing in his basket- ball shorts and was embarrassed by it, thankful they were in the dark. In his peripheral, he noticed Will scratching his crotch and wondered if Will was playing with himself. Luckily, the scratching didn't continue. At least, he didn't think so. Logan stared at the screen, his eyes bloodshot and aching by the end.

He never spent the night at Will's house again, and they barely talked at school once Logan started hanging out with the team. These days, Will did most his shit-talking on the subject of the Nowhere Devils. It came from a place of jealousy, but after what had happened to Kelvin, Logan couldn't brush it off.

Before he retorted, Larry chimed in on the team's behalf. Good thing too. As loose as things got at Wheelman's, Logan still might have lost his job had he ripped Will's ear off with his tongs.

"They can still win it all," Larry said. "Takes more than one person to make a team."

"It's not over until it's over," Logan agreed. He didn't want to talk about the game or his team, not with his coworkers. Wheelman's was supposed to be his escape from basketball, one he really needed right now, when all his mind wanted to do was replay the injury over and over again.

"You know what you could do." Bird pulled the fryer basket with the mozzarella sticks out of the grease. "You could go to the wishing well."

"Don't listen to him," Melinda said. "He's killed every brain cell he's got, and all that's left is his superstitious bullshit."

"No, I know," Logan said. "I've been there."

"What well?" Will asked.

"You ain't heard of it?" Bird turned to Will. "It's out by Nowhere."

Logan wasn't surprised. Will had lived in Nowhere his whole life but never left his house except for school and work and to hate-watch the Nowhere Devils. The well was one of those places you had to be invited to, and no one invited Will Roebuck to anything.

"There's this abandoned house down Snakeback Road," Logan said. "In the kitchen, there's a well. Supposedly, you can—"

"In the *what*? There's a *what*?"

"It's not that uncommon," Jessica said from where she had been listening at the answering station. "Back in the day, lots of houses had water wells in the kitchen."

"And at this one," Bird added, "you shout your wish down the well. If you hear it echo back towards you, the wish comes true."

"You're more likely to stab yourself with a broken needle," Melinda said, "than see a wish come true."

Logan knew she was right from experience, but he didn't say anything. He and his teammates had gone to the abandoned house two different times, including last year, when they had wished to win the STATE CHAMPIONSHIP.

The Basketball Gods had had other plans.

In the championship game against West Mann, Logan had battled inside with their best player, Daryl Roper, holding him to six points and four rebounds. But that night, their guards hit every three they put up. Even so, Kelvin had kept Nowhere in the game.

The two teams went bucket for bucket until the final minute, when West Mann triple-teamed Kelvin, and Marshal, Doug, and Alex missed every shot. With thirty seconds left, Logan clamored for an offensive rebound but missed the putback to tie the game. The Devils had intentionally fouled until the final buzzer saw them lose by six points.

Logan had dragged his feet across center court with his head down. He didn't notice the West Mann bench storm the hardwood, where it was customary to dogpile at center court.

Despite being the tallest guy out there, Logan was trampled by the excited 2003 champs. At the bottom of their pile, hands gripped him, and the smell of B.O. was repulsive. Boys he didn't know shrieked in his ear. Their exuberance hit him vicariously. He wanted to experience it for himself more than anything.

"Maybe I'll go check it out," Will said.

"You should," Bird agreed, "and make a wish for the team while you're at it."

"Fuck that. That's the last thing I would wish for."

"We don't need magic wishes," Logan said. "It'll be tough without Kelvin. No doubt. But we can band together and win it." He thought about his aunt. "It's happened for other teams. It can happen for us."

Will snorted. "Are you gonna start putting up thirty and ten every night, Shaq?"

Logan wiped the sweat from his face and took as deep a breath as he could manage over the hot grill. "Let's go tonight," he said to Will. "You and me. I'll show you where the house is, and you can wish for whatever you want."

Will looked skeptical. "Don't you good boys have a curfew or some shit?"

"You want to go or not?"

Will laughed it off, but his eyes gave him away. "Sure, whatever."

"Watch out for creeps," Melinda said.

4

Logan led the way, with Will's Camaro close behind him—too close. His headlights glowed brightly in Logan's rearview mirror. Will's car was much nicer than the old Ford he drove, and Logan didn't have insurance. The last thing he needed was the Camaro rear-ending him and fighting Will over who was at fault. Then he might really go through with murdering his coworker.

They exited the highway and turned onto Snakeback Road. The curves of the dirt road turned so narrowly and sharply, the road almost disappeared entirely, overtaken by the thick brush on both sides. At night, Snakeback Road seemed even more perilous. Logan drove with confidence, though. He had taken the route plenty of times. This was the way to Marshal Lovegood's house and a shortcut to Turner's barn, where parties were being thrown every weekend.

This weekend was no exception. Tim had called him on his landline that morning to see if he was going to Turner's barn tonight. Logan couldn't believe there was going to be a party after what had happened to Kelvin.

"We won, didn't we?" Tim said. He was never shaken by anything. Not even the most gruesome thing any of them had ever seen.

Logan was envious. He wished he could brush aside Kelvin's injury. At least the trip to the kitchen well would distract him. He wasn't quite sure what the plan was. Logan wasn't a mean or vindictive person, but he'd had enough of Will's shit-talking. His patience had worn out; he was tired of pretending nothing bothered him.

It wasn't long before his headlights reflected in the remaining windows of the house. He turned down what used to be the driveway but was now an overgrown grassy path through the trees. Tall pines surrounded the little house. Roots protruded from the earth, some twisting beneath and making the structure lopsided. Vines crawled up the busted siding. Some windows were spiderwebbed, while others had the glass completely blown out. All that remained of the entrance was the screen door, its broken latch dangling from the doorframe.

Logan remembered many of these details from the first time

he had come out here during daylight. The second visit, they had intentionally come after dark to scare Doug. He was a devout Christian and believed angels and demons were everywhere, engaging in a spiritual battle. Doug refused to go into the house, so Alex stayed outside with him while Logan and Kelvin went to make the wish.

They did it just the way the old legend instructed. Logan shouted, "I wish we were champs," down into the hole, and his own voice echoed toward him. He hadn't really believed it would work, but there had always been a superstitious part of him which believed in the meddling of the Basketball Gods. So why not a magic wishing well?

Now he knew better; Will didn't.

"Gnarly," Will said when they exited their vehicles.

Logan had a tiny flashlight on his keychain, and he beamed the small light onto the house. It was a pitch-black February night. Below freezing, as it had been much of the month so far. Two weeks ago, the electricity had been knocked out across Nowhere by freezing rain and hadn't come back on for five days. Logan had spent much of that time at Kelvin's house because the Harrises had a generator.

Those five days had been a blast; it was the most time the two had spent together since Kelvin started dating Emily. Logan didn't like his best friend dating his sister. Of course, his feelings about it seemed insignificant now compared to Kelvin's life being turned inside out. He wondered if North Texas had already revoked his basketball scholarship.

"Pretty creepy, isn't it?" he said.

"Are you scared, Tramer?"

"Fuck off. I'm the one who's been here before." Logan had been the first of his friends to go inside the house both previous times, like it was a test of his masculinity. Being as big as he was, he had sensed the pull often in his young life. Most times he passed the test, but sometimes he failed, like when he was asking out Macy Goode or trying out for the Tuskahoma Warriors football team.

He was already six-four his freshman year, and the coaches had hoped he would be a great tight end, but his clumsy grip had disqualified him, and his lack of footwork made him a pushover at any lineman position. When Logan didn't make the team, his classmates started eyeing him funny, and his insecurity was at an all-time high. He had been happy to move away from Tuskahoma. They needed a fresh start away from football and the home in which he had grown up with two parents.

"Do you think anyone is squatting in there?" Will asked

"No, Melinda's just paranoid."

Logan beamed the light through the windows anyway before they entered. As dark as it was outside, the interior was worse—an unwelcome black hole. His clammy hands held onto the tiny flashlight, which only shined onto a small portion of the house at any given time.

Get ahold of yourself. But rational thought took a backseat to a superstitious mind when faced with the darkest time of night.

Logan became a turntable, making sure the light hit everything it could. The house only had two bedrooms and one bathroom, with a laundry room behind the kitchen at the back. The living room was a small square. A La-Z-Boy recliner and a couch remained there, covered in dust.

"Whoa, shine it over there again," Will said.

Logan beamed the light into the front room. Grubby looseleaf pages and old magazines were spread across the couch.

"Oh yeah, those were here before," he said.

"And you never looked at them?"

Logan shrugged. "We were here to see the kitchen well, not some Anthrax-infected letters."

Will crossed the room to the couch.

"You sure you want to touch that?"

"Don't be a pussy, Tramer."

Will picked up one of the folded pages and opened it. Cursive handwriting filled the sheet, but dark smudges made some of it indecipherable.

"Is that blood?" Logan leaned in close with the flashlight.

"Gross," Will said, but he continued to hold the letter.

"What's it say?"

"Just some boring 'I'll always love you' sort of shit." He dropped the letter. It floated to the floor like a feather. "Let's see this well."

On the left side of the front room, a door led into the kitchen. Where there might have been a dining room table in any other home, here there was a large well.

"Holy shit." Will circled it.

Logan ran his hand along the brick and beamed his light down into the hole. In the dark, his hand touched something besides brick, and he whipped it away, horrified by the feel of rugged shin bone.

He shifted his light to the object. It was a thick rope descending into the well. A knot looped around a railroad spike jammed into the side of the brick exterior. Logan had forgotten about the rope from his previous visits. He supposed it had a bucket at the other end.

An idea formed quickly. A swift way to get back at Will for all the times he had been a prick. Could Logan convince him to climb down?

A putrid smell rose from inside the well.

"Here's your chance, Tramer. You want to win STATE? Just say the words."

"Seems like you've got something on your mind you want to wish for."

"C'mon. It's bullshit."

"It's not, man. It's just most people don't know how to do it."

"What're you talking about?"

"The old legend is you yell down into the well, and if you hear your wish echo back, then it will come true."

"That's what Bird said."

"That's the way the story goes, but it's not the truth. If you really want your wish to come true, you have to climb inside the well. Make your wish at the bottom, then come back up."

"Who the hell would go inside that dirty-ass thing?"

"I thought *you* might. Will Roebuck's not afraid of anything."

"I mean...I'm not a big-ass pussy like you. But I don't know what gross shit's down there. There might be literal shit."

"You got your work clothes on. Who cares if those boxes on your feet get dirty. They're non-slip, right? At least you know you won't fall."

"You're just messing with me."

"Why do you think this rope is here? Think about it. There's always some truth behind every myth if you dig a little deeper. Or in this case, *climb* a little deeper."

"You're such a nerd, Tramer. You're lucky you're a goddamn giant."

"I don't care if you go down there or not. I'm just telling you, don't waste your breath making a wish up here."

Logan shifted the flashlight away from Will, giving him a moment in the dark to consider what he was going to do. He aimed the light inside the well, as if making Will's decision for him.

"Fuck it," Will said. "I'll go down there. Show you how to be a man."

"You're the man," Logan said.

"You better hang onto that rope, Tramer. If I fall and break my neck, I'm haunting your ass."

Logan laughed. "I got you."

Will stepped over the brick wall of the well and began descending, with his hands around the rope. Logan held tight to the other end, although the spike seemed to hold Will's weight, and pressed his feet firmly against the floor. His free hand beamed the flashlight into the open space around Will. The light only went so far.

Soon, Will descended past where the little flashlight could reach, and Logan stuffed the keychain into his pocket so he could use both hands on the rope.

"Goddamn, it stinks," Will said. His voice echoed up toward Logan.

Logan was giddy. He imagined Will's body covered in whatever sludge he would find at the bottom, then catching some disease from an animal carcass. "Are you at the bottom yet?"

"I don't know...I think I'm close...Why didn't you give me the light?"

"You didn't ask for it."

"Fuck you, Tramer—Oh shit—"

"What?"

"There's no more rope."

"No bucket on the end?"

"Nope."

"So...you must be at the bottom."

"My feet are floating, man."

"Just jump down. It's there. I promise." A tinge of guilt. He didn't know why the rope was in the well, so he wasn't confident Will was anywhere close to the bottom. Logan imagined Will listening to him, falling another twenty feet, and breaking his leg on a rock. He pictured Will's shin bone snapping in half and folding until a jagged end of bone punctured his skin, pointing toward Logan—the guilty party.

"Whoa!"

"What?"

"I'm down. The bottom was just a few feet further."

"Can you still reach the rope?"

"If I jump for it, yeah. It's no problem. Oh, the smell is horrible!"

Logan stifled his laughter. "You better make your wish."

Will was silent for a minute. Logan acted on instinct, Will's insults repeating in his mind, revving him up. He yanked on the rope. It came up some. He pulled some more. And continued. The rope dropped into a circling pile at his feet.

It was longer than Logan expected. How deep was this well?

"All right," Will said. "I did it. God, it's gross down here. I think I saw a used condom and a goddamn milk carton. I'm coming up now."

A splash echoed from the bottom.

"I can't reach the rope."

"What?" Logan asked.

"The rope. It's not there."

"It should be right where you left it."

"It's not fucking there."

"Let me see if I can move it down some more...Try it now."

Another splash, some scuffling. "It's not there, man."

Logan backed a few feet away from the well. His belly cramped from stifled laughter. The shakiness in Will's voice excited him. Senior Night finally faded to the back of his thoughts.

"Tramer? What's going on, *man*?"

Logan leaned against the doorframe where the kitchen met the hallway and looked through the other opening into the front of the house. The night air blew through the broken windows and somehow circled behind him like a warm breath on the back of his neck. Something inside told him to leave Will there.

He'll be fine for one night. You can come get him in the morning.

"Logan? You there?"

He didn't answer. One foot in the front area, the screen door half-open three steps away.

"Answer me," Will hollered. "This isn't funny."

Logan's smile stretched across his face. He was excited and in a good mood finally. Hopeful, even. They could still win it all, just like the Green River Lady Bullfrogs won it all without their best player—his aunt Jocelyn.

"*Logan!*" The voice didn't sound like Will.

It made Logan jump and left a residual buzzing on his skin, all the while that tickling breeze on the back of his neck. He wanted to laugh even harder. What a thrill it was to listen to Will scream like that.

Just go. It'll be hilarious.

"*Logan!*" Will shouted again—a high-pitched panic.

A step toward the screen door. The ultimate prank. *Leave him.*

But Will's panicked voice echoed in his mind enough that it made Logan nervous. He shook away his strongest desire. There was no more wind against the back of him as he returned to the kitchen.

"Will? You there, man?" Logan started moving the rope back down as quietly as he could.

"What the hell, dude!"

"I thought I heard something, so I went to look. Did you find the rope yet?"

"No, fucker. Where's the light?"

"Oh. Right."

Once the rope was far enough down, Logan clicked on his

flashlight again. He couldn't make out Will in the darkness, but Will could possibly see him peering into the well. He kept as straight a face as he could.

"Goddammit," Will said. There was a tug on the rope.

"You got it?"

"Yeah...I swear it wasn't here a minute ago."

"You were in the dark," Logan said. "You probably got turned around."

Will didn't say anything else until he had climbed out, breathing hard. His shoes and the bottoms of his black work pants were covered in mossy water. He stank like the rot inside the well.

Logan scratched at his face when a smile twitched at his mouth. It was hard not to laugh, thinking about the way Will had screamed his name.

He wasn't down there more than a couple of minutes, and he freaked the hell out. And I'm the pussy? Logan thought he would sleep soundly, but by the time they left the house, his mind had returned to Senior Night, the broken leg, and crushed roses.

DISTRICTS

AREA IV DISTRICT 6 BRACKET

NOWHERE

(BYE)

NOWHERE

@NASHOBA
Sat, Feb 21 @ 7:30pm

COTTONVALE

@NASHOBA
Fri, Feb 20 @ 6:00pm

NASHOBA

Winner and Runner-up
advance to Regionals

TWO
LOSERS

1

THE FOLLOWING MONDAY, Logan took forever to get ready for school. By the time he arrived, everyone had gone to class except for some of his teammates. Tim stood in the gravel parking lot with Alex and Marshal. Logan's old Ford appeared minuscule next to Tim's monster truck: an S-10 pickup raised on tires as tall as he was.

They were hanging out by the outdoor court, unconcerned with being late to class. The hoop had a metal backboard on a rusty pole and a crooked rim. Tufts of grass escaped from wide cracks in the concrete. Even during the coldest months of the year, the students played on the court before class and during lunch breaks. Everyone got in on four-on-four pickup games or a game of Twenty-One, whether they were on the team or not.

"What's up, big man?" Tim lit up his cigarette. "I thought you'd skip today."

"Why would you think that?" Logan asked defensively.

"I mean…Kelvin's fucking leg. It's not like you came to Turner's barn Saturday night."

"Was anyone there?"

Tim surprised him with a vigorous head nod.

"Everyone but you and Marshal."

"I went with Emily to see Kelvin," Marshal said.

"On Valentine's Day?" Tim smirked.

"Not exactly a normal Valentine's Day, Springer," Marshal said defensively.

"I was at work," Logan replied.

"Well, you boys missed out. Guess who made out with Mal Turner?"

"Alex?"

"I wish," Alex said.

"The saint himself," Tim said.

"Dougie? You can't be serious."

"Hell yeah. Fucking Doug Mooreland. They were out behind the barn, hooking up half the night."

"But Dougie never even goes to parties."

"That's where Satan is," Marshal joked.

"Well, he was at this one," Tim said.

"Must be more shaken up than any of us."

"How do you figure that?"

"Kelvin's injury made him lose his faith," Marshal said, like it was obvious. "Now he's a hedonist."

Logan guffawed. "You don't even know the meaning of that word."

"I used it correctly, didn't I?"

"Look at us," Tim said, "comforting each other in a time of crisis."

"There's no crisis," Alex said. "Kelvin got hurt. It happens. We can still win the chip."

"You scare me with how good you are at lying, Spruce."

"It's true. You, me, Logan...We've been on this team as long as Kelvin has. We know what it takes to win."

"I know what it takes too, numbnuts," Marshal said.

"Coach Park doesn't even believe we can win STATE," Tim said. "He's thanking his lucky stars we get to skip the first round of Districts."

"Name one team we can't beat," Alex protested.

"How about Nashoba? Might play them Saturday night."

"God dang it," Marshal said.

"What?" Logan asked.

"I really hope Cottonvale can beat those fools."

"No confidence, Lovegood?" Tim asked.

"No, we'll beat their asses," Marshal said, "but God, do I hate playing Nashoba."

Logan knew all about Marshal's history with the Nashoba Wolves. The whole town hated the Lovegood's because Marshal's dad, John, had cracked open the head of Nashoba's star player in the 1979 District Tournament. Supposedly, it had been an accident. That player just happened to be Jay Kemp, older brother of Marshal's mom. His mom did not like her brother and might have even dated John because of the whole incident.

His mom's family loved to badger Marshal when the teams faced off. They heckled him when he missed a shot and booed whenever he touched the ball. A Kemp cousin even mooned Marshal once when the referees weren't looking. Regardless, Nowhere's rival had only beaten them once in four years.

"Alex is right," Logan said. "We just have to take things one game at a time."

"We'll see." Tim threw down his cigarette butt, and the four of them started to walk to the high school building.

Nowhere Public Schools was made up of a series of tin-roofed rectangular trailers: one for high school, one for middle school, and one for elementary, as well as a shop building and cafeteria. Other than that, there was the gymnasium—the largest building on the school grounds—a baseball field, and a playground.

There were less than a hundred students in all of kindergarten through twelfth grade. Logan's class of 2004 would be a big one—fifteen students. Alex, Kelvin, Tim, and Logan were seniors, and the other starters, Doug and Marshal, were juniors. Tim would move into the starting lineup next game.

The single long hallway of the high school trailer was lined with lockers and classrooms on either side and double doors on each end. Doug was standing at his locker next to Marshal's when the four of them approached.

Tim began bowing in mock humility. "Oh, great and mighty Dougie, please accept me as your loyal servant."

Doug laughed, red-faced. Tim gave his hand a sharp yank and kissed it over and over again.

"Stop! What the heck, Tim?"

Doug had stopped cussing since dedicating his life to Christ before eighth grade. Logan had been at Rome Bible Camp the same summer Doug got saved. When Logan returned from camp, he learned his parents were getting divorced.

"Oh, let me kiss the hand that fingered the lovely goddess," Tim said.

Doug tore away his hand and peeked over his shoulder. They were alone in the hallway, late for their various classes.

"Did y'all actually hook up?" Marshal asked.

"Just necked a little."

"Then why the hell am I kissing your fingers?" Tim said.

"Cause you're a fag," Doug answered because he didn't consider it a cuss word.

Logan did. Larry Unders was an openly gay man and had been verbally hounded by some rowdy customers one night at Wheelman's. Three of them were out-of-towners, but one was a local who had grown up with Larry.

Because of his size, Logan had considered this another test of his masculinity. He had stormed outside, his apron tight around his waist, and threatened to beat the shit out of them. Logan figured the four brutes would pummel him if it came to blows, but he would get in a few good licks first. He had been in two fights before and had been surprised by how easy it was to level someone with his enormous fists.

Of course, he had broken his hand in one of those fights because he didn't really have a clue what he was doing. Luckily, the out-of-towners didn't know that and drove away.

The double doors banged open at the end of the hallway, like someone hit them shoulder-first. Everyone jumped, apparently thinking the same irrational thought: *Is Kelvin back?*

Of course, it wasn't him. He was still in the hospital.

"Damn," Tim muttered.

"I'll be honest," Marshal said, "I thought it was Kelvin walking in here, one-legged."

"It is kind of surprising they didn't amputate it."

"It was just a broken leg." Logan downplayed how he really felt.

"I read on the internet you can get back on the court in eight weeks after a broken leg," Doug offered.

"That wasn't a typical leg break," Alex said.

"I was right in front of him, going for the rebound," Marshal added. "I almost backed right into it."

"Couldn't have made it any worse," Tim said.

"Guys." The conversation was making Logan's mouth go dry. "Chill. We got this."

"Say it all you want, big man," Tim replied. "It doesn't change anything."

"Logan's right," Alex agreed. "We got the bye in the first round, so we're automatically in the District finals. It's double elimination, and Nashoba sucks this year. We've got time to adjust to life without Kelvin. Time for this guy"—he pointed at Doug—"to get right with God."

"Excuse me?" Doug said.

"We all know you got some repenting to do after Saturday night." Marshal chuckled.

"Listen," Logan said. "Kelvin wouldn't want us giving up. He would want us winning STATE. So, let's do it."

"What are you even doing here, Logan?" Doug asked. "I figured you would skip today."

"Why does everyone think that? I'm fine. Okay?"

"I don't know…" Tim tilted his head, and Logan felt exposed by his intent stare. "You look a little peaked there, Tramer." Tim reached for his face, and Logan slapped his hand away.

"I saw one of my best friends snap his leg in two. Yeah, I'm a little *peaked*. I'm surprised you even know that word."

"Emily's a total mess right now," Marshal said.

"You been seeing a lot of her this weekend?" Tim cracked a presumptuous, sleazy smile.

"Screw you, Springer," Marshal said.

Logan was annoyed that Marshal knew more about how his sister was doing than he did. Marshal Lovegood and Emily Tramer had been inseparable since becoming fast friends after the Tramer's moved to Nowhere. They had both been in the eighth grade, but Logan still thought it was weird she had not bonded with girls, but instead with a guy who had become known for having a different girlfriend every couple of months. But three years later, their friendship had remained platonic despite Tim's insistence Marshal was in love with her.

Emily hadn't dated anyone ever. It was a shock when she and Kelvin were walking down the hallway one day, holding hands. Logan hadn't had a clue his sister and best friend were into each other. That meant they had at least flirted behind his back. Who knew what else?

He began to question all the times Kelvin had come to hang out at his house. Was he simply wanting to get closer to his sister? Logan was angered by it, distancing himself from Kelvin and Emily these past six weeks. Now, he felt bad.

While the others went to class, Logan stopped by the restroom and peered at his reflection. His skin was splotchy; he hadn't showered since Friday night. His eyes were bloodshot. He almost left Will trapped in the kitchen well. His whole world had been thrown off-balance.

There was only one way to set things right.

Win STATE. *You have to win* STATE.

The road to the championship started Saturday night in Nashoba.

2

It was said the two communities of Nashoba and Nowhere had been founded by two brothers who had a rift. They had been the greatest rivals ever since. Nashoba was more of a town than Nowhere and had a higher Native population than other towns in Shappaway County. There were two convenience stores, a bank, three churches, a post office, and a bar.

The Nashoba Wolves seemed to float around a .500 record year after year, but they were always tough. No matter how good or bad Nashoba was, their two rivalry games each season —three games during those years they had met up in the District Tournament—came down to the wire, games which could swing either way until the last two or three possessions. All but once it had swung the Devils' way in Logan's career, and that one loss was back in 2002—Logan's sophomore year, when Nashoba spoiled Nowhere's unbeaten home record with an overtime victory.

The two times the teams had played in the regular season

this year, though, Nowhere destroyed the Wolves, 88-35 at home and 76-42 in Nashoba. The Devils had beaten just about everyone badly this season. At the midseason Red Dirt tournament, they slaughtered the number two ranked team in Class B, the Olney Mustangs, by thirty.

Their games against Cottonvale had been two of the closest they had played all season, so Logan was thankful Nashoba had beaten the Tigers in the first round of Districts. Despite the rivalry, Nashoba was a much better matchup for Nowhere, and the Wolves' home court advantage wasn't much of one.

After making STATE the past two years, Nowhere had gained more fans than ever before. The whole community and then some traveled to their away games. Two-thirds of Nashoba's gym was crowded with Nowhere fans for the District finals tonight. The Nowhere Lady Devils' season had ended two nights ago. They had the unfortunate draw of going up against the Cottonvale Lady Tigers, who seemed poised for a run to STATE themselves.

The crowd was antsy while the boys were going through their warmups. Everyone wanted to see how the Devils would fare without Kelvin Harris.

It wasn't long after tipoff that Logan realized how false his confidence had been. He was a shell of himself. He missed shots at the rim and gave up offensive rebounds. Kelvin wasn't there to deliver the ball perfectly, so Logan turned it over more than any other game this season.

"Uninspired basketball" was what Coach Park called it at halftime. Things didn't change in the second half, leading Coach to yell, "Get your head out of your ass," even with all the parents right behind the bench.

The rest of the team didn't play much better. The Nashoba Wolves—especially their peskiest piece-of-shit hustle guy, Bolan Grimes—were talking trash all game, whether they were ahead or behind. It was getting to the Devils. Everyone but Alex, anyway.

Alex was playing like the poor man's Kelvin he had always wanted to be. He was taking the opportunity to establish himself as the best player on the team. Only problem was, Alex didn't understand what had made Kelvin great besides scoring: tough defense, incredible vision. Getting his teammates involved had been the key to Nowhere's success because it kept everyone engaged.

Even Logan had been known to get careless when he hadn't touched the ball much. Alex was scoring all right, but he wasn't finding his teammates when they were open. And it was one thing to miss Marshal or Doug for an open three—they were streaky shooters—but he didn't even get the ball to Logan while driving the lane with the defense crowding. The few times Logan could get the ball, he fumbled it out of bounds, or Bolan Grimes came out of nowhere and stole it.

Nashoba's tallest player was barely six feet. Logan should have had his strongest showing of the season. In fact, in their two previous games, Logan had been unstoppable.

Although he couldn't completely blame Alex for his poor play, it didn't stop Logan from getting into it with him late in the second half. "Get me the ball, Spruce," or "You missed Tim in the corner."

But when Tim airballed it, or Marshal or Doug missed, Alex spat back, "You see what happens when I give Tim the ball," or "If you're gonna miss that badly, then give me the fucking ball back."

It was a horrible night. Alex had twenty-nine points, but Nowhere lost by twenty. Nashoba let them hear it too. There was nothing they could say or do to stop it. Their undefeated streak had ended.

3

On the bus ride home, Tim cracked some jokes to lighten the mood, but no one even humored him with a courtesy laugh. Logan was thankful for the dark winter night. He could cradle into the corner of his seat and sulk.

Kelvin had come home yesterday morning, and it was all anyone at school could talk about. Logan had had a hard time swallowing the past two days. Something was lodged in his throat, and when he managed to get it down, he grew queasy.

The inevitable fact bothered him: Kelvin was home, and Logan would have to go see him. The guilt was too much to deal with, so he ignored it and then played like shit.

Now the Devils would move into the consolation bracket of the Regional Tournament next week. One more loss and the season was over. It was difficult to imagine it ending any other way.

Logan didn't say a word on their return trip to Nowhere.

His mom was awake when he got home. She sat on the sofa, reading one of the *Left Behind* books beneath the lamplight.

"What're you doing up?" he asked.

"Waiting on you. Tough loss."

"Yeah. You know we hate playing Nashoba. We'll adjust. Just getting used to life without Kelvin."

"Sure." She closed her book. "Want to talk about it?"

"It's one game, Mom. It's a tougher path to STATE now, sure, but we'll get there."

"I mean Kelvin. I hear he's home."

"Oh, right, yeah. Em says he's doing good."

"I thought you might go over there with her tonight."

"I'll go see him. I will. Soon." Logan started to move toward the bedrooms. His was across from his sister's, while his mom was down the opposite hallway. It was a nice home. His mom called it "the Indian house" because it was a manufactured home paid for with a Choctaw Nation housing loan. He had watched them haul it down the dirt road in two halves.

Logan paused in the hallway next to his aunt's basketball photo on the wall.

"Hey, Mom?"

"Yeah?"

"Aunt Joss's team…It's kind of like now, isn't it?"

Her mouth twitched. "I don't know…I hope not."

That confused him. Didn't his mom want them to win STATE? Then it struck him what she meant.

"Right," he said. "I don't think we need to worry about Kelvin."

She forced a smile. "That's good, honey."

4

The loss in Districts was the talk of the school. Everyone looked at Logan and his teammates like they were cursed, and it pissed him off. It had only been one game. Didn't they have faith in a team that had made it to STATE two years in a row? *Not without Kelvin* seemed to be the answer.

He was thankful their first game of the Regional Tournament would be against Picard. The Wombats were in a rebuilding year, with a team of freshmen and sophomores who were even skinnier and whiter than all the other "skinny and white" teams in Class B Oklahoma basketball.

Of course, they would still have to win two games after that to get to the Area Tournament. And at Area, they would have to win three games just to reach STATE.

The more Logan thought about it, the more daunting it became. He even started to second-guess if they could beat Picard. The plucky, young team might smell blood in the water after the beatdown Nowhere had suffered on Saturday. In Logan's four years on the team, they had never lost Districts, never found themselves on the consolation side of the bracket. His aunt's team had *won* their District Tournament without their star player, so maybe the Devils were nothing like the Lady Bullfrogs.

At the front of the classroom, Mr. Tune wrote random words onto the chalkboard. Logan had lost track of where they were in history, even forgetting momentarily if this was U.S. History or Oklahoma History. Mr. Tune taught both subjects.

"Yes, Jessica?" Mr. Tune said.

She sat in front of Logan, her hand sky-high.

"So, what would happen if a man showed up in this town?"

"Well, supposedly, one man tried to enter Bathsheba, and he was run out of town with a shotgun. He was a reporter from Kansas, and his record of the event is the only proof this town ever existed."

"I'd love to sneak into a town of only women," Tim said.

The boys guffawed, and the girls scoffed. Tim was seated to Logan's right, Marshal behind him. There was an empty seat in front of Tim. A spotlight might as well have been on it—Kelvin's seat. No one else would dare sit there the rest of the year or risk a curse as instantly violent.

Kelvin's wasn't the only absence. Will Roebuck had not been in school all last week and was still missing today. Logan was probably the only person among the students and teachers who noticed. Did he have something else to feel guilty about? Was Will that shaken up by being trapped inside the kitchen well? He had only been in there for a minute.

"The experiment didn't work," Mr. Tune said, "but we can only speculate as to why Bathsheba, Oklahoma, disappeared so quickly."

"They were missing that 'D'," Tim whispered.

Logan laughed nervously. He had never been comfortable around his teammates' displays of bravado, perhaps because he didn't have any sexual experience.

Jessica heard Tim's comment and turned to face Logan. He felt the redness of his face. It pulsed hotter than the rest of him. "Hi," he said, unable to think of anything else. They rarely talked at work and never at school. She rolled her eyes and turned back around as Tim and Marshal snickered.

Logan couldn't leave fast enough and hurried to his next class. It was a virtual language class done over a TV and webcam with other small schools in Oklahoma, taught by a teacher from the Choctaw Nation. At this point in the year, the teacher was mostly speaking Choctaw during class, and Logan spent the hour asking Emily and Marshal to interpret. Those two were much smarter than him. Each had their sights set on attending the University of Oklahoma.

When Logan sat down, Marshal said, "So, I already told the others. We're gonna skip school tomorrow and go see Kelvin."

"All right." Logan felt sick to his stomach. "It'll be good to hang out with him."

Emily stared at her older brother, seeing right through him. She had been ignoring Logan since the injury, mad at him for not visiting Kelvin at Arrow Regional.

"Don't sweat it, Logan," Marshal said after muting the microphone.

Most of the TV screen was filled with Mrs. McKinney at her desk, staring into the webcam. Little squares at the top of the screen showed the other small schools and the three Nowhere students at their desks. Mrs. McKinney began class with a hardy "Halito!"

"Don't sweat *what*?" Logan asked.

"You didn't go see Kelvin in the hospital. It's all right. I was only there a couple times."

So it wasn't just Emily who noticed.

"Oh, I wasn't—" he attempted before Emily interrupted him.

"He's been asking about you, Logan." She clicked the microphone off mute and recited, "Achukma hoke!" along with the other small schools. "Chishnato?"

Now Logan was annoyed. His sister was trying to make him feel guilty.

"Achukma akinli," Mrs. McKinney said, followed by another response from the schools.

This time, Logan muted the microphone.

"I'm gonna go see him. I've been busy with work and practice. The playoffs have started, for Christ's sake."

"Of course, big man," Marshal said. "It's barely been more than a week. We'll see him tomorrow."

"You could come see him tonight with me," Emily offered.

"I know that, Em," Logan said.

Marshal put a hand on his shoulder to comfort him. Logan wanted to slap it away but didn't even shrug him off. Marshal's hot palm warmed through his shirt.

Mrs. McKinney began speaking about what they were working on today in Choctaw. The bus driver and custodian, Marcus Ludlow, passed the room and poked his head inside curiously. The three of them stared at him. He maintained a big smile, like he always had, but his eyebrows furrowed.

"She's saying it wrong," he noted, then disappeared.

"Wrong or right, can someone tell me *what* she's saying?" Logan asked.

Emily explained Mrs. McKinney wanted them to work on their group project for the rest of the period. They were writing and illustrating a Bigfoot story. It had been Kelvin's idea because he had supposedly seen Bigfoot when he went on a camping trip with some cousins.

Logan didn't want to work on the project. He didn't want to see Kelvin. He wanted to win Regionals this weekend and Area after that. In two and a half weeks, he could be playing for the STATE CHAMPIONSHIP again.

If Green River can win it all after losing Aunt Joss, then we can do it without Kelvin.

But it remained difficult to convince himself this was possible. They had lost to Nashoba, and it hadn't even been close. The team needed the good fortune Green River had had. Supposedly, the Lady Bullfrogs had a lot of luck in their run to the title.

No one deserved good fortune more than Nowhere. The Basketball Gods owed the Devils.

5

Logan didn't go see Kelvin the next day. He had started to drive in the direction of Harris Hill but soon turned down the road toward school. His underclassmen teammates were in the high school building Tuesday morning, but none of his fellow starters were. He was nervous about seeing them tomorrow, but that thought disappeared when he noticed Will sitting at the front in his first class.

Logan peered at him, hoping Will would give him some indication of where he had been the last week. He thought Will might still be pissed about being left in the well, but when Will turned to look at him, Will's eyes lit up and he smiled.

What the hell does that mean?

After class, Logan tried to catch up to him but ended up face-to-face with Jessica Fromm.

"Can you take my shift tonight?"

"What?" he asked, his voice cracking. Logan stood a little taller to compensate. "I'm not a carhop."

"Oh, come on. You could do it."

"I can barely take orders."

"It's easy. You just have to turn on the charm and hand people their food. You'd be surprised how much I make in tips each shift."

"That's because you're an attractive girl."

Her cheeks brightened. "Oh?"

He looked away and cleared his throat. "I'm not charming like that."

"Sure, you are. You're quiet, but you've got a nice smile. That goes a long way for guys. It's easier for y'all."

"Why do you need off? Do you...have a date or something?"

"A family thing. Why would you assume I have a date?"

He was tongue-tied, only able to shrug in response. Jessica smiled and touched his arm.

"Thanks, Logan. I appreciate you helping me out."

"I—Okay."

Jessica walked away, and Logan peered at her until she was into the next class. He hated the idea of carhopping but was thankful to work tonight. It made time pass more quickly.

Logan continued through his next two classes. By fourth period he was starving, counting the minutes until lunch break, and he couldn't pay much attention to Ms. Fletcher's teaching, even though English was his favorite subject. She turned to write something on the blackboard, and a note found its way back to him. He hoped it was from Jessica.

In his mind's eye, he could picture the large, swooping letters of the note in her gorgeous handwriting:

Thank you so much for covering my shift tonight. Will you take me on a date, Logan?

But it wasn't from Jessica. It was from Will. He wrote it in all caps, giving his note an urgency:

MEET ME AT CLEARWATER CREEK ON LUNCH BREAK

6

Will Roebuck was unpredictable. Logan had no idea what he was walking into at Clearwater Creek. What if Will realized Logan had been playing a prank on him and had revenge on his mind? Of course, Logan would never admit that Will scared him, so he left school on his lunch break. The creek wasn't far.

Trees towered over either side of the country road while he rounded a long curve. The bridge over Clearwater Creek had seen better times. Lots of graffiti and cracks, which suggested the bridge might collapse one of these days. The penis drawn on the back of the Clearwater Creek sign pointed like an arrow toward the muddy turnoff leading down to the creek bed.

Logan took the turnoff. It sloped in a steep descent until he reached the grassy area where everyone parked. Any further and his truck might not have the horsepower to get unstuck from the mud.

The water was as muddy as the creek bed. Like it always had been. Whoever had named Clearwater Creek had a real sense of humor. It was surprising there was running water at all. The big ice storm had frozen it over, and there had been few days above freezing since.

Icicles clung to the pines running along both sides of the creek. Logan was reminded of the woods around the abandoned house, but that was simply recency bias. Tall pines and cypress swamps were all around Nowhere. Even the Indian house was obscured from the road by a line of trees.

The spindly branches of the pines blocked most of the sunlight, so the temperature dropped another ten degrees a few feet into the woods. Logan's Lakers jacket wasn't thick enough, so he bounced up and down to warm himself. Then he skipped rocks until Will finally arrived.

"There you are," he said. "I'm starving, man, and we're gonna miss fifth period."

"Like you give a shit," Will said. "The rest of your team isn't even here."

"They went to see Kelvin."

"And you didn't?"

Logan shrugged.

"Well, you'll be glad you skipped that visit. I got something important to tell you."

"So important you couldn't tell me at school, huh?"

"Too many nosy bastards."

"It's just us out here."

"That's right."

"So...go on, then."

"It worked."

"What?"

"The wish. It worked."

Logan stared at him, waiting for Will to crack. "You're messing with me, aren't you?" he finally said. "Is this because I left you down there? It was only a minute, dude."

"What do you mean, you left me down there?" Will seemed genuinely confused. "Shit..." It dawned on him, a clear demarcation between an expression that didn't know something and then realized everything. "You fuckhead."

"Wait. So...you're not messing with me?"

"Like I'm telling your ass anymore. You were gonna leave me in that hole! You took the rope away, didn't you?"

"There's no way the wish worked, Will. I made up the shit about climbing into the well."

"Looks like you stumbled onto the truth, then, asshole."

Logan still struggled to believe Will wasn't messing with him, but he would have to be a hell of an actor for that to be the case. "Why do you think your wish came true?" he asked.

"Because it did. That's what I'm trying to tell you. Why we're out here. We don't want anyone else knowing about it, right? Imagine all the things we could wish for. But if others were doing it too, it might...I don't know...run out of magic or something."

"Why'd you even tell me, then?"

"Because I thought you already knew! I didn't know you were just being a psycho."

"I'm not—I was just returning the favor. You're always shit-talking the team because you're jealous."

"I talk shit because y'all are posers. You proved that much Saturday night."

Logan held tight to his skipping rock. He imagined slinging it at Will's face.

"You think I give a flying fuck about playing basketball?" Will continued. "I got a nicer ride than any of you fools."

"And less friends too."

"Fuck you, Tramer."

Will started to walk away.

Logan's vision began to clear, and he dropped the rock. "Wait. Will. Come on, man."

Will hesitated and kicked some mud with the toe of his sneaker.

"You gotta tell me...What did you wish for?"

THREE
THE BASKETBALL GODS

1

LOGAN WAS COMPLETELY outside his comfort zone as a carhop. It was too frantic—too much running back and forth, too much smiling. Even the weight of the change belt around his waist felt strange. He was terrible at counting change. After handing customers their food, he had to lay every bill on his tray slowly and count it again. The wind threatened to blow the cash away and succeeded twice, forcing Logan to chase the bills down, crawling under a customer's vehicle like he was changing the oil.

Melinda and Will kept laughing at him from the kitchen. Larry Unders patted him on the back supportively, but it was clear he was frustrated with how slow Logan was. His shift manager's time record was shot on this Tuesday night.

It wasn't just Logan. The kitchen was shorthanded because Bird had no-called, no-showed. Larry tried calling him on the landline, but there was no answer and no voicemail set up. Bird didn't have a cell phone—no one at Wheelman's did, except maybe the Holdendecker carhops.

Melinda had reached the point of "fuck it." Instead of letting the stress ruin her, she goofed off while working through the backed-up orders. Larry slumped at the "Order Up" station, watching the minutes accumulate on the orders-in-progress screen. Eventually, he started clearing orders before they were ready, so he could speed up his time. Will, of course, was on Cloud Nine. Not even a busy, shorthanded Tuesday could ruin that.

Logan couldn't wrap his mind around what Will had told him at Clearwater Creek. His blind grandmother could now see.

"I wished for it," Will had said. "It was the first thing that came to mind when Bird mentioned a wishing well. I crouched down at the bottom of that well in the dark, felt the breeze on my face, and said it. And then, apparently, you pretended to run after some made-up noise. That's a fucked-up thing to do, Tramer. You don't know what it's like down there…"

Will had kept talking about how terrible the bottom of the well was, but Logan didn't listen. He was already considering where the story would go next.

If he wished for his blind grandmother to see, and he's claiming it came true, then: "You're telling me your grandma can see now? What are we talking about here? She can see a little better? Was she fully blind?"

"Of course, she was fully blind," Will had said. "And no, not 'a little better.' She couldn't see. Now she can. 20/20 vision. My parents and I went to Texas last week to see it for ourselves. She looked at me for the first time ever. It was so hard not to tell her, not to take credit for it. It's a goddamn miracle, and it's thanks to that well. Imagine what we can wish for, Tramer."

Logan didn't go back to school after meeting with Will at Clearwater Creek. He wished he hadn't agreed to cover for Jessica. He wanted to be at the kitchen well. He already knew what he needed to do.

After a couple of hours, the Tuesday night rush was over. Logan took out fewer orders, letting the other carhop, Darcy, a Goth senior from Holdendecker, go more often for the tips. He kept wanting to talk to Will, but Will cut him off every time, motioning toward Melinda or Larry's ears. The secret had to stay between them. Logan couldn't imagine the well running out of wishes; surely, magic didn't work that way. But if they were going to make more wishes, he agreed they couldn't take any chances.

Then Alex pulled into a stall in his Jeep Wrangler—a mid-90s model. The answering station squealed when Alex pressed the order button, and Logan ducked into the kitchen.

"Are you gonna get that, Logan?" Larry asked, juggling an ice cream and drink order.

"Can you get it, Mel?" Logan whispered.

"Excuse me? You're the carhop, big man. You've got the tips to prove it."

"It's Alex. He's on my team, and I can't talk to him right now."

"Why not?"

"Haven't you heard?" Will said. "The Devils lost in the District Tournament. They're about to bow out of the playoffs in the first round of Regionals."

"Okay…Is that somehow your fault, Logan?"

"No." He stretched his neck to look at Alex's Jeep through the window. Alex peeked his direction, and Logan darted out of sight. "It's something else. He can't know I'm here."

The squeal continued to reverberate through the building. "Someone better answer that goddamn order!" Larry shouted over the mixer's whir while he spun chunks of Reese's Peanut Butter Cup into vanilla ice cream.

Melinda sighed and went to answer it.

Alex ordered mozzarella sticks and a Dr. Pepper. Logan peeked out at him again.

"You can at least drop those motts for me," Melinda said, and Logan rushed to do so.

After she read back the order, Alex's voice came through the intercom again: "Can you have Logan Tramer bring that out to me? Please and thank you."

Melinda glanced into the kitchen.

"I'm not here," Logan said. He splashed the basket of mozzarella sticks into the sizzling fryer oil.

"What are you hiding for?" Will asked. "You haven't been any worse than the rest of your team."

Melinda pressed the side button. "I'm afraid Logan isn't working tonight, but we've got great carhops who can help you out, sir."

"I know you're here, Logan," Alex yelled through the intercom. "Hey, you come out on roller skates, and I'll give you a big, fat tip."

Logan cursed under his breath. "Thanks anyway," he muttered to Melinda. When Alex's order was ready, he went out to face his teammate.

"Where the hell were you?" Alex demanded.

"That'll be $4.33."

"Fuck you. You're paying for it. Why'd you bail on us? Kelvin was acting cool, but I know he was disappointed."

"I had to work—"

"At nine a.m.? Are you pulling a double there, working man?"

"Something came up. A family emergency."

"A family emergency that your sister doesn't know anything about? Marshal already asked her—"

"Goddammit. Why does everyone know everything in this town?"

"We ain't from town. We're from Nowhere. Remember?"

"Yeah, yeah."

"Seriously, big man. I'm not trying to be your daddy. I just want to make sure you're good."

"I'm good. Why wouldn't I be good?"

Alex paused, lowering his gaze like he was saying, *Really?*

Logan, well aware of how profusely he was sweating, sighed and delivered the truth as best as he could manage. "I set the screen that got Kelvin open, all right?"

"And?"

"And then I watched him break his leg. All-out. Not like that time your cousin fractured his arm when he fell off that four-wheeler. You saw the leg."

"I saw it when he was lying on the floor."

"Yeah. Well, imagine having to see it bend like that up close. After you're the one who got him open for the shot."

"You've gotten him open for a million shots, Logan. You don't have to blame yourself, man."

"It doesn't matter."

"It does if you're gonna keep playing like shit."

"I'm playing like shit?"

"Don't look at me like that. I had twenty-nine."

"And how many assists?"

"Screw you, butterfingers."

"I'll see him after we win STATE."

"Does that mean you're gonna play better?"

"You pass the ball, and I'll play better. But I got something else that'll help."

"You found a way to make Tim stop shooting with both hands?"

"That could be part of it. Meet me here in an hour. We're going to the kitchen well."

2

Logan cast his apron into his truck while he waited for Alex to arrive. It thudded on the sofa from all the coins he had collected as tips. It was enough to cover his gas for at least a week, including a trip to Arrow, should they win Regionals and want to celebrate in the college town on Sunday. As bad of a carhop as he was, he wondered how much Jessica would make in tips if Logan could pull in this much.

All the other staff had left, but Will lingered. Normally, he was the first one out of the gravel employee parking area, peeling out when his Camaro hit the main road.

"What's up, Will?"

"Oh, now you're tightlipped? You don't want to talk about the kitchen well with me anymore like you did all night?"

"I'm good."

"I wonder why."

"Speak your mind, Roebuck."

"I heard you talking to Alex."

"How did you—You asshole. You were listening to us?"

Will shrugged. "I thought it might be funny since you were trying to hide from him. Didn't realize you were gonna mope about setting piss-poor screens for Kelvin."

"So, when you were talking about the nosy people at school, you were talking about yourself."

"You're gonna tell him about my wish."

Logan kicked at the gravel. "And?"

"I told you we have to keep it secret."

"Alex won't tell anyone."

"Except everyone on your goddamn team."

"I'll swear him to secrecy, man."

"Mmhmm."

"He'll keep it secret. And even if he doesn't, it's not like anyone on the team will be out there making wishes."

"Of course they will."

"Nope."

"Why?"

"Because they want the same thing as me, and I'll be making the wish for all of us tonight."

"What if it doesn't work that way?"

"If it can heal your grandma's blindness, it sure as hell can help us compensate for the loss of Kelvin."

Will shook his head. "All the things you could wish for and you only care about basketball."

"You wouldn't understand."

"Well, I agree with you there."

Alex pulled into the loop around Wheelman's. He honked his horn when he approached the employee parking area, shining his brights in Logan's face to mess with him.

"I'm coming with you," Will said.

"What?"

"Yeah. I'm going back out there tonight."

Logan sighed, exhausted by Will's persistence. "Fine. But I'm the one who gets to make a wish tonight. It's like you said, right? We don't want to deplete the magic."

"I agree." A smile crept across Will's face. "I still can't believe it's real, man."

We'll see, Logan thought.

3

"This is ridiculous." Alex stood before the abandoned house with a Maglite beaming onto the screen door.

Logan had told him everything about Will's grandma, and Will had been there to confirm. The three of them followed each other out toward Nowhere, up Snakeback Road, and to the house where, supposedly, wishes came true.

The house hadn't changed, but this time, Logan felt different. He wasn't here to play a prank. His hope felt like lighting the match on the eventual bomb of disappointment that would go off.

"It's going to work," he said.

"You really think you can trust what Will Roebuck says?"

"I'm standing right here," Will said.

Alex beamed the light onto him. "Oh, right. Sorry. Listen, it's great that your grandma can see again, but winning STATE is a little bigger than one old lady's eyesight."

"You're really looking forward to peaking in high school, aren't you, Spruce?"

Logan cut in before Alex could respond. "Have y'all ever heard of Green River?"

"Doesn't ring a bell," Alex said, one murderous eye still on Will.

"It's near Fort Todd, outside of Tuskahoma. A ghost town nowadays but used to be a lot like Nowhere. My aunt grew up there."

"And?" Will said, annoying Logan like usual.

"*And*...in 1990, the Green River Lady Bullfrogs were rolling through the season, undefeated. My aunt, Jocelyn Horn, was the best player in the state. Then, with four games left before the playoffs, Aunt Joss breaks her wrist. She's out for the rest of her senior year. Sound familiar?"

"I guess so." Alex beamed the flashlight through one of the broken windows.

"Do you know what Green River did in 1990 after their best player was injured?"

"I'm guessing this is a rhetorical question."

"They won STATE."

"Good for them," Will said, spitting in the dirt.

"You're not listening to me. Aunt Joss was badass. She averaged almost thirty a game. If Green River can win it all after losing her, then we can win after losing Kelvin."

"Nice pep talk," Alex said, "but what's that have to do with this creepy ass place?"

"My mom says Green River didn't just band together and win STATE. Weird shit happened. Opposing teams getting food poisoning. Missing shots they would normally make. Basketball Gods kind of shit."

"So, what does that mean?" Alex said. "They have their own 'magic' well?"

"It means unexplainable shit happens. It means maybe Will's right."

"You're goddamn right I'm right," Will said.

"Whatever. Let's just get this over with."

"Hand me that flashlight," Logan said.

Alex hesitated.

"Come on, Spruce. I'm not going down in that hole without a light."

Alex handed it over, and they moved through the house quickly. Logan's teammate stood close by him, either afraid because of how dark the house was or eager for him to make the wish. If anyone wanted to win as badly as Logan, it was Alex. For both of them, it was their final year. Neither had scholarships to play in college.

As much as Kelvin had wanted to win it all this year, he had Division I basketball to look forward to. Also, hadn't the star player proven he didn't care as much about STATE when he started dating Logan's sister before the season was over?

An anger simmered beneath Logan's hope, and he wondered for the first time if he was avoiding Kelvin for another reason besides his guilt.

Why couldn't Kelvin wait until the season was over? Logan asked himself. But another question resided there too: *Why did he have to date my sister?*

The well was right where they had left it, with the rope hooked around the thick railroad spike. Logan hadn't noticed before that the looped end was a noose. His aunt's basketball photo burned through his mind's eye. He stared into the hole, grateful Alex had shown up at his workplace tonight. Logan couldn't imagine climbing down with nothing but the rope around the spike to support his weight.

He beamed the Maglite into the hole. The flashlight would be too heavy, too unwieldy, to climb with.

"Shit." Logan handed it to Alex. "Just be sure to keep it aimed down there when I'm at the bottom."

"Not even a Maglite will reach the bottom," Will mumbled.

"Of course it will," Alex said.

"I've got my keychain light if it doesn't," Logan added. "It's all good."

"Okay, pussies," Will said.

"And fuck you too, Roebuck." Alex turned toward Will. "What are you even doing here?"

"I'm the one who discovered it, fool."

"People have been coming to this well since before you were born, numbnuts."

"Guys, come on." It was silent while Logan stepped over the edge. He held tight to the rope and pushed his feet against the curving brick wall.

The well moaned in response, and the rope whined as it stretched—a sound of protest if there ever was one.

"You got it?" he yelled to the top.

Their silhouetted faces peered down at him. Alex's Maglite lay on the edge of the well, pointing behind them while they held the end of the rope.

"Yeah, you're good," Alex said, gritting his teeth. "Just don't lose your grip."

Logan guided himself with his feet. His hands rubbed against the coarse rope, and heat burned through his palms. Down he went until the light at the top of the ring appeared impossible to reach. He imagined something at the bottom, waiting for him, its jaws unhinged and wet teeth ready to gnaw on his ankles.

Logan paused and pulled out his small keychain light. He pointed the meager beam toward the bottom. Something reflected against it.

The sludgy water.

"I'm almost there." Soon, Logan reached the end of the rope. He hopped down a short distance. Not the drop Will had experienced, since Logan was so much taller. In fact, he could easily touch the rope, with his feet on the ground and his arm outstretched.

Water sloshed at the thick soles of his shoes. He was thankful to still have on his steel-toed work shoes, which kept his socks from getting soggy. Above, the Maglite created a bright circular light, like a train coming down a tunnel, but it didn't reach the bottom. All he had was his keychain flashlight, and he shined it around the claustrophobic space.

His wingspan was barely shorter than the width of the well. He only had to take a step with both arms outstretched to reach either side. The light seemed to grow fainter by the second, like it was a flame being snuffed out.

"Look for the hole," Will shouted. "Don't forget the hole."

A hole within a hole.

Logan laughed at the thought, going a little crazy from nerves. Will had told him there would be a smaller hole with air coming through, which was where Will had spoken his wish. That had seemed ridiculous, but now that he was here and his light hit the small hole, Logan was being drawn toward it.

He crouched. His work pants soaked through at the knees.

The hole opened in a half-moon at the side of the well, like a crawl space barely big enough for an adult to slide through. Logan beamed his light into it, but it didn't go far, disappearing in the dark.

Air blew through the hole. A slight breeze, hot despite it being the dead of winter.

He took a breath and spoke his wish. "I wish for the Nowhere Devils to win the 2004 Oklahoma Class B Boys State Championship."

He felt like he had to be specific, although who knew if that was the case. Perhaps the Basketball Gods could read his mind and knew his wish without him saying a thing.

Logan waited, but for what he wasn't sure.

When he was finally about to stand, his own voice whispered back toward him—a tiny echo of his wish. With it came the strong smell of burning trash and sulfur. He stood quickly, stumbling until his back hit the opposite wall. Logan dry heaved and spit into the standing water. He wiped at his runny nose and cleared his throat.

"I'm coming back up," he yelled.

Will and Alex must have held tight to the rope because Logan had no trouble climbing out. His heart raced like he was in the middle of an important game.

Already, Logan was ready to tell everyone. He didn't care that they wouldn't understand.

The wish would work because there were no coincidences. If the Basketball Gods were responsible for Kelvin's injury, then they wanted Logan down here. They wanted him to make this wish.

We're gonna win STATE, *like we've been destined to do all season.*
The Basketball Gods had wanted him to set that screen.

REGIONALS

AREA IV REGIONALS - CONSOLATION BRACKET

FOUR
HOME COURT ADVANTAGE

1

On Wednesday after school, Logan watched the *TRL* countdown before heading into work for the closing shift. The show hadn't been the same since Carson Daly left, but he still wanted to see if Britney Spears's "Toxic" would be number one again. Boy bands and pop stars weren't as cool as when he was in middle school—not that they were cool to the other seventh and eighth grade boys, but unlike them, Logan had never cared for Eminem or Korn—and he secretly still loved the pop icons.

He had an hour before he needed to leave for Wheelman's. His sister was at Kelvin's, and his mom was either working or at her new boyfriend's house; Logan couldn't keep track. He had met only one of her boyfriends in the three years since she left his father.

Logan didn't enjoy being around the man. It felt strange to hear a man call his mom by her first name or see *Janice* cuddling on the couch with someone who wasn't his father. Maybe Logan would have gotten over it if his father had still been in his life, but Bill Tramer only ever called on holidays or their birthdays. He promised to call more often, but as a long-haul trucker, it was hard to find the time.

Bill Tramer paid his child support. It came every month, along with a letter to his children. Emily had been as pissed as she had ever been when Logan ripped up the latest one. That had been a breaking point for him—an acceptance that he might never see his father again.

Emily, on the other hand, kept all the letters and eagerly awaited his calls on her birthday. Bill always called; Logan had to give him that. But Logan lacked his sister's optimism. Some-day, their father would forget to call. And then he would forget two years in a row. Then he would miss holidays too.

Logan was looking in the fridge when his mom showed up holding Subway sandwiches.

"What're you doing here?" he asked.

"Hello to you too. Are you going somewhere?"

He pointed at the logo on his work polo.

"Oh, right. Burger Night. Where's your sister?"

"Same place she's been every night."

"So I have to eat all these sandwiches by myself?"

"Oh, I've got time to eat."

Logan ate and hummed.

His mom sat down to eat her sandwich too. "Logan Ray Tramer. I'm gonna sit here all night alone, with that dumb song driving me crazy."

Logan shrugged and kept eating. When he had almost finished his sandwich, his mom stood. Her chair scraped back, surprising him. There was a quiet pause before she belted out the chorus of Britney Spears's "Toxic," with a dramatic dance.

Logan laughed until his eyes filled with tears, then started singing along. Before he knew it, he was dancing with his mom. They spun each other around and sang off-key. He was much taller than her but still managed to twirl beneath her arm.

He couldn't recall being in this good of a mood since Kelvin's injury and the loss to Nashoba. He wanted to call in sick—and would have, if it hadn't been Burger Night. Instead, he gave his mom a hug and said goodbye.

When he arrived at Wheelman's, though, an unsettling energy hung in the stifling air. Everyone was much quieter than usual, especially for Burger Night. No music played in the kitchen. No carhops gossiped. Will didn't even shit-talk him when he walked in.

"What's going on?" Logan asked Melinda. "Is the health department shutting us down or something?"

As soon as he said it, he peered past Melinda. Bird wasn't at the fryer station.

Another no-call, no-show?

Melinda's expression fell when she turned to face him.

Something worse.

"It's Bird," she said. "He's dead."

2

Regionals were held in Nowhere for the first time, after the team's back-to-back STATE TOURNAMENT appearances and their number one ranking in Class B this season. Home court made the embarrassment of losing in Districts and ending up on the consolation side of the bracket all the worse. But the fans' nervous energy only made them cheer louder during warmups.

Nowhere's gym was too small to host Regionals. In theory, they only had to accommodate two teams' worth of fans at a time, but it didn't play out that way in practice.

The first game tonight was from the winner's bracket— Nashoba versus Fort Todd. Even though Nashoba lost, all their fans stayed to watch Picard complete Nowhere's downfall—a task the Wolves had started—and the Fort Todd fans stayed because they had nothing better to do.

The crowd spilled over from the bleachers into the two entryways. Each one led from either side of the baskets to the expansive lobby with the trophy cases. Folding chairs were brought out for people to sit in the entryways, leaving just enough space for a single-file line to the restrooms. Nowhere's eighth graders manned the concession stand, stealing candy bars and popcorn when no one was looking.

Logan was nervous and excited, eager to find out if Will Roebuck was full of shit or if there was genuine magic inside that well. He pushed Bird's death out of his mind. Logan didn't need the distraction. No one at Wheelman's knew anything anyway. They couldn't tell him how Bird had died, only that he had.

As soon as Logan won the tipoff, he imagined the ways the magic might play out. Would a Picard player twist an ankle or airball a shot from an unexpected angle? Maybe someone would get sick.

Perhaps Tim would light it up from three-point land. There was no way that could happen without magic.

Logan became too focused on the intangible. He missed his man cutting to the basket and did not block out. Alex pounded the ball into the hardwood in frustration, his usual tunnel vision taking over.

The problem tonight was that Alex's shot was off. It surprised Logan—Alex had been unstoppable at practice this morning. Maybe the high stakes were getting to him.

Picard played without pressure. No surprise since they had no seniors. The Wombats were having the game of their lives in the first half. Those skinny underclassmen yelled, cheered, and danced after every made basket.

Alex and Tim looked like they might punch one of them. Marshal seemed like he would rather be anywhere else. Logan, meanwhile, continued to lack aggression. He barely left his feet. Every time he jumped to block a shot or grab a rebound, he imagined coming down on a leg unable to support his weight. In his mind's eye, his leg folded like Kelvin's.

It wasn't just the season on the line, but their whole lives. This was as big a test as any Logan had ever faced. He came out in the second half and put the kitchen well out of his mind. Logan bullied the skinny Picard boys, grabbed offensive rebounds, and gave his team every opportunity to make a shot. They continued to shoot poorly, but his aggressive rebounding gave the Devils far more chances against Picard.

The tide began to turn in Nowhere's favor. They went from a one-point lead at halftime to a ten-point lead at the end of the third quarter.

Alex heated up in the fourth, now with a bit of a cushion. Once his outside shot fell, it opened opportunities for him to drive for layups or pass to the open man. Even Tim hit a three-pointer near the end of the game, giving Nowhere a comfortable fifteen-point lead.

Yet Logan would toss and turn all night, dwelling on an unfulfilled wish.

Why wasn't he happier they had won and were moving on?

3

The next night, Nowhere played Mutton because the Rams had lost to McClinton yesterday in a blowout. McClinton's best player, Ethan Crist, led the way with thirty points—not so different from the beatdown Kelvin and the Devils had put on Mutton on Senior Night.

Mutton wasn't good this year but had benefited from a

weak district, like they always did. For four straight years, they had won their District Tournament, only to lose their next two games at Regionals.

It should have given Logan confidence.

Instead, the bright yellow and green jerseys of the Mutton Rams triggered the trauma Logan had experienced watching his best friend snap his leg. It was Senior Night again, Kelvin lying near the free-throw line, his twisted leg at an impossible angle.

It wasn't that a Mutton defender had challenged Kelvin's floater when his career ended—the defender hadn't even touched him. It was that the Mutton team had stuck around afterward and watched Kelvin writhe on the floor. Their fans had had the audacity to get involved in deciding what was best for Kelvin.

They had all stood there, gawking in their blinding yellows and greens, like voyeurs to the most intimate moment of the Nowhere Devils' young lives, until Coach Reed had the bright idea to cover Kelvin's leg with Sam Turner's towel.

Logan couldn't focus on punishing the Rams in the low block.

"Tramer, you're bigger than those boys. Play like it!"

He couldn't catch a pass.

"Wipe your damn hands off, boy!"

He misread a screen and didn't switch when Marshal needed him to.

"Not good enough."

He could ignore his coach and the fans yelling at him but not Alex, who bumped into him coming out of a timeout in the second quarter: "Where's your fucking magic?"

"It doesn't reward ball hogs," Logan snapped back.

Alex slapped him hard on the ass and started freezing Logan out. But Doug and Marshal played well. When Alex didn't force a shot, but passed to them on the perimeter, the juniors either drove or took the three, making over half their shots. The game was close going into the fourth quarter—Nowhere clung to a two-point lead, never able to put Mutton away for good.

Mutton's center was at least three inches shorter than Logan, but he had the longest arms Logan had ever seen. They were always closer than Logan expected when he went for a rebound or an easy shot. Still, the Devils were winning. They had never led by more than two possessions, but they maintained a lead ever since Mutton scored the first basket.

Then, with about five minutes left, Logan battled the lanky Mutton center for a rebound, and his opponent crumbled to the floor, grimacing.

Immediately, Logan assumed the guy had broken his leg, but the center's calf muscle rippled into a taut position. The center attempted to rub it away, but when he stood, the cramp tightened again. A teammate helped him to the sideline, where he continued massaging it. The cramp eventually went away, but by then, Nowhere had built their lead to eight points with under two minutes left in the game.

Without the Mutton center's lanky arms wrapped around him, Logan was freed up to fight for offensive rebounds. He tipped in two baskets and even hit his free throws when fouled on three different occasions in the fourth quarter.

Another Nowhere victory.

The Devils ran to the locker room after shaking hands with Mutton. A medicinal smell had lingered ever since the paramedics put Kelvin on a stretcher and carried him out to the ambulance. The whole locker room had reeked of it, like Mikey Spruce's insulin bottle had broken in his gym bag. But it was finally gone, replaced with the usual pungent odor of sweaty boys.

"That's how you do it, boys," Coach Park said. "I want you

to bring that same energy tomorrow night. You know the Wolves well. You know how fearless they are."

Everyone groaned. They hated it whenever Coach Park complimented the opposing teams, but especially when he waxed poetic about their rival. It was never lost on them that Coach Park was from Nashoba. The Wolves' coach, James Harjo, had been his coach during his playing days, and it was obvious how much Coach Park admired him.

Coach Park had even gone out to dinner with Harjo last week, after Nowhere lost to them in Districts. At least, that's what Marshal had said.

Logan didn't want to leave the locker room. Instead, he felt compelled to sit on the uncomfortable bench until tomorrow night's game. Alex stayed behind after everyone else left in high spirits.

"So, what do you think?" Alex asked, peeling off his Iverson Reeboks. "Was it the wish?"

"What are you talking about?"

"The guy getting a cramp. We pulled away after he went out. You played ten times better."

"I was fine before that. He fouled me every play—"

"And then the Basketball Gods got him out of the game."

"You sound like a believer, Spruce."

"All I'm saying is, the timing couldn't have been better. Still...I figured your kitchen well can do better than that. Every other game, someone gets a cramp."

"So, you don't believe it?"

"We're just talking, Tramer. Damn."

"As long as we keep winning, I don't care how it happens," Logan lied. He wanted more than anything to see the well works its magic definitively.

Alex paused before leaving the locker room. "Your aunt's team really won STATE without her?"

"That's right."

"Hell yeah. Maybe Kelvin will be able to come watch us at the Big House. See us win it all, like she did."

"Sure, but she didn't see them win it all."

"What do you mean?"

Logan suddenly felt distant from the words he spoke, like he was reading a statement of fact. "Aunt Joss wasn't at the championship game. She had gone home...and killed herself."

FIVE
GAMECHANGER

1

IT WAS HALFTIME of the Regional Consolation Finals against
Nashoba, and the phlegmy sounds of the players catching their
breath was deafening in the quiet locker room. The Devils
trailed by eight points.

Coach Park braced himself and started in on what might
have been his final speech as head coach. "Do you want this?
That's what you have to ask yourselves. Do you want this?
Because if not, then this is your lucky day. Keep waiting for
Kelvin to walk onto the court, and you'll find yourselves done
with the season. Done with your career, for some of you."

"Yes, Coach," Marshal answered.

"Yes, what?"

"I want this. *We* want this."

"Then get out there and show me."

Marshal wasn't as confident as he might have seemed. He
had answered Coach Park because he was tired of no one saying
anything.

His mother's family, the Kemps, had been as annoying as

ever in the first half. Never before had so many of them shown up to an away game to antagonize Marshal. They led the crowd in chants and laughed every time he missed a shot. He saw his parents behind the team bench, glaring from the opposite side of the court.

Folks from Nashoba actually believed their team had a chance to make STATE with Nowhere out of the picture. Barton-Meek were ranked eighth in Class B and likely to cruise through Area, but that left room for one more Area IV team to qualify. McClinton and Fort Todd were strong, but Nashoba had only lost to Fort Todd by four points, despite playing poorly. Losing one game meant they still had another shot at STATE.

The Devils were doing their best to make sure that didn't happen. They played with more fire in the third quarter, but every time they got within a basket, the Wolves drew a shooting foul, took a charge, or scored on a putback. With one minute left in the third, Nowhere down by two, a ticky-tack foul was called on Marshal. He turned to argue the call but stopped mid-breath, distracted by the police officer standing in the entryway.

The folks in folding chairs looked up at the cop like he was a stranger, but he wasn't. Deputy Ryan Holbrook had graduated two years ago and had taken Marshal under his wing when he was a freshman. Marshal had learned Ryan's game so well that, upon Ryan's graduation, he was able to step right into his role in the starting lineup.

The deputy approached Nashoba's coach when the ball was put into play. Coach Harjo looked baffled. Marshal stared at them and missed Bolan Grimes driving to the hoop for an open layup. Bolan got in his face afterward and howled. His breath reeked of nachos and motor oil. He was one of two white players in Nashoba's starting lineup and the only one—Native or white—wearing "war paint" on his cheeks and biceps.

Marshal knew him well. In second grade, Bolan had been his best friend. They explored the woods together, spied on Bolan's sister while she sunbathed, and had sleepovers playing *Teenage Mutant Ninja Turtles* on Marshal's Nintendo. Bolan was Nashoba's most annoying player and was still hollering when one of the refs blew the whistle. Ryan motioned for the referees and Coach Park to come over.

The crowd murmured with curiosity. The players on the court exchanged annoyed glances at the interruption. Then Coach Harjo jabbed his finger toward the deputy's face, less than an inch from poking him in the eye. His olive skin turned maroon, like he couldn't catch his breath.

Ryan stood with his arms on his hips, like Superman. He said something, and Coach Harjo shook his head. The ref called out, "Grimes. Come on over."

Bolan swaggered toward the sideline, and his teammates teased him as if he were being sent to the principal's office. But Marshal could tell Bolan was scared. Bolan used to have night terrors when Marshal stayed over. Marshal would wake to his friend's wild screeches—an experience that still haunted him. He couldn't sleep without music now; the silence was too ripe for those bloodcurdling howls.

"This y'all trying to scare Grimes?" a Nashoba player asked Tim. "Some home cooking?"

"Home cooking with a cop?"

"He ain't just any cop. That motherfucker was on your team."

Tim squinted toward the deputy. "No, he wasn't. When?"

"That's Ryan Holbrook, Tim," Marshal said.

"See?" another Nashoba player said. "Just some shenanigans to get in our heads."

"I'm still not seeing it," Tim said.

Alex stepped up next to Logan, and Marshal overheard him say, "Do you think this is it?"

Logan smiled in response.

What the fuck?

Before Marshal could say anything, Bolan Grimes shoved the deputy in the chest.

The crowd gasped. Nashoba's players on the court ran toward their bench. Coach Harjo stopped them as Ryan held Bolan over the bottom row of bleachers and cuffed him.

Nashoba fans shouted in disgust. Everyone was shocked, but the Kemps didn't let that stop them. They rose as one—a solid, violent wall. Marshal and his teammates stood between the worst of the crowd and Ryan, imagining they'd be trampled. Fortunately, Coach Park, the refs, and Nashoba's two assistant coaches moved to settle the fans, and their thin authority held.

Marshal knew it wouldn't last long. The Kemps had come to Nowhere, and they recognized no authority higher than their family, their God, and their sense of justice. There were eight, maybe nine Kemps in attendance, depending on whether you believed the rumors about Winnie Carr being Adam Kemp's kid. Every one of them, except Winnie, left the bleachers.

One of Marshal's uncles was the first to try crossing the hardwood river, but he tripped over his own feet and rolled toward Alex, his hairy ass crack on full display. Alex started to help him up, but the uncle wriggled away, as though Alex was behind the arrest. Marshal wondered if his teammate was.

A cousin of his was the next Kemp to make a run for it. He juked past one of Nashoba's assistant coaches and darted straight for Marshal. Marshal couldn't tell if the cousin was coming for Ryan or if this was just an excuse to take a shot at John Lovegood's son. He balled his fists, ready to fight. Out of nowhere, Coach Park blindsided the cousin, and the tackle made a loud thwack against the court.

Coach Harjo now played mediator and calmed down his players. The Nowhere five stood close together on the court, like accomplices getting their story straight. Maybe Logan and Alex would need to, but Marshal didn't have a clue what was happening. Why the hell was Bolan Grimes being arrested in the middle of a playoff game?

"You Nowhere motherfucker," Bolan yelled. His face was smushed against the bleachers, where a sweaty ass had been a few minutes ago. "You crooked fucking pig!"

Bolan had no family here to dispute whatever claim the deputy made for arresting him.

Everyone's eyes had fallen on Bolan and Ryan. No one seemed to notice a third Kemp's attempt to cross the court. The coaches and refs on crowd control must have thought he was no threat.

Everyone called him Uncle Thomas, but Marshal wasn't sure if the old man was his great uncle, a distant cousin, or what. He was ancient—old enough that his body had started curling in on itself, like a roly-poly. The man moved slowly with a cane, batting it so hard into the court with every step that Marshal thought he would leave indentions in the hardwood.

Uncle Thomas made it all the way to the Nashoba bench and raised the cane over his head just as Ryan righted himself, with the cuffed Bolan in tow. Marshal imagined the cane coming down on his head, cracking the deputy's skull. He pictured the blood spreading across the court, leaving a crimson stain. Marshal ran to stop the old man but feared he had waited too long.

Emily Tramer—Marshal's best friend, his secret crush—emerged from the crowd and jumped between Ryan and Uncle Thomas. The old man hesitated just long enough for Marshal to reach him.

He gripped one hand around the cane and placed his other

on Uncle Thomas's back. "It's not worth it, Uncle Thomas," he said. "It ain't worth it."

Uncle Thomas looked up at Marshal like he was coming out of a brain fog.

"Let's get you back to your seat. What'd'ya say?"

By the time Marshal had gotten Uncle Thomas back to the other side of the court, Ryan had left with Bolan in handcuffs.

"I recorded the whole thing, Marshal," a Kemp said. She held the chunky camcorder out like it was a murder weapon. "Y'all won't get away with this."

"We had nothing to do with this, asshole," Marshal replied. "Why don't you ask Bolan why he's getting arrested?"

A half hour passed before the game started again. Most of the eight or nine Kemps left. The rest of the Nashoba crowd lost steam without them. They couldn't even boo properly when Nowhere began to pull away.

The Wolves weren't the same. Marshal had never seen Nashoba play without fire before. It made him uncomfortable. Regardless, the Devils took the win being offered them and were headed back to the Area Tournament for the fourth year in a row. Three more wins and they'd reach STATE.

He kept a close eye on Logan and Alex. *What are you hiding?*

2

Emily loved to talk, and Marshal loved to listen to her talk. He knew what boys she had kissed, which girl she had kissed, and that she was a virgin. Marshal knew who she couldn't stand at school and how she and her friends had been kleptos in Tuska-homa. He knew about every fight she ever had with her mom or Logan and how her father didn't give a shit about her or her brother anymore.

Marshal had had a thing for her when they met in the

spring semester of eighth grade, but he got over it. It took a year and a half, but once he hit his growth spurt sophomore year and started dating girls from Cottonvale and Holdendecker, Emily seemed like small potatoes by comparison. He loved her as a friend, as it should be.

Then Emily started holding hands with Kelvin one day at school, and Marshal couldn't believe he was learning about their relationship the same way everyone else did.

Now he knew nothing. Had they hooked up? Were they in love, or just killing time until Kelvin left for Denton, Texas? He had no answers, and as much as Emily talked, she said little about her relationship with Kelvin. It stirred dormant feelings inside Marshal—an unrequited love he couldn't shake. It had gotten worse since Kelvin's injury. Now Emily did nothing but sit next to his bed, holding his hand. And Kelvin had been annoying as hell. Marshal was tired of spending his days visiting a depressed has-been.

Tonight—if ever there was a night—he pushed Emily to go to Turner's barn with him. "We have to celebrate," he said as she drove them toward Kelvin's house. "Can you believe that shit happened?"

"I almost got clubbed by an elder," Emily said. "I'm lucky you were there."

"My relatives, man. They bring out the worst in people."

"I almost can't blame the reaction. You'd think Ryan would wait until the game was over to do that."

"You'd think." Marshal recalled the way Alex and Logan had been whispering to each other. *Do you think this is it?* "Is it possible someone asked Ryan to arrest Bolan in the middle of the game like that?"

"I don't know. Weren't you two close?"

"I mean, he was like a big brother to me his senior year, but I haven't talked to him since then, except when he pulled me over once or twice to fuck with me. What're you insinuating there, Tramer?"

She laughed. "I'm not accusing you. I'm saying you should ask him. Although...now you're acting suspicious."

"Excuse me?" He grinned.

She pursed her lips and tapped on them with her forefinger, evaluating him.

"Okay, Hercule Poirot."

He wanted to kiss her so badly, even if it meant wrecking the Kia. *At least we won't have to go to Kelvin's if that happens. Maybe she wants me to kiss her. Maybe she's been waiting for it since we met.*

"You sure you don't want to at least swing by Turner's barn?" he asked.

"I can't, Marsh. Kelvin's waiting for me to tell him about the game. Imagine the look on his face...I can drop you at home first if you want to go to the party. Might be nice to have some alone time."

Marshal imagined Emily sneaking in through Kelvin's window and cuddling up next to him while his casted leg was hiked up in the sling. He had been wearing basketball shorts every time Marshal saw him, so it was too easy to imagine Emily sliding her hand down Kelvin's waistband.

"No, no, you're right, you're right," he said. "I want to see his reaction too."

He was annoyed on all fronts. Annoyed he couldn't go to the party. Annoyed he had to spend more time with Kelvin. Why couldn't they pull the car over, admit they had always loved each other, and then passionately make out?

The silence made the night seem darker. Bugs pattered into the headlights like rain.

He waited because Emily always filled the silence. Marshal

hoped she would say something he could cling his hope to, some statement alluding to their secret love.

"Do you think Kelvin is still going to North Texas next year?" she asked, her voice softer with insecurity.

Marshal sat up straighter. "Did he say anything?"

"No... I haven't asked."

"They won't take away his scholarship, Em," he said, straightforward enough to convince himself it was true. He'd been counting on Kelvin moving to Denton in the fall. No matter how strong their relationship was, it wouldn't last long distance.

"What if his leg is never the same?" she asked.

"It's a leg break like any other," he said. "It just looked bad."

"The doctors weren't so sure. They said he'd have to do physical therapy—"

"Yeah, I was there too. Do you really think Kelvin Harris won't work his way back onto the court? Why are you asking me about this?" The anger in his voice surprised him. "You want him to lose his scholarship, don't you? You want him staying here in Nowhere."

"Why do you sound so accusatory?"

"You realize, if Kelvin stays here, you'll be the one doing the leaving next year."

"I can always go to Red Oak—"

Marshal scoffed. "Really? You're better than that."

"You don't have to be such an asshole."

Marshal was hot and flabbergasted. "I'm the asshole? I'm just being real with you, Em. He has dreams, and so do you. It's not the end of the world if y'all break up. I've dated four girls in the last year. You get together, you have sex, you hold hands, get all lovey-dovey, and then you break up to try out other fish in the sea."

"Real romantic, Marshal."

"I'm just saying—"

"Uh-huh. And I'm just being vulnerable with the person I thought was my best friend, not some patronizing asshole."

"Yeah, well..."

Emily didn't say anything more, no matter how quiet Marshal got. Without a word, she steered the Kia away from the turnoff to Harris Hill and went down Snakeback Road. For a foolishly hopeful moment, he thought they were headed to the party at Turner's barn, but then he realized they were going to his house.

He didn't argue the decision. A part of him thought the fight was a good thing. Those in the friend zone didn't fight. Fighting bred sexual chemistry. Marshal convinced himself this was the way.

It didn't stop the disappointment he felt when Emily gave a half-hearted wave and drove away. He went back to imagining her "alone time" with Kelvin.

This can't be how tonight ends, he thought as he lay on his bed. He decided to head to Turner's barn, maybe even find someone to hook up with. But then his mind returned to the game.

Did those two really have Ryan arrest Bolan like that?

Marshal picked up the landline in his room and dialed Ryan's number from memory. The phone rang and rang before going to the answering machine. Marshal hung up before leaving a message, deflated that he'd have to wait to know for sure. Then he realized Ryan would be at the station, so he grabbed the phone book.

The receptionist at the sheriff's office was able to patch him through to Deputy Holbrook's desk phone. It rang three times, and Marshal was about to hang up when he heard a click.

"Hello?"

"Ryan?"

"This is Deputy Holbrook. May I ask who I'm speaking to?"

"It's Marshal Lovegood, man. Anything interesting happen tonight?"

3

The entire community of Nowhere breathed a sigh of relief after the Nashoba game. The boys were headed back to the Area Tournament. There was a time that would have been a huge accomplishment.

Tim Springer hadn't been on the team the first time Nowhere made Area in twenty years. He didn't even go to games back then, but he'd heard plenty about the team's surprising, unbeaten run through Districts and Regionals during Kelvin's freshman year. Before the run to Area, Nowhere games weren't very well attended—mostly family members of the players. By the time Tim joined the team in his repeated sophomore year, every home game was a full house.

Even Holdendecker folks started showing up in Nowhere. Tim was surprised they knew where it was. His dad picked up *The Holdendecker Record* every week because they had started putting full-page write-ups about Nowhere in the Sports section. The Holdendecker principal had spent all summer lobbying to annex Nowhere Public Schools by the start of Tim's sophomore year. A run to Area had garnered all this attention, but nowadays it was "what have you done for me lately."

Even without Kelvin, anything less than STATE would be a disappointment. Tim thought everyone in Shappaway County had lost perspective. Basketball was fun, but life was bigger than the game. Take Kelvin Harris, for instance. Even if he never played another game and had his scholarship to North Texas revoked, he still had a sexy girlfriend and two parents who loved him. He was smart enough for college and charming enough to get any job he wanted.

A good life was ahead of him, and Tim understood that would be the case for many of the players on his team. He could never tell them that, though. Tim was known for being unfiltered, but talking shit about the banality of team sports wouldn't go over well. Just look at Will Roebuck. Everyone at school hated him.

Besides, it wasn't like Tim wanted to lose. A trip to the Big House meant staying in a hotel much nicer than his house and eating food on the school's dime, way better than the ramen noodles and Wheelman's takeout he had every night. It also meant opportunities to flirt with girls from Class A and Class B schools that made STATE. And Tim absolutely loved an athletic body.

If they didn't make STATE, at least he still had Turner's barn. Tonight had the biggest turnout for any party this year. Even Will Roebuck showed up. He was talking to Logan, which surprised Tim until he remembered those two worked together. Classmates and alums and random Nowhere people, some as old as thirty, dry-humped on the dance floor, chugged beers, and dared each other to streak across the pasture in below-freezing cold. Normally, Tim would have taken up the challenge himself, but it reminded him too much of finding his father naked in the pasture.

He had been coming home late from a trip to Arrow to go bowling, and his souped-up S-10 pickup's bright headlights had beamed halfway down the driveway, landing on the tall, pale body of Red Springer.

"Dad!" Tim jumped from his truck and ran to get him, shrugging off his coat.

His naked father turned to face him. The pale blue of his eyes was more off-putting than usual. His skin was almost blue.

His testicles curled into his knobby penis. His pubic hair was frosty. His veins shone through his translucent chest.

Tim steered him into his truck and asked, "What're you thinking, Dad?" but he wasn't thinking. Sure, Red gave him a reason: He had been about to get in the shower when he remembered he hadn't put the dogs in the pen for the night and worried the coyotes would get them. But the Springers' dogs had all been killed a year or more ago—either by coyotes or accidentally run over.

At home, Tim chewed out his older brother Daniel, who was supposed to keep an eye on their dad when Tim was at school, a party, or gone to town. But, like usual, Daniel neglected his responsibilities and got high in his bedroom.

Tim's dad recovered surprisingly well. His skin was dry and red, but nothing needed to be amputated. Ever since, Red had remained his confused self until they got him into the bleachers. He would come alive and cheer on the team, berating the refs with the best of them. He never got onto Tim about how he played. He was just happy Tim had joined the team.

Red Springer played himself back in the day. Truth be told, Tim, the youngest of eight kids, wasn't sure how old his dad was. Red had been on his fourth marriage when Tim was born. Tim's mom died when he was six, and it had been just Tim and his dad since then—his siblings lived with their moms or were already adults when his mom died. Daniel had moved in a year ago after serving time at Lexington Prison. It was nice having someone else around to help, even though Daniel did a piss-poor job of it.

Tim had been nervous about coming to the party tonight but threatened to get Daniel arrested for possession if he messed up again.

He approached Logan and Will, who was as giddy as Tim had ever seen him.

"Why're you so excited, Roebuck?" Tim asked. "Don't you hate us?"

"I don't hate anyone," Will said. "But that arrest was something, wasn't it?"

"Sure was," Tim admitted.

"Why ain't there a drink in your hand?" Logan asked. He only ever said "ain't" when he was drunk, which wasn't often.

"Oh, don't worry about me, big man."

Logan shimmied his shoulders to the music. "We did it, Tim. We're gonna win STATE. Can you believe it?"

"Hold your horses, Tramer. We need three more wins just to get to STATE."

"You don't understand, man. It's our destiny."

"What the hell are you on?"

"Let the man celebrate," Will said.

"I gotta say," Tim said. "I'm not a fan of this supportive side of you, Roebuck. It's downright strange."

"I don't give a shit about the team, all right? But if someone's gonna get arrested every game, well, that might make all these awful games I've watched worth it."

Someone punched Tim in the arm, giving him a Charlie Horse. He recognized Marshal's floppy blonde hair in his peripheral before needing to fully see him. "Damn, Lovegood. Where the hell did you come from?"

"I need to talk to y'all," Marshal said. He didn't feel the need to clarify that "y'all" meant Tim and Logan, not Will.

Will got the hint. "See you at work, Tramer."

Tim noticed the look on his face—a longing to belong—but he wasn't sympathetic. Will could have joined the team all these years. It wasn't like Jack Ward was any good at basketball —or Tim, really. Instead, Will decided to hate on the team every chance he got. As few games as Nowhere had lost the past three years, Will Roebuck would always be there the next day at school to berate them about it.

"Since when are you two such butt buddies?" Tim asked Logan.

"We're not. Will's the worst."

"Anyone else here?" Marshal asked. "Alex? Dougie?"

"Around here someplace," Tim said.

"I saw Alex leaving with Letty Prospect," Logan said, smirking and bobbing to the beat as Outkast's "Hey Ya" began to play.

"Really? The sophomore?" Marshal said.

"Hey, hey now, good for him," Tim said.

"I don't know…"

"She's his brother's age. Maybe they got a little trio happening there. You don't know."

"Goddamn, Tim. You're a sicko, man."

Tim chuckled, wishing it was a real laugh. But the party failed to distract him from leaving his dad alone with Daniel.

"There's Dougie," Logan said.

Tim crossed to where Doug was leaning against a wall, chatting with Mal Turner and Macy Goode, and tore him away.

"Hey—" Doug attempted to shrug him off, but Tim was too strong for him. "What the hell? Didn't you see who I was talking to?"

"You can get laid another time," Tim said.

"*Attempt* to get laid," Logan joked.

"It'll be worth putting off," Marshal said. "Y'all want to know why Ryan Holbrook arrested Bolan during the game?"

"What do you mean?" Logan seemed suddenly sober.

"I mean, I've got a place to be in five minutes if you want to get some answers." He leaned closer to them. "I called Ryan—pardon me—*Deputy* Holbrook. He agreed to meet me out here. I barely had to ask before he suggested it like he's dying to tell someone what happened."

"We saw what happened," Logan said.

"Sure, but *why* did it happen?"

"I don't know, man…" Doug said. "I kind of want to get back to what I was doing."

"Keep it in your pants for one night, Mr. Saint," Tim said. "Fuck it. Let's go."

4

"Watch out for the gopher holes," Marshal said. "I almost twisted my ankle."

They marched toward a row of large oak trees at the edge of the Turner property. The stars seemed unusually close tonight and looked like they were moving, the night clouds passing overhead so quickly. Tim thought it might rain later and ice everything over again. He didn't mind. His truck never had trouble with icy roads, and he often spent those days driving around with a chain in the back, pulling smaller cars out of ditches.

They didn't wait long before a Ford Ranger bounced down the bumpy path, its brights blinding them.

Ryan Holbrook exited in jeans and a hoodie, his hood pulled over his head.

"Hey, Deep Throat," Marshal said, laughing.

"Who the hell is with you?"

"Don't you know your old teammates?" Tim said.

Ryan eased his shoulders and took off his hood. "Sure, I do. You still want to kick my ass, Tramer?"

"Water under the bridge," Logan said, reaching out to shake Ryan's hand.

Tim had forgotten all about the time Ryan and Logan nearly

came to blows on the outdoor court during lunch break. Of course, he also had no clue Ryan Holbrook was a Sheriff's deputy.

"Since when did you become a cop?" he asked, also shaking Ryan's hand.

"Over a year now. Got a reason I should arrest you?"

"Not at the moment."

"Never," Doug said.

"I'm drunk." Logan hiccupped.

"Then you have the right to remain silent."

Everyone laughed. Ryan rubbed his hands together, rattled as much by the cold as by the situation. "It wasn't supposed to happen like that."

"You weren't gonna arrest Bolan?" Marshal asked.

"No, we planned to arrest his ass. Just not in the middle of a damn playoff game." He blew on his hands, then the story spilled out. "We've had an investigation going for the last eight months. A big one. We've been working with Bison County deputies on it. A meth operation covering both our counties. The Grimes brothers were involved—Bolan and his older brother Connor.

"We started making arrests last week. Found out they had a cook site out by Chisolm Lake, so we wanted to pick 'em up there. We got Connor this afternoon and knew Bolan was headed to the lake after the game tonight. I was supposed to follow him without spooking him—make sure he went where we expected him to. Make sure he didn't get tipped off and make a run for it. It was supposed to be easy.

"So I'm waiting out by Clearwater Creek when I get this call on my radio. Police channel, but it's staticky as hell. Maybe it's the cold weather, or all these damn cell phones people have nowadays. I don't know. I ask 'em to repeat, and the staticky voice comes on again, a little clearer this time. 'Move on

Grimes,' it says. It sounds like Sheriff Dixon, so I call back and confirm. 'Move on Grimes,' it says again.

"I go to the gym, and y'all saw how that played out. It was a shit show. I was pissed, wondering why Dixon would put me through that alone. Everyone knows how heated these playoff games can get. Throw in the rivalry on top of that? It's amazing I got out of there without a scratch.

"In fact, a couple of Nashoba guys followed me to the parking lot. Yeah, they recognized me from when I put up thirty points on their asses. They start threatening to fight me. Then guess who comes out to confront them?" Ryan jabbed his finger toward Tim. "Your old man, Springer."

Tim's heart stopped. "My dad?"

He recalled seeing his dad and Daniel at home after the game—the distant look in his father's eyes. Like he often did these days, he gave Red Springer as little attention as he would a floor lamp. Tim took care of his dad—fed him, helped clothe him, even picked his naked ass out of a field in the blistering cold. But he never sat and chatted with him like he used to. Maybe if he had made the attempt tonight, he wouldn't have been caught off guard by the news.

Tim noticed Logan scrutinizing him in the dark and played it off. "Can't say I'm surprised. Red's always getting himself caught up in shit."

"Well, he was ready to throw down with those boys," Ryan said. "I shoved Grimes into my car and pulled my sidearm. That's right. I had to pull out my gun to get them to stop chirping at each other and go home. And actually, that didn't even work. Fucking Ms. Fletcher came out to settle things down. They were more intimidated by her ass than me and my piece. She managed to get your old man back in the gym, and who knows where the Nashoba guys went.

"Anyway, I take Grimes to book him. Dixon calls me,

wanting an update. I tell him I got Grimes, just like he told me to do. He's confused and pissed. He didn't give an order, he says. I tell him someone did, and it sure as hell sounded like him. I don't mention it was staticky because I'm already realizing something funny's going on.

"I badger everyone at the office. Someone gave the order, right? But no one owns up to it. And worse, none of the dispatchers heard anyone radio me to arrest Bolan Grimes during the game. I must be losing my mind, right?"

No one answered.

Ryan ran his hand through his hair so much it started sticking up on its own. "I don't know...It's crazy, man."

"What's done is done," Marshal said. "Forget about it. Come over to the party and have a drink."

"Yeah, that's just what I need to do. Go party with the team after arresting a rival player during the game."

"At least have a smoke," Tim said, offering his pack.

Ryan took a cigarette from him, and Tim flicked his lighter to life. The flame glowed on Ryan's frazzled face.

Tim lit one up himself. He hated that his hand was shaking, but at least he could pretend it was the cold. It wasn't the first time Red Springer had gotten into it with fans from the opposing team, but of course, it felt different this time. Maybe Tim could get his dad another dog and it would help. He suddenly wanted to go home and check on him. By the time he finished his cigarette, he did just that.

5

The only light inside the trailer house seeped from under the door to his brother's bedroom. Tim stopped by his dad's room and peeked inside, relieved to hear the old man snoring.

As he lay down in his bed, he let go of the guilt gnawing at him. He wondered if there would come a day when he couldn't party or go anywhere without his dad. Perhaps even a day when Red Springer would need to go to Hurst Manor in Holdendecker. God forbid Tim would have to admit him to the memory ward of Willow Lane in Arrow. He decided he would ask Daniel to call his mom tomorrow.

Daniel's mom lived between Holdendecker and the larger town of Miner. She was the closest family to them. All of Red's siblings and their spouses had passed, and his other ex-wives and children lived farther away. Daniel's mom had put her parents in homes before they passed, and despite practically disowning Daniel when he ended up in prison, she had always been kind to Tim. She'd even let him stay weekends with them when he was younger, when he had no friends other than his dad.

She'll know what to do, he thought as his eyelids grew heavy.

Minutes or hours later, Tim peeled his eyes open. He could have sworn the sound of barking dogs had woken him. Now, there was nothing. *Go back to sleep.* It was three in the morning, pitch-black inside his room, the moon and stars hidden behind winter clouds. He turned to every position he could think of, but nothing worked.

Another sound pierced the silence. Not barking dogs, but coyotes. They yelped wildly, close to the house. They were no dream.

Tim shivered, a sense of doom falling on him, leaving him breathless.

He leaped out of bed and ran to his dad's room, flipping on the light switch, hoping all it would do was wake him. Tim would love nothing more than to be cussed out by his dad right now.

But that wasn't what he saw. The sheets hung over the side of an empty bed. Panic shot through him as he rushed into his brother's room. Daniel was smoking a blunt. He jumped at Tim's interruption and coughed violently, like he was dying.

"Dad's gone," Tim said. "Put some clothes on."

"Fuck," Daniel managed to gasp through his coughs. "Don't he know how goddamn cold it is out there?"

"He doesn't know a fucking thing, Dan. Let's go."

Tim threw on his shoes and coat, grabbed a Maglite from a drawer in the kitchen, and tossed a second one to his brother. Daniel fumbled the catch, and the heavy flashlight landed on his foot.

"Fuck, bro!" he yelped in pain.

"Shut the hell up. You go down the driveway, I'll check the pasture."

Tim didn't wait for Daniel to finish pulling on his shoe. He ran outside and around the side of the house. He froze when he noticed a pack of five coyotes standing near the empty dog pen. Tim hollered and beamed the light at them. The coyotes scattered into the darkness.

He swung the flashlight around, expecting to see his naked father again. Three more steps toward the pasture, his light sweeping across the dark, the tall grass swaying in the cold wind.

"Dad!" he shouted. His voice echoed across the empty land. For a moment, he could have sworn something moved, but when he caught the spot in the light again, there was only a hazy mist over the darkness, making him think something more corporeal had been there. He felt a breath on the back of his neck and swung to tell Daniel to back the hell up. But Daniel wasn't there. Tim scratched at the tingling sensation that wouldn't go away now and continued scanning the light and calling his father's name.

Then a thought occurred to him: *A pack of fucking coyotes that close to the house?*

Tim hadn't seen them that bold since the Springers had small dogs in the pen.

His blood turned cold, the tickling breath gone from his neck replaced with a numb chill. He turned the flashlight back to the dog pen.

It looked just like it had for the past year—the front gate dangling off-kilter, the top hinge broken, a tarp flapping over the cage. He shined the light into the pen and saw a heap.

An image of four pups huddled together to stay warm flickered in his mind, like his dogs used to do when the Springers had dogs. They didn't anymore, he reminded himself. He stepped closer, until he stood over the heap, the light revealing the corpse of Red Springer.

The look on his dad's face made Tim's screams catch in his throat. He stood frozen for a full minute before he shouted his brother's name.

Red stared up at Tim with bulging eyes and a mouth stretched wide, far beyond what it should have been capable of. His whole face elongated in terror.

SIX
THE SIXTH MAN

1

ON MONDAY MORNING, Coach Park made the boys get to the gym early. He attributed their Regional Tournament success to two-a-day practices and was committed to doing it again on Monday and Tuesday. They would take a break the day before their first Area Tournament game.

Logan hadn't heard yet who they would be playing. It was the loser between Barton-Meek and Colesville, but Logan never found out who won. Without internet at home and no one at work yesterday able to tell him, Logan felt out of the loop. If Bird had been at work, *he* would have known.

But, of course, Bird was dead.

Logan was reminded of that when he had arrived at work Sunday. The place didn't smell the same anymore, like everything they cooked was past its expiration date. It was no longer a reprieve from the pressure of winning STATE.

At least the pressure had eased for him. He had a wonderful sense of inevitability. Even the rest of the team felt it. They didn't know about the kitchen well, but they knew the Basketball Gods had a history of picking sides in big games. The team practiced with purpose and swagger, but one thing was missing that Monday morning—Tim hadn't shown up.

It wasn't the first time Tim missed a practice, especially one this early, but the former sixth man had been reliable since he was moved into the starting lineup. The only upside to Tim's absence was that it gave Mikey, Sam, Dylan, and Jack a chance to run with the first unit. Sam Turner practiced like he was gunning for Tim's spot, and honestly, he deserved it. Although Alex clearly was hoping the spot went to his little brother. He yelled at Mikey every time Sam scored on him or stole it from him. At least Alex wasn't yelling at Logan, blaming him for shit. The two were on better terms after witnessing the magic of Logan's wish.

Logan was still wonderfully hungover from drinking so much Saturday night. He thought about the strange voice on Ryan Holbrook's radio—Logan's magic wish ordering the deputy to arrest Bolan midgame.

Basketball Gods shit. Logan loved it.

After the morning practice, Coach Park called the boys to huddle up by the bleachers before they headed to the locker room.

"Who are we playing Thursday?" Logan asked.

"Colesville," Sam Turner said. "They got creamed by Barton-Meek."

"Those boys are looking scary," Jack Ward added. "I got a cousin from Barton-Meek. Says their guards haven't missed a three since Christmas."

"Your cousin's smoking something," Alex said.

"I don't know," Marshal replied. "They've only lost four games all season."

"Two of those to us."

"Sure..." Mikey Spruce said. "When Kelvin—"

"Doesn't matter who we play," Alex cut in. "Colesville, Barton-Meek. We could play last year's West Mann and kick their ass."

"That's the spirit, Spruce," Coach Park said, meeting them at the bleachers. "It's not about our opponent. It's about us. Aggression. Focus. Those are always the keys to our success, especially without Kelvin. Now, I didn't call you over to talk about Colesville. They're feisty, but nothing we can't handle. I called you over because you may have noticed Tim's absence this morning."

"I told y'all he'd miss practice," Jack Ward joked. "Partied too hard this weekend." He was Tim's third cousin, and they hung out on occasion, but Jack Ward had not observed Red's mental decline. He mostly got high with Daniel and watched Denzel Washington movies with Tim.

"Tim didn't oversleep," Coach Park said. "I'm sorry to say his father passed away early Sunday morning."

The only sound left in the gym was Alex bouncing the ball on the bleacher in front of him. He seemed incapable of stopping, like he didn't realize he was doing it. Logan wished Alex would look at him and signal everything was all right—that this news had nothing to do with—

Already, Ryan's story rattled around Logan's mind.

"I know you boys loved Red as much as I did," Coach Park said. "We're gonna miss seeing him in the stands."

"What happened?" Doug asked.

"He was old, dummy," Marshal said.

Coach Park shushed them when they started arguing. "I don't know the details, but...well...Red was old."

Everyone looked like they might laugh, but Logan didn't find it funny. His lips were dry and cracked, and he couldn't stop licking them.

"Is Tim coming to the game Thursday?" Alex asked. He hadn't returned Logan's gaze.

"I don't know."

"Who's starting if he doesn't?" Sam asked.

"Calm down, Turner," Alex said, then nodded at his little brother.

"I haven't decided anything yet," Coach said. "The funeral is tomorrow. I've gotten Superintendent Walker to let you boys miss school so you can go. We won't practice in the morning, but I expect you all to be here this afternoon and tomorrow afternoon. I want to run some actions I think will work well against Colesville's weaknesses." Coach Park dismissed them.

Logan pulled Alex aside in the lobby. "Yo," he said.

"What?"

"Red Springer's dead."

"And?"

"He was the one getting into it with the Nashoba guys in the parking lot."

"Ryan broke it up. Who gives a shit?"

"What if they followed him back to his house?"

"Dude, we would've already heard about it if it was murder. That shit would've spread so fast through Nowhere, even the Amish would be talking about it."

Alex had a point, but Logan couldn't shake the sudden guilt. "My coworker died," he said.

"What?"

"My coworker Bird. He died last week."

"His name is Bird?"

"That's what everyone called him. He died unexpectedly."

"Well, that sucks, man, but what's your point?"

Logan hesitated. He wasn't sure what his point was anymore. "Nothing," he said.

"You're stressing yourself out for no reason, Tramer. Get

some rest. Go see Kelvin. Get laid. Something. If it's the playoffs that's got you cracking, don't worry, big man. All you have to do is catch passes and get rebounds. I'll do the rest to get us back to STATE...with a little help from that wish you made. How's that sound?"

"Yeah," Logan said, "all right."

Winning STATE wasn't a remedy to anything. His life might not look much different with or without a championship. Logan was going to Murray State, the nearby community college, then getting a job, then buying a house within driving distance of his mother. He knew what was waiting for him.

But how he *felt* while going through his life would be different if they won STATE. He remembered being trampled at center court by West Mann, feeling for a moment what they felt.

Alex headed to the locker room, and Logan stood outside in the cold, wondering why he had been so quick to think some guys from Nashoba had killed an old man.

The day turned gray as he went through the motions in class, but he tried to take Alex's advice. He approached Jessica Fromm at her locker before next period.

"Are you sorry you worked instead of coming to the game Saturday?" he asked.

"Honestly, yeah. How does a minor get arrested in the middle of a game like that?"

"He must have been a serial killer or something," Logan said. "Marshal knew him from back in the day. I'll have to ask him if he ever saw Bolan Grimes killing barn cats."

"Maybe he was wearing people's skin around the house, like, while he was doing dishes or folding laundry."

"He certainly *smelled* like he'd been wearing someone's skin."

They laughed together, and Logan cleared his throat. "Are you coming to the game Thursday?"

"I'm riding with your sister actually. I managed to get off work through Saturday, so if y'all keep winning, I'll be there."

"Oh, we'll win all right."

"Okay then." He could tell she liked his confidence.

"Maybe after we win STATE…" He forced the words out. "We could go bowling together."

"Oh?" She looked surprised, like she had never thought of Logan that way before.

He felt insecure, stupid for thinking—

"Oh." She smiled, her cheeks turning red. "That would be cool…" She glanced around the quickly emptying hallway. He wondered if it was too soon after her breakup with Tom Bomber to ask her out; maybe it was too soon for him as well after learning there had been another death…

"But?" he offered for her.

"But nothing," she said abruptly. "You win STATE, and it's a date."

Logan pushed Red Springer and Bird and Ryan Holbrook—and the air blowing in his face at the bottom of the well as he spoke his wish—out of his mind and smiled.

"STATE. Date. I like the sound of that."

Jessica rolled her eyes but returned a smile of her own before walking away.

It was worth being late to his next class.

"Why're you grinning like an ass?" Marshal asked, muting the microphone as Mrs. McKinney asked another student a question.

Emily squirmed in her seat on the other side of Logan. He noticed the two hadn't been talking like usual when he walked in.

"I'll tell you later," Logan said.

It started to snow, tiny flakes outside. It rarely snowed in Nowhere; they only ever got freezing rain. In fact, Logan's elation over his date seemed to last about as long as the snowfall.

By the time Emily finished reciting their Bigfoot story in Choctaw, Logan felt a sense of foreboding. He imagined Red Springer's body lying in the grass, blanketed in white flakes.

2

The basketball boys sat in the back pew. Logan couldn't speak for the others, but he didn't want to get too close to the body. It was a closed casket, and he imagined the lid flying open, the zombified corpse of Tim's dad pulling him inside.

Alex, Doug, and Marshal sat next to him as the service began. Brother Maxwell White delivered the sermon. He was the funeral director in addition to being the pastor of Holdendecker Baptist Church. Logan only knew him because he was his coworker Melinda's father. He was too soft-spoken to be a preacher. Listening to him made Logan tired, but Brother Maxwell slammed his fist on the pulpit on three different occasions to wake up the crowd. When he finished, the choir sang a few hymns. Everyone filed into a long line to offer condolences to the family.

Logan followed the others reluctantly. At least the family stood between him and the closed casket. Tim was there, next to people Logan didn't recognize, wearing his Sunday best: starched Wranglers, a black pearl-snap western shirt, and his dad's boots. Logan had never seen him dressed like this, nor had he ever seen Tim with his hair combed.

"I'm sorry, Tim," he said, feeling queasy.

Tim stared vacantly. "Thanks, big man," he replied flatly.

Logan felt uncomfortable and quickly moved away from Tim and the casket. He met his teammates outside.

The four of them seemed uneasy, stuffing their hands into their pockets and kicking at the gravel in the parking lot. They were a good thirty yards from the building, closer to the basketball court behind the Holdendecker fire station than the church now.

"Fucking funerals," Alex muttered.

"You got that right," Marshal agreed.

"I think there's something beautiful about them," Doug said.

"You would, Dougie. You think everyone's going to Heaven."

"Not everyone," Doug argued, which wasn't the best thing to say at someone's funeral—especially at Red Springer's, who no one had ever seen at church before today. "What if Tim doesn't play?" Doug asked.

"That'll leave us with only eight players, half of which are dimwit underclassmen," Marshal said.

"Good thing we know how to play without fouling," Alex said.

"Maybe you can play the whole game, but Logan?"

"Screw you, Marshal," Logan retorted. "I can play a whole game if I have to. Regardless, Sam's just as good as Tim, and it's about time y'all's little brothers step up."

"Yeah, Dylan's not exactly sixth man material," Marshal said about his freshman brother. "I was surprised to see Mikey getting outplayed by Sam, though. I thought you've been 'training' him, Alex?"

"He'll be ready," Alex said.

"We all will be," Logan added.

"You're not concerned at all?" Marshal asked.

"Why would he be?" Alex replied. "Y'all need to gain some confidence."

"Maybe Kelvin will be back by STATE," Doug said, and everyone badgered him.

"What makes *you* two so confident?" Marshal asked Alex and Logan.

"Why wouldn't we be?" Alex said. "We survived Regionals. Nashoba's as tough as anyone we'll face before STATE."

"Are you expecting someone to get arrested every game?" Marshal narrowed his eyes.

"What the hell's your problem?" Alex asked.

"You two know something."

Logan stared into the distance.

"What would we know, Marshal?" Alex said. "You think we got Ryan to arrest him?"

"His story didn't make sense. Some voice on the radio told him to do it?"

"You were the one who was friends with Ryan," Logan said. "Maybe he was lying on your behalf."

"I'm the reason he met us out there Saturday night, fool." Marshal shook his head. "No, it's you two for sure. Y'all didn't seem surprised when Bolan got arrested."

"Bolan's a meth head," Alex said. "Why would it be a surprise?"

"Come on, Marsh," Doug noted. "You sound a little paranoid."

"I distinctly remember hearing you"—Marshal jabbed his finger at Alex's chest—"say to this fucker, and I quote, 'Do you think this is it?' And then you"—he waved his hand toward Logan's face—"gave a *big* stupid smile, like you just got the toy you wanted in your Happy Meal."

"You've lost your mind," Alex said.

Logan sighed, the awkward silence stretching longer than it should have. He hated having to lie, and it had been Will's stupid, pointless idea to keep it secret, anyway. Logan knew his teammates. They wanted the same thing he did.

"We might as well tell them," he said.

Alex just nodded, so Logan told Marshal and Doug everything. About the prank, Will's grandma, and the wish that had led to the mysterious voice ordering Ryan to arrest Bolan Grimes.

The four of them were silent. The cold wind whistled through their huddle while people carried the casket out of the church. Tim's blank stare remained as he climbed into the hearse.

Finally, Doug spoke. "It's a miracle."

"Do what now?" Marshal appeared offended.

"You heard me," Doug said. "It's a blessing from God."

"That ain't what I heard."

"What do you mean?" Alex asked. "Isn't that what you were after, Detective Dickhead?"

"Are you kidding me? I thought you assholes had planned it with Ryan. Now you're saying you made a magic wish and some creepy-ass voice told Ryan to arrest our opponent?"

"Just because something's creepy doesn't mean it isn't God," Doug said. "In the Bible, when people saw angels, they were terrified."

"And not just any opponent," Alex said. "The fucking worst. You hate Nashoba."

"And Bolan would've been arrested anyway," Logan said. "The voice just sped up the process."

Marshal crossed his arms. "And I'm supposed to believe this?"

"It wouldn't be the first time a team won despite the odds," Logan said. "Green River. 1990. My aunt's team." He quickly told them the story.

Doug hung on every word. Marshal kept shaking his head.

By the end of the story, Logan was back to thinking about the funeral. "Does the Bible say anything about curses?" he asked Doug.

Alex punched him in the arm. "I told you to let it go, Tramer."

Logan leaned into their huddle and whispered, "It's Tim's dad. Ryan said he went outside to fight those guys from Nashoba."

"So?" Marshal asked.

"So, Logan thinks those Nashoba guys murdered the old man," Alex said.

"There you go," Marshal replied. "Creepy. The whole thing is creepy."

"No one murdered anyone," Alex maintained.

"Yeah," Doug agreed. "As far as we know, those guys were your cousins, Marshal. They wouldn't murder someone over a basketball game."

"If it was the Kemps in the parking lot," Marshal said, "you better believe they might follow him home and kill him."

Alex waved him off. "Don't stress Logan out more than he already is."

"I'm fine."

"Sure, big man."

"What's your problem?"

"Oh, come on…"

Logan gave no reply because he didn't know why Alex was suddenly on his ass again.

Alex scoffed, then said it. "You stood up Kelvin. You're his best friend, man, and you couldn't even go see him. Now, you want to ruin this, talking about Red Springer getting murdered, when not even the police are saying that's the case. He's old, man. Old people die."

The procession started to leave, car after car filing out of the church parking lot, soon to leave the town of Holdendecker for the small cemetery in Nowhere, a couple of miles from the school.

"What held you up last week, Logan?" Doug asked. "I'm not trying to piss you off. Just saying...Kelvin asked about you."

Logan took a deep breath to calm himself. He could see his teammates clearly again and said, "I'm gonna see him. I will. Soon. I just want to see us win a few more games first."

"Saturday night," Alex said. "If we make STATE, we all go see him Saturday night before the party. Agreed?"

Alex stretched his hand out like they were breaking from a timeout. Doug and Marshal placed their hands atop Alex's.

Logan blew out a deep breath and watched the air billow coldly in front of him. Then he stuck his hand in. "Agreed," he said.

"Win on three."

The four of them counted down, then yelled, "Win!"

3

Wheelman's was dead on Tuesday night. If Bird had been around, he would have found a way to make the night fun. In his absence, everyone was quiet, and the night felt as boring as things got around here.

Melinda had left early because it was so slow, and she was struggling with Bird's death. Logan and Will were left to close in the kitchen. They started their chores early.

When Will was washing dishes and Logan was slicing tomatoes for tomorrow, it felt like they were the only two in the building, so Logan updated him.

"I told Doug and Marshal about the well."

Will dropped the pan he had been scrubbing. It splashed

loudly. The soapy water ran over the side of the sink, spreading beneath their work shoes.

"You did what?"

"We were at Tim's dad's funeral...Felt like I had to. Marshal was suspicious."

"I don't give a shit. What was there for him to find out without you telling him? Do you really think he would've guessed you made a magic wish?"

"What's done is done," Logan said. "You don't have to worry about it. I told them we can't make any more wishes until we win STATE."

"Like they're gonna listen to you once they realize it's legit."

"They might already believe it. We saw Ryan Holbrook the other night at the party."

"So, that's what Marshal wanted to talk to you about? Damn. I knew I should have stayed put."

Logan told him about the voice on the radio. Will continued washing the dishes on autopilot. When Logan finished, Will simply said, "Incredible."

Logan didn't mention his concerns about Tim's dad. He was trying to move on. Will's excitement was contagious. Something had given Ryan the order to arrest Bolan Grimes and save Nowhere's season. Logan didn't know what to think.

They waited for the clock to hit eleven p.m., already finished with their tasks, expecting to leave within ten minutes. Then an order rang into the answering station. Larry Unders took it, and Logan snapped out of his boredom when he heard Tim's voice on the intercom.

"I'm looking for the big man, Logan Tramer. Also, some mozzarella sticks."

Logan went out to see Tim. His teammate stood in a stall to the side of the building, his gigantic truck parked in the employee lot. He still wore his outfit from the funeral, but the boots were dirty now.

"What's up, big man?" Tim asked, smoking a cigarette and eyeing Logan's feet.

"Hey, Tim. How're you holding up?"

"Holding up? Well...I'm on my way out of town if that tells you anything."

"Seriously?"

"Gonna stay with my brother at his mom's house for a while. Out near Miner. Got a hankering for cheese sticks."

"You stopped at the right place."

"Figured you'd be here too. Thought you might tell the boys I won't be around."

"I guess you won't be at the game on Thursday."

Tim bit down on his cigarette and took a long puff. "You wouldn't understand, man. I just...I'm sorry I can't be there."

"No need to apologize, bro. Take all the time you need. You can join us when we make STATE."

"STATE. Right...Do you believe in the afterlife, Logan?"

Logan shrugged, and Tim chuckled.

"Exactly," he said. "Never could wrap my mind around it myself. You know, I don't really remember my mom much. She died when I was six. I have this vague idea of her singing, but I don't know if I just made it up to have a nice memory of her.

"But I can remember right after she died. I remember folks telling me she was in Heaven and had earned a gold crown. Not a halo. A crown. I was fixated on that detail for years. What do you have to do to earn a gold crown in Heaven? No one gave me a straight answer. They wanted to talk about Jesus and believing in him, but I just wanted the crown."

"Is it good deeds or something?"

"It's horseshit, is what it is. There are no gold crowns. If there's an afterlife, it ain't Heaven."

Logan grunted, half agreeing, half placating.

"I found him, Logan. I found my dad and…I can't help but wonder if, just before he died, he saw what was waiting for him afterward. The look on his face…"

"You can tell me, Tim. If you want."

He flicked his cigarette away and shook his head. "Forget it, man. Just tell the others they'll have to win without me. I know it won't be easy since I'm the second coming of Kelvin, but you fools got this."

"Sure, Tim. I'll tell them."

Soon, Tim's order came, and Logan went inside. He wished Tim would have told him more. Logan wanted to know why the casket had been closed, and Tim had gotten him as close as he could to the answer.

AREA

AREA IV BRACKET

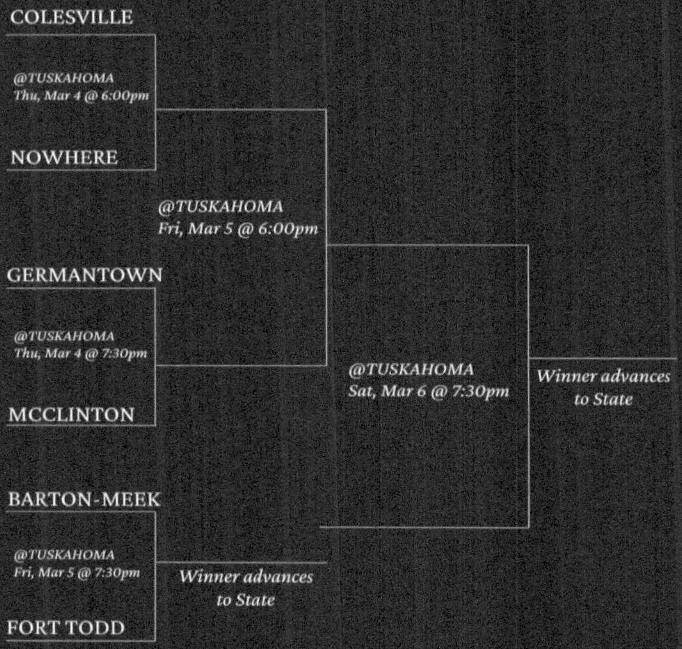

COLESVILLE

@TUSKAHOMA
Thu, Mar 4 @ 6:00pm

NOWHERE

@TUSKAHOMA
Fri, Mar 5 @ 6:00pm

GERMANTOWN

@TUSKAHOMA
Thu, Mar 4 @ 7:30pm

MCCLINTON

@TUSKAHOMA
Sat, Mar 6 @ 7:30pm

Winner advances
to State

BARTON-MEEK

@TUSKAHOMA
Fri, Mar 5 @ 7:30pm

Winner advances
to State

FORT TODD

SEVEN
WISH FULFILLMENT

1

Southern Oklahoma University's gym made Logan wish he was good enough for college ball. It wasn't as big as the dome at Red Oak University, but it was three times the size of Nowhere's gym. The bleachers ran up from the floor to the ceiling, and Logan couldn't make out who sat in the nosebleeds. He tried to stay calm, but he was antsy to see how the wish would help this time. Staying calm was crucial, especially since Colesville liked to run, and they did just that.

As the biggest player on the court, Logan struggled to keep pace. He took advantage of his size in the half-court, but there were very few opportunities for that in the first half. Colesville pushed the pace on offense whether Nowhere made or missed a basket.

Logan tried to get his teammates to slow it down when they had the ball, but everyone got caught up in Colesville's speed, especially Doug, who preferred an up-tempo game. He was speedy and at his best in the open court. The style reminded Logan of when they went full-court during four-on-four scrimmages. It was awful. Logan had to call for a sub more often than usual just to catch his breath.

Without Tim and Kelvin, that meant putting in Mikey or Dylan with Sam, who had gotten the start over Mikey, already in the game. They didn't even have hair under their arms yet. As soon as one of them turned the ball over, Logan would check back in.

The Colesville Tornadoes were athletic and fast. Because of the many weekends Logan had spent dragging Main in Arrow, he knew Lucas Rush and Allen Reed—a younger second cousin of Coach Julia Reed who was from Arrow. Colesville was right outside of the college town, so it was where the Colesville high schoolers went every weekend. Allen was the only outgoing guy from Colesville—Lucas was his shy best friend—so he interacted with others in a friendly manner. Sometimes, high schoolers from rival schools would get into a fight in the Dollar General parking lot but never Nowhere and Colesville.

Four of their five starters were six-feet-tall with long arms. Luckily, the Tornadoes weren't very skilled outside of Lucas Rush. Nowhere trapped him every time and the others would turn the ball over on a four-on-three situation, and they missed layups as much as they scored. The game stayed close into the fourth quarter.

Logan took a final sub on the bench. He sat, sucking in breaths, sweat falling onto his shoes, as he watched his team score to tie the game with three minutes left. Sam Turner made the basket, then followed it up with a defensive stop. The sophomore was growing up right before Logan's eyes. Before Logan could check in, Alex pulled up for a bad shot over two defenders and clanked it off the backboard.

Then came a late whistle. The Colesville fans booed so loudly that the large gym felt claustrophobic. Logan, surrounded by jeers from fans who didn't see a foul, had to admit he hadn't seen one either.

Alex hit both free throws, and Logan came back into the game.

The Tornadoes came right at him after another Lucas Rush trap. The rest of his team hardly shot from outside, relying on banking it in off the glass for every layup and midrange shot as if they knew they lacked shooting skill and hoped for a nice bounce off the backboard. Logan went for a block and hacked his opponent across the arm. He snatched the ball from the air, then paused, expecting a whistle.

None came.

The Colesville crowd erupted, stomping so hard in the bleachers that the hardwood floor vibrated. Logan made the mistake of passing Doug the ball. Despite having the lead with two minutes left, Doug sprinted ahead like the game was still a track meet. Logan shouted for him to slow down, but Doug had already gone too far. Doug pulled up for a bad floater and airballed it when Logan was just crossing half-court.

The whistle blew. Foul on Allen Reed.

He turned and shouted at the ref, earning himself a technical foul.

The crowd was as rowdy as Nashoba's had been when Bolan Grimes was arrested. Logan had a clear view this time. There had been no foul.

He didn't know the referee making the calls for Nowhere, but Mr. Tune, apparently, did. He stared at his referee friend in confusion, who glared back at him defiantly. Logan wondered if the ref saw a foul the same way Ryan Holbrook had "heard" an order on the radio.

Doug took his free throws, including an extra one for Allen Reed's technical, while the Colesville crowd's boos transformed into a unified chant: "A ROPE, A TREE, HANG THE REFEREE! A ROPE, A TREE, HANG THE REFEREE!"

Logan had never heard that one before. What he knew about Colesville was, they had an abundance of pecan trees, and he supposed many of those were mature enough to handle the weight of one poor-sighted ref.

The chant continued for another possession until a different referee called a foul on Alex, giving Colesville free throws. Alex didn't argue the weak call. Clearly, this other ref was trying to keep the crowd in check.

Colesville made both free throws but were still down by three with only a minute and a half left. As long as Nowhere was disciplined and didn't let Lucas Rush get free for a couple of threes, the Devils would win as long as they hit their free throws. They did, winning by four.

The Colesville crowd began throwing drinks and paper baskets with leftover nacho cheese onto the court. The chant started up again: "A ROPE, A TREE, HANG THE REFEREE! A ROPE, A TREE, HANG THE REFEREE!"

The referees left quickly, escorted by a campus police officer. Mr. Tune followed, wanting some answers.

Logan already knew the answer. It was his wish. Once again, he was responsible for Nowhere's success.

One win down, two to go.

2

The middle schoolers had made new posters for the high school hallways after the unlikely wins against Nashoba and Colesville. A renewed energy filled the country school grounds. Marcus Ludlow, Principal Jacobs, and all the teachers he passed clapped Logan on the back. A banner stretched across the hallway, declaring the Devils were soon to be three-time Area IV champions.

Logan didn't think winning the consolation bracket counted as being "champions," but he wasn't about to stamp out the middle schoolers' fun. Everyone was dressed in team colors. Many students still wore face paint from last night's game.

Logan couldn't believe the referee had made those phantom foul calls, giving Nowhere the cushion they had needed, but of course they had. The Basketball Gods would never let it come down to a final shot. He knew how awful an outcome that could lead to. Two years ago, in the STATE SEMIFINALS, Nowhere had missed a game-winning three in the final seconds. It was the kind of thing he would dwell on for the rest of his life if they didn't win it this year.

Logan and his teammates joked about the phantom calls and the kitchen well while they headed to class, late as usual. He assumed Mr. Tune would glare at them when they entered, but the history teacher wasn't there. Instead, Superintendent Walker watched them take their seats.

The boys immediately quieted, sensing something was off.

"Boys, I was just telling your classmates that Larry—Mr. Tune—is out sick today. I have a lot of work to do, so I'm going to put on a movie. I trust you to behave yourselves. Hope to see everyone at the game tonight."

Superintendent Walker rolled a TV on a cart forward, turned on *O Brother, Where Art Thou?*, and left the room.

With the lights off, the TV's glow didn't reach Logan, so no one could see how pale he turned.

"He left with that ref," he murmured, more to himself than to Marshal.

Marshal leaned over, halfway out of his desk. "What?"

"Mr. Tune rushed out with the other refs after the game. He was friends with them."

"And?"

"And..."

A ROPE. A TREE. HANG THE REFEREE!

"I don't know."

A ROPE. A TREE. HANG THE REFEREE!

Logan hated how paranoid he felt. He tapped Jessica on the shoulder. She turned and smiled at him.

"Maybe we shouldn't wait," he said.

"What?"

"For us to win STATE. Maybe you and I shouldn't wait. What're you doing Sunday?"

"No plans...but I don't know if I...Well, I don't know."

"We'll go to Arrow. Just have a bite to eat. No pressure."

Her head blocked the TV, creating a halo around her and shadowing her face. He wished he could see her expression better. Was she thinking it over or searching for an excuse to shoot him down?

Does it matter? Why are you in a hurry?

But he didn't want to answer that. He waited.

"All right," she finally said. "Sure, Logan. Let's go out on Sunday. But you better win tonight."

"Tonight. Tomorrow night. We'll win for sure."

She tilted her head. "I like this confidence, Logan. What's gotten into you?"

That he could answer. "I feel like I can't lose."

3

Nowhere had beaten the McClinton Chiefs twice during the regular season, but McClinton was no pushover. The Chiefs had only lost three other times besides those two defeats.

One of Nowhere's games against McClinton had turned into a shootout between Kelvin and Ethan Crist, each player scoring over thirty points. Nowhere won by nine, but Ethan made them sweat it out.

Logan knew Ethan beyond the court because Doug talked about him. The two were both juniors and attended Rome Bible Camp every summer. Logan remembered the McClinton boy from the summer after eighth grade, when he went to Camp Rome for the last time. He didn't know Doug then, still more than a year before he moved to Nowhere, but he knew all about Ethan Crist. Even as a seventh grader, Ethan was legendary.

He was the most Christlike person at camp. Blonde and blue-eyed like the paintings of Jesus in Oklahoma Baptist churches, Ethan had long hair, was tall and good-looking, and waiting until marriage to have sex. He led Bible studies when he could have been swimming or practicing archery. Doug's lunch-hour Bible study at Nowhere was modeled off Ethan's at McClinton. Other campers joked they wanted to be more "Crist-like."

It was annoying that someone like that could also be good at basketball. Ethan actually had the audacity to go toe-to-toe with Kelvin and backed it up. Before the game, he gathered his team around center court for a prayer and invited others to join. Two of the three refs, Coach Park, the McClinton coaches, and Jack Ward joined in. Even some of the fans from both teams stepped down from the rows of bleachers, widening the circle to the top of the arc on both sides of the court. Doug was in the prayer circle, of course, but Logan chose not to join.

Logan hadn't really believed in God since his parents' divorce. He wouldn't attribute his loss of faith to their split—that would be too dramatic—but it had been around that time he began questioning his assumptions about life, family, and death. He had always wanted to believe your spirit lived on after death in some form. He imagined Bird's spirit watching the Area Tournament from the shadowy back bleachers of SOU's gym.

Logan was surprised to see some of the folks who had traveled this far for tonight's game. The team bus had led a caravan of vehicles, like a hearse at a funeral. Even more Nowhere folks were here than last night.

Some of the older Nowhere supporters looked like they might collapse after the long drive. One elder coughed harshly into his hand, then clasped Ethan Crist's as everyone bowed their heads for the prayer. Ethan didn't look appalled to take the old man's phlegmy hand. The guy was even more of a saint than Doug.

By halftime, Ethan had shown his holiness on the court. He scored twenty-four points in the first half, and his team led by twelve. Coach Park reamed into the Devils in the locker room, but his motivating insults lost some of their bite. The farther they advanced in the playoffs, the more obvious it was they needed Kelvin to get them over the hump. Logan was starting to lose his faith in the Basketball Gods. He couldn't stop thinking about the consequences of his wish, or if it was just a horrible coincidence that Mr. Tune had missed work after leaving with that ref.

When the third quarter began, Logan noticed Ethan Crist was late returning from the locker room. The star player arrived just in time for the ball to be inbounded. He moved gingerly, almost as though he were clenching his ass cheeks. His face, usually glowing Christlike, was pale and thin-lipped. He missed a three-pointer and immediately called for a sub. He ran back to the locker room.

By the time he returned, Nowhere had cut the Chiefs' lead to four. Ethan was sharper, driving for a tough "and one" layup over Logan, then burying a three-pointer in Doug's face. Soon, though, he called for another sub. He seemed frantic, desperate as the game continued without a break. Logan wasn't sure if his teammates noticed, but when he caught Will's eye in the crowd, his coworker certainly did. Will smiled confidently at him.

"Alex, Alex," Logan called, and Alex set a cross screen for him on the low block.

Ethan switched onto Logan, and he posted him up. Logan called for the ball as desperately as he ever had. He felt Ethan on his back, the star player holding one hand against his stomach before pulling it away when Marshal tossed the ball to Logan. Logan caught it cleanly—a miracle in itself.

He turned to throw up a hook shot, but not before planting his elbow in Ethan's gut.

Ethan hit the floor, and the ref blew his whistle. It was a foul on Logan, but that didn't matter. The wounded yelp Ethan had made told Logan he had accomplished his goal. Ethan didn't reach for his stomach but clapped his hands against his ass cheeks.

He rocked to his feet gingerly and shimmied off the court while his sub entered the game.

A foul stench rose from the spot where he had landed. Something damp puddled against the hardwood.

The sub gagged, then others dry-heaved.

Logan smiled.

Ethan Crist had shat his shorts.

EIGHT
DESIRE

1

THREE WEEKS AGO, Doug Mooreland discovered a superpower he hadn't known existed. His longtime crush on Mal Turner was an open secret. Even she had known about it for years, and he had hoped she would make a move because of it. She never did, and Doug didn't either because his confidence had waned ever since the other boys kept growing while he stopped at five-four.

He was the fastest player on the team and the second-best three-point shooter behind Kelvin, yet he was even shorter than the underclassmen. The girls at Nowhere never seemed to look down—or even straight ahead—or they might have noticed him. Doug didn't mind too much; he knew God would present him with the love of his life when the time was right.

When he wasn't playing basketball, Doug focused on the Word. He attended every church and youth group service, participated in every church outreach, and performed skits. He led his small group Bible study during lunch breaks. He planned to be a preacher someday when his time in the Army was over, but he needed much more spiritual growth before then. He was a sinner. Doug couldn't fight the urges inside him and, frankly, didn't want to.

Since he had been born again between seventh and eighth grade, everyone assumed he was a virgin. But Doug had actually had sex three different times with three different girls. Ironically, the first time was at church camp the summer after seventh grade—three days before he gave his life to Christ.

Beyond the prayer garden at Camp Rome was the infamous make-out spot. Many campers had fondled each other out there under the stars. Camp security could never catch them in the act—that alone was enough to make one believe in God.

Doug was not caught the first time, and he wasn't caught when he had sex at camp after ninth grade either. The third time he'd had sex was Christmas break his sophomore year, when he had spent a week with his grandparents in the Oklahoma panhandle. It was with a neighbor girl he had liked for as long as he had been coming to his grandparents' house. She looked a lot like Mal.

Yet no one in Nowhere knew about Doug's sexual experience. He could have corrected them years ago, if he didn't have such shame about it. The shame did not stop him from making out with Mal Turner three weeks ago, and it wouldn't stop him from taking things to the next level if given the opportunity. That night had been when he discovered the superpower: Pity.

Everyone was in the gym when Kelvin's career ended: every girl from high school, most of the teachers, various alumni, the players' families, and area locals. They all witnessed Kelvin struggling on the court with his unmoving, twisted leg. They also saw the other boys in shock. Everyone must have thought the same thing Doug had: *This could happen to any one of you.*

Suddenly, the Nowhere Devils were brave warriors willing to sacrifice their bodies to the greater cause of winning the STATE CHAMPIONSHIP.

After that Mal approached him like he had always wanted, and Doug rode the wave of pity, following her behind the barn where they sat in the dark, kissing. He ran his hands along her legs and had them slapped away when he reached for her breasts. It had been a wonderful night, and he was sweating horribly in anticipation of another like it while he sought her out.

Doug had missed his chance last weekend, thanks to Marshal and Ryan Holbrook. He arrived as early as he could tonight, hoping there would be no interruptions, but there were already plenty of excited students and locals at the barn, celebrating Nowhere's latest win. Once Ethan Crist went down for good, Nowhere ran away with the game in the fourth quarter. Doug had never seen Ethan in such a pathetic, vulnerable state. He felt bad but also a little excited by it. God was humbling the "perfect" Ethan Crist, using the wish Logan made in the kitchen well. It was a miracle. God had blessed Nowhere to go all the way. Doug wondered if he and Mal would go all the way tonight.

He moved through the crowd. She stood on the far side, playing host by the drinks. By the time Doug got to her, Mal was talking to Reba Jacobs and Marshal's little sister, Autumn. Another person had approached them, and Doug nearly turned around and left.

It was Allen Prospect.

The dropout would have been a senior this year. He was Doug's height but had long, lanky arms. Despite how scrawny Allen was compared to him, Doug had been intimidated by Allen ever since being bullied by him in elementary school.

When Doug was in fourth grade, Allen nearly drowned him in a toilet bowl. In fifth grade, Allen shoved a grass snake down his pants.

By middle school, Allen had stopped bullying Doug and

mostly ignored him. He hung out with older kids because he had an older brother. He never played basketball or went to the games. Instead, Allen rebuilt cars and drag-raced down country roads. He had a knack for mechanics and had always wanted to join the Air Force to work on military aircraft at Tinker Air Force Base in OKC.

Instead, he dropped out sophomore year and did little now besides show up at every party like he was still in school. He lived with his older brother after his mom kicked him out. No one knew why, and his younger sister Letty never told anyone the reason. She never seemed to hate Allen the way their mother did. Perhaps Allen had the Pity superpower too.

Though Doug hadn't been bullied since elementary school, that old fear never went away. Allen spotted him before he could turn around, so Doug joined the group.

"I don't believe you," Reba said.

"Ask Dougie," Allen said. "He'll tell you the God's honest truth."

"What's that?" Doug glanced at Mal, who waited for him to vouch for Allen with a smirk on her face.

"I slept with Coach Reed," Allen said. "When I was a freshman."

Doug laughed.

"Seriously," Allen said. "They keep telling me she's having an affair with Coach Park, but she would never. She prefers younger men. She and I had a very mature, serious relationship that entire year, thanks to 9/11."

"Oh God," Mal said. She looked at Doug and shook her head.

He smiled at her.

"Don't leave me hanging here, Dougie. You know it's true."

"I barely saw you that year, Allen."

"Bro, I don't know who you're trying to impress by lying.

You don't remember Coach Reed consoling me when the planes flew into the Two Towers?"

The girls snickered.

"What?"

"It's the Twin Towers," Doug said. "This isn't *Lord of the Rings*."

Allen started laughing too, bigger and uglier than everyone else. He took a step toward Doug, and Doug fought the urge to flinch. It was too easy to imagine Allen taking a swing at him.

"You sly, little fucker," Allen said, reaching out to twist Doug's nipple. Allen could always find Doug's nipple, even back when he wore baggy And 1 t-shirts. He had a gift for it.

Doug made the task easier these days because he always wore tight American Eagle polos that showed off his biceps. His nipple stung. Doug slapped Allen's hand away but laughed to show he wasn't trying to start a fight.

Allen continued smiling, making him even more menacing. He could strike in an instant—shove Doug to the ground, sit on his face and fart, or pin him to the floor and hit him in the kidneys until Doug pissed himself. No one else could see Doug's fear, but Allen could. He still had Doug's number. It was enough of a win for him tonight. He backed off, whispered something in Reba's ear, then wandered off.

"What did he say?" Mal asked.

"You don't want to know," Reba said.

"He's so gross," Autumn added.

"He cleaned up a little nicer back in the day," Mal admitted.

A jealous rage gripped Doug.

"Hell, before he dropped out," Reba said, "I think he might have actually been kind of hot." She laughed, embarrassed.

"He's always been slimy," Doug said through gritted teeth. "Trust me."

"Wow, Doug, I've never seen you hate anyone. Do you think God would approve?"

"Don't be an asshole," Mal said.

Reba smirked, glancing between them. She took Autumn by the arm. "Let's go get another drink," she said and wandered away even though the drink table was behind them.

Doug took a deep breath and slid a little closer to Mal.

"9/11...really?"

"If there was ever a reason for a teacher to sleep with a student," Mal joked in return.

He felt lighter now. They drank and chatted about the game. He wanted to tell Mal all about the miracle, but he was sworn to secrecy. It was probably for the best. Mal had never come to his Bible study. She was Church of Christ, but he didn't know anything about her relationship with Jesus. It was better not to talk religion, or risk losing the superpower. He could see Pity in her sparkling eyes.

Doug didn't want to seem eager, so he waited for her to make a move.

"Walk with me," she said, taking his hand. She led him out of the barn.

He thought they might go behind it again. Instead, she took him to her truck.

"Do you fancy a drive around my family's land?"

"I'll go with you anywhere," he said, and meant it.

2

Mal's truck wheezed and groaned while they bounced through the pastureland. It was an old work truck with over 300,000 miles. She had driven it to school every day since freshmen year, long before she had her license, but this was the first time Doug had ever been in it. It smelled like Mal—a pleasant pineapple scent he had gotten familiar with three weeks ago.

There was a worn path in the grass where the Turners had driven back and forth, repairing the fence. It was where Doug and his teammates had met Ryan Holbrook last weekend because the deputy knew the path well. His father owned the property on the other side of the fence where large oak trees ran along it, bucking the Turners' posts.

"My grandpa has been yelling at Mr. Holbrook for years to cut those trees down, and he refuses. Can you imagine those two old farts getting in a fistfight?"

"My money's on the shop teacher. No offense."

"None taken. Mr. Holbrook's a mean son of a bitch."

"And his son's a cop. Don't want to cross him. Besides, I gotta admit, they're nice trees."

"Some of the biggest in Nowhere, I'd bet. Yeah…don't tell my grandpa, but I like them too."

Mal parked the truck next to the fence. The branches of the oak trees reached over the property line, looking like spider-webs in the moonlight since no leaves remained this winter.

"I like the company too," she said.

"It's not too shabby."

Mal crossed the gear shift, and Doug thanked God these weren't bucket seats. Before long, their bodies were lying across the long, cushioned seat while they made out.

They were warm despite the bad heater in the truck. Doug and Mal started necking, but this time, she didn't slap his hand away when he touched her breasts. He was hard against her leg. They dry humped, Doug on top, gyrating without shame or insecurity. He reached his hand under her shirt and felt warm bare flesh. They moaned like they were already going all the way.

Then something banged against the back of her truck,

a wild boar ramming into it. Doug shot up so quickly the back of his head bounced off the hard metal of the roof. He was momentarily blinded. Mal slid into a sitting position, and both of them darted their eyes around in the dark.

A silhouette approached on the driver's side.

"Hey, hey, Malorie!" It was Allen Prospect. "I love this old truck." Allen pressed his face against the driver's side window. "Who ya got in there?"

Doug's familiar fear came immediately, but with it was a rage that clouded his sight. He shoved the door open, and Allen stumbled to the ground.

"Dougie?" he slurred drunkenly. "Hell yeah, little Dougie."

Doug didn't register what Allen was saying or that he was drunk. He lunged from the truck, slamming down on top of Allen like a pro wrestler.

"What's that?" Allen cackled. "What's that little hard thing against my leg?"

Doug hit him across the face. His hand smarted—a pain he felt even through the hazy rage. Allen laughed. Doug hit him twice more. The more his hand pained him the more Allen laughed. Doug rolled under him and put him in a chokehold. He squeezed on his throat until Allen could no longer laugh or joke about his erection.

Allen finally seemed to understand what was happening. He slapped at Doug's arms, reached back and scratched his face. Doug was hot and cold all over.

Mal started yelling for him to let Allen go. It made Doug angrier. He squeezed tighter. Doug wanted Allen to stop squirming, stop laughing, stop bullying, stop...existing.

Then Allen fell limp. Mal pulled at Doug's arm until he finally loosened his grip. Allen's head thumped against the dirt when Doug crawled out from under him.

"Holy shit," Mal said. She squatted in front of Allen and shook him. "Wake up, Allen. Allen."

Doug stepped away and leaned against the truck, breathing fast and hard. Angry tears rolled down his cheeks. Then he laughed, mostly to himself, a loud cackle he couldn't stifle.

"What's wrong with you?" There was no pity in Mal's eyes, nor any of the affection she had shown him a minute ago.

Doug's giggle turned into sobs while he ran from the oak trees through the dark pasture. It wasn't long before his tears froze on his cheeks in the cold air. The barn lights guided his path, and he reached the parked cars in the darkness beyond the barn. Movement caught his attention.

"Dougie?"

Alex stood near his Jeep with Letty Prospect. They had been kissing—possibly more. Letty looked embarrassed until she saw Doug more clearly, then concern replaced her expression. The sight made him feel guilty for choking out her brother.

"You all right?" Alex asked.

"Fine," Doug muttered, continuing toward his car, a hand-me-down Toyota Corolla from his mom. He was almost home-free, except he couldn't get his keys out of his pocket.

That gave Alex enough time to say goodnight to Letty and run to Doug's side. "You don't seem fine to me," he said.

"It's over," Doug replied.

"What is?"

"Me and Mal. I screwed it up."

"I'm sure it's not that bad—"

"I'm serious, Alex. She's done with me. She looked at me like I murdered someone."

Maybe I did. An unwelcome thought.

"What happened?"

"I gotta go." Finally, Doug managed to get his keys out and unlocked the door.

"Hold up."

"I'm done, man."

Alex pushed the car door closed, and Doug imagined jumping his teammate, putting him in a chokehold.

He couldn't get Allen's voice out of his head: *What's that little hard thing against my leg?*

"I'm not playing, Alex. I need to go right freaking now."

"You're not thinking straight, Dougie."

Doug squeezed the car keys in his palm so hard it broke his skin.

"F-fuck you."

"You can win her back," Alex said calmly. "It's easy."

"What are you smoking, man?"

"The well, Dougie. You're forgetting about the well."

3

Doug reeked of the awful smell from the bottom of the well. His pants and shoes were damp with sludge, his shirt sticky with sweat from his climb. He should have gone home to change, but he was too excited. Instead, he went straight to Turner's barn, hoping his wish would come true. It didn't occur to him that it might not work immediately—or not in the way he expected.

He had no doubts about the kitchen well, believing it was from God. And how could he question anything which came from God?

God had even put Alex Spruce in his path tonight. His teammate had gone to the abandoned house with him, supporting him when he descended into the well to make his wish.

"Would you do it for me?" he had asked, foolishly.

"You got this, Dougie," Alex had said. "You have to be the one."

"Will Logan be mad at us? He said we couldn't make any more wishes until the season's over."

"You really think the well can't handle more than one wish at a time?"

Doug snorted. "I guess that'd be like saying God can't answer more than one prayer at a time."

With that, Doug descended into the well and made his wish. It briefly crossed his mind to wish Allen Prospect out of his life, out of existence, but Doug wasn't cruel. His anger had been a fleeting moment of possession, his demons briefly gaining the upper hand over his guardian angels. Doug didn't want Allen dead; he just wanted Mal, his longtime crush, to like him again, the way she had before Allen showed up.

So, he knew exactly what to wish for when he put his face near the halfmoon hole, a breeze pushing toward him like God's breath. Then he climbed out as Alex held the rope, then rushed back to Turner's barn.

By the time Doug arrived, the party was in full swing. He didn't see Mal's truck and feared she had driven Allen home after he choked him out—and that the bully now had the Pity superpower.

The crowd was chanting when he walked through the open barn doors. "ONE MORE WIN! ONE MORE WIN!" If they were smart, the team would have rested tonight and saved their energy for tomorrow's game. But there they were, leading the chant—Logan, Marshal, Sam, Jack, and Dylan. The underclassmen never came to Turner's barn. They were practically shunned from doing so. But tonight, they were the life of the party. Not Mikey, though. Alex probably made him stay home.

Doug searched for Mal, dodging clusters of people talking, dancing, and making out.

All around he went, unable to spot her. He asked Reba Jacobs if she had seen Mal.

"Last I saw her, she was with you."

Doug climbed to the loft, but she wasn't there either. He went to the Corolla and drove the path Mal had taken him through the pasture, testing the bumper on his car with every gopher hole he hit. Then he drove along the large oak trees by the fence line. Mal's truck wasn't there. He drove around the property, scanning his surroundings.

No truck.

Doug was losing his faith so quickly, he decided to go home. He told himself to be patient. He needed sleep anyway before tomorrow's game. He also needed a long shower. It had been cold inside the barn, so he cranked up his car heater until he was sweating again, bringing with it a moldy smell as strong as if he was still inside the well.

Everyone was asleep when he got home. He went upstairs in the dark, straight to his room, to grab his change of clothes for his shower. Moonlight glimmered bluely through his bedroom window. Doug nearly jumped straight out of his muddy shoes.

Someone was standing next to his bed. The silhouette became clearer, and he pulled his bedroom door closed behind him.

It was Mal.

She clicked on the lamp by his bedside so he could see her. Mal was completely naked, her hair falling over one shoulder, resting against her breast. She had more freckles than he would have imagined from her shoulders to her legs. It turned him on.

"Hey, Doug," she said. "I'm sorry Allen interrupted us. Please forgive me."

"Of course."

"The way you beat his ass...it was so sexy."

"Yeah?"

"Oh yeah."

Doug tore off his American Eagle polo and stonewashed jeans. He wrapped his arms around her and kissed her deeply. It was perfect—a wish come true.

4

While Alex Spruce held tight to the rope and lowered Doug into the well, something hovered behind him, breathing down his neck. Hot, foul breath. At least, that's what it felt like.

He glanced over his shoulder but saw nothing.

When Doug reached the bottom, Alex let go of the rope and turned fully around. Only the moonlit dark of the abandoned house greeted him. The feeling lingered, a soft tickling sensation. He lifted his hand to reach back, pissed at himself for his tremor, and slowly raised his arm over his shoulder.

Nothing but air.

Alex turned quickly, again and again, but whatever was behind him never came into view.

"What the fuck?" he muttered to himself.

He wasn't entirely surprised. Alex had felt something similar when he came out here with Logan and Will. It hadn't been as strong then, easily dismissed when he thought his teammate was crazy for climbing down the well and making a wish. But now that he believed the wish had come true, he was more aware of whatever clung to him.

The sensation only seemed to arise by the well, so he tapped his foot impatiently, ready to escape to his Jeep.

"Hurry up," he called down.

"I'm looking for the hole," Doug said.

"Should be easy enough for you, ladies' man."

Alex's eyes had adjusted to the dark, and he could make out nearly everything in the dilapidated kitchen. Cabinet doors hung from the counter, old pots and pans filled the sink, a small window above the sink was caked with mud, a sliver of moonlight poking through the lone clear spot, and a refrigerator stood without a door, exposing empty shelves. A pungent odor came from the fridge, though it was nothing compared to the breath against his neck.

He considered going to the Jeep for a flashlight, but then Doug called, "Okay, it's done!"

Alex held the rope and brought his teammate back up, ignoring the presence behind him. Once they left, the feeling vanished, but he couldn't relax. He dropped Doug off at Turner's barn and then went home. Alex needed to rest before tomorrow night's big game against Fort Todd. He had to be the responsible one, the leader, the man with the ball in his hands. So far, he hadn't played as well as he wanted since Kelvin's injury.

As good as Kelvin had been—and Alex would never deny it—the hype had become overblown. Kelvin had been good every year of high school. Alex was a late bloomer, not hitting his stride until he became a starter his sophomore year. But there was no denying he was just as good as Kelvin their senior year. He just didn't have the hype machine behind him.

Kelvin's injury had been gruesome and unsettling—a reminder that every dream could end abruptly—but it also gave Alex a jolt. It was his time to show everyone, including scouts. He hadn't received any attention from colleges.

Kelvin had been offered basketball scholarships from every regional university in Oklahoma after their runner-up finish last season. But it was the surprise offer from North Texas that pissed Alex off. If Kelvin could play basketball at a D-1 school, then Alex should at least be getting offers from Red Oak and SOU.

He wouldn't let that stop him. Alex would walk on somewhere if he had to.

After Kelvin's injury, everything was there for the taking. In fact, it was hard not to think of it as taking everything Kelvin had been promised: a STATE CHAMPIONSHIP, a basketball scholarship, a name people would remember in Shappaway County for ages like he was an ancient legend.

Win or lose, Nowhere Public Schools would shut down in a few years, and in a decade, the school would be a distant memory. Their STATE CHAMPIONSHIP would become mythological, making Alex the Hercules character. It was all there for him. He had been the team's leading scorer since Kelvin's injury, but he hadn't dominated a game yet. If Logan's wish hadn't taken Ethan Crist out of the game tonight, the Devils would be done, Alex's dream future along with it.

There was still time. Beat Fort Todd and they'd have three more games in the STATE TOURNAMENT. The Big House was where legends were made.

He expected his parents to be asleep when he got home. His mom was, but Rob Spruce had waited up. He sat in his La-Z-Boy in the living room, a plastic cup in his hand. Alex could smell the bitter stench of the mixture of saliva and chewed tobacco from across the room.

Alex braced himself. "Hey, Dad."

"Bad night for a party."

"I didn't drink."

"Don't care. What would Coach say? Y'all are acting like you already made STATE."

"We got this, Dad. Don't worry."

His dad hocked and spit into the cup. He swiped at the spittle on his bottom lip, bulging with dip on the inside like a kangaroo's pouch.

"You need to take this seriously if you want to play college ball. Do you know what you shot tonight?"

"Yeah."

"Four for eleven. Only one three-pointer."

"I hit my last three shots."

"So, you were one for eight before that? Not great, son."

"It's like you say. I gotta shoot myself out of the slump."

"To do that, you gotta shoot the ball. You should be taking more than eleven shots."

"I will."

"Don't say you will. Because you keep saying that and you keep not doing it. Just fucking do it, son. Stop being so got-damn passive."

"All right."

"You don't want to lose again this year. Next thing you know, you'll never play college ball, never have a chance at the pros, and then you'll be working alongside me at Wrangler's."

"I know, Dad."

Rob Spruce turned to face him, his face bright red, his voice slurring and guttural. "Stop saying you know! Just—"

"Fucking do it."

His dad's rheumy eyes softened. He leaned back in his chair again. "Go get some rest."

Alex released a held breath when he reached his room. Mikey was already asleep in the bed on the other side. Alex had not had a room of his own since he was two years old, when Mikey was born.

He muttered as many insults at his dad as he could think of.

Who the fuck does he think he is? I've already done more than he ever did in his basketball career.

"Alex?"

"Go back to sleep, Mikey."

"That was a crazy game tonight, wasn't it?"

"It shouldn't have come down to one guy getting the shits. We have to play better, Mikey. *You* have to play up to your potential."

"I'm trying, Alex—"

"Sam shouldn't be starting over you. It's bullshit of your own making."

"I know. You're right. He talks a lot of shit in class—"

"I don't care. Let him jaw at you all he wants. You talk your shit on the court. Don't let him push you around in practice anymore. Show Coach you're ready. And when you get in the game, demand the damn ball. You're just as fast as Doug and as good a shooter and you're three inches taller than him."

"I'm open in the corner all the time. Look for me—"

"You stop playing like a pussy and I'll get you the ball."

Mikey fell silent. Alex rolled over but couldn't sleep. He didn't want to end up like his father, putting zippers on Wrangler's jeans for a living at the factory outside of Holdendecker. Alex wanted more. Whether he walked on or got a scholarship, he would play college ball, keep getting better, and declare for the NBA draft. Dennis Rodman had gone to the NBA from a regional university in Oklahoma. So could Alex.

He saw the path, but his dad was right. Alex had to play better. He had to show out. He was done letting his teammates gaslight him into thinking he was a ball hog. But it didn't make sense to let worse shooters take shots he could score on more easily. His teammates had thrown him out of rhythm. He had to get back to playing his game. He was Kelvin now. Every Kelvin play was run for Alex, so he had to convert more.

As he lay in bed, his imposter syndrome hit him hard. What if he wasn't as good as Kelvin? What if he couldn't shoot himself out of the slump? He decided he couldn't leave it up to chance.

Alex waited for his dad's snoring from the living room, which came soon enough, and then he left.

5

The abandoned house gleamed brightly under his headlights. The exterior was so well-lit, the windows seemed even darker —a black void like the bottom of the kitchen well. Alex didn't want to be here alone, but if Logan, Doug, and goddamn Will Roebuck had gotten a wish, he deserved one too.

This time, he remembered to grab his Maglite from the glove compartment, though he left the Jeep's headlights on. His shadow stretched in front of him while he walked into the house.

Inside, the light from the headlights dissolved completely.

The moment he entered, he felt the presence behind him. Alex clicked on his flashlight and spun around. Of course, he didn't see anything, but he beamed his light into every room anyway, making sure he was alone.

He went into the kitchen last and triple-checked the noose at the end of the rope. The spike in the side of the well was thick, solidly wedged into the brick.

He set the Maglite on the ground and waited for his eyes to adjust. Alex hated standing in the dark but knew he couldn't climb with the light in his hand. He slapped the back of his neck, trying to shake off the tickling sensation. It was like the presence wanted to lean closer and whisper in his ear, but it never did.

When his eyes finally adjusted, he climbed down the well. The presence followed him. His shoes splashed in the standing water as he hit the bottom. He found the small hole on one side of the circle and leaned down, feeling the warm breeze against his face. The phantom breath stopped behind him. He was about to speak when he realized he wasn't sure what to wish for.

Logan had already secured their championship hopes. Alex wanted more. He wanted to be seen, to be the hero.

He spoke the only wish he could think of that might get him where he wanted: "I wish to be better at basketball than Kelvin Harris."

It felt right.

His words echoed back, carrying a fierce stench that wasn't so different than his dad's chaw. His eyes watered.

He climbed out of the well quickly. So excited, he thought he might not sleep tonight. But that was all right. He didn't need sleep anymore.

Alex reached his house. His dad was still passed out in his La-Z-Boy. He walked quietly to the bedroom and heard Mikey's soft, sleeping breaths.

His good mood ended as soon as he laid down. The presence at the back of his neck had followed him home.

6

It had been a very long week for Deputy Ryan Holbrook. The only desire he had was to wish away his arrest of Bolan Grimes midgame. All week, older officers side-eyed him like they couldn't decide if he should go in the drunk tank for the night or be taken straight to the mental institute, Willow Lane, in Arrow.

Word had gotten around the office about the "order" Holbrook received to arrest Bolan on his own. Everyone thought he was lying. The Nowhere boy doing his old team a solid. No matter how many times he denied it no one would believe him. He gave up on convincing them. The best thing he could do was what his parents told him to do: Be thankful Sheriff Dixon wasn't investigating the matter further and move on.

After visiting with his former teammates, he'd gone home

and stayed awake all night, second-guessing himself. Had he actually heard a voice or had his mind conjured it? What if he was going crazy because he was so broken up about losing in the STATE SEMIFINALS two years ago. That was ridiculous, of course, but it had been a golden opportunity squandered—losing because he missed the last-second three to win it.

Seeing the team hadn't helped. Telling the story out loud convinced him he needed to see a shrink.

Then he responded to a dispatcher's call early Sunday morning. Tim Springer had found his father dead behind his house. Sudden heart failure. Ryan had seen it plenty in his year as an active deputy, but he had never seen a body like Red Springer's. The skin of Red's face was stretched like someone had pulled him from the top of his head. His mouth was crooked, and his eyes bulged, his irises ice blue. His skin had an ashy discoloration, perhaps because of the cold.

Tim sat on the front porch, drinking from a hot cup of coffee. He said nothing. It was hard to believe he was the same former teammate Ryan had been talking to a few hours earlier. Ryan was overwhelmed and looked for a distraction while they waited for Holdendecker Baptist pastor and funeral director, Maxwell White, to collect the body.

There was something off about the whole thing, and it wasn't lost on him that Red had been the one to confront the Nashoba folks in the parking lot. He wanted to talk to Tim about it, but Tim's brother Daniel was nearby the whole time. Then Brother Maxwell arrived and sighed and said, "Another one."

"What do you mean?" Ryan said.

"Last week, my daughter's coworker Corbin Williams died of an overdose. Still had the needle in his arm. But...his face looked the same as Red's. It wasn't like any overdose I'd ever seen, and this isn't like any heart attack I've ever seen. Lord, have mercy."

After that, there was no convincing Ryan his brain was broken because of an airball. He'd heard a voice and seen a body that should not have looked the way it did. And, apparently, Red's wasn't the first.

He considered consulting Sheriff Dixon about all this, but he was already in the shithouse and wasn't about to make it worse. His mom said he should take a week off, maybe go watch the team at Area or rent a fishing cabin at Chisolm Lake. But he kept working, thinking his absence would only allow the rest of the office to shit-talk him openly instead of behind his back.

Then came another call on the following Saturday morning. Lydia Jacobs, the principal at Nowhere Public Schools, went to talk to her neighbors before she left for Tuskahoma, but they weren't answering the door. When he was on duty, Ryan responded to most calls from Nowhere since he was from there and knew everybody. He especially knew Principal Jacobs. She had paddled him several times when he was younger which created a sort of intimacy between them.

Her hair was completely white nowadays. Seeing it made him realize how quickly the years passed. She was dressed for the Area Consolation Finals game. She had on her Devils hoodie and bright red earrings and bracelet. "What time's the game?" he asked.

"Not until this evening but I was gonna meet a friend from Tuskahoma for lunch. I'll probably be late now, but I couldn't leave without knowing they're all right."

"What seems to be the problem?"

"Well, every morning I have breakfast with Pauline and every morning Ed is sitting on the front porch when I walk over. He wasn't there this morning. I knocked and knocked but no one's answering."

"Could they be out of town or at a doctor's appointment?"

"I thought about that too since their daughter takes them to their appointments, but Pauline always calls me if she can't do breakfast. Or she walks over the evening before and tells me. Besides, they wouldn't be at an appointment on a Saturday."

"Out of town then?"

She shook her head. "If they went out of town, they would've asked me to feed their cats."

"When was the last time you saw either of 'em?"

"Last night. They rode to the game with me. Pauline was so excited for the boys. There'd been plenty of time to tell me if they were going out of town."

Ryan and Principal Jacobs walked over from her house, and Will Roebuck met them from where he lived a hundred yards away on the other side. "What're you doing, Roebuck?"

"I came to ask you the same thing."

"Police business."

"Like arresting that guy from Nashoba?"

"Have you seen the Beaumonts this morning, Roebuck?"

"No. Should I have?"

"Okay. You can get lost now."

Will put his hands up in surrender but didn't walk away. Ryan couldn't help being short with him. The boy had annoyed him since his school days when he liked to argue with Ryan about his stats after a game. Apparently, Will Roebuck kept track of turnovers in his head and would convince Ryan he had twice as many turnovers in a game as the stats sheet said he did.

Ryan climbed the porch steps and glanced around at the rocking chairs and furniture on the wraparound porch. No sign of any disturbance. He knocked. "Mr. Beaumont? Mrs. Beaumont? It's Ryan Holbrook from the Sheriff's department."

"You grew up quick, Ryan," Principal Jacobs said as they waited. "I'm so proud of the young man you've become."

"Thanks Ms. Jacobs."

"What about me, Ms. Jacobs?"

"You'll hit your growth spurt someday, Will."

Will acted offended.

Ryan knocked again, even louder. "Ed? Pauline? Anyone home?"

"You ought to come to the games," Will said to him. "I mean, without arresting anyone."

Ryan ignored him.

"One more win and we're back at STATE," Ms. Jacobs said. "Can you believe it? Three years in a row."

"Actually, this year, I *can* believe it," Will said.

Ryan banged on the door again. Still no answer. "Well, I don't want to break their door down. They give you a key or anything?"

"Only when they've asked me to feed the cats, I'm afraid."

"Cats, huh? Those cats come and go? Day and night?"

"Sure. They're always chasing mice away from my house."

Principal Jacobs and Will followed him around to the back of the house. "I already tried the back door," she said. "It's locked too."

Ryan looked for an open window. "There we go." The window at the side of the house was half-open—an entrance and exit for the cats. Ryan hoisted himself up and through the window.

"Be careful," Principal Jacobs called.

He slid through and adjusted his gun belt. "I'll meet you around front," he called through the window and watched them walk away. He didn't immediately go to the front door. He had the familiar uneasy feeling he'd had at Red's house. He supposed it was fear, but it wasn't like any time he'd been scared before. In high school, Ryan had gotten caught in bed with his girlfriend by her father who immediately went for his shotgun—that was fear; he'd crashed his older brother's Firebird after avoiding a deer—that was fear; he'd stood in the corner lining up a three-point shot to win a game in the STATE SEMIFINALS—that was fear.

Each of those times there had been an immediate electric jolt warming over his body like a worse version of the tingle one felt when they hit their elbow on something.

This feeling was not the same.

This feeling dwelled deeper and so it was subtler and longer lasting, a hair off from the normal nerves he felt at any crime scene. He knew what he would find when he went upstairs, so he kept Principal Jacobs and Will waiting at the front door. He called their names, anyway, as the stairs creaked beneath his boots. "Mr. Beaumont? Mrs. Beaumont?" A halfhearted effort that elicited no response.

They were waiting for him in their bedroom. A cat circled between his feet, nearly tripping him. He picked up the cat and rubbed it. It quickly became a stress ball. Without realizing it, he'd squeezed the cat so tight it yowled at him and jumped away, drawing blood from deep scratches in his arms.

The Beaumonts lied dead in their marriage bed. Their bulging eyes stared at him like he was the one who brought this curse upon them. Maybe he was. Their faces stretched too long, and they had the same ashy complexion as Red's corpse despite dying in their warm bedroom.

Ryan needed to call for backup. It was wrong to be here alone. He half-expected them to rise from their bed and prompt him to join them. He backed out of the room, found their upstairs bathroom, and threw up in the toilet.

He froze in the bathroom doorway. Down the hallway, Will

Roebuck stood at the entrance to the master bedroom. He stared at the corpses.

NINE
CONSEQUENCES

1

THIS SEASON HAD BEEN full of off-the-court distractions for the Fort Todd Mariners. They entered the Area Consolation Finals with a 17-9 record—not bad, considering they had been in the news for all the wrong reasons last spring.

This year, their fans continued to distract them with poster board banners reading, "GO SAVAGES!" and retro t-shirts that said, "Fort Todd, Home of the Savages," featuring a caricature of a Native warrior.

At home games, this wouldn't be too confusing for attendees from neighboring towns. A large sign in front of the school read, "Fort Todd Savages: 1978, 1981, 1985, 1995 Class B Boys Basketball State Champions." Away games were more confusing for those unfamiliar with the history, especially if they didn't tune into the local news. The small town of Fort Todd had made waves because of the fight for their mascot.

Pressure came from the tribe—Fort Todd, like Nowhere, was in the Choctaw Nation—after a young history teacher shed light on the offensive name. The insult was compounded by

Fort Todd's history as a military outpost, established after the tribe's removal from Mississippi. The soldiers at Fort Todd had "maintained peace" between the removed Choctaws and the Plains tribes.

It took three school board votes before a compromise was reached: The school would change its name, but the banner could remain for its "historical importance." The students voted on a new name, but instead of choosing from the provided options, the majority wrote in "Savages."

Some students were in favor of changing the name, but most protested. It really came down to which side of the issue their parents were on or which clique they were in at school. The school board, fed up with the students' indecision, chose a name themselves. Inexplicably—or perhaps out of spite—the Savages became the Mariners, despite being in landlocked Oklahoma.

At least the jerseys looked good. They reminded Logan of the Orlando Magic jerseys from the Penny and Shaq era.

Logan won the tip-off. Right away, Alex knocked down a three-pointer. Logan darted to the post, ready for Fort Todd's guards to drive quickly. Alex crouched at the top of the key.

Then everything stopped.

The crowd went silent in confusion.

Fort Todd's guards stood just across halfcourt, passing the ball back and forth whenever Alex or Doug approached them. Marshal followed a third Fort Todd player, who dashed to the free throw line and raised his hands performatively, but the guards didn't even look to see if he was open. They had no intention of shooting.

Alex glanced at Logan and Sam, but they were waiting for him, their best on-ball defender, to make a move. Coach Park gave Alex a "settle down" motion.

"Wait and see," Logan said. "Let's just see what they're up to."

Fort Todd's center laughed.

They were up to nothing.

There was no shot clock in Oklahoma high school basketball, so they were free to not play the sport. It wasn't basketball —it was a game of "keep away." The ball floated back and forth, and Alex sidled from one guard to another. Eventually, he motioned for Marshal to come in for a trap, but the ball was already back to the other guard, and Coach Park called for him to settle down again.

Logan glanced at the scoreboard:

HOME: 0 AWAY: 3
TIME: 3:03 QUARTER: 1

Five minutes had already passed while the two guards tossed the ball to each other. The same third player cut across the lane with his hands up, then down, up, then down.

At one point, Doug tried to shoot the passing lane, displaying how minuscule his vertical leap was when the ball went over his head. He looked like a little brother.

With thirty seconds left in the first quarter, Fort Todd started to run a play. The Devils were sluggish from standing around—and because half the team was hungover. They were late on their rotation while the Mariners hit a corner three. Marshal heaved it full court when the buzzer sounded.

The crowd expressed support, but their energy had depleted. Even the Fort Todd fans seemed half-asleep in slouched positions, bunching up their Fort Todd Savages t-shirts, the Native caricature now sporting wrinkles.

"It's all right," Coach Park said. "They're trying to get under your skin. Patience, all right? In a game like this, every possession matters."

"What possessions?" Alex said.

Everyone agreed.

"Should we trap again?" Marshal suggested.

Coach Park said to try it and see if the Mariners sped up.

They didn't. Even when Fort Todd broke the full-court trap in the second quarter and had a free run to the basket, they pulled back into their "keep away" game. Alex managed to cause one turnover and scored a layup off it, but it was the only turnover of the quarter, and they took a 5-3 lead into halftime.

Nowhere had the ball to start the second half. Doug's missed jumper felt like missing a game-winner. The Fort Todd guards tossed the ball back and forth, no change in their strategy. Nowhere fans began to boo.

"This ain't basketball," someone shouted.

"You call yourself a coach?" another Nowhere fan belted.

Logan imagined a Dr. Pepper bottle flying out of the stands, aimed at Fort Todd's coach, or maybe a chant like the one the Colesville fans had. But instead of the refs, it would be a threat against the coach.

The frustrated murmuring of the crowd continued, like grasshoppers chittering at midnight, until a singular voice rang out, cutting through the noise. The voice drew everyone's attention. It broke the unwritten rule that you could complain about the refs and coaches all you wanted but never threaten a player. This Nowhere fan apparently didn't care about the rules.

His voice carried across the SOU gym, clear and direct: "I'm gonna gut you fuckers!"

It was enough outside the norm—even in a game of keep-away like this—that everything stopped. No one in the crowd murmured, the coaches turned their heads, and the Fort Todd guards gazed into the crowd.

Prompted by the distraction, Sam sprinted away from his man to steal the ball. In his excitement, he missed and slapped the guard across the arm.

The guard was startled—the slapping sound was like a gunshot after the threat from the crowd. The referee had a delayed reaction and didn't blow his whistle until Sam had collected the loose ball and was off in the other direction for a layup. Sam complained while he came back up the court, reluctant to give the ball to the ref.

Coach Park was pulled into a conversation with Superintendent Walker, and they glared at the crowd, trying to spot the culprit of the threat. Logan called Alex, Marshal, and Doug into a huddle on the court. Sam's foul had given him an idea.

"How many fouls put them in the bonus?" he asked.

"You think that'll work?" Alex asked, understanding right away what Logan intended.

"Four more," Doug answered.

"I'd love to play basketball too, Tramer, but it seems a little risky."

"It'll work."

"What will?" Doug asked.

"No..." Marshal's face lit up with realization. "Fuck that," he said. "Let 'em run out the clock and we win."

"That's more of a gamble than fouling," Logan said. "They're smart. They know they're not as good as us, even without Kelvin, so they take away most of our chances at scoring. We're only up two. All they have to do is catch us sleeping again, and they might win this thing."

"I'd rather try and stay awake than intentionally foul them," Marshal said.

"You want to send them to the free throw line?" Doug squeaked, then covered his mouth and glanced around to make sure no one heard him.

"Think about it…"

Doug was smiling when he pulled his hand away. "The well."

"Exactly."

Alex shook his head. "All right, magic man. Let's try it."

The ref blew the whistle, and Fort Todd put the ball into play. They went back to their game of "keep away," and Alex started the slew of fouls.

2

While Fort Todd continued to miss free throw after free throw, Logan felt lighter on his feet. He bounced up and down, even when standing still, and ran down the court, "frolicking." Logan didn't care if people saw how happy he was.

With each missed free throw, the truth sank in deeper: The Nowhere Devils were going to STATE.

Between the rest of the third and fourth quarters, the Mariners took fourteen free throws and made only two. Nearly everyone who was fouled bent their knees correctly, had a nice rotation on the ball, and a good arc. But a dozen times, the ball went in and out.

Some shots "toilet-bowled" around the rim and rolled out, others rattled and popped out at the last second. A few looked like they were about to swish through the net when the ball tilted upward, as if a shot of air had hit it from below, and bounced off the back of the rim. Fort Todd fans cried conspiracy, claiming Nowhere had someone hiding beneath the floorboards with a giant magnet controlling the ball.

Coach Park hadn't approved the strategy and was furious at first, but he changed his mind after seeing Fort Todd's poor free throw shooting. After that, he paced back and forth, jotting tally marks on the back of his clipboard next to each player's poorly scrawled name to track fouls.

Marshal and Doug fouled out, putting Mikey and Dylan in the game. There was a fear two others would foul out, leaving the Devils in a four-on-five situation, but Nowhere only intentionally fouled enough to gain those extra possessions. Once their lead grew to double digits, they were satisfied.

Alex took nearly every shot on offense, but Logan didn't chastise him. The boy was red-hot. Every shot swished through the net. He even hit a three off the backboard at an impossible angle for fun late in the game.

The final buzzer sounded, and the team hugged each other and screamed.

A chant began in the crowd: "STATE! STATE! STATE!"

The players lined up and shook hands with the Fort Todd Mariners before dispersing into the crowd to celebrate with their families. Logan's mom gave him a big, wet kiss on the cheek and attempted to wrap her scrawny arms around him. He stood back to his full height after their embrace and spotted Jessica with his sister, coming down from the top bleachers.

Of all people, Allen Prospect was with them. Logan had never seen Allen at a Nowhere game before. The dropout had a purplish bruise around his neck, starting to turn yellow.

Logan met them halfway up the bleachers. Jessica surprised him with a hug. She smelled nice which made him insecure about his own body odor.

"I can't believe we're going to STATE again!" she said.

"I told you we would make it."

"I'm just glad you didn't let those fuckers keep up their bull-shit," Allen said. "That ain't basketball."

The way he said "fuckers" was so obvious, Logan didn't even need to ask. His eyes widened, and Allen knew what he was thinking.

Allen scanned the bleachers. People looked at them because Logan couldn't go anywhere without being noticed at his height, but no one seemed suspicious.

"I just couldn't stand watching them throw the ball back and forth like that anymore," Allen said. "My first b-ball game in five years and I gotta watch that shit?"

"Thanks for coming," Logan said with a sly smile. He meant it too.

If Allen hadn't shouted that surprising insult, catching everyone off guard, Sam might not have fouled the Fort Todd guard, and then Logan might never have thought to intentionally foul, giving the Basketball Gods a chance to help Nowhere.

"I gotta thank your little sis here for giving me a ride home."

Emily didn't look happy about the arrangement. Jessica was less annoyed, giddy, in fact, hopefully about their date tomorrow and not the prospect of Allen Prospect riding to Nowhere with them.

"How'd you get here in the first place?" Logan asked Allen.

"My brother came to town, so I thought I might as well come watch my boys make STATE."

"Glad we could oblige."

"Hell yeah. Makes me wish I was still in school. I'd be on that court with you."

Allen Prospect had never played sports. Logan recalled the few times Allen had played on the outdoor court before school, and he was no athlete. He was far worse than Tim, who at least had some height and muscle.

"Strange finish, wouldn't you say?" Emily said after being so quiet.

Logan shrugged. "I guess they couldn't handle the pressure."

"They missed twelve out of fourteen free throws. I counted." She glared at him suspiciously.

"Obsessed much?"

"I'm just saying it was weird."

"Who cares?" Jessica said. "We're going to STATE."

Emily wasn't satisfied but didn't press any further. Her gaze made Logan nervous, as conspiratorial as the Fort Todd fans.

It was not a conspiracy if it was true.

But why would anyone in their right mind think I caused them to miss their free throws? What powers does Emily think I have?

Then it struck him: Emily had grown up hearing the same Green River story he had. She was thinking about the way the Lady Bullfrogs had won in such an unexplainable fashion. He wondered if he needed to bring her in on the secret.

Will would be pissed, but who cared? It wasn't like Emily was going to rush out to make a wish at the kitchen well. Or would she? What if she wished for Kelvin to be healed? Logan was amazed he hadn't thought of that as a possible wish until now. If the well could heal Will's grandma from her blindness, surely it could heal a broken leg.

He wondered if he should go straight away and make the wish himself. But then he thought about Tim's dad and Bird. He didn't want to risk what could happen if he compounded his wishes.

An immense guilt washed over him again, a feeling that lingered no matter how excited he was after each victory. He didn't want to leave Jessica in the bleachers, but it was customary to ride the bus to and from away games, win or lose. And the team had to celebrate their third straight trip to STATE.

During the hour-long bus ride back to Nowhere, they played music and danced, rocking the bus. Folks from the long line of cars in front of and behind the bus waved their arms out the windows and flashed their lights in celebration. The basketball boys leaned out the windows to their waists and hollered at the fans, not caring how cold it was outside.

They freestyled, cracked jokes, and wondered aloud who was getting laid that night. When they reached the school, Alex reminded Logan, Doug, and Marshal that they were going to Kelvin's house before Turner's barn.

Logan could think of no excuses. He couldn't stand them up like last time. Besides, there was no better time. They were going back to STATE, and he was taking Jessica on a date tomorrow. The wish was proving its power.

Everything was perfect—and Logan was scared.

3

He drove from one dirt road to another before heading up Harris Hill to Kelvin's farmhouse. The driveway was long, and the gravel always came undone no matter how many times a dump truck delivered more.

There seemed little point to it, considering how often Wendall Harris drove work trucks and tractors up and down the drive, but Belinda had insisted on spreading new gravel to cover as many of the potholes as possible. In his hurry, Logan managed to hit every one of them. He needed to get to Kelvin's house before he changed his mind.

Logan parked next to Alex's Jeep. Kelvin's mother greeted him excitedly.

"It's so good to see you, Logan. Kelvin will be happy you came."

He was surprised she was awake, but he supposed everyone in Nowhere would be, buzzing about how the team was going back to STATE. "We listened to the game on the radio," she said as she led him into the kitchen for a glass of soda. "I've never heard of such a cowardly strategy before. They must have been frightened to play actual basketball against y'all."

"That's how he knew to foul them. Figured they'd choke on their free throws."

"Smart thinking." Mrs. Harris poured Dr. Thunder over a stack of ice cubes. She hadn't needed to ask Logan if he wanted some before filling a glass. It was like he had been coming over every day, the way he used to.

"How's he holding up?" he asked.

"You know Kelvin." She shook her head playfully at her son's stubbornness. "He's doing exactly what he told the doctor he'd do. 'I'm gonna be out there supporting my team at STATE,' he said. 'They can get there without me, but I want to be with my team when we win it all.'"

"And here we are," Logan said. "Guess he'll be with us next week then."

"Don't think any doctor or worried mama could keep him from it."

Logan smiled at her and sipped from his drink. The glass of Dr. Thunder began sweating before he reached Kelvin's room. The door was open, and he heard Doug's voice, followed by everyone else laughing. The drink threatened to slide from his loose grip. He imagined dropping it on the hardwood floor, letting its crash announce his arrival.

Instead, he tightened his grip and cleared his throat before he entered Kelvin's bedroom.

"What's up, big man?" Marshal said.

Logan expected to see Kelvin in bed, his leg in a long white cast elevated in a sling. But Kelvin was standing among the others, crutches under each arm, with a new, shorter cast from below the knee down to his toes. He looked almost like his old self, except for the dark circles making his eyes appear to be sinking into his skull.

"Well, look who it is." Kelvin bounded toward him, his crutches squeaking with each step.

Logan dapped him up.

"It's good to see you, bro," Kelvin said.

"You're looking right as rain."

"Getting there."

"Doug was just telling us about his latest rendezvous with Mal," Alex said. "Look at his goddamn hickeys."

Doug looked sheepish but pulled down his collar so Logan could see the welts on his neck.

"He didn't even have to make STATE to get laid," Marshal said. "Lucky bastard. I guess all that praying paid off."

The joke had a bite to it. Logan sensed jealousy—a strange feeling coming from Marshal who always seemed to have a sexually active girlfriend around. Come to think of it, though, Logan hadn't seen Marshal with any girl lately, not even Emily.

Kelvin crutched his way to the other side of the room, peering out his window into the night. "Y'all really did it," he said, as much to himself as to the others.

"Fucking A," Marshal said.

"You should've seen the way Fort Todd played tonight," Doug said. "I'd heard of teams running down the clock like that, but never thought it'd happen to us."

"It's like I told you earlier this season, Dougie," Kelvin said. "Teams fear us now. You have to embrace being the best team in the state. You have to accept it quickly so you can start focusing on how to handle the pressure."

"Imagine the pressure we've been under," Alex said. "No one thought we'd do shit without you."

"Can you blame them?" Doug asked.

"It was this guy here." Alex pointed at Logan. "He was always confident we could win."

Logan could have taken the opportunity to tell Kelvin about the kitchen well. It felt strange that everyone in the room knew something Kelvin didn't. That wasn't how things usually went.

For most of Logan's high school career, it had been Kelvin who had the insight, who told his teammates how to guard a certain team or whether to play fast or slow depending on the matchup. Now, the four of them had the ultimate advantage in any game, and Logan couldn't bring himself to tell his best friend.

The others followed his lead. Once it was clear Logan wasn't going to share about the well, they shifted topics, asking Kelvin about his PlayStation 2.

"I didn't know you had the new one." Doug snatched up the case for *NBA Live 2004*. Inside the plastic DVD case was the cover art—Vince Carter in his Raptors jersey, seemingly driving the ball in for one of his otherworldly dunks.

"Got it for Christmas."

"Where have you been, Dougie?" Marshal asked, as though he had been the one spending day and night with Kelvin since Christmas.

Before the injury—and before Kelvin started dating his sister—it had been Logan who was here all the time. Logan had a metallic taste in his mouth. He tried to dismiss the oncoming resentment. He couldn't be mad at someone who had lost the only thing he'd ever cared about. He wondered if North Texas had already called to cancel Kelvin's scholarship.

Logan had seen up close the way his leg broke. Even if Kelvin played again, he would never be the same as he was. His own leg began to ache, being in close proximity to his old friend.

"How long have you been moving around?" he asked.

Kelvin shrugged. "Just a couple of days."

"They switched out your cast, what, a week ago?" Marshal asked.

Kelvin seemed annoyed, but if Emily knew something, Marshal definitely did too.

"Yeah," Kelvin admitted. "I've been getting used to the crutches since then. I should be able to get back to school soon."

"Next week?" Alex asked.

Suddenly, it felt like everyone was standing over Kelvin.

"Soon," Kelvin said vaguely.

He was scared to leave the house, Logan realized.

"You're coming to the STATE TOURNAMENT, though, right?" Doug asked.

"Of course," Kelvin said quickly, then added, "Do y'all know who you're playing yet?"

"The schedule won't be out until Monday," Logan said.

"Got to watch out for Barton-Meek. They've been on fire."

"We're not worried," Alex said dismissively.

"Good...good."

"This is the year, Kelvin," Doug said, taking a step closer. "You have to come watch."

"Don't worry, Dougie. I'll be there." Kelvin wrung his hands around the padded handholds of his crutches. "Do y'all remember when we played Olney at the Red Dirt Tournament? Don't forget about the way the Mosely brothers will hook your arm when they're in the ref's blind spot—"

"We remember," Marshal said, cutting Kelvin off, joining Doug and Alex, enclosing Kelvin by the window.

"Awesome." Kelvin gave them a weak smile. He seemed to be running through other advice in his mind that they didn't need.

Logan watched his best friend lose his confidence in real time as the four of them crowded him. It was sad to see, but it also gave Logan pleasure. He was the one who would bring Nowhere their first championship.

In Logan's moment of self-congratulation, Kelvin turned to him and said, "It's good to see you, Logan."

"Yeah, man," Logan said.

The bedroom door flung open, startling him. Logan's skin vibrated, like he couldn't let go of an electric fence. He almost laughed at how much he jumped—until he saw the look on Belinda Harris's face. She gripped the cordless phone tight.

"What's wrong?" Kelvin said.

His mom stared at Logan. "There's been an accident."

4

Emily drove everywhere. Now that the girls' season was over, she didn't need to worry about team bonding on the bus before and after games. She was free to drive her Kia to her brother's games.

For the past three weeks, she and Jessica had frequently left school to grab lunch in Holdendecker. Jessica would use her employee discount at Wheelman's for both of them: two orders of large Dr Peppers and large fries with ranch. Turned out they were very similar. Emily wished Jessica had broken up with that asshole Tom Bomber a long time ago. Jessica was one of those girls who spent all her free time with her boyfriend. Now that she was single, she finally hung out with her teammates and other classmates outside of school, having something to say that wasn't about Tom.

Of course, Emily asked her about her relationship. Jessica was a wealth of knowledge, and Emily felt new to dating despite how long the past nine weeks had been. Especially the past three. She was thankful Kelvin could get out of bed on his own now. She had started to feel like she was tagging in for his mom anytime she visited, waiting on him hand and foot. She started getting short with him when he asked for a glass of water or to switch out the discs in his PlayStation 2. She felt bad when she finally snapped at him to do it himself, but it was the motivation he needed to get out of bed. He was still in a funk but at least she didn't feel guilty about leaving him alone for an evening or two. She even planned to go to Turner's barn tonight.

Emily hadn't talked to Marshal much this week because he had been such a dick about her desire for Kelvin to stay home next year. That wasn't the only reason she distanced herself from him—Marshal had been a dick plenty of times before. She sensed something else from him: jealousy. Which was laughable. Marshal had years to ask her out but decided to date girls from Cottonvale and Holdendecker instead. He had no right to be jealous.

So, she befriended Jessica and they drove to every game of the Area Tournament together. Emily loved driving. Her 2004 Kia Sportage had been a gift from her mom—a fulfilled promise from three years ago to soften the blow of moving from Tuskahoma to Nowhere.

Logan was resentful. He was offered no such promises and drove his old Ford, which could fulfill their dad's favorite joke at any time: F.O.R.D. — Found On Roadside Dead. But he didn't need a promise to move. He had no friends he was leaving behind like Emily did.

Logan bugged her all the time about borrowing the Kia, most recently so he could take it on his date with Jessica if they won their game Saturday. She found it weird that Jessica would be sitting in the passenger's seat, like she was tonight, but with Logan driving. It was one thing she and Jessica didn't talk about: the fact Jessica said yes to a date with her brother. It was gross but, deep down, Emily was happy to see Logan putting himself out there. He had been so confident since the strange arrest at Regionals.

After tonight's game, she understood why.

The Green River Lady Bullfrogs. 1990 Class B State Champions.

Emily was a toddler during the run. She had no memory of the strange circumstances that led to her aunt's team winning the title, just as she had no memory of her aunt. She wished she did. Her mom had told her she and Jocelyn not only looked alike but they had the same personality. Emily joked that she wished they had the same skills on the court. Emily was Nowhere's best player but only reached 20 points five times this season. She thought the team would be good next year, assuming the school didn't shut down before then.

She couldn't concentrate on recalling the stories her mom had told her about Green River because Allen Prospect wouldn't shut up in the backseat.

"Did y'all see that shit?" he said, sitting in the middle so he could lean over the console and poke his head between Emily and Jessica. He smelled like cigarette smoke, popcorn, and B.O. She didn't hide her objection to it, scrunching her nose anytime he turned toward her, wafting the smell in her direction.

Jessica seemed amused by him. Emily suspected she was attracted to Allen, but she didn't see the appeal and felt territorial on her brother's behalf.

"It wasn't that big of a deal," she said.

"C'mon, Tramer," Allen said. "As soon as I called out those fuckers, they started shitting themselves. Why else would they miss all those free throws? They were scared shitless."

"You gotta admit, Em," Jessica said. "It makes sense."

"It also makes sense that they felt the pressure of reaching STATE and choked."

"Think what you want," Allen said, leaning back, satisfied, and stretching his arms.

Thank God, Emily thought, hoping her car vents would push the smell back with him.

"So I heard a little story about you," Jessica said, looking over her shoulder.

"Finally heard about my lovemaking skills, did ya? Well, it's true, ladies."

"Nope. Definitely not that. I heard you got in a fight last night. That's the reason for your little—" She ran on her finger along her throat like she was threatening him.

Emily couldn't see his face when he was sitting back. The glow from the digital clockface of the Kia certainly didn't reach that far. The moonlight shined through the back window, illuminating his jeans and shirt, but above his collarbone, Allen was shadowy in the rearview mirror.

She gazed into the mirror for too long to try and see his reaction, then quickly looked at the road ahead when her heart did an intuitive skip to remind her that she was driving seventy on a highway at night. Ever since getting her Kia, she had been worried about deer. A couple months removed from deer season and there were already plenty scrounging in ditches across southeastern Oklahoma. The highway was pitch-black aside from the beam of her headlights. There wasn't even light pollution in a town the size of Tuskahoma, albeit they were half an hour away from SOU.

"Is it true?" Jessica asked. "Did Doug choke you out last night?"

Emily had heard the story from Reba Jacobs who claimed to hear it from Mal, although Jessica said Mal didn't know what she was talking about when she asked her directly. Emily didn't believe Doug Mooreland would do that. He led Bible studies during lunch break for Christ's sake.

Allen threw his arms out and shook his head. "It's true," he said. "Little Dougie got his revenge when I was compromised."

"What?" Emily blurted out.

"That's right. Dougie ain't so scrawny anymore. Or innocent. You should've seen the 'compromising' position I found him in."

"I'm surprised you didn't jump him after the game," Jessica said. "That's what you would've done when you were in school. Catch him behind the shop building."

"Jesus, Jessica. Don't give him any ideas."

"I'm not saying he *should* do that. You hear me, Allen? Do not attack Doug. We need him to help us win STATE."

"Oh, but after that, have at it," Emily said sarcastically.

"Don't worry your pretty little head," Allen said. "Honestly, I respect him more now."

"So, what's this compromising position?" Jessica leaned further over the center console, pressing her side against Emily, causing her to swerve a little.

"Sorry," Emily said when the other two protested.

Allen leaned forward, out of the dark, where Emily could see his face in the moonlight. He was close to Jessica's face now, and Emily had the dreaded premonition they might make out. He didn't look at Jessica when he spoke but into the rearview mirror where Emily was glaring back at him. "He and Mal were in her truck, fogging up the windows. I heard 'em before I saw 'em. Gruntin' and moanin'."

"Ew," Emily said. But she kept staring at him in the mirror, as excited to hear the story as Jessica.

"Nice," Jessica said, flirting more blatantly than she had all night.

A part of Emily imagined them kissing and her heart beat a little faster. She pictured Allen reaching his arm between Jessica and the console and cupping her breast, the side of which was currently pressed against Emily's arm. She shifted in her seat and checked the road ahead again when her fast-beating heart gave its warning skip.

Nothing.

No reflecting eyes or silhouetted bodies along the side of the highway.

Only the next exit sign to her right. White font across the green background reflecting in her headlights:

GREEN RIVER
EXIT 1 MILE

Eerily fitting, given she had finally drawn the connection between Nowhere's playoff run and her aunt's team tonight.

Also, that means we got a long way to go before I can get out of this car.

But she wasn't as desperate to escape Allen as she had been. She found herself peering into the rearview mirror again as he continued leaning close to Jessica over the center console.

"You know me," Allen continued. "I had to get a peek. I pressed my face up to the window and saw Doug with his pants down, pumping like a jackrabbit, and Mal had her top off. He was sucking on her nipple."

"Bullshit," Jessica said.

"Scout's honor," Allen said, his eyes gazing up at Emily in the mirror. He had a cocky grin and started to lean even closer to Jessica.

Oh my god, they're really gonna start making out.

But then Allen's eyes flicked to his right; Emily saw it in slow motion. A moment later, his body followed, whipping back into his seat, his head twisted to the right, his eyes narrow as he stared out the passenger's side window.

Her slow-motion observation had not kept her from being startled, and Emily jerked the steering wheel like this time—for sure this time—there would be a deer in the road ahead of her. But there wasn't.

"Goddammit, Em." Jessica fell back into the passenger's seat and put on her seatbelt.

"Sorry," Emily said, straightening the Kia in her lane. The solid yellow line glittered blurringly in her headlights.

"Did y'all see that?" Allen continued staring out the window, the moonlight glowing on his face. He looked concerned.

"What?" Jessica asked.

Then he squinted, turning his eyes into dark slivers. "Something flew by my window. Maybe it was an owl or something."

"An owl? Really?"

"Hey, you don't know."

"*Right.*" Jessica drew out the word. "I'm sure that's exactly what it was."

Allen laughed nervously, then shook it off, and leaned over the center console again, his face next to Emily's arm. He looked cartoonish, like a turtle stretching its neck out of its shell. It helped her shake the intrusive vision of them making out while she drove.

Why the hell would you torture yourself imagining that?

She wondered if she should go see Kelvin tonight instead going to Turner's barn. Sure, he annoyed her when he treated her like his nurse, but he was a great kisser. His injury had not stopped them from fooling around.

"So," Allen said. "Where were we?" He looked back and forth between the two girls.

Jessica shook her head but smiled. Emily glanced down at him, and he held her gaze.

"Woah!"

Jessica this time.

When Emily looked ahead, it was no false alarm. Her warning heartbeat had failed her.

In the middle of the highway was no deer. It was—

She couldn't make sense of it.

She swerved into the other lane just in time to miss it. Allen was thrown back against the backseat hard. Headlights blinded her—the first car they had seen in ages.

She yanked the steering wheel, the Kia rocking back into her lane in time to miss the oncoming car. A horn blared at them as the car passed and was muted by distance quickly enough because Emily never slowed down, never even hit the brake. Stupidly, the Kia remained in cruise control.

Her heart pounded in her throat, and she considered taking her car off cruise control, being more prepared along the dark highway with no shoulder. Instead, she and Jessica looked at each other and simultaneously said, "Holy shit!" Then they laughed wildly, a belly laugh laced with adrenaline.

"Ya'll are some crazy bitches," Allen mumbled from the backseat but was barely heard over their laughter. Finally, they settled down, and Emily looked in her side mirror as if what was in the road followed them. But even if that was the case, she wouldn't see it. Now she had a moment to think about what it had been, and all she knew for sure was that whatever it was had been clouded in a dark mist. It was nothing more than a black spot in her headlights.

"You all right, Allen?"

He sighed. "Oh, ya know. Tramer's trying to kill me. But you ought to know by now. I'm indestruct—"

Suddenly, Allen spasmed and let out a sharp gasp.

A shared moment of frozen confusion before Jessica unbuckled and reached back as Allen screamed and seizured. A deep gurgling sound rattled from the back—

In the darkness, where Allen's face was hidden.

Jessica climbed as fast as she could over the seat, trying to hold him down. "Allen, Allen, Allen," she repeated, getting louder each time to match the rising inhuman sounds coming from him.

Emily's hands wrung the steering wheel, her rearview

mirror a peephole into a world of horror that she couldn't peel her eyes away from.

Allen's moonlit body rose from his seat—

Levitating. She was sure of it.

Jessica held his hands to the seat cushion like she was a stake in a hot air balloon preventing him from floating away.

His arms stretched against her resistance, his skin pulling tighter and tighter.

"Em! Help!"

What could Emily do but stare at them in the rearview mirror—

A red light flashed in the moonlight, and she locked eyes with Allen for a long, horrible moment, as his glowed red, reflecting the flashing light that covered the moon.

Emily tore hers away from the mirror without her heart needing to skip a beat—an impossible feat at the current speed of her heartrate—just in time to see the same *thing* in the middle of the highway.

A black spot.

Another flash of red blinding her.

This time she didn't swerve into the other lane but toward the ditch.

5

There would be no Kia for Logan to borrow. No date anyway. Not that Logan was thinking about that.

Emily had wrecked her car on the way home from tonight's game. She, Jessica, and Allen Prospect had left the gym after the procession of vehicles with the team bus because Allen kept talking to people he claimed to know from other schools.

Along the dark highway, they glided through a ditch and smashed into a telephone pole.

Jessica had been the luckiest. She was mostly unscathed—a cut along her cheek requiring three stitches, some bruises and possibly a concussion, a dislocated shoulder from slamming into the back of the driver's seat. But she was released from the hospital after a couple of hours.

Allen was the least lucky. From the backseat, he somehow went through the front windshield and cracked his head open on the pole. He died instantly. What even the paramedics didn't know was that he had died before his head collided with the pole, before his body sailed through the windshield.

Emily was somewhere between lucky and unlucky. She wasn't dead—lucky, considering the speed they'd hit the pole —but she wasn't unscathed. She had lost consciousness on impact and hadn't regained it. A traumatic brain injury put her in a coma. She had fractured her right arm and broken some ribs. The paramedics rushed her back to Tuskahoma.

When Logan saw her in the ICU, he started to cry. His mother held him until he could control his breathing again. He couldn't look at his sister any longer. Fluids were needled into her arm, and a tube disappeared down her throat. Her face was half-covered in bandages. It was too much for Logan, so he paced around the hospital, hoping his brain fog would subside, but it didn't.

In the waiting room, his teammates sat nervously. Kelvin had finally left his house although Logan was sure he wished it was under better circumstances. A line of cars had left the Harrises' farmhouse together, Logan's truck in front taking the same highway back to Tuskahoma. No one was hanging out their car windows celebrating this time.

Kelvin stared at his outstretched leg, his crutch resting against his cast. Doug nibbled on his fingernails. Marshal tapped his foot wildly. Alex stood against the wall with his arms crossed.

Others were there, including Coach Julia Reed. She had been the one to find the Kia in the ditch. Despite the car being totaled, she recognized it was Emily's. She rushed to help, only pausing when she reached the ditch and saw the car a little better.

Buzzards pecked around the roof of the Kia, already looking for a way in.

Coach Reed rushed to the car, fearing the worst. She called 911, thankful she had finally gotten a cell phone before the start of the basketball season.

Since Jessica was the only one conscious, Coach Reed pried open the passenger's side door and helped get her out. Jessica went around the back of the Kia to get to Emily's side while Coach Reed approached Allen Prospect's body.

Two buzzards squawked and flapped at her until she shooed them away from the body.

She took a long look and wished she hadn't, but she had to make sure her intuition was right. Allen was dead, his face unrecognizable beneath his squashed head.

Like a deflated basketball.

She finally moved away from him.

Coach Reed waited at the hospital with everyone else.

Now the sun was beginning to rise. Logan's mom thanked everyone for coming and letting them know they could leave. Coach Reed asked where things stood, and Logan's mom was surprisingly calm when she told them Emily was comatose.

"Are they going to perform surgery?" Coach Park asked.

Dr. Warren had told Logan and his mom that there were no signs she had bleeding or swelling on the brain, so no surgery was required. Logan had known Dr. Warren since he was a kid. She was married to a distant cousin of his mom. Dr. Warren had a way of calming everyone down in stressful situations, but not even she could sell this as good news.

No surgery, sure, but it left him feeling like there was no gameplan to save his sister. Emily was left alone to decide if she would live or die.

He feared it wasn't her decision. No one had died in Nowhere in no telling how long before Tim's dad a week ago, and now this.

Logan's mind was too clouded to dwell on it but being present was worse. He couldn't handle the way everyone stared at him and his mom. They weren't leaving soon enough for him, so he left to find a vending machine and wandered the halls some more.

When he actually saw a vending machine, he stopped and unfolded a dollar bill. Over and over again, he inserted the dollar, but the machine wouldn't take it. Finally, Logan slammed his fist into the machine, sending an echoing whap down the hallway.

"Easy, killer." Alex came around the side with Doug and Marshal. He took Logan's bill and shimmied it back and forth on the rounded edge of the vending machine.

The machine took the dollar, and Logan punched the orange soda tab.

He stood against the wall and sipped the drink. His teammates looked around to make sure they were alone.

"This is our fault, isn't it?" Doug ran his hand through his hair. "Your sister—"

"Emily's gonna be all right," Logan lied. "She'll wake up and be all right."

"But Allen...I killed him." Doug put a hand over his mouth.

"Jesus, Dougie," Alex said. "You didn't kill anybody."

"You know I did."

"What're you talking about?" Logan said.

"Alex and I went to the well last night and made a wish."

"You did what?" Marshal's bloodshot eyes widened in

surprise and disgust. He had been speechless since learning his best friend was in a car accident and unconscious, only brought to the present by Doug's admission.

"I told you not to do that," Logan said. "I said not to make any more wishes until we won STATE."

"I just wanted her to like me," Doug said. "That was all. It was a simple wish. It wasn't like curing the blind or wishing for a championship or anything. It was just Mal liking me."

"Your wish didn't kill Allen, Dougie," Alex repeated. "It was an accident."

"Was it?" Marshal wondered aloud.

"Of course it was. Y'all need to calm the hell down."

"Don't you see?" Doug pleaded.

"Shut the fuck up." Logan squeezed the can until orange soda spewed out of the open tab. Immediately, the liquid dried into a sticky goop on his hand. "Everyone just shut the fuck up."

He closed his eyes to focus. He couldn't think through the haziness of his mind. He had been floating since arriving at the hospital. The lights were too bright, the hallways too clean.

"Doug, you didn't kill Allen," he finally said.

"I told you so—" Alex started to say before Logan cut him off.

"—Allen was the one who made the threat. 'I'm gonna gut you fuckers.' That one. That was Allen...and Mr. Tune, who apparently is missing now, left with that ref who whistled Colesville for all those phantom fouls. And Tim's dad wanted to fight those guys from Nashoba. And Bird...he told Will about the kitchen well. Will would have never made the wish if Bird hadn't brought it up. So, no. You didn't kill Allen, Dougie...I did it."

"Come on, big man," Marshal said, but Logan was as clear-headed as he had been all night.

There was a surprising relief to saying it out loud, to admitting he might be responsible.

"You're wrong," Alex said. "I get what you're saying, Tramer, but you're wrong...Think about it, man. No one died after we beat Picard or Mutton—"

"We didn't need the magic to win those games."

"Of course we did."

"No, Logan's right," Doug said, his face emptying like a glass of water. "I would have noticed if anything miraculous happened. I'm always looking for signs from God. I would have noticed like when Bolan got arrested. I was on my knees praying that night, thanking God for helping us win, even before you told me about the well."

"The center for Mutton had a cramp," Alex said, refusing to be stumped.

"A cramp can happen to anyone," Logan said. "Compared to what we've seen the wish do, do you really think there was anything magical about that?"

"Definitely not," Marshal agreed.

"So, it *is* our fault." Doug's head dropped shamefully.

Alex was beside himself until his eyes widened a moment later. "What about McClinton?"

"Ethan Crist?" Doug asked, lifting his head again hopefully.

"Dude was shitting himself on the court," Alex said. "You're telling me that wasn't the well's magic? And did anyone die or go missing after that game? No. They didn't. Because it's a coincidence, man. An awful coincidence."

Logan's hands fell over his face because he thought he might cry again. He slid to the floor, overwhelmed and tired. His face felt warm in his hands—a small comfort during the worst night of his young life.

When he pulled his hands away, he had no response for Alex other than to shake his head. His hands dangled from where he rested his arms on his bent knees. He wanted to believe his teammate, *needed* all this to be a coincidence. But it was almost worse to think his sister was in a coma because of an accident, that the recent deaths were meaningless.

"I'm right," Alex said. "Right?" He looked to Doug and Marshal for support.

Marshal had been staring at his feet, pondering, until then. "Who fucking cares?" he said, shocking the others. "It doesn't matter if it's the wish snuffing these people out, or if this is all a coincidence. There's nothing we can do about the people who died. But Emily...she's not dead. And there's something very obvious we can do to help her right now."

Logan caught on first. He began to stand.

It hit Doug next. "You can't be serious."

Finally, Alex understood. "Holy shit." He peered at Logan. "It'll work, won't it?"

A warmth rose from Logan's gut, cutting through the fogginess of his thoughts. "Yeah...it will."

6

The abandoned house looked different than at night. The slanted morning light shot through the trees. Every blemish on the house's exterior was more obvious. The chipped paint was a light blue, not the off-white Logan had previously thought it to be. He discovered carvings in the paneling—crude drawings and words like "dick" and "fuck" put there by visitors over the years, and dozens of initials including some he recognized: LT and KH. His and Kelvin's.

They moved straight to the kitchen and gazed into the well. It was as pitch-black inside as it had been at night. Logan was ready to climb down again, but Marshal volunteered.

"Fine by me," Alex said. "You couldn't pay me to go down there."

"It was your idea, Marshal," Logan noted. "Go for it."

Marshal planted his feet against the inside of the well, while Logan, Alex, and Doug held the other end. As he descended, Logan felt the strain on the rope. It turned and tightened in his grip.

Marshal shouted when he reached the bottom, though the splashing sound of his drop told them that much.

Logan made the wish in his mind: *I wish for Emily Tramer to be saved.*

It wasn't as specific as his last wish, but it was what he and Marshal could come up with. It was what they wanted, after all.

They pulled Marshal out a few minutes later. Logan crossed the house quickly, eager to return to Tuskahoma and find out if his sister had been instantly healed. The others moved slowly, intrigued by the rest of the house.

In the light of day, it looked more like a home that had once been lived in. Its history lay in its destruction: old letters, blown-out windows, a chevron-patterned couch, and clear glass doorknobs in the back bedrooms. The kitchen well, of course. Doug and Alex explored the house while Logan stood with Marshal in the front room, waiting.

Logan stepped on one of the old letters and realized it was the one Will had read the night of the prank. He picked it up and scanned it. The ink had faded, and the cursive handwriting was almost indecipherable. Bloody fingerprints dotted the page. He tried to avoid touching those parts.

He read what he could make out: *"My heart still aches that you would return to that place. Even sending a letter to the address makes me shiver."* Further down, it said: *"I blame myself. It was I who took you there, and you trusted me. Trust me now. Please. Like you once did. You have to leave that place."*

Logan couldn't make out what was written after that. He narrowed his eyes, trying to focus on each swooping letter—

"Look at this dump." Doug shuffled the magazines on the couch with one finger. "Hey"—he approached Marshal, his forefinger jabbing toward him—"smell my finger."

"Fuck off," Marshal said, slapping Doug's hand away. "Can we go now?"

"We should've left ten minutes ago," Logan responded.

7

"I can't explain it," Dr. Warren said, perplexed. "Not only is she awake, but she's completely lucid. No memory loss. Her reactivity to light is great, and her reflexes are fantastic. X-rays show the break in her ribs and arm aren't as bad as we first believed."

Logan's mom finally felt safe enough to cry, and Logan couldn't stop smiling.

"I want to keep her here for a few days and run some tests," Dr. Warren continued.

Logan's first thought was disappointment, that Emily would miss seeing him win STATE.

"And you should know," Dr. Warren added. "Emily remembers the crash, so she won't just be healing physically. I'll provide you a good therapist recommendation before she leaves the hospital."

Logan's mom unexpectedly hugged Dr. Warren, and the doctor briefly dropped her professionalism to embrace her husband's cousin.

"Thank you, thank you, thank you," Logan's mom repeated.

"Of course, Janice. I'm so happy and relieved too."

Logan thanked Dr. Warren too.

While hospital staff moved Emily out of the ICU, Logan and his mom shared the good news with everyone in the waiting room. Kelvin hugged him, the embrace as intimate as the night Logan had held his best friend's hand.

Marshal, Doug, and Alex stood to the side, looking proud of themselves. Coach Reed had stayed since last night. Some of the girls' team had come this Sunday morning, eager to see their friend.

Logan asked if anyone had talked to Jessica, and Reba told him she had gone to see her earlier. "The doctor told her to stay home and rest for a couple of days, but she seemed okay."

"Good," he said. "That's good. I'll have to go see her."

Reba glanced at her friends and smiled. "I'm sure she'd like that, Logan."

"Oh? Did she...say anything about me?"

Reba pushed him away teasingly. "Go see your sister, lover boy."

Logan followed his mom to Emily's room, feeling energized. The others stayed behind so they wouldn't overwhelm her all at once.

The hospital room was warm, and an orange light glowed above Emily's bed like a heat lamp. A rerun of *Smallville* played on the TV in the background.

The bandages were gone from Emily's head, leaving only a small scrape. Her right arm was in a cast, and the bruises on her face had vanished. She beamed when they entered. Logan couldn't find any words, so he just grinned stupidly.

His mom couldn't stop talking, worried Emily's miraculous healing was some cruel joke from God. "Where are you hurting, honey? Do I need to turn off this light?"

"I'm fine, Mom," Emily said.

"You always say you're fine," their mom replied, "but you were in a wreck, sweetheart. You wouldn't wake up."

"I'm awake now, and I feel fine."

Their mom started to cry again.

"I really am, Mom." Emily glanced at Logan for help.

"Uh, should we get you some water?" he offered.

"Yeah," Emily said. "Yeah, that'd be good."

"Right," their mom said. "Let me get you some water."

She left the room, and Emily sighed in relief. "Good call," she said. "Maybe Mom will be a little calmer when she gets back."

"We're just happy you're all right, Em." Logan choked up.

"C'mon, you big crybaby." She pulled him into a hug.

When he straightened, she held his hand to keep him from getting too far away. "I have to tell you something, Logan."

"Anything." He wiped a warm tear from his eye.

"Well, I'm not really sure how to say it. I've heard that people sometimes can't remember when they've been in a car wreck. But I remember everything. At least, I think I do. It feels... like a nightmare. And I wonder if that's how everyone who remembers their wreck feels."

"I'm sure it is. That's an awful thing to—"

"I really mean it, Logan. It feels like a nightmare because what happened can't be real."

"All right..." His throat went dry. "Go ahead, Em. I'm listening."

"We were driving along. As you know, Allen was with us. I couldn't believe I'd gotten roped into giving him a ride home. I think he has—*had*—a crush on Jessica. He saw us at the top of the bleachers and homed in on us. I keep thinking...what if Allen hadn't come to the game? He never comes to games. Not the regular season, not the playoffs. Why the hell was he there last night?"

"It's not your fault, Em. It was nice of you to give him a ride—"

"Just listen. We were driving along. Allen was being a dick but then—"

Emily stared past Logan, like she was seeing what happened the night before. She squeezed his hand harder.

"I'm here, Em. You can tell me anything."

"I swerved to miss something in the road. I thought it must be a deer. We'd been on the highway for a while already, near the exit for Green River. It was about time to see some, right? Well, it wasn't a deer. It was...like a black cloud. But I didn't go through it because I just knew it was solid. It doesn't make sense...and Jessica says she didn't see it so the whole thing must not be real, right, Logan?"

Her face turned red, her eyes bloodshot and welling up. Logan placed his other hand over their interlocked fingers and crouched.

"Then Allen started having a seizure. The sound was horrible. And so *loud*. Jessica climbed into the backseat to help him, and he started floating until I could see his face in the rearview mirror, lit up by a red moon—

"It was a nightmare...It had to be. Because his arms stretched like that Stretch Armstrong toy we used to fight over, but there was nothing fun about it. His eyes scared me the most, though. The skin on the sides was being pulled back so his eyeballs looked loose from their sockets. I should have slowed down. I should have pulled over."

"You didn't do anything wrong, Em—"

"Shut up! I did! I could have stopped. I could have hit the fucking brake. But all I could do was hold onto the steering wheel until I flashed my eyes back to the road and saw it again! That *thing*. I swerved, then my stomach dropped when we hit the ditch. Of all the things, it was a rollercoaster I thought of. And then I didn't think of anything. By that point, I didn't even see the telephone pole. I just saw whatever I thought I saw in the road...until I blacked out."

He gave her a moment to catch her breath, then hesitantly

asked, "If it was smoke or mist or whatever, why do you think it was solid?"

Emily stared ahead, past Logan, like she was looking right at it. "I just know something was hidden behind the black cloud...a living thing...I just know, Logan."

Finally, she looked at him again, squeezing his hand tighter. "It's not real, though, right? It was a nightmare?"

"Of course it was." He patted her hand, hoping it was comforting and not dismissive. "The way Allen had a seizure like that must have been the scariest thing ever. Your mind blacked out, and your imagination filled in the rest. I'm sorry, Em." He stood, feeling queasy. "Why don't I get the others? Kelvin's here. He actually left his house—"

She wouldn't let go of his hand, taking her casted right arm and gripping his wrist with it.

"It felt so real, Logan. And the way Allen looked at me...his face...and his arms. He was being pulled—"

"A nightmare. Our minds do crazy things in distressing situations."

"I don't want to go to sleep."

"You don't have to—"

"I mean, ever, Logan. I don't ever want to go to sleep. What if I don't wake up? Like last time."

"That won't happen. The doctor says you're healing so fast. You're all right now, Em. You're safe."

"That's just it, Logan. Nightmare or not...I don't feel safe."

8

A low red line divided the sky from the earth as evening settled into Sunday night. It was the first time Logan had left the hospital since Emily woke up. His mom had asked him to run home and bring back a change of clothes for the three of them, along with everyone's toothbrushes. They wanted to make Emily more comfortable as soon as possible, even if she had to stay for a few days. The anomaly of it kept Dr. Warren from sending her home right away. He could read between the lines: Emily had been in a coma and what if she slipped into another.

But Logan wasn't concerned. He wouldn't be surprised if her broken bones healed entirely within days. That was the power of the kitchen well.

He drove north, the red line splitting the world to his left. His teammates had left after a couple of hours, along with the coaches and some other community members. Kelvin only left when Emily insisted he go home and rest. He said he could sleep at the hospital, but his casted leg was too stiff, and he was far from healed himself. A part of Logan wanted to go to the well and wish for Kelvin to be healed, but he couldn't shake Emily's story from his mind.

He didn't drive home immediately. At the four-way stop in Nashoba, he turned toward Holdendecker instead of right for Nowhere. He couldn't keep Emily's story to himself but didn't want to go to one of his teammate's houses.

Doug would freak out and think his wish had killed Allen all over again. Marshal might get nervous about the repercussions of his wish to save Emily. Alex would dismiss it, but it wasn't smart to dismiss it. For Emily, maybe, but not for Logan. He needed to question himself, consider the implications. Logan had to clear his head by talking it out with someone.

Wheelman's was slow when he arrived. Melinda gave him a hug, and Larry Unders offered condolences as if Emily had died. Even the Holdendecker carhops showed sympathy and mentioned how Jessica had stopped by and said she was feeling better.

"Sorry about your sister," Will said.

"Yeah, well...she's gonna be fine now. Can we, uh, talk outside?"

Will followed him into the employee parking area, and Logan braced himself for another Will Roebuck overreaction. "We, uh, we made another wish."

To his surprise, Will remained calm. "You wished for her to get better?"

"Exactly."

Will shrugged. "Fair enough."

"You're not mad?"

"Under the circumstances, how can I blame you? I'm not a monster, Tramer. Besides, it's better than wishing to win STATE. What a waste—"

"Emily told me how the wreck happened. She remembered everything."

Logan repeated Emily's account as closely as he could, lightheaded by the time he finished, feeling like he might vomit.

He waited for Will to yell at him. Maybe his coworker would have if he mentioned Doug's wish, but Will stood silently with his hands in his pockets. His cold breath billowed in the air. The temperature had dropped significantly now that twilight had arrived.

"Consequences," Will said. "It's like each time a wish is fulfilled, it requires a sacrifice."

"I thought so too, but...no one died after we beat McClinton, so I don't understand."

"McClinton?"

"Yeah. You could argue the wish wasn't needed for the Picard and Mutton games, so no surprise no one died then. But Ethan Crist was kicking our ass until he had the shits. That had to be the magic, right?"

"You didn't hear about Mr. and Mrs. Beaumont?"

"Who?"

"My neighbors. Ed and Pauline Beaumont. Elderly couple."

"From Nowhere?"

"Like I said, they're my neighbors, so yes. They never had kids, so I guess you wouldn't know them. They rode with Principal Jacobs to the games against Colesville and McClinton. She lives on the other side of them. Ed was sick but insisted on going. We didn't think he had anything life-threatening, but at their age, everything is life-threatening. Anyway, Jacobs called the cops yesterday morning because she always has breakfast with them on Saturdays, and they weren't answering the door."

"Yesterday morning?"

"That's right. When Ryan Holbrook showed up, I went over to the house too. He looked scared, like he knew what he would find. I wanted to ask him if anything else like the radio voice had happened, but with Jacobs there, I didn't. The front door was locked so Ryan climbed through an open window and told us to stay outside. But you know me. As soon as he was out of sight, I climbed through the window too. Jacobs yelled at me, but it's not like we were in school. I climbed the stairs and heard him blowing chunks in the bathroom. That's when I knew. Someone had died.

"I walked over to the master bedroom. Apparently, it wasn't just Ed who was sick. Both of them were dead, right there in their bed. They must have had a stroke or something. They looked unreal, man."

"So, they died overnight? After the McClinton game?"

"Afraid so."

"Goddammit."

"The Beaumonts were both well into their eighties. Much older than Tim's dad. Could've been natural causes."

"So, then what? This is all a coincidence?"

"Could be."

"But what about what Emily saw? Do you think she imagined it?"

"It's possible...What's the alternative? You killed all these people? I killed Bird?"

"I don't know...I can't think straight anymore."

Will blew on his hands to warm them. "There was something you said from Emily's story. Something about driving near Green River when they wrecked."

Logan hadn't realized he had been that specific when he relayed the story. He was overwhelmed, his headache biting, eyes throbbing. It didn't help that it was so cold out here.

"Do you think it means something?" he asked Will.

"Not necessarily, but it does make me think about what you told me and Alex. That was your aunt's old school, right? When she got injured and the team still won STATE?"

"My mom said weird shit happened."

Will tilted his head, as if asking, *Do you see where I'm going with this?*

"Do you think they made a wish?"

"I don't know, but if they did, it worked. They won STATE. Would your aunt know something about it? Could we ask her?"

"We can't. She died...She killed herself." In his mind's eye, Logan saw the basketball photo of Jocelyn Horn. With his sister's recent near-death experience, he couldn't help but focus on how much Emily resembled Aunt Joss in her own basketball portrait from the beginning of this school year.

"Oh...sorry, Tramer...And your mom can't tell us anything more about Green River?"

"She's told me the story a hundred times. If she knew about some local legend, she would've said so."

"We need to talk to someone who wasn't just a spectator watching Green River win the title. Maybe someone from the team lives there."

"The school shut down ages ago. Green River's a ghost town."

"It was never a town to begin with if it was like Nowhere." Will started bouncing, his latest attempt at warming up.

"True...I suppose when Nowhere shuts down, folks won't just abandon the area. I could see any one of my teammates staying in Nowhere." Logan paused, thinking. *I could see myself staying there.*

"Exactly," Will said. "People will always be in Nowhere. It's not Roanoke, for fuck's sake."

"What's Roanoke?"

"You really don't pay attention in school, do you?"

Logan shrugged. "I'm not an idiot. I like to read."

"Really?"

"What?"

"I didn't know you could."

"Fuck off, Roebuck," Logan said, but he laughed. "I'm going back to Tuskahoma this evening. Why don't we meet at the hospital tomorrow and then go to Green River?"

"I can't just skip school. I'm not on the basketball team. I don't get that kind of favoritism."

"C'mon, it's your idea."

Will seemed pleased at that. "Fine," he said. "Tomorrow, then."

1989-1990 GREEN RIVER LADY BULLFROGS ROSTER

Jocelyn Horn

Lana Red Hawk

Betty Bromide

Rebekah Hines

Olivia McCullers

Susanna Hines

Jacqueline Soo

Debbie Hines

Maggie Miles

TEN
GLORY DAYS

1

IT WASN'T easy to find Green River, Oklahoma, because most of the buildings scattered across the land were abandoned. Will spread a Road Atlas across his lap and pointed this way and that. Had it been Nowhere they were looking for, they would never have found it among the pines, but Green River was mostly open plains. The narrow river, which gave the town its name, ran along the country road as a guide. Of course, it was dried up.

They saw the school grounds from a distance. When they neared, they realized only one building stood unscathed.

The gym was as imposing as a haunted house—one of those places that triggers your primal intuition for danger even though you can't pinpoint why. It was sturdy, but vines crept up the sides, like the earth was trying to keep the building from collapsing. Every other building had burned to the ground, either completely gone except for a pile of ash or left charred, like the blackened rectangular trailer in the center of the school grounds which reminded Logan of Nowhere's high school building.

In fact, the entire campus reminded him of his school, including the outdoor court. The only difference was Green River's court was far more overgrown with weeds, the concrete barely visible. It was the only space where the grass grew tall. Fire had left the land barren.

Near the entrance to the school grounds, a sign remained high above that read: "GREEN RIVER PUBLIC SCHOOLS." At the bottom, in smaller marquee letters, it read: "1990 Class B Girls Basketball State Champions." The sign looked surprisingly pristine.

"Damn," Will said. "Guess this is what our school will look like in a few years, huh?"

"Hopefully without the fire."

Once they drove up to the school, they had a better view of the surrounding area. Trailer houses were scattered about the land. Most appeared abandoned as they passed by. When they came upon one that seemed occupied—a dog in the yard and an old El Camino—they stopped.

A Private Property sign was nailed to the trailer, and the German Shepherd barked at their arrival.

"Not the most inviting place," Logan said. "Should we try somewhere else?"

"Don't be a pussy, Tramer. You're big enough to take the dog if it comes to it."

"Screw that. I'm not messing with that dog."

"It's fine." Will opened the passenger's side door. "I'm good with animals."

He stepped out, and the German Shepherd rushed toward him, growling and slobbering.

Logan could already see how it would play out. The dog would jump on Will and clamp down on his throat. Blood would splatter on his windshield. Will was about to become the next "coincidental" death among people from Nowhere.

But an owner came out of the house and hollered. Logan hadn't expected such a commanding voice from such a small man.

The German Shepherd cowered and ran beneath the El Camino.

The man was shirtless, his jeans curling around his scrawny waist because of how tight his belt was. He was barefoot too but didn't seem bothered by the cold when he stepped down the concrete stairs from his trailer. The man also held a pistol in his hand.

"You trying to get yourself killed?"

Will came around the front of Logan's truck. Logan stayed inside, both hands on the wheel as if the man were a cop. He told himself he was staying in the car because it might make the man jumpier if he also got out, but in truth, he was scared shitless.

"We were hoping you could help us," he heard Will say.

"Are you lost?" The man pointed his gun northeast. "Highway's that-a-way."

"We're actually right where we want to be. This is Green River, right?"

"Used to be."

"Right. My friend there…" Will pointed at the truck, and Logan waved as friendly as he could. "His aunt is from here."

"And who might that be?" the man said.

"Jocelyn Horn," Will said. "You know her?"

While the man's hand remained on his pistol, his shoulders relaxed. "*The* Jocelyn Horn?"

Logan eased his hand to the door handle and climbed out of his truck. "I'm her nephew," he said. "My mom is Janice Horn."

"Goddamn. I haven't seen Janice in decades. And Jocelyn…

God rest her soul. You look like quite the ball player yourself there."

"Not nearly as good as my mom or Aunt Joss. But I'm all right. My team just made STATE."

"Is that right? Hell yeah."

"Were you around here when the girls won the title?" Will asked.

The man spat in the dirt and tucked his pistol into the back of his pants. It took him a solid thirty seconds to do so since his pants were belted so tight. "Oh yeah. The tenth of March 1990. School shut down three years later. And your aunt...still the best I've ever seen on the court."

"We were hoping to find some of my aunt's old teammates," Logan said. "I thought it might be nice to hear some stories, you know."

"I hear ya. I'm afraid I ain't seen any of 'em in a long ass time. I doubt any of 'em are still around here. Hardly anyone stayed after what happened."

"You mean the school fire?" Will asked.

Recognition showed on the man's face, but there was something else too. A look of closed-off suspicion. The man was deciding what to tell them, and it wasn't just about the fire at the school.

"We drove by the school," Logan offered. "Just about everything was burned to the ground."

"Everything but the gym," the man said. "That gym ain't ever coming down."

"And the fire made everyone move away?" Will asked.

"Plenty was already gone by then. They's saying Green River was cursed long before someone set fire to the school."

"Cursed?"

The man spat again and shook his head. "You might try Betty Bromide. I don't know if she'll be there, but the Bromide farm's still around, and her parents are getting up there in age. She might be staying with 'em. Someone said they saw her not long back."

"Betty," Will said. "Alrighty, then."

"Where's the farm?" Logan asked, and the man reluctantly gave them directions.

When they returned to Logan's truck, the man said, "Don't stay around here for too long. Wouldn't want you catching our troubles."

2

They passed two other homes that appeared to be occupied and a child rollerblading down the dirt road. Logan expected her to fall at any moment, but she waved and kept going.

"Just like Nowhere," Will said. "Except the last time I saw a kid rollerblading on a dirt road, she was Amish."

"Sounds about right," Logan replied. "That must be the farm up ahead."

The farmhouse stood atop a hill. Slender cows nibbled at what little grass remained. Logan wasn't sure if the scarcity was due to the winter or if the curse was to blame. He and Will hadn't discussed what the man had said. They were focused on finding someone from the 1990 team. Once again, they found themselves driving up to a stranger's home.

The farmhouse reminded Logan of the Amish houses in Nowhere: a barn nearly as large as the house next door, a wrap-around porch on both the upper and lower stories, and a chicken coop beside the house. The only thing missing was a horse-and-buggy by the barn doors. Beyond the house, pastures stretched out, and a wide line of trees marked the horizon. The sight of the evergreens put Logan at ease. It reminded him of home.

For a second time, someone emerged from the house when they arrived. Country folk didn't like strangers pulling into their drive. It was a woman with hair down to her waist, blue jeans tucked into work boots, and a floral sweater.

This house also had a dog barking at his truck, but it was a mild cow dog, so Logan felt safer getting out with Will. They waved at the woman. He slouched, aware his height could be intimidating.

"Are you Betty Bromide?" Will asked abruptly.

Logan winced, worried she wouldn't respond well to being called out by name by a stranger. Who knew if anyone else was around. The country life was wonderful if solitude was what you were after, but it also meant vulnerability if some strange person decided to show up unannounced.

She stared at Logan, making him feel insecure.

"You look familiar," she said, then her eyes widened. "You wouldn't be related to Jocelyn Horn, would you?"

"She's my aunt," he said.

The woman smiled. "I'll be damned...You look just like her." She crossed her arms and shivered from a cold gust of wind. "Come inside," she said. "It's nice and warm." The woman disappeared into the house before they could say anything.

Now the boys were left to feel vulnerable.

"Should we be worried?" Will asked.

"I thought you weren't afraid of anything."

"What if she wants to chop our dicks off or something?"

"Come on, man. You're the guy who climbed down the well first. Remember?"

"You'd love for me to forget, asshole. I'm gonna get you back, by the way."

Logan ducked his head to pass through the doorway. The screen door slammed closed behind them.

"My parents are napping upstairs," Betty said. "We don't have to whisper, but inside voices would be appreciated."

"Of course," Logan replied.

"Sweet tea?" Betty asked when she went into the kitchen. She returned with a pitcher and three glasses filled with ice, then poured the tea over the ice. Steam rose from the glasses. "I just brewed it."

Now seated across from her, Logan noticed she looked a decade older than someone in her mid-thirties. Her skin was sunbaked, while her hair was naturally bleached and damaged. She didn't seem like someone visiting her parents from a nicer town, but like someone who had lived her whole life in the all-but-deserted country community, working the land.

"Thanks," Will said, taking a glass from her. "I'm thirsty as hell."

Logan watched him drink, wary the tea might be poisoned. When he was satisfied Will wasn't going to drop dead, he took a sip. It was perfectly balanced—not too sweet.

"Tastes good," he said. "Thank you."

"It's simple," Betty said. "You just add the sugar while it's hot."

"That's how my mom does it."

"Your mom's Janice, right?"

He nodded. "Did you know her?"

"Not well. She came to the games, but she was ten years older than us, and your family didn't move from Tuskahoma until Joss was in eighth grade."

"That's what I've heard."

"Jocelyn sure looked up to your mom, though. Said she was a hell of a player. We all looked up to Joss. Oh wow—"

"What?"

"You were at some of our games, weren't you? You were itty bitty."

"That was me. I was four when you won STATE."

"Fourteen years ago this week..."

"Must have felt amazing." Logan shifted, jittery from the sugar.

"You can't even imagine. The best feeling I've had was holding that trophy." She shrugged. "But I've never been married or had kids. Maybe that compares. I'm sure it does."

"I don't think much about being married or having kids. But I sure as hell think about winning STATE."

Betty offered a weak smile, then took a sip of her tea. She nodded toward Will. "Do you play too?"

"Just the team's number one fan," Will said sarcastically.

"We earned our trip to the Big House this past weekend," Logan said. "Third year in a row."

Betty's eyes flickered. "Congratulations," she said.

"Last year we made it all the way to the title game and lost in the final minute." He guffawed weakly. "It sucked. Big time. But we brought back every starter, including our best player." He noticed a picture of the Green River Lady Bullfrogs on the wall. "Kelvin's amazing. He's got a D1 scholarship and everything. But he got injured on Senior Night. Broke his leg."

Betty paused, setting down her tea. "I'm sorry to hear that."

"Truth be told, we sucked without him. The rest of us aren't bad, but he unlocked everything for our team. He communicated best on defense, got us the best shots on offense. Gave us confidence and chemistry."

"You're being hard on yourself," Betty said. "You made STATE without him, didn't you?"

"That's true...just like Green River."

She blinked in an unusual rhythm, first quickly, then slowly —a nervous tic, he supposed.

"I guess you're right," she said.

Logan glanced at Will, but Will had nothing to say. Logan cleared his throat.

"May I?" He pointed at the picture, ready to stand and look at it, but Betty reached over and took it from the wall.

She handed it to him on the couch. The frame had a smaller portrait window in the top left corner. The wider window, which took up most of the frame, showed Betty and the rest of the Lady Bullfrogs posing with the championship trophy, a cut-down net draped over the gold ball. The smaller window had Jocelyn Horn down on one knee with a basketball pressed against the court next to her.

It was the same portrait from the hallway at the Indian house—the same one he had woken up thinking about the day after Kelvin's injury.

"Joss was special," Betty said, collecting herself. She sat back down, and the blinking stopped. "We needed a lot of luck to do it without her."

"Same." Anxious to get to the truth, Logan added, "In fact, just about every playoff game, we've won in some weird way."

"He ain't lying," Will said, finally backing him up. "In the Regional finals, a guy got arrested during the game."

"Oh wow." Betty forced a smile.

"Not just a guy," Logan said. "Someone from the other team."

"A player?"

"Believe it or not," Logan said, gesturing with his big hands. "Right in the middle of the game, a cop came onto the court and arrested him."

"That's…insane." Betty turned her drinking glass between her palms like she was molding clay.

"Anything like that happen for y'all?" Will asked directly.

Logan noticed Betty start to pull away.

"The Basketball Gods do get frisky this time of year," he said with a laugh, hoping to put her at ease.

"Basketball Gods...No, nothing that crazy. I'm sure your mom told you about it."

"Sure, but nothing specific."

"Specific. Right." She seemed to relax as her eyes glazed over with nostalgia. "Well, I'll tell you one story." Betty held up her index finger like a referee indicating a foul call. "It's not like someone getting arrested, but it's a fun one. We were playing Germantown in the first round of Regionals. We got through Districts, no problem. Even without Joss, it wasn't tough. Fort Todd had a terrible girls' team back then, and they were second best in our district.

"But Regionals was a different story. Germantown had this giant sophomore. I can still smell her. She never wore deodorant. Or maybe she did, but it didn't work on her. She was an ogre but had the best footwork I'd ever seen on the court aside from Joss. She was like Hakeem the Dream, I'm not kidding. She was killing us all game, but we kept it close. In the fourth quarter, we're down five, only four minutes left. I remember it exactly. The ogre posts up, makes her move with a pump fake and a spin, and then—"

Betty let out a surprising yelp, making Logan jump.

"Her shoe exploded! The sneaker just tore off her foot completely. It was in two pieces on either side of the low block. She ran to the sideline, scrambling to find a shoe that fit. Her teammates on the bench started passing her their shoes, but nothing fit. It was like Cinderella or something.

"Meanwhile, we start scoring and take the lead. The ogre yells out her shoe size to all the Germantown fans, and now the crowd starts throwing their shoes down to the bench. She finally gets one that fits, and she runs back onto the court with a sneaker on one foot and a loafer on the other." Betty snorted with laughter. "But by then, there wasn't enough time for them to catch us, so we won the game."

Will and Logan laughed along with her.

"That's amazing," Logan said.

"I would have loved to see that," Will added.

"It was incredible. We had four games like that in the play-offs. Once in Regionals, once in Area, and twice at the Big House."

"We've had four already," Logan said.

Betty stopped laughing and took another sip of her tea. "Did someone get arrested at all of them?"

"No. It was different each time. Any idea why y'all got lucky in those four games?"

"It wouldn't be luck if I did."

"We were driving around and noticed the school campus was burned down," Will said.

"I wouldn't call it a 'campus.' Just some trailers and the gym. Unfortunately, everything caught fire about ten years ago."

"Not everything. The gym looked untouched."

"Oh yeah. A miracle."

"What caused the fire?"

"They say some kids who used to go to Green River did it. Supposedly, they were pissed that they were being bussed to Fort Todd because the school shut down the year before."

"*Supposedly*," Logan muttered.

Betty forced another smile, then refilled her glass. The pitcher was nearly empty now.

"We talked to this guy who lives a mile up the road from the school," Will said. "Has a mean dog."

"Oh. Yeah, that's Charles Wanamaker."

"Well, Charlie said Green River was cursed, and that's why everyone moved away."

"Everyone moved because they shut the school down. It happens."

"So, you don't know what he's talking about?" Logan asked.

She glanced down at the picture. Logan gripped it tight in his hands, sweat soaking into the wooden frame. Aunt Joss wasn't in the team photo. He had always wondered why she killed herself when she did. She was depressed—battled with it since she was a little girl, according to Logan's mom—but it still surprised him that she would choose to end her life the night before the championship game.

Now he wondered something else: if his aunt had killed herself at all.

Betty's smile was completely gone. In fact, she had a sour look on her face, like the sweet tea was making her sick. She pushed her glass away from her on the coffee table, disregarding the coaster she had been careful to use before.

"If there's something you're wanting to say, you should just say it."

Logan looked to Will because Will had been adamant about keeping the well a secret. The two hadn't discussed what they would do if they actually talked to one of his aunt's teammates.

"Might as well tell her," Will said.

"All right," Logan said, unsure how to go about it. "We live in Nowhere. It's not so different than here, or how here used to be. In Nowhere, there's this old house with a well in the kitchen. This is gonna sound crazy but—"

"You made a wish." She looked at them with pity—an expression he recognized from somewhere.

"And it came true," Will said.

"Of course it did."

Logan realized where he recognized the look. It was the same way the crowd gazed at the boys while Kelvin writhed on the court.

The picture frame slipped through his sweaty fingers, just like the ball often did on the court. The hardwood floor wasn't far below, and yet the glass shattered. Shards painted the floor and spread to the rug under the coffee table.

The broken frame was only a momentary distraction. When Logan glanced at Betty, she was staring at him. She hadn't even watched the frame fall.

"You did it too, didn't you?" Will said. "You made a wish."

"Not me personally, but I was there. All five of us were."

"My aunt?" Logan asked, ignoring the broken frame at his feet.

Betty shook her head. "It was me, the twins Rebekah and Susanna Hines, Lana Red Hawk, and Olivia McCullers, who had been the sixth man before Joss got hurt. We had lost two games in a row to end the regular season, so we went to the well in the woods."

"Holy shit," Will said. "There's a well?"

"There sure is. My classmates weren't familiar with it, but I grew up hearing about the well. It was an old family legend."

Logan was speechless, and a silence lingered until he reached down to grab the frame.

"You can leave it," Betty said. "It's all right."

"I didn't expect you to have a well," he said.

"What did you expect?"

"I don't know. Some other way the Basketball Gods would make up for Aunt Joss's injury, I guess."

"The Basketball Gods...You keep saying that."

"Do you call it something else?"

"You could say that."

"Did someone climb down the well to make the wish?" Will asked.

"Rebekah volunteered. We didn't actually think it would work, but figured, why not have some fun if our basketball careers were about to end anyway? She was the most stupid and fearless of us, so she went to the bottom and asked for a STATE CHAMPIONSHIP.”

“Did you tell Aunt Joss?”

“Lord, I wish we did, but no, we didn’t.”

“Betty...did the wish kill my aunt?”

Betty leaned down and started to pick up glass shards, intently staring at the job at hand.

“Maybe if we’d told her, she would have been protected. I think she would have. The wish took the unsuspecting. The witnesses to our glory. It took your aunt.”

A hidden piece of glass in the rug cut her, and she rose, sucking the blood from her thumb. She seemed surprisingly at ease when she sat back up.

“Do you want to see it?” she asked.

Will was excited. “The well is still out there?”

“Where else would it be?”

3

Betty went upstairs to check on her parents before they began their trek into the woods.

“You sure about this?” Logan asked.

“Are you kidding?” Will said. “We have to see this thing.”

“I don’t care about another damn well. I just want to know more about the curse.”

“We know what we need to know, don’t we? People die because of the wish.”

“Maybe Betty knows how to stop it. She did say if you know about the wish, you’re protected.”

“She was just guessing, Tramer.”

“Still.”

"It's a long walk to the well. We can ask her whatever you want."

Betty came back downstairs, rifle in hand.

Logan's stomach twisted with nerves. He thought he might shit himself.

"Coyotes have been aggressive lately," she said. "It's good to be safe."

"My dad's the same way," Will said. "Coyotes killed three of our dogs."

They left through the back door and began walking through the pasture. The woods seemed far from the house but closed in quicker than he expected. Logan didn't like that Betty was leading them into a dark forest with a rifle slung over her shoulder. He had never been comfortable around guns.

He had gone deer hunting with his dad and uncle once, when he was eleven. They had been excited for him to join them after he got his hunting license. It was a rite of passage for any young man in southeastern Oklahoma to bag his first deer, but Logan didn't feel right about it.

His dad had never looked more ashamed of him than the day before the hunt, when Logan thought he was talking to his mom alone and said it was ridiculous that killing something was some sort of important ritual for a boy. That's when his dad stomped loudly from around the corner. He didn't mention what Logan had said until the next morning, then insisted Logan would understand once he shot his first deer.

"There are a lot of important moments to becoming a man, Logan," his dad had said. "This is your first."

Logan's uncle had come because he was visiting from Missouri. But, really, Bill Tramer was incapable of spending time alone with his kids. When Bill was mad at Logan's mom, he would admit he could only be himself around his brother, as if Logan's mom were forcing him to be someone he wasn't.

The day was mostly uneventful in the deer stand until a young buck appeared. Logan aimed the rifle at it. The buck had the smallest set of antlers poking out from its head. The gun felt much heavier than it had during target practice. His eyes blurred, and he couldn't tell if his scope was on the buck. He didn't pull the trigger, and the buck ran off when Bill let out a guttural groan.

He never asked Logan to hunt with him again. Logan had failed his first test for being a man.

This isn't a deer hunt, he reminded himself.

When they reached the tree line, he continued his inquiry from the living room. "You said you only needed to use the wish to win four times."

"That's right."

"And someone died after each of those games?"

She sighed. "Or went missing. They never found Dale Jennings."

"Mr. Tune wasn't just out sick on Friday," Logan said to Will.

Will's eyes lit up. He hadn't thought about that.

"Do you think Dale Jennings is dead like the others?" Logan asked Betty.

"I'd have to assume so. But I always wonder why his body wasn't found. *It* wanted the sacrifices to be seen. Just like the wishes."

Logan recalled the few details about Aunt Joss's death. She had been missing during the championship game. They searched her hotel room and asked if anyone had seen her. Another high school student said she had let Jocelyn borrow her car. The car was found at Jocelyn's house in Green River. She was hanging from a rope in her bedroom.

Her death differed enough from the deaths in Nowhere that Logan hadn't connected it before. Everyone in Nowhere seemed to die of fright, caught off guard—*by whatever was hiding behind the black cloud...*

He thought about the closed casket for Red Springer. There was an extravagance to the way his wish had played out during the games. Was that why the "sacrifices" looked the way they supposedly did; why Brother Maxwell couldn't fix Red's face well enough to open up that casket?

Ultimately, it didn't matter if they died of fright, were taken somewhere else to be killed, or hung themselves in the most private place for any teenager. All Logan needed to know was how to prevent it from happening again—

...and still win STATE.

He couldn't escape thinking about it.

"What about the games you won without the magic?" he asked.

"Nothing. No consequences."

"Was it true what you said?"

"About what?"

"You said everyone moved because the school shut down, but Charles Wanamaker said it was because this place is cursed. Which is it?"

Tall pines rose around them, the foliage thick at the top, forming a canopy that made the woods darker than when they had been at the Bromides' farm. Logan zipped up his Lakers jacket. By mid-March, the outside air had begun to warm, but in the shade of the pines, it felt like the last vestige of winter.

"Winning STATE was all we wanted," Betty said. "It was everything. And like I said, there's no better feeling I've experienced. But what happens once you've won everything you wanted? Does your life change because you're a champion? Do you live the rest of your life with no desires, no dreams?"

"I haven't thought about it," Logan admitted.

"We hadn't either. Not until we actually *did* it. You see, I had a problem after we won STATE. I hadn't convinced my team-mates that the wish came with consequences. They wouldn't admit there was a connection."

"Not even after Aunt Joss's death?"

"Everyone on the team knew she was in a bad place after the injury. They grieved our friend's suicide but thought nothing else of it. That's why her death had to look different. She wasn't old like Henry Miles or Mr. and Mrs. Peak. Not easy to dismiss. Sure, Dale was our age, but I could never convince my teammates he was dead. They thought he ran away. Well, Jocelyn wasn't old or flighty, but she was depressed, so *it* had to make her death look *right*."

Betty picked up her pace, and Will and Logan power-walked to keep up. Broken branches and dried leaves rustled beneath their feet. They came to a clearing.

The well in the woods was larger than the one in the kitchen. A wide, low brick oval with moss growing between the bricks. On top were cinder blocks stacked on a thick block of wood, wrapped in chains that blocked the hole. A sizable padlock held everything in place.

"No more wishes, huh?" Will said.

Betty ran her hand along the chain. "What do you think people do, Logan, when they realize life continues after you win STATE?"

He shrugged. "They accept life will never live up to that moment."

She barked a loud laugh that echoed through the trees. Spittle landed on her bottom lip. Logan stared at it. She made no attempt to lick or wipe it away.

"Do they?" she said.

"Don't they?" he asked weakly.

Betty looked almost sympathetic, her hand gripping the

rifle strap over her shoulder. "In my experience, they do not. They make more wishes. They cause more harm."

"Charlie wasn't wrong, was he?" Will asked. "This place *is* cursed."

"Let me tell you about my teammates. The girls I once trusted more than anyone." Betty sat on the wood block, rifle across her lap. "The Hines twins and their little sister Deb started a successful law firm in Denver. They had a suspiciously easy time getting through law school. Now they live in nice houses, with husbands who fish in the mountains every week-end. Vacation homes in the Rockies, and perfect little children.

"Olivia McCullers is a model. When she's not in her fancy LA condo, she travels the world.

"And the last of us who knew about the well—Lana Red Hawk. Well, Hawk was never satisfied. She'd come home, make a wish, and then change her mind. She never knew what she wanted. Did she want to travel the world like Olivia? Or have children, a nice house, a respectable job like the Hines sisters? She figured she could try it all because, why not? She had as many wishes as she wanted."

Betty stood suddenly, gripping the rifle in both hands and pointing it at the dirt. Logan took an involuntary step back. He glanced at Will, who looked nervous too.

"I tried telling her," Betty said. "She wouldn't listen. None of them would. Maybe they thought I was crazy. Maybe they were in denial. Maybe they saw the truth but didn't care who suffered for their gains.

"But they didn't have any family left in Green River to worry about. Who cared how many died or went missing? I didn't have that luxury. I couldn't let Lana make another goddamn wish because what if *it* came for my parents, Logan? What if they were next because they were among the few left?"

"What happened to Lana, Betty?" Logan asked, knowing the answer.

"She made it to the bottom of the well one last time…I put her there."

"Oh fuck," Will said.

Betty slowly raised the rifle. "I'm sorry, but I can't let you go. You won't listen either. You'll keep making wishes until everyone you care about is gone."

"Betty, don't—"

Will ran before Logan could finish his attempt to reason with her. A shot clapped from the rifle hitting a tree to the left of Will. As Logan's ears began to ring, he ran too.

4

Betty fired three more shots, and Logan expected any one of them to hit him. He kept moving, everything a blur. He didn't look back.

Betty shot at him from who knew how far—or close—away. Trees seemed to close in around him. Logan found himself dodging them, then ducking behind. His eyes remained on Will's back. His coworker was much farther ahead after his head start.

When they emerged from the woods, the Bromide farmhouse in sight, he was relieved and terrified. His truck was so close, and yet the open field they had to run through would provide Betty with as clean a shot as she could hope for, if her aim really was to kill them.

He sprinted faster than he ever had on a basketball court. Will zigzagged ahead, knowing Betty could simply stand at the edge of the tree line and line them up in her scope.

Logan was too clumsy to zigzag. He ran right for the house, peering straight through the place as if it was invisible and he could see his old reliable Ford on the other side. Another shot clapped in his ears.

Maybe this one hit him, and his adrenaline kept him from feeling it. He wouldn't know until he reached his truck. Logan wasn't about to bleed out in this goddamn pasture in goddamn Green River.

Moments later, another shot seemingly missed. The house was so close now—

Logan's foot landed in a gopher hole. He fell to the ground. Weeds stabbed at his face and hands. A jolt of pain throbbed in his twisted ankle. He leaped up, getting a good long look toward the trees. Logan didn't see Betty until something reflected in the sunlight.

He ducked when another shot cut through the wind. Logan couldn't be certain, but he somehow knew the shot would have hit him if he had been standing his full height.

Why do I have to be so fucking tall? Then he ran as fast he could while crouching and unable to put his full weight on his sprained ankle.

He expected another shot, but none came. Maybe she was out of rounds. Perhaps Betty had given up. Either way, he had never been so happy to see his beat-up truck before.

The cow dog growled and barked, slobbering and baring its teeth but keeping its distance, like they were the ones with the gun.

Will bounced up and down by the passenger's side of the truck. "Why the hell did you lock it? Why would you fucking lock it?"

Logan struggled to dig out his keys.

"C'mon, c'mon, c'mon," Will repeated.

The dog's warning cries continued, loud as the gunshots.

Logan finally jammed his car key into the door lock and opened it. He reached across and yanked up the lock on the passenger's side door. Will was in the truck before Logan could even start it.

He banged on the dashboard. "Let's go, let's go, let's go."

Logan peeled out, dust and gravel billowing in front of the truck. He reversed down the entire driveway, afraid if he took the time to turn the truck around, Betty would come around the corner and shoot him in the back of the head through his rear windshield.

He reversed onto the dirt road at the crest of the hill, and then they were off. He hoped to never see Betty Bromide or Green River again.

ELEVEN
A THOUGHT AND A PRAYER

1

DOUG WENT to the men's prayer breakfast at Holdendecker Baptist Church every Monday morning before school. Fellowship with his mentors was a great way for him to start his week. He especially needed the reprieve this morning. After the weekend he'd had, good food and the Word would replenish his soul, perhaps clear his mind too.

He hadn't been thinking straight since Friday night with Mal. It had been a wonderful night. He had never felt so much passion directed toward him.

His previous three sexual experiences were quick and awkward. The nervousness between him and each of the girls lingered between them until near the end. When he climaxed, he gave thought to nothing else in the world. Friday night with Mal made him feel that way the entire time they were hooking up.

Since then, though, things had gotten complicated.

Allen's death should have been his warning but Logan's explanation as to why Doug's wish hadn't caused Allen's death made sense to him. He was more relieved than anything when he left the hospital in the early dark of Sunday morning. Doug couldn't have Allen Prospect's death on his conscience, no matter how much he hated his former bully.

And he did hate him. Even now that the dropout was dead, Doug felt no empathy toward him.

Allen was always going to die young, he reasoned. In the back of his mind, Doug also wondered: *If I didn't kill Allen with my wish, does that mean I killed someone else?*

He should have thought about it more seriously but focused on getting home and showering quickly because he could still make it to church. Once he cleaned up, he felt better. Doug told himself Alex was right: the deaths were a coincidence.

When he left for church, Mal was waiting outside of his house, her truck parked next to his Corolla. She wanted to go to church with him. He couldn't have hoped for anything better. Doug finally had a girlfriend to sit with him during the service. He had dreamed of this since his first kiss. His prayer at the bottom of the well had been answered in more ways than he imagined.

But while Brother Maxwell lulled the congregation to sleep with his slow, monotone style, Mal put her hand on Doug's leg and crawled her fingers toward his penis which was already growing toward her hand like it wanted what she was offering. Discreetly, he shoved her hand away but she kept smiling and pressing, like they were in a dark movie theater instead of a well-lit sanctuary.

He wasn't sure if any of his family members saw her. Doug didn't dare look at them.

Eventually, he squeezed her hand with both of his and held it like that until the service was over. They left in the Corolla, but when he went to tell her how inappropriate she had been, Mal began rubbing her hand against his crotch. He darted his eyes back and forth, wondering how well cars in the other lane could tell what was happening because he couldn't resist her outside the Holdendecker Baptist Church sanctuary.

It was nerve-wracking but exciting, so Doug said nothing about how she had attempted to do the same thing in the middle pew.

They spent another wonderful day together, putting the wider world out of his mind. No basketball, no friends in the hospital, no kitchen well, no dead Allen Prospect. Just Doug and Mal on a perfectly cool and sunny Sunday.

Monday morning, though, everything burdened him. Basketball, Emily in the hospital, the kitchen well, Allen Prospect. But most of all, the new and improved Mal Turner.

When he left his house for the men's prayer breakfast, Mal was outside waiting for him again. She climbed out of her truck.

"What're you doing here, Mal?" he asked.

"I thought we could ride to school together," she said. Even her voice was different than before his wish. His very own Stepford Wife.

"It's six in the morning."

"And it's a good thing I'm here so early because you're leaving already."

"How long have you been here?"

"Doesn't matter."

"Well, I'm not going to school yet. Men's prayer breakfast at the church is Monday mornings."

"Oh, wonderful. Can I come?"

"It's...for men."

She rolled her eyes. "Oh, a boys' club, huh?"

"No, it's not like that. It's just breakfast."

"Well, is there a women's prayer breakfast?"

"There's a...No, I don't think so."

"Exactly."

He took her hands in his. "Tell you what? I'll see you at school, and then after basketball practice, we can hang out this evening. How's that sound?"

"That's a long time from now, Dougie."

"I know, I know, but it's also *not* a long time from now."

With a little more encouragement and small kisses, Doug convinced Mal to go home and clean up. He had noticed a sour smell on her and was convinced she had been outside his house all night.

Doug wondered about Saturday night, when he had visited Kelvin and then gone with his teammates to the Tuskahoma hospital. Mal had not been there with the other girls. He worried she had been at his house, waiting for him, until he returned Sunday morning. Did she hide her truck in the woods and wait for him to leave for church?

Shame gripped him by the time he reached the prayer breakfast. It was one thing to be a sinner, but there was a difference between his weakness for women and praying for his own dedicated sex slave. He told himself she was simply in love with him; this was what love looked like.

Doug ate a tall stack of pancakes and conversed with the other men at the breakfast. He was the only teenager consistently there every Monday. That had to count for something. It had to go a long way in overcoming his sins. But it was silly to think that way. Only Jesus washed away your sins. Doug wasn't here for salvation, but to grow in his walk with God. Yet he didn't feel like he was growing much. Other than inside his pants anytime he got close to Mal Turner.

Doug felt as low as he had in a long time by the time he finished eating. Others left, but he stayed to help Brother Maxwell clean up.

"Were those flapjacks everything you dreamed they'd be?" the preacher asked him.

"They were wonderful, as always."

"I'll be sure to let Mrs. Brennan know you approve."

"I figured she'd come over from the church for cleanup."

"She was happy to cook our meal, as usual, but she headed out of town to see her sister afterward. I told her cleanup was the least I could do. I need the break from downstairs anyway."

"Downstairs" referred to the morgue of the funeral home next door to the fellowship hall.

Doug hadn't thought much about Brother Maxwell's work with the bodies since Tim's dad's funeral. So much had happened since then.

"Are you leading Allen's funeral, Brother Maxwell?"

"I am."

Doug wondered what Allen's body looked like.

"The Beaumonts as well," the preacher added.

A cold river ran through Doug's body. "The Beaumonts from Nowhere?"

"Oh, dear…You didn't hear?"

"They died? *Both* of them?"

"I'm afraid so."

Doug had to stop what he was doing to keep himself from shivering. "Do you know when they died?"

Brother Maxwell paused from wiping down the table and raised an eyebrow. "Early Saturday morning."

Doug forced an empathetic smile. "I'm sorry to hear that. They came to all our games."

Had he seen them at the McClinton game? He wasn't sure he wanted to know. Two deaths just to give Ethan Crist the runs? It couldn't be. Had to be a coincidence.

Doug pictured Red Springer's closed casket in his mind's eye and wondered again about Allen's body.

"You must be really busy," he said to Brother Maxwell. "I'd be happy to help with anything I can."

Brother Maxwell took a deep breath, like he was considering it.

"I haven't had the time to tidy up," the preacher said, "and you really want to keep that kind of space clean...but no, no. You've got school, Doug. I couldn't impose."

"I'm free my first two periods." Doug hated lying, but he had to get to that basement. He felt the answers were there. He had to know what sins he had or had not committed. "That leaves plenty of time to help you clean up."

Brother Maxwell turned him down again, but Doug insisted, and it wasn't long before the preacher accepted his help. They finished cleaning the fellowship hall and walked over to the funeral home.

The first floor was the worst shop he would ever want to browse. Doug passed by samples of coffins and urns for sale. Brother Maxwell unlocked a door, and they moved downstairs.

"Obviously, I can't let you in the morgue," the preacher said, "but the work room could use some cleaning. I'll show you what needs to be disposed of and what needs to be stored. Then you can wipe down the counters."

Plastic sheets, empty buckets, and dust covered the tables and chairs in the work room, but it wasn't as bad as Maxwell made it seem. The preacher pointed out what Doug could clean. Doug insisted he could finish it quickly.

"You must be tired, Brother Maxwell," he said. "If you want to get some rest, I'll just leave when I'm finished."

"I appreciate your offer, Doug, but I don't think it would be appropriate. Besides, downstairs can be a little unsettling if you're not used to it."

"Actually, I find it fascinating. I've mentioned I want to be a preacher, but I was thinking about being a funeral director too. It seems like the two go hand in hand."

"Well, it's a lot of work. You should only do it if you feel the calling."

"I do, sir. It's an admirable thing you do. Helping families grieve. Making their loved ones look so at peace."

Brother Maxwell smiled. "It's a hard thing, but a beautiful thing." He shook his head. "Too many closed caskets lately."

Doug started to clean like he was fine either way, if Brother Maxwell stayed or not. The preacher glanced at his watch and yawned.

"All right, Mr. Mooreland. I think you're right. A little rest would be good."

"Absolutely. Anything else you want me to do after the work room?"

"Just this. Thank you."

Doug waited ten minutes after Brother Maxwell left, fighting against the Holy Spirit's warning the whole time. Then he set aside the cleanup and went to the morgue.

I have to see them, he told the Holy Spirit. *Just one time, then never again.*

After that, he could ask God for forgiveness if that was what he needed to do. But he wouldn't know if it was a sin or not until he looked.

2

Emily hardly talked to Marshal all last week. It wasn't simply his refusal to apologize for judging her over her selfish desire for Kelvin to lose his scholarship and stay in Nowhere—although, if he had come to her with his tail between his legs, it certainly would have helped. It was that she knew why Marshal had judged her, and he knew that she knew. Emily had replaced him with Jessica Fromm because, if she and Marshal kept on as best friends, the tension would runneth over and she would cheat on Kelvin. Marshal was sure of this, but it didn't make him feel any better. He wanted to confront her, get her to admit she had just as big of a crush on him as he had on her. Instead, he gave her space.

Patience.

Patience would be his superpower.

It was more difficult to wait after saving Emily's life. Marshal had crawled into the well, sucked in that moldy, cancerous air emitting from the halfmoon opening, and thought, *I wish for Emily to be healed.* Before he could say his thought out loud, his words echoed toward him, perhaps only in his mind, and he knew the wish was granted.

He was there with everyone else at the hospital, piling into the room against Dr. Warren's orders to see Emily after she had woken up. But he also skipped school on Monday so he could go see her again. Alone this time, he hoped—although fat chance of that with Kelvin lurking.

But alone was exactly the way he found her.

He arrived at the hospital in the afternoon, an hour after Logan and Will left from Tuskahoma to go to Green River. When Marshal walked into her room, Emily was facing away from the door, her bare back exposed between the flaps of the gown. A line of freckles ran along her spine. A warmth trickled through Marshal's fast-beating heart, then down below the belt. He rapped a little rhythm on the door. As she turned, he caught a flash of where her lower back met her panties and gulped dryly.

"Hey, Marsh," she said, her voice more pleasant toward him than when they sat next to each other in Choctaw class last week.

"Where's Kelvin?"

"I sent him home to rest. Poor guy's been up since Saturday."

"Poor *him?* What about you?"

"I've gotten plenty of sleep." She could never keep a straight face when she was being funny.

The desire to kiss her returned; maybe had never left. "How're you feeling?"

"Bored. I keep telling them I'm fine but they won't let me leave. Now I'm gonna miss STATE. And who knows how much it costs to keep me here. Mom has been playing phone tag with the Choctaw billing department. She keeps saying she's gonna call the Chief."

"Benefits of having a cousin who works in his office."

"Did I tell you that?"

"You did."

"What good it does me. Not even the Chief could break me out of here. Apparently, I'm a medical marvel." She crossed her eyes, blew a raspberry, and gave a thumbs down.

Marshal laughed. "Count your blessings, I guess."

"Count my blessings? Have you been reading *Chicken Soup for the Soul?* What happened to Marshal Lovegood, the proud atheist?"

"I'm just saying, you were in a coma, like, twenty-four hours ago. Now you barely have a scratch on you."

"So you believe in God now?"

"I didn't say that."

"Did you pray for me, Marsh?" She smirked playfully.

No, but I made a wish, he wanted to say. An irresistible desire to tell her everything passed through him. And then, on top of it, he could confess his love for her. Surely, she would reciprocate his feelings if she knew he had saved her life.

He resisted the desire.

Patience...be patient.

"Very funny," he said.

"Have you seen my brother?"

"Can't say I have."

She sighed in an overly dramatic way. "Men have a tendency to disappear at the most important times, don't they?"

"I'm here." He drew close to her bedside.

Her pleasant demeanor gave way to a cautious exterior, although Marshal didn't see it as cautious. He saw it as cold and immediately felt insecure, like he should take a step back. His insecurity made him angry and he knelt down even closer to her out of protest.

"I'm really glad you're doing better, Em. I missed hanging with you last week and if you had…if things had turned out differently after your wreck, I would have—

"…I guess I'm trying to say sorry for being a dick after Regionals."

"You're my best friend, Marsh. I don't want that to change." Her face paled and her eyes had a vacancy to them, like she was caught between being awake and a troubled sleep, her mind returning to the wreck as it often had since she woke up. But all Marshal saw was the girl of his dreams trying to keep him where he had been the past three years. A fever-heat rose to the top of his head. He clinched his jaw and inhaled deeply.

Patience…

"Me neither," he said, then took her hand.

She let him but patted the back of his in a "there, there" fashion.

How long are you gonna let this friend zone last?

He ignored the devil on his shoulder. It would last as long as it needed to. Worst case scenario, there was next year when Kelvin was out of the picture. Gone from Nowhere, one way or another. Even if Marshal had to wish him away.

3

Doug felt like a changed man by the time he left the church, although not in a good way. The dead faces flashed before him on his drive to school. He wanted to tell his teammates about it but was also scared to do so.

Being a changed man was nothing like when he had dedicated his life to Christ. It was the opposite. A despairing fall from grace. If the corpses of Allen Prospect and the Beaumonts could look the way they did in this world, then this world might be crueler than he had believed an hour ago. He decided against saying anything and went through the motions of his school day.

Practice was a throwaway scrimmage. Logan was still in Tuskahoma, and Doug supposed Marshal was too. The Devils would match up with King-Marlow in the first round of the STATE TOURNAMENT on Thursday. Coach Park decided to wait until tomorrow to talk strategy. He seemed annoyed that the boys weren't here today even though the death of a former classmate and serious injury to two others was plenty excuse, not to mention it was Logan's sister. Maybe Park was perturbed because he didn't get to flirt with Coach Reed today. Doug didn't want to read into her absence. She was far from the only teacher not in school. In fact, most classmates and teachers who had been at the hospital Saturday night weren't here, no doubt sleeping off the late night/early morning.

After school, Doug wanted to go home and climb into bed himself. The sooner he slept, the sooner he would reach tomorrow. Maybe by then he would forget all about what he saw in the morgue.

Mal waited for him in the school parking lot. She leaned against his car with her arms crossed. "There you are," she said. "You weren't here this morning."

"Sorry, I got stuck at the breakfast longer than I thought I would."

She put her arms around him. She still had that sour smell to her. "I missed you," she said.

"I missed you too," he lied.

"You know what we should do now?"

"What's that?"

She bumped her forehead against his. Her eyelashes nearly tickled his own. "Let's go to Clearwater Creek and fuck in the woods."

"Mal...We got STATE coming up—"

"Exactly. You don't want to be backed up when you go to the city on Wednesday. You should be relaxed and focused. I'm here to help."

"I need to go home."

"Come on." She reached for his crotch.

Doug shoved her hand away. "Mal, stop!" He scanned the parking lot and squinted at the windows of the high school trailer on the opposite side of the outdoor court. He just knew Ms. Fletcher would be watching them from her classroom. "What the heck are you even doing here? School got out over an hour ago."

The shove seemed to make her somewhat more normal, although she still had the same hypnotized look in her eye. "I was waiting for you, Dougie."

"You were supposed to go home and clean yourself this morning. You smell awful."

"I was going to, but I just kept thinking about how much I wanted to see you at school. So I came here...and you weren't in first period. Or second."

"You came straight to school after I saw you? That was, like, six in the morning."

"And?"

He shook his head. "You're acting crazy."

"Crazy? Because I want you?"

"Listen, Mal. I—I just need some time to myself."

She snatched his arm and dug her nails into him. "*Please*," she said. "Don't you want me too?"

"Get out of my way, Mal."

"All right, all right. We don't have to go to the woods. There's no one at my house. You want me to shower? Why don't we shower together?"

"Let's talk later."

"You don't want me?"

"Let's talk—"

Mal wrapped her arm around his neck and forced him into a kiss. She bit down on his bottom lip. Doug pushed her off and felt his skin pull away. She was smiling with blood on her teeth.

A deep gash stung in his lip.

"What the fuck, Mal?"

"I'm just teasing you."

"I'm going home."

"I'll come—"

"No!" He shoved her to the ground and threw his car door open. Doug slid into the driver's seat and pulled the door closed fast.

It connected with something. He heard a loud crack like the initial snap of rolling thunder.

Instantly, Mal howled in pain.

Doug's scream caught in his throat, as if he were choking on the blood from his lip. Her arm wriggled up and down until, finally, he opened the door. She pulled the arm out swiftly. He closed the door, afraid to look out his window.

Mal wailed outside of the Corolla while Doug put it in reverse. Dust billowed, shadowing the heap which remained squatted by the outdoor court.

He tore his eyes away from her and drove home.

4

Doug couldn't remember the drive. One moment, he was breaking Mal's arm in his car door. The next, he was sitting in his parked car outside his house, his three-year-old sister waving at him from behind the screen door.

Kayla always greeted him when he got home unless it was a late night. Doug wished she were napping. He wasn't sure if he could greet her with his usual affection.

He sat in the Corolla for a full minute, processing...nothing. His mind was empty.

Someone knocked on his window, and he jumped. He cranked down the window, muttering some choice words under his breath he would have to ask forgiveness for later.

"What're you doing, weirdo?" his sister Cindy said. She was one of the middle schoolers who had designed the banners for the playoff run.

"Nothing," which was true. He wasn't thinking or moving, just staring until Kayla gave a confused look and walked away from the screen door.

"Are you coming or going?" Cindy asked.

"I just got home."

"Then will you come out back and tell Joseph he's shooting it wrong?"

"I'm busy, Cindy."

"C'mon. He keeps shooting with two hands, and I told him you have to pick one."

"Is he making any shots?"

"I guess so."

"Well, Tim Springer shoots with two hands, and he's a starter on my team."

"No, he's not."

"He was. Listen, if it feels right to Joseph, then he can shoot with two hands. It's probably the only way he can get it over the rim at his age."

Cindy huffed and stomped away.

Doug went inside.

Dinner was already on the table, mostly eaten. Kayla had a meatball on the end of her fork, nibbling until she saw him. She smiled, sauce smeared across her cheeks.

"Doug!" She ran over and hugged his leg.

"About time you came inside," his mom said from where she was washing dishes in the sink. "Kayla was starting to think it wasn't you out there."

"I's scared," Kayla said.

Doug leaned down. "You don't need to be scared, Kay. You were right, and here I am!"

She gave him a "fish" kiss, and sauce stuck to his cheek. He went over to his mom and gave her a hug. She pulled back to study him.

"You look so tired, baby." She took her kitchen towel and wiped the sauce from his cheek.

"I am. I'm probably going straight to bed."

She put a hand on his forehead. "Maybe you're coming down with something."

"No, I'm still recovering from the night at the hospital. I'll be fine tomorrow."

"Well, rest as much as you can. Big game on Thursday."

"Huge," he agreed. "Did Dad get off work for it?"

"Believe it or not, he did. Even with that farm's dire straits."

Doug's father was the accountant for Rush Family Farms and commuted three hours total each day to and from Kiamichi County. Rush Farms was a name everyone in southeastern Oklahoma knew but the company had peaked in the nineties and grew far less produce nowadays. His dad had been looking for a new job, and Doug had prayed hard he could find something in Arrow or Tuskahoma.

"Whole family will be there," his mom added. "So, yes, you better get your beauty sleep. I have a good feeling about the team's chances this year."

Doug grabbed a piece of garlic bread. "I got a good feeling too," he said, although it didn't ring true in the aftermath of what had happened at school. The cracking sound haunted him. He kissed his mom on the cheek and wandered off. The garlic bread was the first thing he had eaten since the men's prayer breakfast, and it didn't settle well inside him.

The evening sun left an orange haze in his bedroom. It was March 8th but still cold enough to see your breath most days. The only giveaway they were any closer to spring was the sun staying out a little later each day. No longer full dark by five p.m.

Doug closed his blinds, leaving only lines of orange among the darkness. His bed felt extra soft, like the night he and Mal first slept together.

He focused his thoughts on Friday night, recalling her warmth, the softness of her skin, her breath in his ear—

A more recent memory interrupted the pleasant image— the sound of Mal wailing in pain. The crack. Bone colliding with metal. The way his car door lurched in protest to him yanking it closed.

He felt queasy. Too many pancakes. The garlic bread roiled in his gut.

"Lord, help me," he muttered. Then he clasped his hands together and prayed for God to take away the stomachache.

But it wasn't just a stomachache. His mind knew what he had done. Her howling wouldn't stop even when he hit himself in the head.

Please, God, take it away. I'd rather be empty. Please, God, save me from my worst self. A prayer as desperate as the one he made at the bottom of the well, the prayer he wished he could take back. Time passed quickly as he lay there with his hands clasped together and eyes squeezed closed—*please close your eyes and bow your head as we pray together.*

This was no Invitation on a Sunday morning, though. It was a prayer more like Jesus in the Garden of Gethsemane—*Father, if you are willing, take this cup from me.*

Doug was sweating and muttering to himself as his ears pounded with the thud of his car door catching on the meat of Mal's arm and then—

Crack!

Please God, take it away!

Minutes or hours passed but it *was* full dark when he finally opened his eyes. He had a lightheaded feeling like he had been sleeping—or was sleeping now. Dreaming, maybe.

He lay on his side, facing the closed bedroom door. A sliver of light beneath and the shadow of feet pattering back and forth as his siblings chased each other. It couldn't have been too late then. Unless this was a dream. His siblings could stay awake all night in a dream.

Suddenly, he felt a weight in his bed behind him.

"I'm sorry, Mal," he said, knowing it was her.

Her warm breath tickled the back of his neck.

"Please forgive me, Mal."

A cold, hard hand, like a block of ice, ran up his back, then wrapped around his shoulder. Her right arm was no longer broken.

"There, there, Dougie. You will always be forgiven. Isn't that the point? To give yourself permission to do whatever you want, knowing forgiveness is always there."

"Of course not." He hated the rise in his voice. Shame

coursed through him. He was hardly aware of how cold her body was, only that she was naked, when she pressed against the back of him.

"It's okay, Dougie. If you can't be honest with me, then who can you be honest with?"

She patted her hand against his chest. With every word she spoke, he felt her breath closer and closer to his neck. A putrid trash smell clung to the air.

"But you should be happy, you know. Your prayer was answered. And all it took was a little tithe. Do you want to know what you left in the offering plate?"

"A tithe? I—I don't have anything to tithe. Mom said I don't have to tithe until I'm on my own. When I'm in the service, I can send—"

"You already left it in the offering plate. When you said your prayer. Isn't that how you put it? You prayed for me to want you. Well, haven't I wanted you? Haven't I answered your prayer?"

"I didn't mean it like that—"

"Don't you want to know what you tithed?"

"No...no, I don't."

"Look." The sliver of light beneath the door and his siblings' pattering feet were gone. It was a solid black wall before him.

He squeezed his eyes closed. "I don't want to." He could hear his bedroom door creak open.

"Look."

Her fingers cut into the thin skin of his eyelids and pulled them open. His vision blurred from the pain of her jamming those fingers against his eyeballs as she forced him to—

"Look!"

A vertical red line formed where the door was now ajar. The bleary lump of a silhouette crawled through the slight opening. There was something odd about the way it moved and he realized it was dragging itself on its side, one arm pulling it forward like a soldier who'd had his other arm and both legs blown off by an IED in Afghanistan—the kind of soldier a couple of years from now Doug would be demanding take Jesus into his heart before he died.

The silhouette slid like that across the carpet and the door creaked closed, once again forming the infinite black wall.

Doug wanted to close his eyes but those cold ice picks pulled at his eyelids, peeling them further from his cavernous sockets, numbing his entire face.

The body reached its lone hand over the side of his bed, as dark as the black wall behind it and yet Doug could somehow see it clearly now.

"The offer of a lover for a lover's prayer," Mal said behind him, her breath stabbing at his neck so cold it felt hot.

The arm held tight to his blanket, pulling itself up. A face rose above his bed, twisted like a melting photo, the same face he had seen that morning: the Beaumonts and Allen Prospect. Another victim of the kitchen well. *His* victim.

Had this been a normal nightmare, Doug would have woken up right then, but he had rejected his answered prayer, so the nightmare continued, Mal holding his eyelids open the whole time as the face grew closer and closer and kissed him.

It was the worst kiss of his life.

TWELVE
CONFLICTED

1

FOR SEVERAL MILES after escaping Green River, Logan and Will didn't say anything. They ran their hands along their bodies to make sure they weren't shot. Logan ignored the growing pain in his right ankle, using the same foot to pump the gas pedal.

As soon as they were out of what had once been a township, and onto the same highway that had nearly killed Logan's sister, they finally breathed again. With their exhales of relief came laughter. Will started it, laughing like an idling engine, his body shaking, and Logan joined him, his laughter coming out phlegmy.

They laughed and laughed, loud and obnoxious, until they reached Tuskahoma.

"Oh my god," Will said, wiping tears away with shaking hands. "We almost died."

"Yeah," Logan agreed. "I guess we did."

"Your ankle is jacked up."

"I don't know how I don't have a bullet hole in me."

"The wish."

Logan paused at that. "You really think so?"

"Yeah," Will said. "Your wish isn't finished yet. You can't die."

"And what about you?"

"I had you between me and her."

"I noticed, asshole. You took off without me."

"Every man for himself, Tramer. No offense, but if it's between you and me, I'm choosing me. And I expect you to do the same."

"Well, you're lucky I didn't get shot. You'd be shit out of luck without my car keys."

"Not luck. The wish, remember?"

Logan shook his head and took a deep breath. He laughed a little more.

"So, the Basketball Gods have saved me *and* my sister now."

"And cured my grandma."

Their miraculous fortune was almost enough to make him forget the consequences, but Logan couldn't ignore the reason they had gone to Green River and been shot at. He was jealous that Will's wish was fully realized. Will only had to deal with one repercussion.

Logan wondered if Will thought about his responsibility for Bird's death. Maybe Will still doubted that the wishes and deaths were connected. It's not like they could trust the crazy woman who had shot at them. But Logan didn't ask Will about it. He feared whatever answer Will gave wouldn't satisfy his own dilemma.

They returned to the hospital at dusk, and he dropped Will off at his car.

"When I'm back in Nowhere, I'll talk to the guys about what happened."

"Do you really think Betty Bromide killed her teammate?" Will asked.

"The way she was shooting at us, I'd have to say yes. Her teammate's body is in that well."

"Damn…We have to tell someone, right? Maybe Ryan Holbrook—"

"That would mean telling him about the well."

"We wait, then. We don't tell anyone else about the well."

"Just like we started this, right? We keep the kitchen well secret."

"Something you're an expert at, Tramer," Will said sarcastically, but there was no snark in it.

They both smiled.

"No one else," Logan said. "I won't tell anyone else."

Will left, and Logan went into the hospital. He was ready to see his sister and mom, to spend all night in the little hospital room, comforted by his family's presence, thankful to be here.

When he stepped into Emily's room, though, the air felt thick, charged with a different energy than he'd expected. He saw why soon enough.

"Hey, bud," his father said.

2

Logan's mom and Emily both wore the same expression, one of excitement tinged with the inevitable disappointment. Bill Tramer had one hand tucked in the waistband of his blue jeans near his hip, his thumb poking out, but his other arm was extended for Logan to embrace him.

His father had never been one for hugs, but these circumstances called for it.

Emily had almost died, and that had a way of bringing a family together. Even Logan wasn't immune to the urge to bring his father back into the fold. He had shown up. And goddammit, wasn't that enough?

Not really, Logan thought, reluctantly returning the hug. His father's hand in his waistband never came out, even though Logan had both arms around him.

Bill Tramer smelled the same, talked the same, dressed the same, but in other ways, he had changed. The last time Logan saw him, three years ago, he had been a little taller than his father, but today, he towered over him. Logan had grown only an inch since then. His father had been over six feet but now seemed to have shrunk, like he had spent three years crammed into too small a space and had slouched to fit into it.

"I got here as soon as I could," Bill Tramer said. "And your sister looks as pretty as ever."

"I feel much better," Emily said. "I don't know why I'm still here."

"Dr. Warren wants to be sure you're all right," Logan's mom said. "You're not supposed to heal so quickly."

"Good genes." Bill Tramer elbowed Logan in the ribs and winked at him.

Logan laughed without smiling.

"I can't believe I'm gonna miss the Big House for this."

"You don't know that yet," their mom said. "And if you do, it's not the end of the world. Better we know for sure you're okay."

"How long are you staying?" Logan asked his father.

Bill seemed caught off guard, and Logan's mom eyed him, like it was rude to ask.

"Well, I was thinking I might stay all week and watch you play. Can't believe y'all are back in the STATE TOURNAMENT again."

"They've played well," his mom said. "They really came together as a team after Kelvin got hurt."

"Hardest thing I ever did was make STATE once," Bill said. "Can't imagine three years in a row. That's a hell of a thing, Logan."

His father had played basketball himself at Briar Christian —a Class 2A school on the opposite side of Tuskahoma from Green River. That was how Bill Tramer and Janice Horn had started dating.

Janice had led Tuskahoma to the Area finals in 1980—when girls' basketball was still six-on-six—and they had lost in over-time. Bill had put up ten points and ten rebounds in a first-round loss in the Class 2A State Tournament. Janice had watched him play his heart out, and always told Logan and Emily that she fell in love with him because of how much he cared when the rest of his team had given up.

When Janice saw him the next day near one of the concession stands during the semifinals, she approached him. He had heard of her because she was Class 5A All-State, and soon, they started dating off and on until they married four years later. Two years after that, Logan was born.

As much as they fought, their chemistry was undeniable. They had passion for each other that wasn't meant for the long haul.

Logan hadn't seen it at the time. When he returned from church camp and his parents sat him down to announce their divorce, he had been shocked and angry. Emily seemed much more at ease than Logan, who had started shouting and crying.

Later, when he understood the truth of his parents' limited love for each other, he felt ashamed of his reaction. He was left wondering if his father never visited because of the way Logan had reacted. As if he had been so embarrassed, he had to move to Missouri and start a new family. Logan had no idea if his father was dating anyone or had more children—anything.

"Why don't you two go to Krebs' and eat something?" Logan's mom said. "Then you can bring me and Em some takeout when you're done."

"I second this plan," Emily said.

Logan had no desire to go to the diner. His father seemed just as uneasy. But neither would admit it. Another test of their manhood, Logan supposed.

Silence meant strength. Expressing reservations was for the weak.

Did the tests ever end?

3

When they had lived in Tuskahoma, Logan's family ate downtown at Krebs' Diner every Saturday. They sat in the same booth, Logan always on the inside next to his father, with Emily and his mom sitting opposite them.

He liked sitting next to his father, even when he had grown too big for it to be comfortable. His father's hairy arms would brush against him, and he would smell the spicy musk of the cologne his father only wore when they went out.

This time, Logan sat across from him, but he still caught the scent of the cologne over the basket of fries between them. Logan had been starving after running for his life earlier. He scarfed down his burger and onion rings, then shared the fries with his dad, who had eaten much less.

Bill had done most of the talking, a nervous stream of consciousness about the diner, Tuskahoma, and his days of coming here with the boys from Briar Christian.

Despite being students at a church school, they had been hellions—kicked out of movie theaters, bookstores, and even Krebs' Diner once.

"Much different story than when I came here with your mother," his dad said. "The same waitress who shoved me out of here when I hit on her as a teenager was telling me and your mom how lovely of a couple we were. She was so excited when your mom came in one day with the biggest pregnant belly you've ever seen. It's no wonder you ended up so big, Logan. She had the worst back pain in the world."

Logan dipped the same fry into ketchup over and over again, listening, trying to think of something to say, but he was determined not to humor his dad. Admittedly, it became harder the longer he was around him. He found himself excited to hear Bill's stories, pleased by the nostalgia his dad's presence evoked. It made him angrier, though—annoyed at his father for not being around to tell him stories like this all the time.

He didn't want to hear more about the past, so he said, "My friend from school says Germans dip their fries in mayonnaise."

Bill cleared his throat, his face red like he regretted talking about the good old days. "Is that right?" he said. "I like to mix mayonnaise and ketchup. You ever try it?"

"I've never seen you do that."

"It's a new thing. A friend of mine showed me." Bill squirted some mayonnaise and ketchup together, mixing it with a fry.

Logan wondered about this "friend." He dipped his fry into the concoction.

"Yeah, that's good," he said. "Damn good—Uh, sorry."

"It's goddamn good, son...You ain't gotta worry about cussing in front of me. Your mom's not here."

"Right." A smile threatened to spread across Logan's face. "How's the truck driving?" he asked. "I was thinking about doing something like that."

"Oh, you don't want to do that, Logan. Your mom said you were wanting to do something with computers."

"She told you that?"

"We've had all day to talk. She said you'd just left when I arrived. Said you had something to do with a friend."

"Yeah. Just some prep work for the game Thursday."

"Is that how you rolled your ankle? Prep work?"

Logan shoved a fry into his mouth. "I was being stupid. I'll be fine."

"Looks swollen as hell, Logan. I didn't want to point it out in front of your mom, though. She might freak—"

"It doesn't hurt."

"Well, I'd go home and elevate it as much as you can until Thursday. From what I hear, your team needs you, if you're gonna win it all." Logan must've had a look on his face because his dad said, "What is it?"

"Nothing...You just never seemed like you liked basketball much."

"It was all right, but frankly, my team was never gonna win STATE. We got lucky with a weak region my senior year and were just happy to be there. The best thing ever happened to me at the Big House was meeting your mom."

"Right. For sure. For sure. You were more of a football guy, right?"

"You know it, boy. Tight end. Most TDs on the team my junior and senior years. Briar C. never had a good football team —our coach was lousy—but if I'd gone to school at Tuskahoma, who knows. Maybe I would've played college football. Maybe NFL."

"Yeah, you used to say that."

"But basketball's good, boy. Nothing better than making STATE. I'm excited to see you play."

"It'll be the first time."

"That's right." Bill guffawed. "I'm shocked, to be honest. Never thought you'd be any kind of ball player after how tryouts went for the football team."

"Practice makes perfect," Logan said, grateful for the reminder that his dad could be an asshole. He didn't want to miss his father. It needed it to be easy when the man disappeared again.

A part of him doubted Bill Tramer would actually stick around until Thursday.

What if he does? If your dad's in the crowd, you have to win, right? And if you win, what if he stays for the other games? What if he really wants to watch you win STATE?

It was a pleasing thought, complicated by the encounter with Betty Bromide. He was conflicted on how to proceed and had done his best not to think about it. He wondered if it would help to talk to his teammates. And should he tell Kelvin about the well?

Logan hadn't felt like he was lying to Will when he said he wouldn't tell anyone else, but Betty Bromide's comment about his aunt kept replaying in his mind. She'd said, *Maybe if we'd told her, she would have been protected.*

His dad threw a fry at him. "Well, what do you think?"

"About what?"

"About me coming to your game? Aren't you excited about your old man watching you win STATE?"

Logan feared telling Kelvin or updating his teammates. He didn't want to do anything to deter the team from reaching its goal. He was convinced he could still win STATE without hurting anyone. He just had to figure out how.

"Yeah, Dad," Logan said, admitting it to himself as much as Bill Tramer, "I am."

4

On Tuesday morning, Logan planned to return home on his own. His mom and dad would stay in Tuskahoma until Wednesday night, then get a hotel room in the city—separate rooms, of course—for Logan's game Thursday morning. After much convincing, Dr. Warren agreed to release Emily tomorrow so she could go to the tournament too. "As long as she continues to feel this way," Dr. Warren had said. "I honestly can't explain it." She said it as if it were a bad thing, but Logan supposed that was because doctors didn't like not having an explanation for something.

His mom had finally spotted his swollen ankle this morning and freaked out. She insisted he go straight home and spend the day with his ankle elevated. *He* insisted he couldn't miss practice.

"If you want any chance of playing Thursday, don't even dare run up and down a court until then," she had said.

But even if he didn't participate, Logan had to go to the gym this afternoon. He needed to see Alex, Doug, and Marshal and update them. After sleeping hard the night before, Logan woke knowing he had to tell them about Green River. It was necessary to brainstorm ways they could win STATE without losing any other Nowhere folks.

He missed Bird, felt bad for Tim, and wondered if he would ever see his history teacher, Mr. Tune, again. Allen Prospect hadn't been easy to like, but he was too young to die. All of this had happened because Logan had climbed down the well. He was responsible.

Yet, a part of him reasoned that accidents happened and people died every day from heart attacks and strokes. Long lives weren't guaranteed, and it was almost comforting to think there was a reason for the recent tragedies, rather than some random cruelty.

After letting these thoughts circle in his head all morning, he had to tell his teammates. He couldn't deal with this alone. Finally, Logan convinced his mom to let him go to practice, as long as he agreed not to play and spend the rest of the day with the heating pad.

"You're a great teammate," she said. "You're supportive and quite the leader. I'm really proud of you."

As he was leaving the hospital, he crossed paths with Kelvin in the parking lot.

"Yo," he said. "Going to see Em?"

Kelvin rocked on his crutches and dapped him up. "Yep. Even got here myself. First time driving again," he said. "My mom freaked out. Made me finally get one of these things." He flipped his cell phone open and closed.

"Is that the Razr?"

"Nah, that doesn't come out until the fall. I was gonna wait until then when I moved to Denton, but..."

Logan didn't know what to say. Kelvin moved on for both of them.

"Tell the boys I won't be there to watch practice today," he said. "But I'll be on the bus tomorrow evening. Coach has you and me rooming together."

"Word?" Logan swallowed hard. "That's awesome."

"For sure. We need to spend some time together, man."

"Yeah...Sorry I haven't been over much. Between work and the playoffs, I've been hella distracted."

"I get it, Logan. You didn't miss much. Truth be told, I probably wasn't very pleasant to be around."

"And now look at you. Zooming all the way to Chahta County. Beaming like an idiot."

Kelvin laughed. "Yeah, things are looking up. Especially with Emily awake and feeling better." His eyes glazed over. He was only two inches shorter than Logan, but on crutches, he seemed smaller. "I wish I could be out there on the court with y'all. More than anything."

"At least you'll be on the bench. You can't imagine how much that will mean to the team."

"Can I be honest with you for a sec?"

"Of course."

"I could've been at the Area games. Hell, I could've been

back in school last week too. I guess…I'm afraid to be seen like this."

"Dude, what?"

"I know. I know. It's just, people looked at me a certain way before, and now they don't. Now I'm damaged goods."

"Some people are fools. Everyone knows this is temporary."

"Do they? I think they're scared of me."

"What?"

"Yeah, I think…people think I'm cursed or something."

"No one believes—"

"C'mon, Logan. It's just me and you here."

Logan stared at the sky. The sun broke through the clouds like spring was finally ready to rid Nowhere of the long winter.

Kelvin chuckled. "Exactly. But my point is, I'm ready to get out of the house. What happened to your sister, to Jessica… fucking Allen Prospect dying…It's time for me to rejoin my team, is what I'm saying."

"Hell yeah," Logan said, choking up.

He decided Kelvin had to know the truth. Logan didn't know if Betty's theory about accomplices versus "witnesses to our glory" was true, but he couldn't live with the thought of someday looking at Kelvin's basketball portrait the way he looked at his aunt's. So, he asked Kelvin to stay in the hospital parking lot a little longer and told him about the kitchen well.

5

"What the hell, dude?" Alex was angrier than Logan had expected.

Logan watched his team practice, and each player looked stressed when they saw his discolored ankle. He assured them he would be fine by Thursday, and the wish might have been the only thing putting them at ease. Mikey, Sam, Dylan, and

Jack didn't know about the kitchen well, so the underclassmen looked scared as hell, worried they might have to step up in a STATE TOURNAMENT game, if Logan's ankle kept him sidelined.

Of course, Sam was a starter now, but it was hard to imagine Dylan and Jack playing key moments in a big game. Mikey was certainly more talented than Sam, but he had yet to get out of his own head. It didn't help that Alex yelled at him every time he screwed up.

When practice ended, Logan stayed in the locker room with Alex, Doug, and Marshal. He started by telling them about his conversation with Kelvin.

"What did he say?" Doug asked. Something was different about him today. His skin was ruddy, his lips chapped, his eyes raccooned. It could've been lack of sleep like the rest of them, but there was a nervous manic in his eyes, a jittery quiver to his lips.

"He thought I was messing with him at first," Logan replied. "He said I made the same wish last year at the kitchen well, and we lost in the finals. I told him you had to climb to the bottom if you wanted the wish to come true. I told him about Will's grandma and how the wish helped us win."

"Did you tell him the rest of it?" Marshal asked.

Doug bit his fingernails.

"What would there be to tell?" Alex said, sticking stubbornly to the belief that the deaths and disappearances were just coincidences.

Unsurprisingly, Mr. Tune hadn't been back in school this week.

"I didn't get into it," Logan admitted. "I was focused on convincing him I wasn't pulling his leg."

"His good leg, I hope," Marshal joked.

"There's something else I need to tell you guys." Logan dove into the story of his trip to Green River, starting with what

Emily had said about Allen's death. He tried to quote Betty Bromide as closely as he could remember, but it wasn't precise. The gist would have to do.

When he reached the end of the story—his and Will's escape—all his teammates wanted to talk about was how she had shot at them.

"You could be dead, Logan," Doug said, his eyes darting around wildly. "Thank God I pray for y'all every night."

"It isn't your prayers that kept him alive, dumbass," Marshal said. "It's the wish."

"Going with Will Roebuck was your mistake," Alex said. "We would've jumped that bitch if she dared raise a rifle at us."

"Sure, tough guy," Marshal said.

"Guys, focus," Logan said. "Don't you get what this means? People are dying because of us."

"Easy, Tramer."

"Seriously, Marshal. We can't live in denial. We have to be responsible."

"You're jumping to conclusions," Alex said. "Even if the Beaumonts died after the McClinton game, it doesn't mean—"

"Do you think Emily lied about how Allen died?"

"She said she might have been having a nightmare, didn't she?" Alex shot back.

"Nightmares can be vivid," Doug said, chewing the inside of his mouth.

"And what Betty Bromide said about Green River?" Logan pressed.

"You mean the psycho chick who tried to kill you?" Alex asked.

"My wish came true," Marshal said. "So did Dougie's. No one died after those."

"No one yet," Logan added.

"Fucking stop it!" Doug's voice startled them. He never

cussed, never yelled. His upper lip glistened with nervous sweat. "We can't keep debating this. We need to face the truth."

"And what's that, Doug?" Alex asked.

"We don't know jack shit."

"Oh, ye of little faith," Marshal joked.

"This isn't the time to joke around," Logan said.

"Marshal's right," Doug agreed. "I don't know what to believe any more. My wish...Mal's not herself. And I know I said just because the well is creepy doesn't mean it's not God because angels terrified people in the Bible...but so did demons."

Alex guffawed. "You can't be serious."

"Is it so hard to believe?" Doug asked, his voice high and on edge. "We've seen wishes come true. Something told Ryan to arrest Bolan Grimes. An actual *voice*."

"It doesn't matter what it is," Logan said. "We need to focus on what we can control."

"And that is?" Marshal asked.

"How do we win STATE without killing anyone?"

Doug nodded too quickly. "Exactly. No matter what you say, Alex, we can't be a hundred percent sure it's a coincidence. So, we have to err on the side of caution."

"Picard and Mutton," Alex said, agreeing without vocalizing it. "We beat them without the magic. Nothing happened to anyone we knew."

"Can we actually beat King-Marlow without magic?" Marshal asked.

"Now who lacks faith?" Doug smiled for the first time all afternoon. The conversation had brought him a little closer to himself again, and Logan appreciated his support.

"We can," Logan said. "We would've destroyed them with Kelvin. Without him, we just have to win convincingly enough that the wish doesn't come into play."

"And if we can't?" Alex asked, already knowing the answer. They all did.

Logan didn't want to say it. They had worked too hard to give voice to the worst-case scenario. He felt the same shock and gut-wrenching sadness he'd had when Kelvin was injured.

"Then we lose on purpose," he said. "We accept it's the end of the road."

He glanced at Alex. They were the two seniors on the team, accepting the game against King-Marlow could be their last. Alex wanted to win STATE as badly as Logan did, maybe more.

"Agreed?" Logan held out his hand.

Marshal and Doug stood and put their hands over his.

"Fine," Alex said, putting his hand on top. "But it won't come to that. We got this, guys. We just have to stick to the game plan and not let our nerves get to us. Focus on your mechanics when you shoot. Breathe through your nose whenever possible. Right?"

"We got this," Logan agreed. "Win on three."

THE

STATE

TOURNAMENT

STATE

OLNEY
Winner Area II

LITTLE SAHARA
Runner-up Area I

GOLDFINDER
Runner-up Area III

BARTON-MEEK
Winner Area IV

KING-MARLOW
Winner Area III

NOWHERE
Runner-up Area IV

ALABASTER
Runner-up Area II

WEST ARCHER
Winner Area I

THIRTEEN
THE BIG HOUSE

1

The team dinner was a state tournament tradition. Superintendent Walker had booked a local Italian restaurant with a private area in Bricktown, and the team, along with anyone else from the Nowhere community, would have dinner together on Wednesday night.

More Nowhere folks than ever before showed up. Logan was shocked by how many came. They might have emptied the community of everyone, except the Amish.

Brother Maxwell came because every Sunday half of the Baptist church in Holdendecker was filled with congregants from Nowhere. He said the prayer before they ate, which he cut short when his cell phone beeped loudly. He glanced down at the phone, frowned, flipped it closed, quickly said, "In Jesus's name, amen," and stepped out to return the call.

Ryan Holbrook was also there with his parents. He wasn't in uniform or hiding himself beneath a hoodie. He looked better than he had the night after arresting Bolan Grimes.

The food was good, though Logan didn't eat much. Their

STATE TOURNAMENT games were always early in the morning, and this year was no different. They would play King-Marlow tomorrow at nine a.m. He worried about his ankle, but with another night on the heating pad, it should be fine.

Logan greeted four old teammates from his freshman and sophomore years who were sitting by Ryan. He thought they had moved out of state, but two of them lived in the city, one in Shawnee, and one in Tulsa.

After going to the bathroom, Jessica greeted him on his way back to the table.

"You're here," he said, his voice cracking. His face reddened until she surprised him with a hug.

Jessica had a taped patch of gauze on her forehead and bruises on her cheek. "You stood me up on Sunday," she said.

"I—um—"

"I'm fucking with you. Sorry, bad joke."

She had a nervous energy unfamiliar to her. Although she seemed in good spirits, there was sadness behind her eyes.

"No, no, it's a good joke," he said. "How are you feeling?"

"I was a little busted up, but yeah, I feel fine now. Just these ugly bruises."

"You're still gorgeous."

She stuttered, surprised by his compliment. He was surprised he had blurted it out too.

"W-Well, thank you."

Logan cleared his throat. "So...if your parents were okay with you driving to OKC to watch us win STATE, does that mean you're clear for a trip to Arrow this Sunday?"

"No, I think I'll stand you up this time."

He laughed. "Fair enough."

Jessica ran her hand along his arm. "Seriously, though. I'm looking forward to it."

"Me too."

Another sad look on her face, and he finally realized the obvious: she had been next to Allen Prospect when he died. *That's right, idiot. Don't forget it wasn't the crash that killed him. Never forget what you're up against.*

What he was up against? Was that really how he felt about the kitchen well now, Logan wondered.

Jessica returned to the table she shared with Macy Goode, Reba Jacobs, Letty Prospect, and Mal Turner. Logan was surprised to see Letty here. He had heard Allen's funeral was rough. Allen's mom had attempted to open his casket and was restrained by Allen's brother and a couple of cousins. Maybe Letty needed the distraction, which made Logan even more determined to win STATE. Then there was Mal Turner who had a long cast on her arm.

Doug's wish?

Logan shook the thought away.

Take it seriously, but don't be paranoid.

Still, it was hard not to be paranoid when she sat there, glaring angrily at Doug across the room.

Logan had focused on not limping all day, tricking himself mentally into feeling no pain in his sprained ankle. He caught sight of his sister with his parents and waved at them. Logan had talked to them when they first arrived, surprised his dad had stayed after all.

Before he reached his seat, he spotted Will Roebuck through the open door, eating alone in the main area. Logan went out to talk to him and saw another team at the restaurant. They had no private area, no community members surrounding them. It was the Olney Mustangs—about a dozen athletes in cowboy hats, along with their head coach and assistant coach. The three Mosely brothers recognized him and gave him a nod. He returned the gesture, then sat across from Will.

"Even Will Roebuck came to the team dinner. Hell must be frozen over."

"Technically, I'm not at the team dinner," Will said.

"Right. You'd rather eat an awkward dinner alone than admit you're here to support the team."

"I'm here to see what happens. I've been watching everyone go into the room, making note of who isn't here."

"All of Nowhere showed up, man. Would've been a great day to break into everyone's houses."

"Not everyone," Will said.

"We already know Mr. Tune's missing because of the Colesville game."

"Not just him. Ms. Fletcher isn't here."

"No surprise there. She only goes to home games."

"She went to your STATE TOURNAMENT games last year."

Logan took a breadstick off Will's plate and ate it. "Anyone else?"

"Oh, just the biggest absence there could be. Coach Park's been looking sulky all week because of it. Coach Reed isn't here."

Logan paused mid-chew. "Really?"

"She wasn't in school on Monday or Tuesday either."

Logan shook his head. "But we haven't played any more games since Area. No more magic since then. Why would anyone else be dead or missing?"

"Marshal made a wish, didn't he?"

Logan had trouble swallowing the bread. He grabbed Will's water and drank the whole glass.

"Hey—"

"Doug made a wish too," Logan admitted.

"What?"

"Doug made a wish Friday night. He and Alex went to the well. I didn't know anything about it."

"Goddammit, Tramer. This is why you weren't supposed to tell anyone in the first place. *'Oh, the team's cool, man. Why would they make any wishes? They want the same thing I've already wished for.'* Fucking idiot."

"You were right. I was wrong, okay? I told them any other wishes had to wait, but they didn't listen. It's done."

"And who's paying the price, Logan?"

"You sound like Betty Bromide."

"I've had a few days since being shot at. Time to think."

"Well, you can stop judging me. I have a plan. I convinced the guys to go along with it. We win without the magic. If we can't do that, then we lose on purpose."

Will considered it. "No magic, no sacrifices."

"Exactly...Why do you look so surprised?"

"No reason. I just can't imagine you losing at the STATE TOURNAMENT on purpose."

"Yeah. Well."

Will wrote something on a napkin. "Here's where I'm staying and my room number, in case shit hits the fan and you need to find me."

"It won't, but all right. Whatever." Logan crumpled the napkin and stuffed it in his pocket. He returned to the private area, peering at the different Nowhere people passing by the team's table, greeting them, wishing them luck.

There were too many of them, he thought. Too many had come.

2

Ryan Holbrook had finally taken his parents' advice and requested time off work. After finding the Beaumonts in bed— not quietly dying in their sleep, but a present death, a disturbed death, a look of pain and terror on those ruined faces—he couldn't sleep. He kept thinking about Red, then thinking about the Beaumonts.

But that wasn't what kept him awake last Saturday night. It was the voice from a week earlier.

The memory replayed in his mind: sitting in his unit at Clearwater Creek, the winter night too dark for his eyes to adjust, then a green glow from his police radio blinding him as the voice ordered him to arrest Bolan Grimes. The more he replayed it the less the voice sounded like Sheriff Dixon. The voice was distorted to begin with, but now it twisted into something even less human, a rigid and rough modulation of multiple voices edited together inexpertly: *Move* on GRIMES.

Then came the car wreck. He only heard about that one. What a mess. Allen's body had been delivered to Brother Maxwell to prep for his funeral, and Ryan went to see it. The head was smashed in, causing his face to fold inward. It made it difficult to tell, but Brother Maxwell pointed out tiny details in what was left of the loose skin in Allen's cheeks that suggested his face would have been like the others before he hit the pole.

Another memory, another voice haunted him after that. When Ryan waited with Tim after Red's death, and Brother Maxwell came to collect the body: "Another one," he had said.

Ryan could only sleep two hours a night, tops.

Move on GRIMES.

Another one.

His parents saw the toll the job took on him, so they suggested the three of them go to the city for the STATE TOURNAMENT. Neither Ryan nor his parents had been since he missed the game-winning basket in the semifinals two years ago, as if the Big House was cursed.

He was surprised Sheriff Dixon agreed to the last-minute request, but Ryan's lack of sleep had given him the look of a madman.

Move on GRIMES.

Another one.

He was only aware of how bad he looked yesterday morning —his first day of leave. It had been enough to make him go back to bed and sleep the entire day.

He felt refreshed today. Excited to see the boys play tomorrow morning. The community dinner was going great too. He hadn't seen Foster Miles or Greg Foster or Eric Sands in ages. They talked about the good old days, the tough matchups and playoff runs and Kelvin Harris—that *young* shit—who was the best player with whom they had ever shared the court, even during his freshman and sophomore years. Ryan's dad, the shop teacher Jonathan Holbrook whom all his former classmates knew well—he was often everyone's favorite teacher because he'd let you cuss during class—chimed in with stories of fights breaking out in the crowd during rivalry games. "Those shit-for-brains over in Cottonvale wouldn't know a full-court press from three-two zone. They'd argue just to argue. If I held up a basketball, they'd try and convince me it was a soccer ball. I almost put a boot in this son of a bitch who threw popcorn on me." Ryan's mom scolded his dad for his "potty mouth," but he had Ryan's former teammates rolling.

And yet Ryan couldn't relax after Brother Maxwell prayed over the community dinner. During the prayer, the preacher had been interrupted by his phone going off and then quickly left the room to return the call.

Ten minutes later, he hadn't returned.

"I'm gonna step out," Ryan said.

"Hurry back," his mom responded, a look of concern on her face. Even when Ryan was having a good time with his old friends, she could tell something was wrong.

He offered an unconvincing smile and hurried out of the private event room. He passed through the restaurant, worried

Brother Maxwell had returned to his hotel room, that Ryan had missed his chance to find out what the call was about. Deep down, he knew it was connected to all the deaths.

Move on GRIMES.

The strange voice that had once sounded like Sheriff Dixon but now sounded uncanny echoed in his mind over and over again, the inflection shifting each time.

MOVE *on* Grimes.

Move ON *Grimes*.

He stepped outside into the cold night air. His breath billowed before him like an arrow pointing toward where Brother Maxwell White stood at the corner of the long building, smoking a cigarette.

Downtown OKC was bustling with foot traffic, folks headed to nearby bars and nightclubs and other restaurants. A homeless man asked if he had change, and Ryan dug in his pocket and offered some. Two women his age passed by him in short skirts and smiled, and Ryan smiled back and glanced at their asses over his shoulder after they passed. A thirtysomething wife said to her husband, "That smells good! What is that?" and Ryan told them it was the Italian place he had just come out of.

The distractions seemed designed to keep him from reaching Brother Maxwell, but also Ryan indulged each one like he was afraid to actually speak to the preacher. Were all these deaths somehow his fault? He couldn't help but think it was, although his mom would say that was his ego talking. "The world doesn't revolve around you, Ryan Peter Holbrook." How many times had she said that to him?

Finally, he reached the end of the block. Brother Maxwell was still there, the tip of his cigarette glowing orange. A yellow light reflected on his face, then turned red as the stoplight changed.

"Hello, Ryan." The preacher tapped his foot rapidly but his voice was as calm as Sunday morning.

"Hey, Brother Maxwell. How are you?"

"Well, I'm smoking a cigarette from a pack I've kept for ages just for special occasions like this."

"How's it taste?"

"Terrible." He held it out to Ryan.

Ryan laughed and took a drag. "It's the case, isn't it?"

"Not much of a case, really." Brother Maxwell raised one eyebrow. "Haven't you heard? Everyone is dying from natural causes."

"Except...are they?"

Brother Maxwell took the cigarette back and tilted his head as if to say, *That's the million-dollar question, my boy.*

"There's a couple of missing people in Nowhere too," Ryan said. "An Amish boy and my old history teacher."

"Larry Tune?"

"Yeah. But I've been ordered to keep it quiet."

Ryan was surprised at the preacher's surprise. He assumed Maxwell would have heard anything he heard, regardless of his orders.

"Sheriff Dixon and Superintendent Walker are old buddies," he continued. "So, Dixon's doing him a solid."

"Ridiculous. We should be forming a search party. Or, or, something—"

"Not until the boys win STATE, apparently."

"You sound like you might agree with them."

Ryan shrugged. "All I know is this is spooky. Feels like two people from Nowhere going missing has to be connected to the deaths, but without a body to look at, who can say?" He nodded down at the preacher's hand like Maxwell was gripping his cell phone. "Your phone call. It's why you're out here, isn't it?"

Brother Maxwell sighed. "There's another body. My coroner friend in Arrow told me about her."

"Arrow?"

"She commutes to work. It's Julia Reed, Ryan."

"Coach Reed?"

"I'm afraid so. Her sister hadn't heard from her since Sunday when Julia called her on her way home from the hospital in Tuskahoma. She went to Julia's house this morning and found her."

"Geez-sus. Oh, sorry, pastor. I just—what the hell is happening?"

"I'm going to put on a happy face and finish dinner. And then I'll drive out to the funeral home tonight. I have to see the body, Ryan. Find out if she's like the others."

"Of course you do." Ryan snatched the cigarette and took another drag. "We both do."

"You're off duty, my boy."

"Not anymore. I'm coming with you."

The preacher chuckled. "I don't think your mother would approve. She told me how worried she is about you when I last saw her at church. Did you know you're on our prayer list?"

"No. I didn't know that." Knowing it made him feel guilty, but he shrugged off his mom's concerns. "She'll be fine. This is big. Maybe Coach Reed's death will be enough to get more eyes on what's happening. The Sheriff's department in Hereford County certainly have more resources than we do. I'm sure Dixon will keep it quiet until Saturday, but maybe we can do more behind the scenes now instead of pretending it's normal for so many Nowhere folks to punch their ticket in such a short period of time."

"Hope you didn't eat too much." Brother Maxwell took the cigarette back and stomped it out. "Sorry, sorry, mortician humor."

"No, it's a good point." Ryan grabbed his stomach, wishing he had eaten less. He already felt ill because he knew what they would see at the funeral home in Arrow.

Another one.

3

The night before their first-round game against King-Marlow, Logan attempted to go to sleep early. His ankle throbbed dramatically, keeping him from even closing his eyes. He stared at the purple nugget bulging from his skin.

"Keep staring at it and it'll never stop hurting," Kelvin said. "Trust me." He sat down on his side of the bed and hoisted his casted leg up. He tossed Logan the heating pad he had forgotten about in his duffel bag. "Don't forget this," Kelvin said. "There's a wall plugin on your side. Don't use the plugin on your lamp."

Logan followed his orders and had to admit the throbbing dulled when he could no longer look at the busted ankle.

"You mind if I call your sister for a sec?" Kelvin asked. "Just to see how she's doing with the travel and to say goodnight."

Logan acted like it was fine, but he underestimated how strange it would feel to hear his best friend talk to his sister in that tone—one only teenage boyfriends and girlfriends used.

He turned onto his side, away from Kelvin, when he heard words like "baby" and "honey," along with declarations of love repeated with complete confidence. Kelvin said "I love you" no less than four times during the conversation and three more when they said goodbye.

There had been a mix-up with the room reservations, so Logan and Kelvin ended up sharing a king-size bed. Logan had never shared a bed with a teammate, mainly because he was too big to do so comfortably. But the king-size bed gave the two six-footers just enough space.

After Kelvin hung up, he said, "Your sister says good luck tomorrow."

"Hmm." Logan returned to lying on his back, his hands under the pillow. The pillow padded around his face. He had two throw pillows from the corner lounge chair propped under his heating pad-covered foot.

"I need to tell you something," Logan said.

"What's up?"

"People have been dying in Nowhere. Tim's dad. Allen. The Beaumonts. My coworker too."

"I guess that's right," Kelvin said, considering it. "And no one's seen Mr. Tune either. I overheard Jacobs and Walker talking about it at dinner. They were nervous."

"It's the wishes, Kelvin. The wishes come with consequences."

He told Kelvin about the trip to Green River, leaving out any mention of his aunt. Logan wasn't sure why he avoided it. There were many differences between Kelvin and Jocelyn Horn. Kelvin wasn't depressed. More importantly, Kelvin knew about the wish. He was an accomplice. Kelvin couldn't be sacrificed. That's what Betty Bromide believed, and Logan knew she was right. He could feel it.

"We have to win without the magic."

"You will," Kelvin said, not seeming deterred by the revelation, but rather empowered. "King-Marlow doesn't have a guy taller than five-eleven. You'll punish them down low."

"I'd feel a lot better about not needing the magic if you were out there."

"If I was out there, you would've never made the wish."

Logan paused, considering how none of this would have happened if he hadn't set that screen. He hadn't thought much about Kelvin's injury since seeing his friend Saturday night. Now, the moment replayed in his mind.

He hesitated but asked, "Do you ever think about why you got hurt?"

"Why I got hurt?"

"Like, if it was fate or something."

"Nope. It was an accident. Plain and simple."

Logan's eyes welled up, and his nose threatened to run. He was thankful it was dark since he suddenly felt emotional. "I should've never made the wish."

"Dude. Are you kidding? We might actually win STATE."

"After everything I've told you, you think it's worth it?"

"Of course. How many people get to say they're STATE CHAMPS?"

"And the deaths?"

"You didn't know, man. Now that you do, you know what to do."

"Yeah?"

"Why do you seem surprised?"

"I don't know...You started dating my sister, and I wondered if maybe you were checking out a little. Thinking about North Texas next year."

"Really, bro? After how close we've gotten these last two years?"

"I was being stupid. I missed my best friend, I guess."

"Fair enough." Kelvin slid down into a sleeping position. "I guess that makes us even. Because these last couple of weeks, I've missed my best friend too."

"Fair enough," Logan said.

4

Logan always felt insecure when Nowhere's janky yellow bus pulled in alongside the colorfully wrapped buses of the other STATE-qualifying schools. It was obvious what it took to be a contender year after year. The investment Class A and Class B schools made in their athletic programs was on full display in the parking lot. Names Logan had grown accustomed to seeing were slapped across the sides of blue, white, red, green, purple, and neon buses in big blocky fonts, with painted mascots at the ends of the school names.

Superintendent Walker had pushed for money to upgrade one of the two Nowhere school buses after the team made STATE Logan's sophomore year, but it was deemed a waste of investment, since the school had an expiration date.

The conversation nearly had the opposite effect, with the school board suggesting the Holdendecker principal might have had a point about annexing Nowhere into the larger district. Superintendent Walker backed off, and two years later, the Nowhere Devils were still pulling up to the Big House in their yellow school bus, with its chipped letters on the school name.

Two years ago, the Big House had been the largest gym Logan had ever played in, and it remained intimidating. Each year, their first-round game had been the lowest-scoring of the season because of the adjustment to the bigger gym.

For one thing, there was no wall behind each basket. Instead, folding chairs for fans ran several rows deep. Cheerleaders tried to distract you, and opposing fans screamed at you. Because the ceilings were so high to accommodate thousands of bleacher seats, the court felt tiny, and the rims and backboards even more so.

Logan supposed he was more optimistic this year because, being on the consolation side of the Area Tournament bracket, they had played three games instead of just one. It gave them more of a chance to get used to a larger gym, not that SOU's compared to this.

Aside from the size of the Big House, there was much more to adjust to. Playing in front of a row of sportswriters along one side of the court was intimidating. The jumble of technology for scorekeepers and announcers between the two team benches could easily distract you from your coach's directions. Everyone from the small towns came to support their schools at the STATE TOURNAMENT, including high school classmates and elementary and middle school kids who wore team colors, painted their faces, held posters, and yelled obnoxiously anytime you had the ball.

Aside from the STATE TOURNAMENT, Logan had never played in a game with a scoreboard above center court. It always looked too heavy not to fall.

He watched the King-Marlow Hornets in their layup lines while sitting on the side, getting his foot wrapped by Coach Park. King-Marlow Public Schools consisted of two incorporated townships, King and Marlow, northeast of Tulsa. Logan didn't think it was fair that the two communities could combine into one Class B school, considering neither King nor Marlow was smaller than Nowhere. They had twice as many students with which to build a team and actually had twice as many players as Nowhere.

Of King-Marlow's seventeen players, five were permanent benchwarmers—the type to be put in during a blowout, where the crowd would go bonkers if they made a basket. The other twelve were interchangeable wings, ranging from five nine to five eleven. The key to King-Marlow's success this year had started with their first-year coach, Ray Blevins, who knew how to use their interchangeable lineup.

Chaos was their ally; an unrelenting full-court press created a frenetic pace only a team with twelve active players could sustain. It was the only way they could make it this far without a player over six feet tall.

Not only had they made it to the STATE TOURNAMENT for the first time in school history, but they had done so without losing a game at Districts, Regionals, or Area. Five straight wins after a 15-7 regular season made them the surprise of the season—aside from Nowhere's remarkable run from losing in Districts to making STATE without the best player in Class B.

It was a hell of a first-round matchup between two under-dogs. Coach Blevins was no doubt getting attention from larger schools by now. Coach Park would be envious, as he was every year.

Unlike other coaches whose teams made STATE year after year, Coach Park never got credit for Nowhere's victories. If he had this year, Logan hadn't heard much about it. He had been too self-absorbed, happy to take credit himself. Logan had never been one for the spotlight, but when folks peered at you with admiration rather than scrutiny, it felt nice.

Coach Park had gone on and on about King-Marlow's full-court press when they practiced on Tuesday. Since Logan had been kept to the sideline, he struggled to remember all the possibilities for breaking the press. He retained information better when he learned it hands-on.

Logan's sprained ankle was interrupting Coach Park's usual pre-game ritual, and if there was one thing a basketball coach or player needed, it was their pre-game ritual.

"What the hell did you do to it, anyway?"

"I was running through a pasture and tripped."

Coach stopped, pulling the tape tight. His other hand squeezed Logan's ankle, causing a nauseating ache.

"You were running through a pasture?"

"You know, playing games and stuff."

"No, Tramer. I don't know."

"We were just messing around, and there was a gopher hole."

"A gopher—" Coach shook his head while he continued wrapping Logan's foot. "You know what the problem is? You kids these days don't take anything seriously. Instead of focusing on the biggest game of your career, you're frolicking around in fields."

Logan laughed. The insult actually put him at ease.

"Don't worry, Coach," he said. "We're gonna beat them."

Coach pulled the last of the tape from the roll and pressed it against Logan's foot. His ankle was stiff and immovable.

"Let's get it done then," Coach said, pleased to see his starting center so confident.

Logan stayed confident as the game began. His height was advantageous in breaking the trap, as long as he kept himself between the pesky King-Marlow boys and any pass coming his way. When Alex or Doug was trapped in the backcourt, they quickly tossed it to Logan at center court. Logan then turned and threw it ahead to Sam or Marshal for a two-on-one layup. They broke the trap this way three times in a row, but Coach Blevins adjusted.

The Hornets trapped Logan at center court, forcing Alex or Doug to throw a more difficult cross-court pass to Sam or Marshal. Alex's passes were sharp and on target, but Doug had trouble against King-Marlow's interchangeable players. They were taller than him and just as fast. They intercepted two passes and deflected two others when Doug attempted to toss it over them. They scored on two of those possessions.

The game remained close as each team countered on the fly. Logan doubted Nowhere would have been able to keep up with all of Coach Blevins's defensive schemes if Kelvin hadn't returned.

The injured star player was an assistant coach on the team bench, something Nowhere had never had. The Devils took more timeouts than usual because Kelvin saw something that could help them win.

He suggested moving Doug out of the backcourt since he

was too short to make clean passes, and his speed would help when they broke the traps. Kelvin also told Coach Park it might help to move Logan's height to different areas of the court, so King-Marlow couldn't predict he would always dart to center court for the trap-breaking pass.

"Keep them guessing, keep them guessing," Kelvin repeated, and soon, Coach Park was saying it in every huddle.

When the pace of the game became too hectic, Kelvin made sure to make eye contact with every Nowhere player on the court and take a deep breath. The Devils slowed the pace, forcing King-Marlow to play offense and defense in the half-court. The Hornets struggled during these possessions. They weren't great outside shooters, and when they drove, Logan was there to contest their layups.

On offense, Nowhere didn't need to take advantage of Logan's size. At first, he was frustrated until he noticed Alex hitting every shot he took. The senior guard was on fire, as close to Kelvin as he had come since the injury. Eventually, King-Marlow threw double teams at Alex, and he found Logan in the post.

His passes were much smoother than usual. Every one of them hit Logan right where he could grab it and shoot without bobbling the ball.

King-Marlow slapped at his arms every time he caught a pass or shot. Although most of the fouls went uncalled, Logan was unperturbed. He had never been so focused. Apparently, Alex hadn't been either. His dribbling, defense, passing, and scoring were all tight and efficient. He even rubbed off on his little brother who started the second half for Sam because Mikey had an easier time breaking the press than the other sophomore.

Soon, the lead grew to double digits, and Nowhere fans erupted in excitement. Logan had refused to look at the crowd the whole game. He didn't want to see the faces of potential sacrifices to the Basketball Gods. But soon it became clear the Devils were headed to the semifinals.

Lives were in his hands, and he was coming through in the clutch.

"With great power comes great responsibility"—the line everyone remembered from the Tobey Maguire *Spider-Man* movie he'd seen two years ago. He was looking forward to the sequel this summer, and he could relate to it like never before. Logan felt like a hero.

As the clock wound down, he allowed himself to gaze into the crowd. He raised his arms and shouted, and they cheered in return. His dad was in the near bleachers, not the student section, where Emily, Jessica, and other high schoolers and middle schoolers from Holdendecker chanted in unison, crying goodbye to King-Marlow, but the nicer padded seats where families and important community members sat. Bill Tramer stood from his seat with an arm around Logan's mom, both cheering and pointing at him.

It was such a perfect image, Logan wondered if any of this was real. Maybe he had been dreaming since watching Kelvin's shin bend backward. A victory had never given him this feeling before. Logan wasn't just giving his team a chance to win the STATE CHAMPIONSHIP, but had also saved lives tonight. Not even Kelvin had not accomplished something so lofty.

FOURTEEN
THE MISSING

1

I_T WAS_ strange to step out of the Big House into broad daylight. Alex's blue eyes never did well in the sun, but today it was worse than ever—sharp pain stabbing at his eyes causing tears to blur his vision. He squeezed them shut and rubbed them again.

Sure, there were windows in the Big House, but they were high above. Down on the court, only the harsh interior lights— the false lights—reached them, and the locker room felt like a cave. Windowless and cold.

There was also the breath on the back of his neck. It hadn't gone away since he had made the wish Friday night, but it grew stronger during the game. The more he scored or passed like Kelvin, the more the presence clung to him, like an embrace. He sensed its lingering aftereffects but didn't mind it anymore. Even the smell wasn't so strong. Alex accepted it came with winning S_TATE._

Not only was he disoriented by the sun, but Nowhere's fans had gathered around to greet the team while they exited the arena, overstimulating him. Alex was surprised by how many people he didn't recognize. He had lived in Nowhere his whole life, yet some of these faces didn't match the names he had heard.

He watched Logan with envy. The tall son of a bitch was surrounded by people, standing among them like he was the best player on the team. Had no one seen Alex's shot-making, his passing, his stellar defense? He must have been invisible because hardly anyone came to congratulate him.

Then Letty Prospect found him.

She was crying, but not entirely happily. She squeezed her arms around him and kissed him with the wettest, snottiest kiss he had ever experienced. Her excitement was grief-stricken, tears of joy, pain, and loss.

Her brother had died less than a week ago. This was the first time Alex had seen her since the party Friday night, when they had made out by his Jeep. Allen's funeral was yesterday, but Alex hadn't gone, too focused on the playoffs.

He pulled back from her kiss and scanned the crowd to see if anyone saw them.

"Hello to you too," he said with an awkward laugh, wiping his mouth.

"That game was awesome. You kicked ass, Alex."

"Two more wins to go. I really feel like we're gonna do it."

"You will. You're too good not to."

Despite his embarrassment, it was nice to be acknowledged by at least one person as the true leader of the team, the reason they won.

"What are you going to do now?" she asked.

"I don't know. We usually watch the other games and then rest up for tomorrow morning."

"Can we do something tonight? You and me?"

"Uh, listen, Letty, I—"

His parents emerged from the crowd to save him.

"Let's catch up later."

"Later, like—"

She turned and saw Rob and Joanna Spruce behind her, waiting to greet their son.

"Of course. See ya."

Letty ran off, and Alex breathed a sigh of relief.

"Oh, honey, you were so good!" his mom said cheerily. But she always told him he did well even when he played poorly.

He waited for what his dad would say.

Rob Spruce looked skeptical for a moment. Then a smile crossed his face. "Damn, son," he said, pulling Alex into a hug. "Goddamn."

Alex was in shock. He scratched his face to keep his smile from looking too eager and waited for his dad to say more.

"And you," his dad yelled, pointing behind Alex.

Mikey broke from a huddle of congratulations and came over to the family.

"You're gonna be starting next game, boy." Rob ruffled his youngest son's hair. "Mark my words, son." He pulled Mikey into a hug that looked more intimate than the one he gave Alex. Of course, that was because he had given Mikey hugs his whole life so there was a natural comfort between them. Alex fought against the jealous feeling and focused on the *goddamn* his dad had given him. He had earned it.

2

He had always wondered why he and Mikey weren't closer. They were only two years apart. Most of the time it was a passing thought he didn't feel too strongly about, but sometimes, like now, as the two of them walked around downtown OKC after having dinner with their parents, he wished he had made more of an effort. It wasn't like Mikey made the effort either, Alex told himself. Mikey had never been a tagalong, always content to hang out by himself, and if he was being honest, Alex had always been offended by that.

"Can't wait to get my license," Mikey said as a lowrider passed, subwoofers making the pavement vibrate.

"How long until you're sixteen?"

"Only two months now."

"Nice."

Alex would turn eighteen in mid-May. He was one of only two out of fifteen seniors who would graduate at seventeen. The other being Will Roebuck.

His mood had soured since the moment with his dad. Having a moment like that only reminded him of the fact it had never happened before. Not Alex's junior year when he put up twenty-five in the Regional finals. Not the first game he started his sophomore year, or any of the games this year when he was hot from outside, knocking down all the available shots that came when Kelvin drew the attention of everyone on the court.

It took a *goddamn* wish to get Rob Spruce to tell him *goddamn*, while Mikey got their dad's love freely. Alex's little brother hadn't even played that well.

They found their way to Myriad Botanical Gardens. Rows of flowers and plants he couldn't name lined the walkways. Canopies of large leaves sprung from tall trees overhead. It would have been a nice place to bring Letty, he thought, feeling a little guilty he didn't hang out with her tonight. He could have skipped dinner with Mikey and their parents, but he hoped to receive more compliments from his dad. He didn't. Instead, Rob Spruce was mostly quiet, looking over the menu as he spit his dip into an empty plastic cup he had brought with him, getting glares from other patrons in the restaurant. Surprisingly, their server didn't say anything about it, and at least he went to the restroom to spit it out before the food arrived. Still, that smell lingered over their table as Alex attempted to eat his salmon.

"You really think I'll get the start tomorrow?" Mikey asked as they passed through the Crystal Bridge, a large greenhouse in the middle of the Gardens.

"Can't say I'm as certain of it as Dad seems to be. But you played better today, for sure."

"Thanks, Alex."

"Just don't settle, Mikey. You got a lot more potential that you're too scared to show."

"I'm not scared—"

"Next year, it's just you, Doug, and Marshal. Sam will be there too, but you're better than all those guys."

When they came out the other side of the Crystal Bridge, they descended a staircase and walked a path along the narrow waterway. Ducks floated in the same direction.

"I'm not scared," Mikey said, breaking the silence. "Maybe I just don't care as much as you."

"Clearly. You know, Mikey, you had an excuse last year but you've hit your growth spurt. Hell, you're taller than me. If you cared as much as I did my sophomore year, you'd put up at least fifteen a game."

"It's not all about scoring."

"It's the only way to be seen."

"Seen by who?"

Alex stopped abruptly and rubbed the back of his neck. They were beneath a bridge. A shadow fell across Mikey's face.

"What?" Mikey said.

"What do you mean, what?"

"You're smiling about something."

"Am I?"

"And why'd you stop walking?"

"You just don't get it, do you, Mikey? You're wasting your opportunity."

"Opportunity for what?"

A mother duck passed by with her duckling following earnestly.

"Don't you want to play college ball?"

Mikey let out an exhausted guffaw and shook his head. "Dude. What are you talking about? I barely want to play high school ball."

Alex scoffed and walked away, leaving his brother standing still. He was fed up with Mikey's inability to understand how important this moment was. He could be winning STATE alongside his big brother in the starting lineup, if he only cared.

"You're a lost cause," Alex called back, taking long strides until the evening sun slanted into his face when he stepped out from under the bridge.

"Alex, stop!" Mikey called from where he'd been left behind.

Alex was startled by the urgency in Mikey's voice. Annoyed, he said, "What the hell, Mikey?"

His little brother was a tall, scrawny silhouette beneath the bridge. "Th-there's something behind you."

"What?"

"Between me and you. It-it was following you."

A cold streak slivered through Alex. Could Mikey see the invisible force that had been haunting him?

"F-fuck you."

"I'm serious. And now it's—oh God—" The shadow of Mikey started backpedaling away from Alex.

Still, Alex saw nothing between them.

His little brother backpedaled too fast and fell hard on his ass. The loud whop had Alex thinking he had broken his tailbone, but Mikey made no sound. Not one of pain or fear. His silence unnerved Alex. He remained rooted, either incapable or unwilling to go into the dark beneath the bridge, like a troll waited there to eat him if he couldn't solve its riddle.

Mikey scrambled backward on his back, his long neck stretched upward as he stared at something only he could see.

Then came a sound—one Alex had only heard from his brother once before. He had been nine years old and they were messing with a beehive out in the woods behind their house. The bees spun around the long stick they were using until they wizened up. Alex managed to keep his distance from the attack, but Mikey got the bees inside his clothes. He jumped up and down, shrieking, and Alex wrestled him to the ground and tore his shirt off. Bees stung his hands but he didn't let up, next ripping away Mikey's shorts and underwear. Mikey had scrambled upright just as he finally did now.

Alex tore his feet from where they had rooted into the concrete path and ran.

"ALEX!"

He barely registered his little brother shouting his name in high-pitched panic.

Mikey ran so fast Alex didn't think he would catch him, the same way he had run naked toward their house with red whelps all over his body almost a decade ago. He had shrieked until he disappeared inside the house, and Alex wondered how long he would continue yelling this time. There was no house in which to escape. Nowhere to go that whatever chased him besides Alex couldn't reach him.

Then, suddenly, Mikey stopped on a dime, planting his feet next to each other so fast Alex thought his locked knees were sure to buckle.

But they didn't, and Alex stopped himself now, afraid to get any closer than the ten feet between them.

"Mikey?"

He faced away from Alex who took slow, deliberate steps

toward him. The tap of his feet echoed around the underside of the bridge until he came out the other side, the red line of evening against his shoulders.

Three more steps.

Right behind Mikey now, breathing down his neck.

"Mikey...you all right?"

His little brother turned and peered at him with glazed eyes, a twitchy smile on his face.

"We have to go," he said in a monotone unlike him.

"Go where?" Alex responded.

The twitchy smile widened. "Home."

3

Alex moved quickly to keep up with his brother. Mikey walked determinedly through the Gardens. Something significant had changed in him, and deep down, Alex knew what was happening to his brother.

He could hear Mikey's screams in his head. It chilled him as he saw a swarm of bees in his mind's eye, only half a memory as the bees seemed to circle in front of him in the darkening dusk. The silence didn't help but so far he had not managed to coax Mikey into saying anything else.

"We can't go home," Alex had tried. "Not until Saturday. After we win the chip."

"What do you need from the house," was another attempt. "Can't it wait until Saturday?"

"I'm not taking you anywhere," a third time. "Not until you answer me."

But each time Mikey ignored him and quickened his pace.

Finally, Alex's concern and fear couldn't equal the anger he felt as he thought about the way Mikey dismissed his dreams of playing college ball.

"I'm winning STATE, Mikey," he said as heat rose to his face. "And you're gonna play so well tomorrow that Coach has to start you on Saturday. I want you by my side, bro."

Mikey remained a few feet ahead of him, moving toward the staircase that led out of the Gardens.

"Do you hear me?" His eyes blurred. "I said I'm not going home!" He snatched Mikey by the arm, yanking him hard to face him. Mikey's shoulder shifted out of socket. "Oh shit!" Immediately, his anger turned to panic. "Mikey. Oh my god. I'm sorry, man. I'm—"

Mikey didn't seem to notice as his arm dangled by his side and one shoulder angled lower than the other.

At least, he stopped walking.

"I have to go home, Alex. Chip or no chip."

Alex softened. The calmness of his brother subsided his panic, even though he knew the calm demeanor wasn't a good thing.

"It's my wish, isn't it?" he asked.

Mikey's twitchy smile returned. "You played really well, brother. And could again. And again. All the way to Red Oak University."

He spoke in a stilted way but it was Mikey's voice, and it was Mikey's face looking at him, and Mikey's busted shoulder above his thin body. It was difficult to think there was anything wrong. Alex had to force himself to remember that Tim had left the team after his dad died, and that Emily Tramer had been in a wreck that killed Allen Prospect, and Allen's little sister had kissed him like he could save her from her grief.

"Why aren't you dead then?" he said out of nowhere, but Mikey expected the question.

"Is our home game ref dead? The history teacher?"

"Mr. Tune?"

"Is that little Amish boy dead?"

"What?"

"You know the one, brother."

Lightheadedness hit Alex. He held onto his little brother's busted shoulder for support. Mikey didn't seem to feel any pain.

"You knew what it would take, Alex. Why are you surprised? But to answer your question: it doesn't matter. Dead. Not dead. We all make the descent."

"The-the what?" Alex fumbled for what to say. He knew there was a right question to ask but couldn't find the fitting words.

Mikey whipped himself free of Alex's grip, his dangling arm swinging around with him, and powerwalked up the stairs.

The Amish boy...

Alex's mouth was dry. Of course, he knew who his brother was referring to.

Before the Fort Todd game in the Area Consolation Finals, Alex had been the first to school, even beating Coach Park. He waited by the outdoor court, putting up shots with the ball he kept in his Jeep. Alex was testing his skills, seeing if he truly was better than Kelvin Harris at basketball. He had hit ninety percent of his shots, but one clanged off the rim and bounced over the railing into the gravel parking lot, rolling to the feet of an Amish boy.

"Oh, hey there," Alex said. "Hit me."

The boy looked confused, his little hands in his pockets, his straw hat perched on his head.

"Um, pass?"

The boy picked up the ball and threw it to him. "Can I play?"

"Sure. Have you played basketball before?"

"With my cousins."

"Show me what you got."

Alex rebounded for the boy, who pushed the ball toward the basket but kept front-rimming it. Alex wasn't great at guessing little-kid ages, but the boy couldn't have been older than seven or eight.

"Move a little closer," he offered. "Right here."

The boy followed his commands but kept missing.

"You're gonna want to give it some arch. Don't aim straight for the rim. Up and over is your best shot."

Alex showed him an example, and the boy began to add some arch. He was small but managed to push the ball up and over the basket with consistency.

"I think you found your spot. You're on fire!"

The boy did a little dance with each made shot, and Alex wondered where he had learned it. When Coach Park showed up, Alex said he had to go.

"You can keep shooting if you want. Hell, keep the ball if you want."

The boy was still shooting—up and over—while Alex disappeared into the gym to help Coach carry things to the bus.

"But that's not my fault," Alex said, hurrying to keep up with Mikey. "My wish had nothing to do with us beating Fort Todd."

"We put 'em on the free throw line, Alex."

"And? They missed because of Logan. He wished for us to win."

"Did you not take advantage of those extra possessions in the fourth?"

"What? So I made some baskets. That doesn't mean I was as good as—"

Alex couldn't bring himself to say Kelvin's name out loud. He was embarrassed by his wish even though it excited him to play so well today. And it was true; he had been better during that fourth quarter against Fort Todd. He hadn't miss a single shot.

"Where are we going?"

"We need a car, don't we?"

Alex knew he should have forced Mikey to go with him to his teammates. They had to figure it out together.

But shame gripped him now—a hand to the back of his neck.

At least they were moving in the general direction of the hotel. Maybe they would cross paths with Logan or goddamn Will Roebuck.

Anyone but Kelvin.

Instead, they crossed with paths with someone who honked the horn of a familiar vehicle and waved at them cheerily, someone he did not expect to see driving Macy Goode's car:

Letty Prospect.

4

"What're you doing here?" he asked, not kindly. The last thing Alex needed right now was to deal with Letty. "Why're you driving Macy's car?"

He stood by the driver's side window, Mikey behind him. Letty leaned out, stretching her neck, like she expected him to lean down and kiss her. Her face was clear, no dry streaks of tears. She had put on eyeliner and lipstick. Despite his annoyance, he had to admit she looked good now that she wasn't a crying mess.

"She said I could borrow it in case you wanted to drive around town tonight," she said.

How the hell did she find us?

"Letty, I never agreed to that," he said. "We're a little busy here—"

"Perfect timing!" Mikey said in a gleeful voice, shoving his way next to Alex. "We needed some wheels."

"Is that right?" Letty said, matching his positivity. "Well, get in then."

"No, you don't understand," Alex said, then stopped. What could he tell her? That he had wished to be as good as Kelvin, and the wish came true, and now Mikey was what? transformed? possessed?

"What he means is we need to leave," Mikey said. "We have to go home tonight."

"Back to Nowhere?"

"Of course."

"We're not going anywhere," Alex said. "We need to rest for the game tomorrow."

"I'll take you!" Letty said. "I can have you in Nowhere before you can say, 'STATE CHAMPS.'"

The twitchy smile returned to Mikey's face. He knew Alex was going to agree to go, just as Alex knew it long before he could admit it to himself. The presence behind him whispered breathily on his neck. Not aloud but in a telepathic language only available to Alex and perhaps those who had been "chosen" in exchange for the fulfillment of his wish: *You did this, Alex. It's time to take responsibility for your actions.*

His mouth went dry. Whether the voice in his head was a guilty conscience or supernatural didn't matter. He was responsible for what was happening to Mikey. And if his brother was telling the truth, then Alex was responsible for the Amish boy too.

Dead. Not dead. We all make the descent.

Mikey had been speaking nonsense, but one thing was clear: he knew where the missing went. He would take Alex and Letty to them, and Alex would save his brother and the boy and Mr. Tune and whoever else.

"Fine," he said. "Get in the back, Mikey. On the driver's side." *So I can see you.*

His brother followed his instructions which Alex took as a good sign as he got into the passenger's seat.

Letty leaned over and kissed him hard. For a moment, he thought they were going to make out right there at the curb of a downtown street with Mikey in the backseat. His heart quickened, blood rushing downward. He was about to push her away when she settled back into the driver's seat and put the car into drive.

Mikey sat completely still behind her seat. Better posture than he'd ever had before. His limp arm lay across his lap.

"We need to fix your arm," Alex said, but he knew popping his shoulder back into its socket was a ways away.

"What happened?" Letty asked, leading them toward the interstate.

"So much," he said, and he decided to tell Letty everything.

5

The sky darkened quickly when they left the city, as if the light pollution had been what kept God from flipping the light switch and calling it a night. Alex didn't know how he felt about God, but he said a prayer anyway as he told Letty about the kitchen well.

He left out the part about wishing to be as good as Kelvin and, instead, offered a generic version, saying he made a wish to be better at basketball than he already was. He also didn't tell her that Allen had been a sacrifice for their winning ways but wondered if she inferred it from what he said about the other "consequences" for making the Devils' dreams come true.

If she did, she kept it to herself. In fact, Letty remained upbeat and cleareyed. Alex wondered what strange stage of grief this was.

Denial? Maybe he was in denial too.

Do you really think you can save him?

He had second-guessed himself—and second-guessed his second guess—many times. But they were well on their way to Nowhere and the closer they got the more confident he became.

"So, it doesn't straight up kill everyone it claims," she said at the end of his story, and he had never heard it put that way: everyone it *claims.*

"Nope," Alex said. "They're still alive. I can *feel* it. Mikey will take us to them, and then we can get 'em out of there. We don't have to let the fucking kitchen well win."

"The kitchen well? Is that what you call what's been granting y'all's wishes?"

"We had been calling it the Basketball Gods, like its sole purpose is helping us win STATE. But it's bigger than that. This whole thing is bigger than a STATE CHAMPIONSHIP."

"You sound like you're trying to convince yourself."

"Don't get me wrong. I'll be at the game tomorrow. I'm gonna lead my team to the title. No doubt. But life goes on after that, doesn't it? College ball? The NBA? A wife, kids. If I can figure out how to stop this thing from taking the people we care about, then I can...control it, maybe."

"Control it?" She took a long, thoughtful pause, then smiled ever so slightly. "You want to make more wishes, don't you?"

"No, no. Not really. I just...it felt good playing so well this morning. It felt like I was finally doing what I was meant to do. And, and-and I've had this feeling ever since I went to the well with Logan and Will. I think I'm *meant* to control it."

"Do you?"

"Yeah, definitely. This...sensation. I hated it at first. But now I understand."

"Good," she said with finality. "That's really great, Alex. I'm so proud of you."

He looked back at his brother for the hundredth time. Mikey

had been eerily quiet the whole drive. *Still there*, he thought as if one of these times he looked back Mikey would be gone. The presence on Alex's neck hadn't disappeared either. Telling Letty the whole story had made him look at everything in a new way. He knew how to stop the sacrifices just as he knew Mikey wasn't taking them to the Spruce family's double-wide.

Home.

Nowhere.

There could be only one place he was taking them.

"We're going back to that shitty abandoned house, aren't we, Mikey?" Alex finally asked as they came to where the plains met the forestland in the Choctaw Nation of Oklahoma. They turned south onto a local highway at a large four-way intersection. If they had continued eastward, they would reach Holdendecker in ten minutes. South took them straight through Cottonvale and later, about halfway between Cottonvale and Nashoba, they would turn onto another small highway, to the east again, and venture into the woods of Nowhere, where they would find the house he both wanted to return to and never wanted to see again.

Either way, he was no longer afraid of it.

You went into the well on your own, no one at the house with you, he reminded himself. *You're the only one of your teammates with the balls to do that. You were meant for this. Meant to be the one to control it.*

"Of course," Mikey said, his voice a whisper. He leaned his head against the window and stared up at the bright face of the moon. In the blueish nightlight, Alex could make out his brother's dazed look beneath heavy eyelids, like the closer they got to the destination the more Mikey became hypnotized.

"What's it like?" Letty asked.

Her face was a shadowy oval as she leaned away from her moonlit window like a vampire avoiding the sun. But, really, she wanted to stay as close as she could to him while still driving. He held her hand. It was cold. He cupped his other over it and leaned down and blew on her hand to warm it, his lips touching her soft skin.

"It's dark in the house," he answered. "Somehow darker inside than coming home after a party."

"And the well?"

"Deep. So deep a Maglite won't reach the bottom. Can you believe that? You could hide a bunch of bodies down there."

"Maybe someone did, once upon a time."

"Yeah, maybe. Maybe that's why it's cursed."

And why I have to save them.

He welcomed the tickling sensation behind him, there even when his back was pressed to the seat. Somewhere along the drive he had realized the presence wasn't whatever magic granted their wish and killed their people. It was that black magic's opposite. It was the Light. It had to be.

He was antsy to reach the house, ready to see where Mikey led them. A subconscious part of him—perhaps the part supported by the presence—knew where they were headed inside the house, but he couldn't quite bring it to the forefront of his mind. Instead, he emptied his thoughts. Breathed deeply as they pulled off Snakeback Road between the tall pines, where tire ruts were barely visible on the rarely trodden path.

A more traveled path lately.

It was the fourth time Alex had come here in the past three weeks, and his stomach bottomed out each time at the sight of the house. A crack in the remaining broken window glistened in the headlights, an unwelcome smile.

"Okay, Mikey," he said, opening the glove compartment to look for a flashlight. "Take us—"

Before Alex could say anything else, much less find a flashlight, Mikey darted from the car. Letty hadn't even fully stopped. The back driver's side door flung shut in response to the way he barged through it with his busted shoulder in his hurry. He rolled across the bald winter grass.

"Mikey!"

Alex's little brother climbed to his feet, dusted himself off, and walked determinedly toward the house.

Alex struggled to unbuckle his seatbelt, unaware of Letty calmly sliding her own off and placing the car in park. Finally, he pushed down on hard plastic and sprung from the passenger's seat, slamming out of the car with his shoulder, the same as his brother, the door springing closed on its own afterward. He ran for the broken screen door as Mikey threw it open and disappeared into darkness. Letty somewhere behind Alex, walking.

Walking—?

His mind only peripherally registered her casual trek as he disappeared into the house himself, the one remaining hinge on the screen door protesting the violent motions of the brothers. It slapped closed behind Alex as he saw the thin figure ahead of him fade around the corner, heading—*of course!*—to the kitchen well.

The complete dark hit him about the time he reached the far side of the front room, and Alex slammed into the wall to the left of the doorway. He grabbed onto the edge of the wall to keep from falling and propelled himself around and to the left.

Into the kitchen.

The slightest bit of light through the mud-caked window above the sink—*the* Light, maybe, what still followed Alex even now—and he saw Mikey vault one leg over the side of the well.

"NO!"

He realized now the well had no intention of keeping the "missing" alive. It only wanted to see them throw themselves to their death—

He had no chance of considering the timeline, that his and Doug's and Marshal's wishes were all made after Mr. Tune went missing

—Alex snatched Mikey by his loose shoulder bone and pulled him against the linoleum floor, inching away from the well from beneath his brother, who hissed like a cat and scratched Alex just below his eye, causing a bloody gash. It felt like his eye was dangling, but he could see through it despite the water pooling, so that couldn't be the case. His skin, maybe. Skin could certainly dangle.

"Goddammit, Mikey!"

Alex grabbed at Mikey's wrist to keep him from scratching again, and shimmied to his feet, pulling Mikey along with him.

The yowl of cats fighting emitted from Mikey's throat as he bit down on Alex's arm.

"GGAAAHHHH!!"

The pain sliced through him, white-hot. He grabbed Mikey by his hair and yanked his head back. Flesh tore away from his arm, along with his brother's grinding teeth. He was certain he felt some teeth break off and, if he'd had time to think anything else, would have feared that he broke Mikey's neck with how hard and fast he pulled him back.

Everything was instinctual as Alex wrapped both arms around his little brother, pinning his arms down, and picked him up and carried him backwards away from the well.

The screen door rattled as wind pushed against it, flowing into the front room where Alex dragged his brother toward that door, like the wind was urging him to take Mikey back to the well.

Just get him out of the house, he told himself.

Just get him—

"It's everything I imagined it would be."

The voice startled Alex, but it made Mikey stop yowling and

writing in his arms. The brothers were both still as they watched Letty do several waltz spin turns around the front room, running her finger over the back of the dusty couch.

Alex had forgotten all about her.

She looked at him gleefully, now leaning against the opening from the front room to the hallway, rooms down one side, the kitchen the other way.

It hit him, and he should have known all along why Letty was in Macy's car waiting for them. He took another step toward the exit, and Mikey planted one foot to resist but didn't wriggle against him.

"Isn't this place wonderful?" Letty asked like they were newlyweds at an open house.

"Letty. We're going outside now. You, me, and Mikey."

"Sorry, Alex," she said. "I don't think we are."

Suddenly, Mikey swung his elbow right into Alex's cheekbone, cracking it.

Alex stumbled back, a numb sting met by the sensation of half his face feeling like it was caved in and the other half feeling like a potato peeler had been taken to it. He both wanted to touch his face and not touch it. He chose the latter, although nothing felt like a choice in the rush of the moment. His head swam, and he couldn't see through the eye above the broken cheekbone and barely saw through the blur of the other.

When he had the semblance of a thought again, Alex panicked, seeing Mikey running off and diving into the well in his mind's eye.

Instead, Mikey snatched him by one arm, and someone else —*Letty, it's fucking Letty, how could it be Letty?*—gripped his other, digging her nails into the groove on the inside of his bicep. Alex screamed as he was pulled to the floor, the pain sawing up and down his body as he struggled to regain any cognizant ability, let alone enough strength to resist them.

"Let go!" Alex cried out, the way Mikey used to when Alex pinned him down and "piano-keyed" his ribs. Big brother shit. Now he was the little brother, unable to shake the two latest consequences of his wish despite how much stronger he was than them. He couldn't get any leverage from the way they pinned him down.

"It's okay, brother," Mikey said, his voice as stilted yet calm as it was hours ago. "We just need you to relax."

"If you had let him go, it wouldn't have to do this," Letty added. Her voice lacked any empathy, and Alex preferred Mikey's, even if it was false.

She laughed a little. "You really thought you were the Chosen One? It just liked the smell of your skin is all. It followed you out of here because of the taste of your sweat. That's all, Alex."

He jerked suddenly, hoping to catch them off guard but the two were gargoyles made of stone.

"Easy," Mikey said. "Don't listen to her. She's just mad her piece of shit brother died. But what did you expect, Letty? We all make the descent."

"We do," she agreed, looking at Mikey like it was just the two of them there. "And I can't wait to see him again. I hate him but I love him too. He's my big brother. He's waiting, isn't he?"

"Not waiting. Praying. Like we all will be soon." The muscles of Mikey's bulging neck strained tightly as he turned to look at Alex. "Except for you. Not for a while, brother. Not for a while still."

"So just chill out," Letty said. "Let it happen and you'll go on with your little life. Sorry, we'll never fuck, Alex. Sorry we'll never have children and never live right here in our trashfuck little house in our trashfuck little town, wishing we could be anywhere else. But, hey. Maybe you'll wish for that next."

The room around him breathed in and out, blackness

coming on the inhales, the semblance of a silhouetted dark on the exhale, like the dilation of his pupils followed the breath. It didn't breathe against his neck. All he felt back there was the fabric of the dirty couch. Its breathing was in him and around him, and as the darkness came and went, he saw a shadow approach from the kitchen, coming around the corner of the hallway, taking its time toward him. Enough time for the dark to breathe in and out several more times, from pitch black to the approaching shadow.

Pitch black.

Approaching shadow.

Pitch black.

Approaching shadow.

Pitch black.

A final exhale.

Before him was an empty black hole of a face.

He stopped resisting the weight of the gargoyles.

He could sense the presence's need for him. It was as strong as Alex's own desire to be seen by the fans. He was seen now—by whatever this was.

Letty and Mikey let go of him, and the presence clung to him. Embraced him.

It held him to the floor. It was heavier than Mikey and Letty collectively. A heavy shadow. Its arms around him like a weighted belt, holding him to the ground.

Then he no longer felt held down. He no longer felt the floor.

Alex floated.

And the presence floated with him.

FIFTEEN

WHATEVER HAPPENS

1

No celebrating took place Thursday night. No team dinner, no playing cards or watching an NBA game. Their semifinal matchup on Friday would also be at nine a.m., and after watching the West Archer Dusters dominate the Alabaster Bats, they would need all the rest they could get.

Unfortunately, Logan couldn't sleep. He buzzed from their victory, specifically the way the crowd showed him love.

"Is that how you felt every game?" he asked Kelvin.

His friend had nearly fallen asleep, but his long, quiet breaths shortened, and he smacked his lips before answering. "Everyone enjoys being celebrated. But not even I know what it's like to win it all. That feeling of everyone staring at you with passion or envy. Legend status, man."

"I remember how I was looking at West Mann last year. Those runner-up medals were uncomfortable and itchy."

"Something tells me the championship ones aren't."

"I wish you were out there, dude." Logan wasn't sure he believed himself.

"Can you say that again, but at the bottom of the well this time?" Kelvin laughed to make it clear he was joking, but the laugh was too big.

"I'm afraid to make more wishes," Logan said, as if justifying his hesitation to wish for Kelvin's healing.

"No sweat, man. I get it. Actually, I've been thinking about that."

"Oh yeah?"

"How could I not? You left out the most important part the other day."

"The consequences...sorry, I-I—"

"It's all good, Logan. Since last night, though, I can't stop thinking about what you said. I mean, think about all the people who come to the games. They're all at risk."

Logan lay in the dark, staring at the ceiling. His eyes adjusted enough to turn everything around him blue. He still didn't look at Kelvin. His guilt seemed to never go away completely, which made him angry.

"Why are you telling me this?" Logan asked.

"Well, I had an epiphany after that."

"An epiphany?"

"Yeah. Everyone who's died so far had some underlying reason. Like, they were really old, had health problems, or were reckless, like Allen. Think about it. If you were betting on which one of our classmates would die in a car accident, who would be your first choice?"

"Allen Prospect. Makes sense," Logan said.

"I'm not trying to upset you or make you feel guilty. How the hell could you have known the wish would work, much less have consequences? I'm saying this because I think we can relax. Our parents, the girls we love—I don't think they're at risk."

"You're saying it only takes people that are what? Near death?"

"In a manner of speaking, yeah."

Logan hadn't told Kelvin about Mr. Tune, but it was possible that his history teacher wasn't dead. Betty Bromide had only assumed her own missing person from Green River was dead, but perhaps Mr. Tune, like Dale Jennings in 1990, sensed the curse of the kitchen well and left town. Wasn't that what Tim did? Logan could see Mr. Tune bailing the same way after talking to the ref from the Colesville game.

Is the kitchen well a curse?

He hated to think about his wish that way.

He rolled onto his side, facing away from Kelvin. He could feel his friend's warmth from the other side of the bed, even though they made sure to keep at least six inches between them.

"No homo," Kelvin had joked the first night, when awkwardly establishing their bed-sharing boundaries.

Normally, Logan would have hated the extra body warmth because he always ran hot. But in that moment, he was comforted by Kelvin's heat. It crossed the six inches between them and pulsed against Logan's bare back. He needed it. Now that the adrenaline from the game was subsiding, he felt defeated.

"West Archer isn't King-Marlow," he admitted. "I don't know if we can beat them."

"You can," Kelvin said. "You will."

"Without the magic?"

"Maybe it's all magic."

"What?"

"I lied to you last night...I don't think my injury was an accident. It was fate. It was meant to happen because whatever is out there—beyond us—the same thing fulfilling your wish—it isn't all good. It can be cruel."

"Sure, but Kelvin, the rules of the well are clear—"

"Fuck the rules. It's the same reason it's been taking people who were already 'near death.' It took my leg because I was scared."

"Dude…"

"I'm serious. I knew I would let everyone down. Our team. College ball. I was afraid I would fail, like I did against West Mann."

"Are you kidding? You were awesome. We failed you."

"I saw the trap coming. Do you remember? Thirty seconds left. I saw those boys coming for me and could've made my move before they reached me. But I was too scared to take the shot, so the Basketball Gods—or whatever it is—decided to take my leg. If I wasn't gonna step up and earn my God-given talent, then what was the point?"

"That's bullshit—"

"I'm saying this for a reason, Logan. My point is, whatever happened, whatever *happens*, it's not your fault, man."

Like every late-night conversation with a friend, this one ended abruptly. Logan could have argued with Kelvin more, but he felt relieved.

Maybe there was no alternate dimension where Kelvin was leading them to the championship, where Logan had never set that perfect screen, where he had never played a prank on Will or made a wish himself. There was no other dimension where Bird and Tim's dad and Allen Prospect were still alive.

Maybe Fate could be as cruel for some as it was awe-inspiring for others. Things played out the way they were meant to, regardless of how Logan played on the court. Maybe… maybe not.

He stayed up all night thinking about it.

2

The next morning felt like the cold February days Logan thought were behind them. He hadn't brought his Lakers jacket. Goosebumps rose on his arms while he boarded the bus. He wore his short-sleeve Nowhere Devils t-shirt over his jersey, with breakaway pants over his game shorts. Aside from changing into his basketball shoes, he was ready for the game.

Logan hadn't eaten anything that morning, despite Kelvin returning to the room with a pile of fruit and toast from the continental breakfast.

"Too nervous," Logan had said. "Last thing I need is to throw up on the court."

"Where's that confidence you had yesterday, Tramer? Y'all can beat those cornfed motherfuckers outright. I'm telling you."

The West Archer Dusters hadn't made the STATE TOURNAMENT in the past two years, so Logan and the Devils had no on-court experience with them. He had read plenty about the team from No Man's Land in the paper and seen how good they were for himself yesterday.

West Archer often bred great teams out in the Oklahoma panhandle. It was the middle of nowhere, even more so than Nowhere, but despite that, West Archer was well-known. Compared to East Archer and the rest of the panhandle, the land was rich and fertile. The town had been dubbed—or dubbed itself—*America's Garden of Eden* and could certainly make a case for it.

The Dusters had made the STATE TOURNAMENT twenty-three times in the past thirty years—more than any other team in Class B—and had won STATE nine times. Their most recent championship had come Logan's freshman year, when Nowhere lost in Area.

West Archer had no players left from that team, but this

year's squad had shooters at every position. They didn't have any seniors, so maybe Nowhere's experience could make up for Kelvin's loss—still, they would have to win convincingly.

Logan was starting to convince himself they could do it, if Alex's hot streak continued. He had never seen his teammate hit so many shots in a row or make such crisp passes, like he had against King-Marlow. If they could win by ten or more, it would be enough. Alex's offense and perimeter defense, combined with Logan's aggression in the paint on both ends, could get them there.

Logan had been the first on the bus, followed by Kelvin, Doug, and the underclassmen. Coach Park bounced onto the bus, energized and ready to go win STATE. What no one knew was Superintendent Walker had chosen not to pass on what he had learned from Brother Maxwell: Julia Reed was dead. He wouldn't tell anyone until after the boys won STATE. And Coach Park awoke this morning, finally deciding he was done with Julia's teasing. She couldn't even be bothered to show up for the STATE TOURNAMENT, so good riddance; no way was he going to leave his wife for her now.

Coach plopped into the driver's seat and cranked the engine. It roared loudly enough that they wouldn't hear much beyond the seats around them.

Logan sat behind Kelvin; Doug was across the aisle. They were waiting on Marshal, Alex, and Mikey. Logan felt a chill that he worried wasn't the cold snap.

Finally, Marshal arrived, looking panicked, confirming Logan's gloomy intuition.

Coach asked him something. Marshal gestured with his hands when he answered.

Coach rose and jabbed his finger into Marshal's chest. "You better not be screwing with me, Lovegood." His voice carried all the way to the back of the bus.

Marshal followed suit, his voice rising into a comically high-pitched warble. "Honest to God, Coach!"

Coach Park sighed, defeated. He started the bus before Marshal had found a seat, and Marshal almost fell into Logan's lap before sitting next to him. Doug leaned over from across the aisle. Kelvin poked his head around the seatback.

"What the hell?" Kelvin asked. "Where's Alex?"

"Me and Dylan's room is adjoining with Alex and Mikey. You know, we have one of those doors between us. So, we've been opening it every morning so we can shoot the shit. But when I opened it up, Alex and Mikey weren't there—"

"Maybe they just—" Logan cut himself off. There was no *maybe* because the Spruce brothers weren't on the bus now as they headed to the Big House.

"I thought they'd gone down for breakfast, so I went and looked for them," Marshal said. "But they weren't there either."

"Oh no…" Doug leaned against the back of Sam Turner's seat. "Please, God, no."

Sam glanced back at him, feeling the top of Doug's head through the seatback leather. The sophomore shook his head, annoyed, like he'd been ignoring the upperclassmen's weird secrecy since the playoffs started.

Kelvin put a finger to his lips and then waved Doug to slide closer. Doug looked like he had the flu. His forehead glistened, and his skin went ashen. He followed Kelvin's command, though, and the four of them whispered in the aisle with their heads almost colliding.

"I thought about telling Walker since he's down the hallway," Marshal continued. "But he would just tell their parents. Dylan was curious, so I just blurted out this lie about finding a note in their room, saying they had a family emergency. When he asked to see it, I told him to fuck off, but then slipped back into their room and forged a note. But Coach didn't ask to see it just now. He's really pissed."

"Of course, he is," Doug said. "Our best remaining player is gone."

"Chill, Dougie," Kelvin said. "Everything is fine. Our goal is the same."

"What're you talking about?" Doug said. "Nothing is fine. Alex and Mikey are missing. Just like Mr. Tune."

"What do you mean, Mr. Tune is missing?"

"He's not," Logan said. "I mean, we don't know for sure he is. It's not like anyone else has gone missing as a consequence for the wish. He may have just left town because the deaths were bothering him."

"What about that guy at Green River?" Doug blabbered, raising his voice until the others shushed him. Then, he whispered: "No one ever found that guy, right?"

"Forget it, Dougie," Logan said. "That doesn't matter right now."

Marshal glared at him. "Of course it matters—"

"We won without the wish last game. You see? There's no sacrifice because the wish wasn't involved."

"Unless we're wrong about that part."

"We're not, Marshal," Kelvin said. "Logan's right. The plan works. Alex probably got scared and made his little brother leave the city with him. The same way Mr. Tune got scared. Hell, the same way Tim did too, after his dad died." He added quickly, "Understandably."

Kelvin didn't even give Logan a questioning glance about the missing. His best friend had his back which made Logan feel guilty about not mentioning Mr. Tune and the Colesville referee to him.

"Nothing has changed," Logan said. "The plan is the same."

"We lose on purpose," Marshal said.

"We win without the magic," Kelvin corrected.

Doug raked his hands over his face.

Marshal scoffed. "Without Alex and Mikey, we're down to six players. Jack Ward's our only guy off the bench for fuck's sake."

"Then it's time for your brother to step up," Logan said. "He ain't no normal freshman anymore."

"Is Dylan gonna have a hot streak like Alex? That's the only reason we beat King-Marlow and you know it."

"You *can* win," Kelvin said. "Trust me. You have the experience over West Archer. And the size advantage. That goes a long way in the semis when everyone's tired and nervous. Their shot-makers may not be shot-makers this close to the title. Word?"

Marshal shrugged. "I guess."

"We at least have to try. We have a responsibility to the community to go out there and try and win before we give up."

"A responsibility." Marshal guffawed. "Right..." He paused and shook his head and then said, "Okay, we'll try. Of course, we will. But don't forget that losing on purpose *is* our second option. And we have to take it if it's the only one left. *Word?*"

He sneered the final word at Kelvin, who ignored his sarcasm and nodded, putting his flattened hand out between them, palm down.

"What do you think, Dougie?" Logan said, attempting to bring him back into the fold. He could tell the junior was about to crack and wondered what had happened with Mal, thinking about her broken arm.

Not now, he told himself. *You can't think about that if you want any chance of winning.*

"I don't know, man..."

"The way I see it," Logan said, "we just have to stay up by at least two possessions when we get into the second half. In the fourth quarter, if we can get up by six or more, there'll be no risk at all. It's not much, y'all."

For a moment, Doug put his hands together in front of his face like he was praying, and Logan wondered how long Kelvin would be waiting with his arm stretched out between them. But, quickly, Doug opened his eyes and repeated Logan's words, "It's not much…" He took a relaxing breath. "We can do it." He put his hand over Kelvin's, then Logan swallowed theirs with his own.

"If y'all say so," Marshal said, adding his hand to the pile.

Kelvin smirked. "On three."

3

While Coach Park wrapped Logan's ankle, Rob Spruce marched straight for him, his wife running to keep up. Logan had always struggled to picture Rob Spruce as a former star basketball player because he carried himself like someone who had never dribbled a ball before. But now Logan could see it.

In his anger, Rob Spruce moved with a confident swagger, like he was dribbling a ball between his legs.

"Where are my boys?" he demanded accusatorily, as if Coach would have kicked him off the team.

Coach Park rose from wrapping Logan's ankle, the roll of tape in his hand. A long strand coiled over Logan's foot, like rope piling outside the well the night he pranked Will.

"They couldn't be here," Coach Park said, confused. "Marshal said it was a family emergency."

"A what?" Rob Spruce's face turned red. He spotted Marshal shooting on the court and stormed toward him.

Coach dropped the tape and ran to stop him, but Rob had already reached Marshal and grabbed him by the collar of his jersey. "Where the fuck are they?" he shouted.

"I don't know! They left a note, man."

Coach tried to de-escalate the situation rather than jump between the parent and his player, but at the sound of her son's frantic voice, Marshal's mom saw what was happening and ran over bleacher seats, yelling, "Let my son go, Rob! I will fucking kill you!"

Logan was reminded of the Kemps storming the court during the Nashoba game in Regionals.

Joanna Spruce tapped on her husband's shoulder. "Okay, Rob. Let him go."

"You're fucking lying," Rob spat into Marshal's face.

Marshal raised one arm. "Hand to God, dude." Of course, he didn't believe in God, but Rob didn't need to know that.

Joanna looked terrified as Emma Lovegood reached the floor and stomped toward them. Logan remained seated, not wanting to screw up his tape job. Not that he was in a rush to get in the middle of the skirmish.

"Easy, Em!" John Lovegood called after his wife, trying to catch up, and Logan only remembered then that John and Rob had both been on the 1979 Nowhere team who almost made STATE.

Joanna Spruce slid out of the way, wanting none of Emma —formerly—Kemp. Emma jumped on Rob's back, wrapping her arms around his neck in a chokehold. He still didn't let go of Marshal's jersey, and her attack freaked out Marshal who scrambled to pull away from Alex's dad, ripping the collar of his jersey in the process. That was when Coach Park finally did something other than calmly ask Rob Spruce to let the teenager go. He pulled from behind Emma and John Lovegood pulled behind him and it was a strange, almost-comically intimate sight of the Nowhere adults wrestling.

It wasn't until one of the game's refs made it to the court and ran toward them, blowing his whistle, that Rob let go of

Marshal like this had been a scuffle during the game and the whistle was king. The group of adults fell onto each other like a dogpile of players who had just won STATE.

The entire thing put Logan at ease. He laughed along with Kelvin who was now next to him on the sidelines. The fight was broken up, and Coach came over to finish taping his ankle.

"Well, that'll get the blood pumping," Kelvin said.

"Fucking parents," Coach said under his breath.

Rob and Joanna Spruce were escorted out of the Big House by the referee but mostly left of their own accord to find their sons.

Watching them leave made it difficult for Logan to put Alex out of his mind. He knew they were missing, just like Mr. Tune and Dale Jennings from Green River. He didn't know how, since no wish had been granted during the King-Marlow game in the first round, but he could sense the truth of it. He caught sight of Will Roebuck in the crowd who had watched the skirmish and seemed to be counting the players now. He locked eyes with Logan and gave him a long, suspicious look.

Logan wanted to flip him off. How dare Will think Logan wouldn't lose on purpose if he had to. Of course, he would.

But what if losing isn't enough? What if it just makes the sacrifice go missing instead of killing them immediately?

His heart was racing, the moment of easy laughter gone.

What if it's like Aunt Joss? She didn't die immediately but then...

Coach gave the tape a final press against Logan's ankle, and he and Kelvin helped him to his feet. Before Logan ran to the court, Coach put his arm around him and leaned in close. "You're the only senior left now, Logan. Go out there and lead your team."

"That's right," Kelvin said over his shoulder.

"I got you, Coach."

Kelvin slapped him on the ass, and Logan joined his team for layup lines.

On the other side of the court, the Dusters didn't bother with layups. All twelve of their players pulled up from three. Their best player buried every one of his.

Warmups isn't the game, Logan reminded himself, but he felt intimidated. He was too big and clumsy to chase guys around the three-point line. He was comfortable in the paint on offense and defense, but not so much anywhere else on the court.

"What the hell?" Marshal said, holding his ripped collar. His chest was exposed down to the bottom of his pecs.

"This is getting too crazy," Doug said.

The three of them were next to each other in the layup line, and Logan held the ball and paused as the underclassmen waited on the other side, throwing their arms up in frustration.

"We got this, guys," he said. "We can beat them as long as we can get them off the three-point line."

"I nearly got murdered by Alex's dad," Marshal said.

Doug added, "And now he's gonna go home and find both of his sons lying on the slab, cold and naked, their faces—"

"What the fuck, Dougie?" Marshal said, and Logan was also disturbingly surprised by the specificity of Doug's imagination.

"Alex and Mikey aren't dead," Logan insisted. "Just spooked. We didn't need the wish last time. And we won't need it today."

"What if it doesn't matter?" Doug asked.

Logan wanted to slap him. "Get your shit together, Dougie. And, Marshal, you don't need to worry about some big, scary has-been."

Both of the juniors laughed a little at the insult to Alex's dad.

"Two more games. That's it. Then it's all over."

"Yeah, yeah-yeah," Doug said, nodding furiously. "You're right. You're right. Let's do this."

"Marshal?"

Marshal nodded reluctantly.

"Okay," Logan said. "Now let's send these assholes back to No Man's Land."

4

They huddled up at the bench before the starting lineup announcements.

Kelvin prodded Logan with his crutch. "You're gonna have to leave the key today, big man."

"Switch everything," Coach Park said in agreement. "Even you, Logan. Switch and stay on them. Make them put it on the floor. They can shoot, but they're not the best drivers or passers."

"Watch out for the offensive rebounds," Logan added. "I may not be down there to get the board."

"We got you, big man," Doug replied.

"This is it, Dylan," Marshal said. "This is why you stay ready."

His freshman brother looked scared. Logan bumped him with his shoulder playfully.

"Just play hard, and you'll be all right," he said.

Dylan nodded.

Soon, the game began. Despite his reservations, Logan managed to stay with his man. West Archer put him in every play, assuming that if he was switched onto a smaller scorer, he wouldn't be able to keep up. The problem was, they didn't want to drive by Logan. They wanted to jack threes. His height made their shots more difficult. Even West Archer's best player couldn't hit shots over Logan's outstretched arm.

Logan's confidence centered him. He felt like a different man—one who never stumbled, as quick as he was strong. Logan even found himself talking trash after the West Archer shooter missed his third three in a row.

"This ain't warmups," he shouted.

The shooter huffed on his way back on defense.

Nowhere took their time on offense, using their size and experience. They not only got the ball inside to Logan, but also knew how to use their elbows when the referees weren't looking and when to argue a call so the ref would call a soft foul the next time down.

Though only a sophomore and in the biggest game of his life, Sam Turner was hustling to get to shooters and knocked down the open shots West Archer intentionally funneled to him. Dylan managed to stay invisible on offense, darting from corner to corner and sneaking inside for the occasional offensive rebound. On defense, he was above average. He was nearly the same size as his older brother, just much skinnier, and fast, hustling to contest every shot near him.

Nowhere led by eight at halftime, and Logan started to believe they were going to win it on their own.

In the second half, West Archer adjusted. Rather than include Logan in their offensive actions, they exiled his man to the opposite corner of the court, practically out of bounds. Meanwhile, the Dusters set their screens and ran handoffs on the other side of the court, freeing up their shooters just enough to start making shots.

As hard as the rest of the Devils were playing, without Alex, Kelvin, or even Mikey, no one was above five-ten, so they couldn't contest the way Logan could.

Logan hated how useless he had become, watching their lead shrink from eight to five to four to two, then one. For every two-pointer West Archer gave up, they made a three to close the gap. It was becoming a game of math Nowhere was going to lose.

Near the end of the third, Logan forced the issue, sprinting to involve himself in the play, leaving his man by the out-of-bounds line. West Archer's star player made the cross-court pass to the guy who conveniently stood inbounds now and knocked down an open three to put the Dusters up by two.

"What the hell are you doing, Tramer?" Coach Park yelled, further frustrating him.

Logan threw his hands up. "Are y'all gonna start playing defense or what?" he shouted at his team.

"You're the one leaving your man open," Marshal responded.

"Only because someone has to stop those other boys."

"Guys, guys," Doug said, "calm down. We got this."

But they didn't.

While the game tightened, old habits crept up on offense: rushed shots and bad passes. West Archer stole the ball from Sam and sprinted up the court, stopping behind the three-point line to knock down a shot. Logan was afraid to look at the scoreboard when the quarter came to an end.

Sam and Dylan sat quickly to catch their breath while Coach Park argued a call with one of the referees.

Marshal tugged on Logan's jersey before he could reach the bench. Logan had hoped to ignore their circumstances and push for the win, but Marshal said, "We're down four."

"So?" Logan said.

"So, that's it, right?" Doug said.

"I'm afraid so," Marshal replied.

They looked to Logan for the final call. He craned his head back to see the score.

"It's not insurmountable."

"It's the fourth quarter, Logan," Doug said softly. "It's too risky."

"If we go for it, the well is gonna help us," Marshal said, his tone unkind. "It's obvious. If you can't see that, you're blind."

Who does he think he is? "It's easy for y'all to say," Logan snapped. "Y'all got another year."

"It's just a game, dude—"

Logan shoved Marshal whose ass smacked hard against the floor. A gasp rose from the crowd. If they had been distracted by conversation or nachos before, they certainly weren't now.

Logan barely registered the crowd's reaction. His vision narrowed onto Marshal's smug face, which turned to surprise, followed swiftly by his own anger. Marshal popped up and ran at Logan.

Doug got between them and shouted, "Stop! Stop!"

His voice jarred Logan from his blackout state. Logan backed away.

Emily and Jessica stared at him. His parents had risen from their seats with concern. Coach Park and Kelvin stopped talking and peered at them.

Embarrassment broke through Logan's anger. He realized this moment was worse than losing. His heart settled. His head cleared.

"You're right," he finally said. "We can't risk it."

Coach yanked him to the bench. "Sit the hell down, Tramer." The bench was cold. "This isn't the time to start blaming each other. We're in this shit together, goddammit."

Marshal still looked pissed.

Kelvin gave Logan a supportive pat on the leg. His best friend knew what they'd been fighting about. Kelvin looked guilty, like it was his fault they had to lose on purpose.

Logan wanted to tell him that was ridiculous, and when they started the fourth quarter, he thought about what Kelvin had said last night: *Whatever happened. Whatever happens. None of it is your fault.*

It angered him to watch Sam and Dylan be the only ones trying on defense. When Marshal airballed a wide-open shot, Logan wanted to hit him all over again. Doug bounced the ball off his foot, and Logan felt a strong desire to kick the ball into the stands.

But they did what they had to do.

Nowhere was playing so much worse to start the quarter that the crowd murmured in confusion and Coach Park berated them openly, calling them quitters. He seemed to think they were screwing up because of a petty feud. Logan supposed it wasn't the worst thing that he had shoved Marshal to the floor. It gave them the perfect excuse to blow the game on purpose.

But if winning STATE made them legends, what did losing on purpose make them?

Logan wished he could tell the crowd they were doing this for them, that they were making the ultimate sacrifice to save lives. He made the mistake of looking at his parents again. They had a much different expression than the last game's fourth quarter. It was the kind of disappointment parents were supposed to hide from their children.

West Archer only led by three because Sam and Dylan's hustle had caused a turnover, and Sam had made a layup on one possession. So Marshal and Doug started to freeze them out on offense.

Mal shouted insults at Doug. Not only did she seem to hate him, but he wouldn't give her little brother the ball when it was clear he was the only one who wanted to win. Boos would come soon enough. Logan could sense it.

Then West Archer's star player went for a rare layup when Sam ran him off the three-point line. Logan pretended like he was running to block the shot, but he moved much too slowly to get there in time.

As the West Archer star drove into the open lane, he fell and screamed.

For a second, Logan's heart stopped. He imagined the guy's leg snapping like Kelvin's. Instead, the guy rose into a sitting position, grabbing at his stiff legs, both feet pointed skyward. His calf muscles tightened in a horrible-looking cramp. Logan wasn't sure he had ever seen both legs cramp at once.

Watching his teammates carry him to the bench excited Logan. *Even now, the Basketball Gods are trying to make my wish come true.* It was like the wish hadn't realized the boys wanted to lose.

They came down on offense and went through the motions of running a play. They couldn't resort to tossing the ball back and forth like Fort Todd. Instead, they took bad shots and turned it over with untimely passes. Marshal feigned like he was going to drive, and one of the refs blew his whistle.

A phantom call, Logan thought, amused.

The foul put Marshal at the free-throw line. He tossed up as bad a shot as he could without it looking too obvious, and it banged in.

Logan shifted his weight. They were only down by two points.

Marshal threw up—and that's what it looked like, a regurgitation of a shot—his second free throw. Once again, it rattled around and fell through the hoop.

One point.

"What're you doing?" Doug whispered while they ran back on defense.

The Nowhere fans shifted from confused muttering to chants of "D UP! D UP! D UP! D UP!"

"I was trying to miss," Marshal said.

"Just let 'em score," Doug whispered.

Each of them faked like they were playing defense and watched their man drive past them. Two more West Archer players fell in pain.

It wasn't just their legs cramping but their arms too. Their fingers stiffened, somehow straight *and* twisted. Their thighs spasmed. Creases in their calves indented their skin, like smiles held for too long.

The ref finally blew his whistle when the ball rolled out of bounds and returned to Nowhere. West Archer fans held their breath, and their coaches ran onto the court. Teammates helped them off the floor while benchwarmers took their place in the lineup.

Logan huddled up with the others. He didn't care that Sam and Dylan were there too.

"Hold the ball," he said.

"For the last shot," Sam agreed.

"No," Logan said, feeling like he wasn't being himself by saying it. "We just hold the ball."

Sam looked confused and was about to speak when he became distracted by a third West Archer player falling to the floor.

The guy couldn't even cry out in pain. His jaw locked, and his body curled in jagged, awkward angles. Now West Archer fans were yelling from the stands like it was a conspiracy.

They pulled the fourth player from the court, leaving the Dusters with one starter and four bench players. Jack Ward clapped encouragingly from the bench while Nowhere inbounded the ball with two minutes left.

Coach Park stared at the West Archer bench, where the four boys writhed, their cramps shifting up and down their bodies. The toothpick he chewed on during every fourth quarter fell out of his mouth.

"Kansas!" Kelvin yelled over the nearby commotion, taking Coach's spot in playcalling. "Take your time."

Kelvin was pretending, for the Nowhere fans' sake, that they were going to run a play to win the game, but Logan also wondered if Kelvin meant it, if his best friend wanted them to go for the win.

Whatever happened. Whatever happens. None of it is your fault. But wasn't it?

Weren't Logan, Marshal, and Doug responsible for resisting the magic?

They ran through the motions of one of Kelvin's favorite plays.

"Kansas" was designed for Kelvin, and Alex had run it lately, but now Marshal held the ball, with a chance to be a hero. It had to be tempting. Logan set the screen for him better than he had meant to. He would venture to say it was as good a screen as he had set since Senior Night.

West Archer's lone starter stumbled around him and chased Marshal, but Marshal had a clear run to the rim. He could go for a layup or floater or stop on a dime to draw a foul from behind. Marshal could even pull it up from the same spot where Kelvin's leg had split in two.

He's gonna do it, Logan realized, sweat tickling his nose, his mouth nearly a smile.

Then Marshal passed it out to his little brother, who had a defender all over him. Logan felt queasy, once again thankful he hadn't had breakfast. He already wanted to cry and felt his face contorting without his consent. His eyes blurred with fresh tears.

This was the end of his basketball career.

Logan had no idea how much time was on the clock when Dylan took the desperate shot that had no chance of going in. He felt like he had to go through the motions. Otherwise, what would folks from Nowhere think? What was the opposite of a legend?

Logan ran toward the hoop with a weak attempt at an offensive rebound.

The ball clanked off the rim toward Logan and the defender who blocked him out. Logan reached up and batted the ball. He wanted to knock it out of bounds, like he had done plenty of times before, like he had done in last year's championship game against West Mann. But the ball popped up toward the basket with unreal backspin.

The horn blared as the ball rolled through the net.

SIXTEEN
THE TRUTH

1

"WHAT THE FUCK?" Marshal said before anyone else could speak.

After putting up pretenses and staying to watch Olney defeat Barton-Meek in overtime, the team returned to their hotel for lunch. Marshal and Doug met Logan and Kelvin in their room—if Alex was still alive, they figured he would call his fellow seniors, but Marshal hardly thought that mattered now. Logan had betrayed them by scoring the winning basket.

"I was trying to knock it out of bounds," the big man said.

"Why even go for it?"

"Are you kidding me? If we didn't pretend to try and win, we'd be run out of Nowhere."

Everyone else seemed to agree, which only annoyed Marshal.

"Who cares? Someone's gonna pay for what you did."

"Now's not the time to judge Logan," Doug said. "Don't forget, you made those free throws—"

"What was I supposed to do? I had to shoot them. I tried to miss as much as I could without taking a granny shot."

"Did you see the way West Archer started cramping up?" Kelvin said. "We can sit here and blame each other, but in the end, the magic wouldn't let us lose. Logan's wish is going to come true."

Marshal could barely stand to look at what Kelvin had become. He bounced back and forth on his crutches like some "cool teacher" commanding his classroom.

What does Em see in him?

He reminded himself to be patient. Now that he was back in her good graces, it was as important as ever to *be patient.*

He glared at Kelvin. "So, what do you suggest we do?"

"Nothing's changed," Kelvin said. "We go out and try to win STATE tomorrow."

"Against the best team in Class B?"

"They barely beat Barton-Meek," Logan said. "They're not as good as they were earlier this year. They're running out of steam."

"They know us better than they knew Barton-Meek. They'll know how to beat us without Kelvin. Hell, we don't even have the poor man's Kelvin anymore."

"Maybe we should try calling Alex," Doug said.

"Good idea, Dougie. Before we pretend like we didn't just murder someone today, let's find out why our best remaining player couldn't be bothered to show up." But he knew why. He and Mikey had been sacrificed. Marshal couldn't figure out what wish it would be for, but he'd have to be as blind as Logan had become to think it was anything else.

Doug called Alex's house and put the phone on speaker. The four boys waited while the line trilled.

"Hello?" It was Joanna Spruce.

"Hey, Mrs. Spruce. This is Doug Mooreland. I was calling for—"

There was a scrambling sound, then her husband took over. "Where are they?"

"Mr. Spruce?"

"He didn't leave no note about a family emergency. You better start talking, Doug. I know your shitass teammate told you."

"We told you everything we know, Mr. Spruce."

"My son would never miss a game this important. Never."

"Sorry, I can't help, Mr. Spruce."

Doug hung up when Alex's dad started threatening him.

"Guess he's not home," Kelvin joked.

"We have to find out what happened to them," Marshal said. "We should go to Nowhere."

"We're not going anywhere," Kelvin said. "We need to focus on the game tomorrow if we want any chance of winning." He crutched his way to the door. "There's really no point debating this anymore. We all know what we have to do. I'm going to lunch with Emily. Let me know if Alex calls."

The door closed slowly behind him, and Marshal listened to the creaking of the crutches with every step.

"It's easy for him to say. He's not the one who has to play the games."

"We don't want to head to Nowhere if he just got scared like Tim," Logan said.

"Scared? You're saying Tim got scared like it's his fault. You're fucking cold, Tramer."

"What if he doesn't call, Logan?" Doug asked.

"Our game's at noon tomorrow. We'll go home after we win the chip. He'll be there. You'll see, Dougie."

Marshal felt defiant. He hadn't forgotten how Logan humiliated him at the end of the third quarter. His ass still ached from hitting the hardwood.

He shook his head and looked directly at Doug. "We can't beat Olney, man."

"I don't know, dude." Doug leaned forward with his elbows on his knees, face in his hands, like it might fall to the floor. Then he mumbled repeatedly, "I don't know, I don't know, I don't know."

"Trust me, fellas," Logan said. "Trust Kelvin."

"What's happened to you, Tramer?" Marshal said.

"Excuse me?"

"You were the one who convinced us there was more to these wishes, and now you're ignoring it."

"I was trying to miss that shot."

"Were you?"

"Screw you, Marshal."

Marshal left the bedroom. He didn't let the door swing shut on its own—he slammed it behind him.

2

Marshal walked the downtown streets surrounding their hotel. The sun burned through the back of his shirt, sizzling his shoulders. The heat felt good, a sharp contrast to the chill of the breeze. On this Friday afternoon, people in business attire bustled about. He liked the anonymity of being alone in a big city.

He couldn't wait to move to Norman for college and hoped to find work in OKC someday. Marshal didn't want to stay in Shappaway County, not unless he was there with Emily.

He scanned every storefront window for restaurants, looking for her and Kelvin. He assumed they were having lunch nearby. If he didn't see them, he could catch up with her later at the Big House, but he was too impatient to not at least try to find her.

When he had left Logan and Kelvin's room, Marshal considered going to Nowhere to find Alex on his own, but he didn't have a car. He didn't want to return to his room with Dylan there, and he didn't want to watch more games at the Big House. He felt alone, and he hated being alone. He wished he could be with his best friend.

Then it hit him: Logan was intent on playing tomorrow, and Doug was a pushover. Kelvin was the worst of all of them, pressuring them to play while he sat on the sidelines, washing his hands of any repercussions.

Marshal needed allies.

It was time for his patience to go fuck itself.

So, he set out to find Emily. It wasn't likely he would find where they were eating, as big as downtown alone was, but when he spotted Kelvin and Emily emerging from Subway, it was almost enough to make him believe in God.

They didn't notice him among the crowd and began walking in the other direction. He followed, staying far enough back to remain out of sight. They didn't head straight back to the hotel. Instead, they wandered around downtown—Emily on two legs, Kelvin on crutches.

Marshal couldn't bring himself to worry about being seen. There was something oddly alluring about watching them. A vicarious longing gripped him.

He had walked with Emily countless times, but this was different. Even the way she moved was different with Kelvin. She leaned into him more, looked at him more, brushed her arm against his. Of course, they held hands, interlocking their fingers like the day they had walked into the high school trailer and shocked everyone.

But that would change as soon as she knew what a psycho Kelvin Harris was; how little he cared about the "community"

—as the hypocrite liked to call Nowhere. She would leave him and be with Marshal.

Finally, they headed back toward the hotel. Marshal kept his distance but stayed close enough to see which room they entered. He assumed Kelvin would walk her back to her room, since it would be risky to go to his for some "alone time," with her older brother as his roommate.

When they got on the elevator, Marshal sprinted up the hotel stairs, stopping on each floor to peek around the corner, listening for the elevator door to open. This method wasn't sustainable. By the time he reached a floor, they had already moved on to the next. But he tried anyway, taking the stairs two at a time.

Out of breath, he reached the fourth floor, opened the door, and peered around the corner. The two of them stood outside a room, only four doors down from where he was. He thought they would see him for sure, but they didn't. They were too focused on each other, which pissed him off.

Patience...

Only a few more minutes of it and then he would wait no longer. He would tell her about the kitchen well.

Marshal thought he would be waiting forever, but finally, Kelvin kissed her goodbye and crutched away toward the elevators.

Marshal knocked on Emily's door, hoping her mom wasn't there since he knew they were rooming together. When she answered, he said nothing at first, thinking if he stayed silent, she might fill the void like she used to, but all she said was, "Oh, hey, Marsh. You just missed Kelvin."

You're done with patience, he reminded himself.

"I need to tell you something."

"Okay. Shoot."

"Can I come inside?"

"You...want to come into my hotel room?"

"Are you alone?"

"Jesus Christ, Marshal. You're being weird."

"Sorry. It's really important. And-and we need some privacy—"

"I'm closing the door now."

"Wait—I'll just say it here. It's gonna sound crazy."

He quickly explained about the kitchen well, Logan's wish, and everything that had happened since then. His mind grew foggy, his throat dry.

He almost said more. Almost told her how he had been in love with her since the eighth grade.

But then Jessica Fromm pulled the door open wider from inside.

"I can't listen to any more of this," she said. "I thought you were at least here to confess your love."

"What the hell?" Marshal ignored Jessica and glared at Emily. "You were hiding her in there?"

"I wasn't hiding," Jessica said. "I just didn't want to interrupt if you were gonna talk about anything fun. But whatever this story is it's crazy."

Marshal squeezed his hand against the doorframe, anger flaring. He had lost his train of thought about the well. Couldn't even remember where he had left off. "You should know better than anyone I'm telling the truth."

"What does that mean?"

"You were next to Allen when he died, weren't you? You must be in denial if you think I'm crazy. I know y'all saw something. Logan told us—"

"Lower your voice," Emily said.

"No!"

She grabbed him by the shirt and pulled him inside the room.

"Jesus, Marsh. Jessica's right. You're acting like a lunatic."

She flung him toward the rolling chair by the desk. Marshal dropped into it, embarrassed by how little he could control his emotions. He took a deep breath and replayed what he had said to her about the well.

"I missed something…" he said. "Wait a second. I said Logan made a wish, but that wasn't how this started. It was Will Roebuck. Logan and Will went to the well one night after work, and Logan tried to prank him by telling him he had to go to the bottom to make his wish. So, Will did it, and his wish came true. He wished for his grandma to be healed. She was blind, but after his wish, she could see."

"I remember them going out there," Jessica said, shrugging. Unconvinced but no longer being snarky toward him.

Marshal had struck a nerve bringing up Allen. Perhaps, Jessica was remembering the way Allen had died in the backseat while she held his hands to the seat, something pulling him toward the roof of the Kia.

"It was the night after Kelvin got hurt," she said. "Valentine's Day. Bird told Will about the well, and Logan dared Will to go out there with him."

"Yeah, that's it," Marshal said. "Will made his wish, it came true, and then this Bird guy was killed because of it."

"'This Bird guy?' Really?" Jessica crossed her arms and paced around the hotel room.

"Should I call him by his Christian name?"

Jessica flipped him off, and he ignored her.

"I made a wish too, Em," he said. "When you were in a coma, I wished for you to be saved."

"What?"

"That's right. I didn't even have to say it out loud, I wanted it so badly. Why do you think you've healed so fast? You don't need that cast anymore, do you?"

She and Jessica exchanged a look.

"I did say I was jealous of how good you looked for being in a coma a week ago," Jessica noted.

"Logan told us this is the same thing that happened with your aunt's team."

Emily's eyes widened. Anger crossed her face. "What do you mean?" she said, but she didn't look confused.

"Logan and Will went to Green River on Monday, when you were in the hospital. They found someone from her team who told them about a well in the woods. After your aunt got hurt, the others made a wish. They won the championship because of it."

"And were there consequences?" Jessica said, suddenly serious, thinking about Allen.

Emily thought about someone else. She stared through Marshal, waiting for his answer. He swallowed hard.

"Yes," he said. "There were."

SEVENTEEN
FATE

1

AFTER KELVIN and then Marshal left, Logan and Doug hung out in his room. Doug laid on the king-size bed while Logan leaned back in the rolling chair and propped his feet on the desk next to the TV stand. He put the heating pad on his throbbing ankle. *Only one more game,* he thought through the pain. *Just last a little longer.*

He tried convincing himself Alex and Mikey were alive because they had beaten King-Marlow without the wish. He couldn't say the same for the game today. There would be a sacrifice, if there wasn't one already.

But if Alex and Mikey were alive, then it was just Tim's dad, Ed and Pauline Beaumont, and Allen who had died. Sure, Bird had died too, but not because of Logan's wish. Only four deaths were his responsibility.

Two of them were in their eighties, and another was destined to live fast and die young. The other one—Tim's dad—Logan felt the worst about. But Red Springer was in his seventies and had lived a hard life. Logan's guilt was somewhat eased by the hope Mr. Tune wasn't dead, though that was far from the main reason his guilt seemed to lessen.

It was Kelvin.

His best friend was back in his life, and he didn't blame Logan for setting the screen. He blamed Fate. Fate had put them in this awful position. Fate had caused the ball to go through the hoop when Logan had tried to knock it out of bounds. Fate propelled them into the championship and took the lives of spectators who were likely at risk of dying anyway.

Logan didn't know who would be taken next, but he assumed another Nowhere old-timer or someone with a drug problem. Maybe Fate had taken enough people already. Maybe they could win it all without any more consequences. Only four lives had been lost for Green River to win STATE. Perhaps that would be enough to fulfill the requirements.

"Can I ask you something, Logan?" Doug had been quiet for a while, and Logan thought he had fallen asleep.

Logan put his hands behind his head and crossed his good leg over the heating pad, causing a little more heat to his ankle. "Go for it."

"Have you had any bad dreams?"

Logan noticed a circular stain on the ceiling above the TV. "Recently?"

"Yeah, like since you made the wish?"

He thought about it for a moment, a little surprised. "No, actually. I haven't really dreamed at all. Not that I can remember, anyway."

"I had this nightmare on Monday and again on Tuesday night...it felt real. And, um, well, I saw Allen's body."

"In your nightmare?"

"No. In the morgue."

Logan sat up to see Doug a little better. "What?"

Doug lay on his back, staring at the ceiling. "Yeah," Doug

said. "I was at the prayer breakfast, and I offered to help Brother Maxwell, and—I was curious, so I snuck in and looked at Allen's body. His head was all jacked up. The Beaumonts were there too. Their faces weren't smashed in, so you could really see what they looked like. It's something I can't describe, but the kind of thing that makes you want to drop down on your knees and pray."

Logan recalled how he had felt at Red Springer's funeral: the fear that the closed casket would pop open, forcing him to stare at Tim's dad. "Shit, Dougie. Well, that explains your nightmare."

"Does it?"

"Sure. I'd be having recurring nightmares too if I saw those corpses. Have you had it since Tuesday night?"

"No. Not since I left Nowhere. Maybe I'm far enough away. Or, or…I shouldn't have made that wish, Logan."

"It's okay, man."

"No, it's not. I rejected my wish. I broke Mal's arm. Slammed it in my car door because she wouldn't let go of me."

"Dougie—"

"It doesn't like it when you reject the wish. And-and I don't blame it. I wasted it. I killed Coach Reed."

A chill passed through Logan as he recalled his conversation with Will at the team dinner.

"Coach Reed?" His voice didn't sound much like him, like the time he had strep throat. "What are you talking about?"

"She came to me in the nightmare to show me what happened. Why it was important for me not to reject Mal. To let her love me. Let her want me."

"It's not your fault, Dougie," Logan said, hoping if he said it out loud it would make it true. "Whatever happened is not your fault."

"Will you pray with me, Logan?"

"Of course, Dougie."

Logan got up, slinging the heating pad to the floor, and limped to the bed. He took Doug's hand, and Doug pulled him onto the bed. His machismo resisted the smaller junior, keeping six inches between them, but Doug kept hold of his hand. He prayed for the nightmares to stop, for God to watch over the team, and let them do his will.

After that, Doug and Logan both lay on their backs and didn't say anything.

Hours passed. A nap was not on Logan's radar. His mind tortured him too much for that as he pondered all the events that had led to him being one win away from a STATE CHAMPI-ONSHIP. But he must have dozed off at some point because he woke to the sound of Kelvin's voice in the room.

"Wakey, wakey, fags."

"What time is it?" Logan mumbled groggily.

"Late afternoon," Kelvin replied. "I ordered a couple of pizzas."

"Good. I'm hungry."

"I don't know how y'all can eat," Doug said, wide awake. Logan felt insecure that he had slept in front of Doug.

"Did Alex call?" Kelvin asked.

"Nope."

There was a lightness in the room without Marshal there. Even Doug seemed more at ease. They played cards while they waited for the pizza. A knock came soon enough, and Logan's stomach growled when he went to the door.

It wasn't the pizza guy.

Emily, Jessica, and Marshal stood side by side.

"We need to talk," his sister said.

2

Marshal smirked at Kelvin. His eyes dwelled on the former star player a little longer than Logan or Doug.

Look at his shady ass, Logan thought. *I can't believe he told my sister.*

"Is it true?" Emily said to Logan, like they were the only two in the room.

He knew what she meant. "Aunt Joss didn't kill herself," he answered.

"How could you not tell me?"

"We only knew the wish was real two weeks ago. Even then it was debatable. Life's been moving too fast."

"Life's been—" She guffawed angrily. "This is ridiculous."

Jessica stepped in. "What are you going to do?" she asked.

Logan felt incapable of speaking. He couldn't tell the girl he liked that they were going to do the exact same thing they had just failed at doing.

Kelvin answered for him. "We're going to go out there and win tomorrow."

Emily turned her attention to her boyfriend. She seemed shocked by his response.

"Who's *we*?" Marshal asked. "You'd just be a cheerleader again."

"You can't," Jessica said. "Emily and I saw what happened to Allen. We can't let another person—"

"Tim's dad!" Emily shouted. "And Mr. Tune—"

"Mr. Tune's not dead," Logan said, not helping.

Kelvin put his hand on Logan, easing him back. He spoke quietly, as if he could calm everyone down simply because he was Kelvin Harris. "We can beat Olney without the magic. We've proven there are no consequences if we win on our own."

"What about Alex and Mikey?" Doug asked.

Logan tapped his foot rapidly. He felt an unpleasant jolt go through him.

Doug's gonna flip sides. He's too scared to play tomorrow. And if he doesn't, and Marshal isn't bluffing, then—

"We don't know that they're missing," Kelvin said, maintaining a professorial demeanor. "We stick to the plan."

"Yeah, because it worked out well last time," Marshal said.

"Shut the fuck up," Logan snapped.

"You want to shove me again, big man. We'll see how it goes for you this time."

Kelvin stepped between them. "Let's all calm down."

"Give it a break, Kelvin," Marshal said. "You're not in charge here."

"I never said I was."

"You're the one who insisted we play tomorrow."

"What other choice do we have? We try to win, and if we can't, we lose on purpose."

"That's not the only choice," Emily said. She seemed to move closer to Jessica and Marshal, further at odds against her brother and boyfriend.

"We've been talking it through," Jessica said, also setting herself against Logan. He was so angry with her he didn't think they'd ever go on a date now. "There's one other option."

"We don't play at all," Marshal said. "We forfeit the game."

"You wouldn't," Logan said.

"Try me."

Kelvin and Doug seemed caught off guard.

This is ridiculous, Logan thought. *You don't forfeit the championship.*

Doug shook his head. "The well doesn't like to be rejected."

"The well?" Jessica said. "Is that what we're calling it?"

"Well, it's not God, is it, Dougie?" Marshal said.

More like Fate, Logan thought.

"What do you mean, 'it doesn't like to be rejected?'" Emily asked.

"It wants the wish to be fulfilled," Doug said. "It gets angry if you don't."

"Like the Hulk?" Marshal said, laughing. Then he quoted the Ang Lee movie they had all seen last summer. "'*You're making me angry.*'"

"What are you saying, Doug?" Jessica asked. "People are dying because you rejected the wish?"

"No, it doesn't kill anyone...It just doesn't like to be rejected."

"Well, it *is* killing people when you fulfill the wish," Emily said. "So, there's really no choice here."

Kelvin stepped between the two sides again. "But there *is* another choice. That's what we're telling you." His crutches seemed to do the opposite of what they had done for him when Logan first visited Kelvin at his house. Then they had made him pathetic. Now the crutches gave him a wide, commanding presence. "We can win tomorrow on our own. We just have to believe in ourselves."

"What a load of horseshit," Marshal said.

"You can give up all you want, Lovegood. Be a coward like Alex. The rest of us? We're not forfeiting the game, are we, guys?"

Logan stood to his full height defiantly. "Jack Ward's as good as you are, anyway."

Doug hesitated.

"We're playing." Logan put his large hand on Doug's shoulder. "Right, Dougie?"

Doug sighed. "That's the plan."

"Unbelievable," Emily said.

"Have a little faith, babe." Kelvin reached for her, but she turned away from him.

Marshal looked pleased.

What an asshole, Logan thought.

A knock rapped against the door. The smell of pizza wafted into the room.

3

Logan and Kelvin kept the thermostat as low as possible in their room. The icy air felt nice against Logan's skin but made his throat burn when he breathed it in. Kelvin lay on the other side of the bed. Less than six inches separated them, as if their bodies knew they needed companionship—solidarity, a like-minded presence for comfort.

Logan had spent the last half hour in silence and darkness, imagining one of the Nowhere spectators going to their hotel room tonight, only to find that dark figure waiting.

He heard Emily's voice in his head: *I just know something was hidden behind the black cloud...a living thing...I just know, Logan.*

He played different scenarios mentally: Ms. Fletcher lying in bed, reading by lamplight, when the cloud rises from the foot of the bed; Mr. Holbrook leaving a restaurant, walking down a dark alley, only to be greeted by the black cloud; Superintendent Walker and Principal Jacobs having a meeting in the hotel conference room to discuss the Spruce brothers' disappearance, when the lights flicker and the black cloud appears, taking both of them; Logan's parents going out to rekindle what they had lost, his dad reaching for his mom's hand, but then the black cloud comes for them.

There were endless possibilities. Logan knew he had screwed up. He shouldn't have gone for the ball. But whatever happened...

"Logan?" Kelvin sounded more distant than the couple of inches between them. "You awake?"

"Yeah. Can't sleep."

"I think I'm in the doghouse, man."

"I'd say so."

"You agree with me, right? We have to go for it."

"Yeah, bro. It's the championship."

"Exactly. After everything we've been through, we can't let it all go to waste."

"Waste... yeah."

"I believe in you, man. I always have. Remember how we'd stay after practice, working on the pick-and-roll? How we'd work on me getting you the ball where you liked it? Our chemistry?"

"Of course."

"That's because I knew you had it in you, Logan. I knew you could be the best big man in the state."

"I don't know about that—"

"I'm serious. You've kicked ass even without me. You can punish the Mosely brothers."

"Okay."

"Okay, what?"

"I can punish the Mosely brothers."

"And you're not scared. That's where you got me beat. You ain't scared of nobody."

"What are you smoking, Harris?" Logan joked.

Kelvin laughed painfully like little shards of glass scraped his throat.

"I went out to the damn house, Logan."

"You...you did?"

"Yeah. Monday night. When I got back to Nowhere from Tuskahoma, after you told me about the well, I went straight there and stood over the damn thing. Stared down into it. Shined my light down, and it's just like you said. Not even a Maglite could reach the bottom. But I didn't go down there. I told myself I was being logical. With my leg fucked up, I could climb down but no way I'd make it back up.

"But that was bullshit. I knew the magic was real, didn't I? As soon as I reached the bottom and made my wish, my leg would be healed. I'd make it to the top, no problem. Nah, that wasn't why I didn't go down there. I just...couldn't. I was as scared as I was in the championship last year."

"You're too hard on yourself, Kelvin. I can't imagine anyone climbing down the well on their own at night. It was bad enough doing it with other people up top." He thought about the way he had pranked Will that first night and felt bad. Of course, if he hadn't done that, they wouldn't be one game away from winning STATE.

"All I'm saying is I believe in you," Kelvin said. "Even if Marshal doesn't come around, you can out-physical Olney. You can bring them down into the muck and beat them. Right?"

"Yeah, Kelvin. We can beat them."

"Hell yeah."

His confidence renewed, Logan found it easier to fall asleep. It started as another dreamless night, until he saw Kelvin near the door. In the dark, he mostly saw his teammate's silhouette. No crutches. Kelvin was standing on both legs.

That's when Logan knew he must be dreaming. He stared groggily.

"It's all right, Logan." Kelvin's voice sounded distant. "Go to sleep."

"Where're you going?"

"Nowhere."

"Then why are you standing?"

"Go to sleep, Logan. Everything's all right. It's not your fault. It's Fate."

EIGHTEEN
THE DEVIL

1

Tim Springer's older brother Daniel had found Jesus. That was exactly the way he'd said it last week when he came out of his bedroom at his mother's house and stood in front of the four people in the household while they attempted to watch *American Idol* and said, "I've found Jesus."

"Where at?" Tim had said. The joke didn't land well.

Finding Jesus was an obvious outcome for Daniel after their dad's death. Daniel had "found Jesus" half a dozen times before in his life, most recently during his stint in prison. How could he not find the Lord Almighty again after the shape of their dad's body? The sight of the corpse had left Tim changed too, hadn't it? But not like Daniel. Tim didn't find Jesus, despite the argument that, if the Devil existed, it meant God had to exist too.

Tim didn't believe in that argument. For what was the Devil but a metaphor for evil. What he saw in the dog pen could only have been done by the Devil. Red Springer had stared evil in the face, seen whatever came after death, and it wasn't God.

By that logic, what is God but a metaphor for goodness? he'd argued with himself while they finished *American Idol*. Didn't that mean God existed too? Tim had experienced plenty of good times in his life: that weekend he had with Reba Jacobs, his team's success on the court, Turner's barn parties, fishing with his dad. But the good times were miniscule compared to his one moment of experiencing evil. There was a power imbalance in this world, or at least in Nowhere, and could God exist if he wasn't as powerful as the Devil?

Tim Springer had changed since his father's death and not for the better.

He had considered going home many times the past two weeks. He went to get the *Miner Daily News* every morning to see how his team did, and every time, they had won. Each Wednesday, he snagged *The Holdendecker Record* because it had a more in-depth recap of Nowhere's playoff wins, and they were quite the story, including such highlights as "fecal matter on the court" and "the crowd threatened the referees with dangerous language." Tim ate it up. He nearly called his teammates on several occasions but was too ashamed. He would rather talk to them when he made his triumphant return.

On two occasions, he almost went home. As soon as he climbed into his jacked S-10 for the specific purpose of driving the forty minutes to Nowhere, his hands began to shake and he got lightheaded. In his mind's eye, he would see his dad's distorted face even more detailed and real than when it haunted him every time he closed his eyes.

He felt like a coward for not going, especially because his subconscious mind had been urging him to return most nights, when the same dream recurred.

He never remembered how the dream started, only that he would feel the rumble of his truck on the bottoms of his bare feet and the vibration of the idling engine on his palms where he held the steering wheel. In his headlights was his naked father. Tim was naked too. He was on his way to get his basketball jersey from so he could rush back to the school bus before they left without him to go win STATE.

His dad faced the headlights. His eyes were a pale dead color. His skin almost blue. His testicles curled into his knobby penis. His toes and fingers were black. His veins shined through his translucent chest.

Tim told himself to get out of the truck, to wrap his father in a coat before he froze to death. But Tim had no coat to give and he couldn't take his hands off the steering wheel no matter how much he told himself to do so.

Then, an awful, poisonous smell filled his truck like he'd clogged the exhaust pipe with deadly intent. He couldn't actually smell it but his dream-self knew the smell was strong and choking. And his dad was suddenly next to him in the cab of his truck.

"Dad!" Tim shouted like his dad was still in the field.

Red breathed out a word: *"Go."*

"Go where?" Tim asked.

"Nowhere."

"I'm in Nowhere, Dad. We're at home."

"Not home. Go nowhere."

"Nowhere?"

"Nowhere."

Then his dad's face began to spread apart, but each time, Tim woke before he saw the uncanny face he'd seen in real life. He also felt like he was late for something when he woke up. Then came the pressuring urge to join his team. So far, he had resisted the urge, letting this fear win out.

Early Saturday morning, he went with Daniel's mom to Nickel Saver. While she went into the grocery store, Tim stayed out front by the news rack. He inserted two quarters into the vending device, opened the latch, and took out a copy of *Miner Daily News*. He went right to the Sports section and saw the small paragraphs dedicated to the Class A and Class B semifinals results.

Nowhere had defeated West Archer by one point.

What a game that must have been.

Sweat sprouted onto his upper lip despite the cold. He wanted so badly to be there with his team. It wasn't like Oklahoma City was Nowhere. Surely, he wasn't too scared to go to the Big House.

Tim insisted Daniel's mom hurry him back to the house. Once there, he got into his truck and started down the drive, dirt spitting out beneath his tires. He turned onto the road and stopped. He felt the rumble of his truck beneath the bottoms of his feet and the vibration of the idling engine on his palms where he held the steering wheel.

He clicked on his headlights even though it was light enough to see without them. For a moment, he saw a shape, then it was gone, probably had never been there.

And an epiphany hit him; a clear interpretation of his dream he hadn't considered before.

Go nowhere.

His dad wasn't pleading with him to return home. He was telling Tim to *stay put.*

Don't you dare go back to the place that killed me. That's what Red Springer was doing in his dream.

It was a warning. For the first time since his dad had died, Tim felt hopeful. His dad was protecting him. Of course, he was. Goodness existed, after all.

Tim turned around and returned to Daniel's mom's house.

If the Devil was real, he was elsewhere.

2

Doug thought he might go mad when the nightmare happened for the second night in a row. Like Monday, it seemed to last forever. The messy remnant of Coach Reed's face stared into his own from on top of his paralyzed body without any more words from Mal or anything said by the figure that he couldn't be sure even had the ability to speak. It was dead, right? If not dead, then unhuman, no longer Julia Reed but the offering Doug had tithed to the kitchen well. The only prayer in his entire life he had ever regretted.

Forever, they remained like that until he was saved by daylight, or perhaps it was the pungent stench of his piss that finally woke him up. His mom would certainly question him when he washed his sheets for the second day in a row. Screw it, he thought and rolled up the sheets, stuffed them into a plastic tub after removing his Camp Rome keepsakes, and threw the tub into the trunk of his car.

The smell had filled the inside of the Corolla by the time he reached school Wednesday morning. He wondered how hazardous it would be when he returned to his car after the playoffs.

Wednesday night, he feared the nightmare would come again, and he would piss himself, and Sam Turner would smell it from his bed. What could he say: Sam's older sister was torturing Doug in his nightmare?

It was awkward sharing a room with Sam, but Sam didn't say anything about Mal's broken arm or about her dating Doug or anything about how strange the upperclassmen on the team had been acting for weeks. From Sam's perspective, why would he? There seemed to be a working method to the madness as they were one win away from immortality. Yet Doug could sense trepidation from Sam anytime they were alone in their hotel room, which was only right before bed because Doug hung out in Logan and Kelvin's room until he was too tired to stay awake. That first night, he dreaded going to sleep, but it turned out his nightmare was confined to his bedroom in Nowhere.

On Wednesday night, he dreamed he was knocking down every shot he took in the STATE CHAMPIONSHIP. Thursday night, he dreamed he was on a battlefield, helping the dying find Jesus. Friday afternoon, when he dozed off next to Logan, he dreamed about a family vacation to Branson—the same trip they had taken five years ago—but now Doug and the rest of the family were their current ages. He hoped he would dream about Rome Bible Camp when he returned to his room Friday night after the "showdown" with Marshal, Emily, and Jessica.

Doug was as on the fence as he'd been all week. He prayed the Holy Spirit would show him the right path.

When they defeated King-Marlow without Logan's wish, it seemed like an answer to his prayers: *Trust in the Lord, and your dreams will come true!* Now the answer had been complicated. Alex and Mikey were missing. And they should have lost to West Archer, but the magic didn't let them.

The kitchen well hated being rejected. He didn't need another nightmare to remind him of that, especially with Mal's violent gaze on him from the crowd every game. Doug feared what would happen if they forfeited, so he couldn't join Marshal, Emily, and Jessica—even if he wanted to—and the last thing he wanted to do was go to Nowhere, so he had to put it off as long as possible. He felt like a coward and wished he had never gone into the morgue. Maybe Logan was right, and what he saw there caused his recurring nightmare. Regardless, the nightmare stayed in Nowhere, so he was safe as long as he remained in the city. Maybe, after the game tomorrow, it would be over. No more deaths; no more nightmares. Win or lose, they could put this behind them.

But when Doug fell asleep on Friday night, he didn't dream about Camp Rome.

"Mal?"

The hotel room door was open. She stood beneath the hallway lights, cast in an ugly fluorescent orange. She wore a spring dress. *That's right, it is just about springtime, isn't it?* His favorite season. Doug loved nothing more than seeing girls at church in their easter dresses. Mal was as beautiful as anyone he had ever met. She beckoned him into the hallway, no cast scaling her slender arm, while Sam snoozed, slack-jawed, in the other bed.

Doug floated to her, the bright lights buzzing above them as if they were the bug-zapping kind. He couldn't quite reach her and, suddenly, found himself in an empty hotel room. No bed, no TV or desk, just a blackened square like the remnants of a house fire.

A cold hand caressed the back of his neck. He felt lips against his ear.

"Go."

"Where?"

"Nowhere."

"I-I can't. It's not safe."

"Dougie, Dougie, Dougie. You still don't get it, do you? You'll never be safe until you commit to something, friend. You *chose this. So, stop fighting it. Stop rejecting what you've already offered up."*

"N-No."

"No?"

"I'm done with you. You're not Mal."

A hot and foul sigh in his ear. Then the hand caressing his neck gripped the back of his head, and Doug was in a bed, his arms and legs stiff at his side, his neck straining as his head was lifted and forced to stare at the end of the bed, where the shadow—*she*—stood.

She—*it*—crawled onto the bed, slithering between his legs, up his body—

No, no, no, no, no, no, no, no, no, no, no, no, no, no, no—

The face drew so close to his own that his eyes blurred into a muddled, spinning image.

A flash of orange like the hallway lights, and Doug was awake.

His eyes burned but he couldn't even blink. Couldn't bring himself to lift a hand and rub the crud from his eyelids.

He was alone in a hotel room that wasn't his.

Alex's. This is Alex's room.

The air reeked—the warning urine smell of a mountain lion. It sizzled in his nose. Then he realized he was soaking wet. Sweat from the nightmare, he reasoned, but it was too sticky to be sweat. Afraid to move, he lifted his head, straining his neck, and saw he was drenched in his own piss. Not just around his groin but all the way from his neck down to his ankles. And the bed around him was soaked too like someone had stood above him with a steady stream for a half-hour golden shower.

It was an impossible amount, enough so that he had to wonder if Mal had gone to the kitchen well and wished for a bucket of animal piss to be dumped on him.

Doug wanted to yell but saw in his mind's eye Marshal rushing through the shared door and finding him here. Only humiliation could match his fear. Finally, he rolled off the bed and cried.

The only thing that made him stop sobbing was the sight of the W.W.J.D. bracelet on his wrist: *What Would Jesus Do?*

Doug knew right away he needed spiritual guidance.

3

Doug showered in Alex's room and put on a hotel robe. He rolled up the sheets from the bed and added them to a trash bag along with the t-shirt, shorts, and underwear he worn to bed last night. There was nothing he could do about the urine that soaked through to the mattress but housekeeping would assume it was the missing brothers who did it. Word may have even gotten around among the hotel staff that two teenage boys from one of the small-town teams had disappeared. It would be another hotel ghost story; Doug was sure there were plenty others. He returned to his room and thanked God Sam was still sleeping. He changed into his clothes, put his room key in the pocket of his baggy shorts, took the elevator up a floor, and headed for Brother Maxwell's room.

At the team dinner Wednesday night, Doug had talked briefly with his pastor. It was an odd interaction as both of them clearly had something on their minds but played it off like everything was fine. Maxwell had mentioned staying in the same hotel as the team and gave Doug his room number, in case he needed anything.

His first thought was that Maxwell was propositioning him —the Catholic molestation case from a couple of years ago was still fresh in Christian circles. He quickly pushed the thought aside, feeling ashamed. It was the same sinful part of him that couldn't resist attractive girls. He was a sex pervert and assumed everyone was like him.

He knocked on Brother Maxwell's door, worried he might be waking the old man. Maxwell was only in his sixties, but being a widower made Doug think of him as older, like a man who might pass away any day now.

The preacher answered, fully clothed and bright-eyed, as

though he had been awake for hours. "Hello, Doug." He didn't seem surprised to see him. He looked contemplative.

"I saw the bodies," Doug blurted out.

Maxwell sighed. "Come in, son."

He ushered Doug into the room and closed the door, pulling out the rolling chair from the desk next to the TV stand. "Have a seat."

Doug sat in the chair, while Maxwell leaned forward on the edge of the lounge chair next to the bed. The large window beside them showed the night lights of downtown. From this high up, they could see rooftops and streets below, other hotels just as tall, where shadows passed by window shades and lamps clicked on and off.

"I'm sorry, Brother Maxwell," Doug said. "You trusted me, and I took advantage of the situation."

Maxwell smiled. "Well, I still appreciate the job you did cleaning up my workspace." He reached out and patted Doug on the knee. "I'm just sorry you had to see what you saw."

"It was...tough to see."

"I can assure you, it wasn't normal."

"I really am interested in being a funeral director."

"Perhaps next year, we can work out an internship."

"I'd like that."

"Try not to dwell on it. You'll want to focus on the big game tomorrow."

"There's something else, Brother Maxwell." Doug hesitated, unsure how to say it without lying. "I feel like I'm in a spiritual battle."

"Hmm, yes. I know what you mean. I'm afraid there is a great evil near our community right now." He paused, considering, then said, "You'll hear this soon enough, and I pray it doesn't affect you in the game today, but Julia Reed has passed away."

As inevitable as it was to hear, a shock of cold struck Doug. He couldn't speak, but it didn't matter because Brother Maxwell continued, peering out the window like he was talking to himself:

"We think Sunday night or Monday morning, when she returned home from visiting Emily Tramer in the hospital, but we can't say for sure. Her sister found her Wednesday morning, and I went to see her body Wednesday night. Sheriff Dixon has kept everything quiet but has already ordered a search in all of Shappaway County for Alex and Mikey, thanks to Ryan Holbrook.

"Things aren't so quiet anymore, though. Julia's death was in last night's edition of *The Arrow Evening News*. Some in the crowd may even whisper about it during your game. If Coach Park finds out before tipoff, be there for him on the court, Doug. Winning or losing isn't as important as the godly comfort you can offer him out there. Like you said, we're in a spiritual battle.

"Unlike the others, Julia's cause of death has remained undetermined, but they all died from the same evil that continues to lurk around us, making it difficult to breath. Lord, help us, I can feel it even now."

The color had completely drained from Maxwell's face, giving him a waxy look, and Doug reached over and squeezed his shoulder. He fought hard to keep his hand from trembling.

The preacher started at his touch, then smiled. "Who's the pastor here?" He winked, then lifted his hand over his shoulder to palm Doug's. For a long moment, they remained like that. "Fear not, Doug," Brother Maxwell finally said, holding his head a little higher. "Though evil comes to our neck of the woods, so do angels fighting on our behalf."

"Of course," Doug said, his voice scratchy from having not talked for a while. "What can we do?"

"Pray."

They bowed their heads and Brother Maxwell led them in a prayer. "Father, we ask for your forgiveness in how we have sinned. We trust that no evil in or out of this world is as mighty as you. We seek your guidance through the Holy Spirit. In Jesus' name, amen."

They were both weepy after the quick prayer.

Doug stood to leave and paused. "What if...what if we're confronted head-on by a demon?"

"Ah—" Brother Maxwell raised his finger, signaling for Doug to wait a moment, then opened his nightstand and took out his Bible.

Doug thought he would quote scripture, but instead, Maxwell slid out a tiny wooden cross, which he had been using as a bookmark, and handed it to Doug.

"It may seem silly to a young person, but the symbol of what Christ did for us is powerful. It can center you, give you courage, and rebuke unholy spirits. If you find yourself afraid, clutch this cross and trust in the Lord. He will give you strength."

"I can't accept this, Brother Maxwell."

"I have plenty of them. Go ahead, Doug."

Doug thanked him and pocketed the cross, feeling only slightly better. He knew that if he confessed the whole truth, he might find the satisfaction he was seeking, but he refrained. It wasn't like he needed to confess *all* his sins to his preacher. He could confess them to Jesus himself and would on his way out of town.

Doug had a very important sin to confess.

As he walked away from Maxwell's room, he reached in his other pocket and pulled out the set of keys. He couldn't believe he had been able to steal them during the prayer without a single jingle. It was dang near impossible, meaning it was meant to be. He had to confront his fear. He was the only one who could stop it.

Be careful what you wish for, he told nightmare-Mal, who had urged him to go to Nowhere.

That was exactly where he was headed in Brother Maxwell's car. It was time to beat the Devil.

4

Marshal woke at the sound of a knock. He had been dreaming about Emily, of course. It was the night after Bolan's arrest. He had convinced Emily to go to the party at Turner's barn instead of Kelvin's house. They had a toke from Reba Jacobs' joint but were mostly riding the high of saving Ryan Holbrook from getting his skull crushed in by Uncle Thomas—Marshal's distant relative.

They found themselves outside of the barn, standing close to each other unconsciously because of how cold it was. Emily told him how much he meant to her, how loyal of a friend he had been all these years. How patient he had been.

She looked up at him with more than friendship and pulled him into a hug, her cheek brushing against his. He was no longer cold because her body pressed against his. Marshal held the hug a little longer. She seemed okay with it.

Finally, they pulled ever so slightly away, her face an inch from his. So close he could feel her breath against his lips. Before he could kiss her, she kissed him. Her tongue slid inside his mouth, and the warmth of her mouth intoxicated him.

The knock ripped him out of the moment, and he was immediately pissed at whoever was banging on the door this early. His little brother Dylan slept through the knock, which didn't surprise him. Dylan was the deepest sleeper Marshal had ever been around.

Marshal didn't even care that he had a boner when he stood and crossed the room with no shirt, only wearing his And 1 basketball shorts.

He rolled his eyes when he saw Logan standing there.

"What the fuck, man?"

"He's gone," Logan croaked.

"What?"

"Kelvin's gone."

"What do you mean?"

"I mean, he left. He got up and said he was going to Nowhere."

"So, he changed his mind?" Marshal felt panicked, worried Kelvin was forfeiting the game to show his love for Emily.

"I don't think so," Logan answered. "I think...he's the sacrifice. He's going home because he's going to die next."

Marshal's panic disappeared immediately, replaced by a surprising giddiness he had to fight to keep from showing. He shushed Logan and pulled the door closed behind them. They went to Logan and Kelvin's room down the hall.

"We don't know that he's going to die," Marshal said to put Logan at ease. "Just like Alex and Mikey. Since they didn't die immediately, we don't know what happened."

"I do," Logan said. "I know what happened. The wish didn't kill Aunt Joss immediately either. It directed her to go back to Green River and hang herself."

"Calm down, Tramer. We already know there's a third option besides what happened to your aunt or Tim's dad. Mr. Tune is still missing. His body hasn't been found. We just have to figure out where they went."

Marshal knew they wouldn't be able to save Kelvin or Alex or anyone, but the wish had run its course. No way Logan would play today without his support blanket on the sidelines. Marshal had done it; he had sided with Emily and gotten rid of

Kelvin. All without having to make another wish himself. His patience had paid off.

"When did Kelvin leave?" he asked.

Logan sat on the end of his bed, rubbing his face. "I don't know. I thought I was dreaming." He motioned toward the door. "He was standing right there without his crutches. He put his full weight on his cast. It had to be a dream. But when I woke up this morning—" He pointed at the crutches on the floor next to the bed, crisscrossed in a giant X.

"So, he's out there without his crutches?"

"He's the sacrifice."

"We need to get Doug and find some wheels."

"What?"

"We have to go to Nowhere."

"I-I can't. The—"

Logan cut himself off, but he didn't need to. Marshal knew what he was going to say and was annoyed at himself for how surprised he was to hear it: *The game.*

After all this, the big-ass psychopath still wanted to play today.

He took a soft approach, recalling how violent Logan had become when Marshal suggested they lose on purpose in front of a crowd. It was only the two of them here.

"Logan..."

Logan gazed up at him.

"It's over, man. We have to go to Nowhere. We have to forfeit."

Logan shook his head. "Kelvin wouldn't want us giving up."

"We don't have a choice."

"Of course we do."

"Even if I played today," Marshal said, "we aren't good enough to beat Olney without the magic. And do you really think the well will let us lose on purpose?"

"We could try—"

"Think about what it did to those West Archer guys. Now imagine what it will do in the championship game if we try to lose."

"The Basketball Gods—"

"It's not any kind of God, Logan. Maybe Dougie's right. Maybe it's the Devil."

"You don't believe that."

"I don't know what I believe anymore," Marshal admitted truthfully. "Maybe we made a deal with the Devil, or maybe Dougie's way of thinking about it is too simplistic. Regardless, we know one thing: Kelvin said he was going to Nowhere, so that's where we should go if you want any chance of finding him."

He leaned down next to where Logan still sat, his final plea that he felt a little guilty saying: "If you want to keep him from suffering the same fate as your aunt, then we need to go now."

"Fate...right."

Logan stood and followed Marshal out of the room. They went to get Doug. It was Sam who answered the door, rubbing his eyes and yawning.

"Where's Doug?" Marshal asked.

"He got up and left in the middle of the night. Figured he was going to be with y'all."

Marshal's giddiness was washed away by the cold river passing through him.

5

The hallway looked different from the opposite direction. Marshal reached the fourth floor from the elevator rather than the stairwell this time. The beige walls were brighter, the doors a dull brown. Each peephole glimmered like a firefly. Logan lugged along behind him like he was exhausted by the constant surprises.

Marshal couldn't blame him. The past two days, the kitchen well had begun to pick off the team. He didn't even know his teammates could be sacrifices. The idea that he could have been a consequence for Logan's selfish tap-in at the buzzer messed with his head and made him boil viciously. He wanted to turn around and tackle Logan, catch him off guard so he could get in a few good licks before the big man pummeled him.

But he remained calm and patient. Marshal had not been taken by the well, and he had saved Emily's life. The two of them could get through anything. He knocked on the door to her room.

Emily answered. Her hair was wet, which nearly sent him into a frenzy. He imagined her taking off the robe, revealing her naked body to him.

Of course, Logan was not part of his imagination.

"What?" she said when she saw him staring.

Logan bumped him aside. "Is Mom here?"

"She went to get breakfast with Dad."

"Logan?" Jessica called from inside.

Logan pushed his way into the room. He seemed stronger than earlier. Purposeful.

"What the hell?" Emily said. "We're getting ready."

"It's all right, Em," Marshal said. "He's come around."

She relaxed and moved aside so Marshal could come in.

"So that's a thing, huh?" Logan said to Emily. "Mom and Dad?"

"It might be," she said.

"What about her new boyfriend? Whatever his name is."

Emily ignored him. "So, you decided to forfeit?"

"We don't have a choice," Marshal said.

Logan scoffed, pretending to cough. Jessica gave him a hug.

"Thanks, Logan," she whispered.

"Kelvin and Doug are gone," Marshal blurted out.

Emily's face paled. "No..."

Logan repeated what he had told Marshal earlier, lingering on how groggy he had been when Kelvin spoke to him. How he had thought it was a dream because Kelvin had put weight on his broken leg. Logan was making excuses for not stopping Kelvin the same way he had made excuses for winning against West Archer.

Hearing the story a second time, it should have been easier for Marshal to stop himself from rolling his eyes, but it was just as difficult—perhaps more so, since Jessica seemed so sympathetic. Even Emily seemed to soften toward her brother.

"We have to go," she said.

"Em, we don't even know where they're going—"

"Of course we do. The house. It has to be that house."

"Shit," Marshal said. "I didn't think of that." It was true enough, but Marshal wondered if he had intentionally been dense. He didn't want to find Kelvin.

But Doug? And Alex? And Mikey who was no different than Marshal's little brother? "You're right. They have to be in that house. We need a ride."

"Mom's car." Emily grabbed the keys from atop the TV stand. "Dad picked her up this morning, so I'll call her cell phone and convince her to ride with him to the game after they finish breakfast."

"Good," Marshal said. "Her car's small, but the four of us should be able to squeeze in."

"I'm not riding with y'all," Logan announced.

Marshal glared at him.

"I have to get Will," he explained.

"Is that really worth it right now?" Marshal asked.

"Will's been with me from the beginning on this. The guy got goddamn shot at for me. He deserves to know."

"Do you know where he's staying?" Emily asked.

"He's here. In this hotel. The presumptuous shithead told me his room number, in case something like this happened."

"I'll go with you," Jessica said.

"No. His Camaro is pretty crammed. Will and I will meet you at the house. We'll be right behind you."

"Just get there as soon as possible," Emily said.

Logan nodded and scanned over the three of them, like he was about to make a speech. Instead, he nodded again and left.

Marshal didn't think it was worth it to get Will, but it didn't matter. They would either get to the house before Kelvin and Doug, who presumably would need time to find a vehicle themselves, and it was possible Kelvin had left the room not long before Logan woke up and realized it wasn't a dream, or they would get to the house after them and have to figure out what to do next. Regardless, Marshal finally felt like he was right where he needed to be. At Emily's side.

6

Alex rose and gasped.

Morning light soaked the abandoned house. For once, the empty front room was filled with light. Dust motes floated around him reminding Alex of the way he had felt just before passing out.

Floating.

He and the presence had floated.

Now he was lying against the hardwood floor, his whole body as stiff as it had ever been.

How long was I out?

He felt disoriented, battling the excited feeling of floating and the tension of wrestling against—

"Mikey," he whispered. His voice was powder.

Blood smeared the floor around him. His arm was bleeding again where Mikey had scratched him, a trickle of crimson running down to his hand. He must have irritated the wound in his sleep.

His eye had swollen above the loose flesh that had made him feel like his eye was dangling from its socket. Pain shot through him when he tried to open it wide. His other eye wasn't much better because his broken cheek bone had bloated that side of his face.

How long was I fucking out?!

His vision was obscured but he managed to right himself.

"Mikey," he called, a little louder this time.

No response. Of course not.

"L-Letty?"

His jelly legs made walking a nightmare, but he managed to run into the rough brick siding of the well.

The black circle within met his gaze like a giant dilated pupil. He reached for the rope.

It was gone.

The railroad spike dug into the exterior as always but no noose was around it.

"Mikey?" He stumbled out of the kitchen. "Letty?"

A tapping sound drifted like a leaky faucet. But there was no running water in this house.

"Mikey?"

The back of the house was as dark as night, but he felt his way toward the bathroom and the two bedrooms, toward the tap, tap, tap. A cold doorknob snipped at his hand, and he turned it. Slits of daylight flooded his vision as he pushed into the first bedroom on his right.

A moment later, his blindness passed and he saw her swinging body in front of the boarded-up window. Her shoes tapped against the rail at the end of the moldy bed.

Tap, tap, tap.

Alex wanted to scream. Instead, her name croaked out of his mouth. "Letty..."

And an insane thought crossed his mind: *How can a ceiling fan support her weight?*

He rushed to get her down, unable to do more than whimper: "No, no, no, no."

And he thought about the way she so easily agreed to drive them to Nowhere, and if he had really paid attention, he would have seen the same look in her eye as he saw in Mikey's. They were no longer themselves, all because Alex had to prove himself on the court.

And, boy, did he. Thirty-six points was the most he had scored in any playoff game in his career. The journalists were along the sideline, scratching on their notepads and nodding their heads with pleasure as he knocked down shot after shot. College scouts were no doubt in the crowd, highlighting his name, seeking out his parents in the crowd so they could offer him a scholarship as soon as he was finished leading the Devils to the championship. He had been more than noticed out there; he had been seen.

He almost smiled thinking about it, and suddenly Letty was limp in his arms on the musty bed, the rope coiled around him like a snake on his shoulders. Her color had changed her completely. She was no longer Letty. She was unreal now, and maybe none of this was real, anyway.

He held her like they had been tragic lovers, but they had never made love. They had never been anything. *She shouldn't be here. She shouldn't be lying dead like her brother.*

The thought of the word—*brother*—caused a panic in him. If Letty had killed herself—

Alex dropped her and ran to the bathroom and the other bedroom, and each time he opened a door, he imagined seeing Mikey unreal too, a prop among junk being used in a high school play. The abandoned house had become just that. Nowhere had no theater arts, no stage to do such a thing on, but now, apparently, they did, and Alex was the star. He would be seen by the crowd gathered to watch the next act. And he knew what the next act was supposed to be.

Mikey wasn't inside the house. He was exactly where he had fought so hard against Alex to get to. Alex's wounds pulsated like a reminder.

He didn't want to return to the bedroom where he had thrown Letty's body onto the bed and missed, leaving her half-on and half-off. But he held his breath and went inside and avoided looking at her body until he had the rope wrapped around his arm.

He went to Macy's car to find a flashlight, and the morning light completely undid him. The world spun, and Alex sobbed. He kept moving in an unbalanced way, lucky the driver's side door had been left open by Letty because he may not have been able to finagle a door handle. It was hard enough unlatching the glove compartment as he reached across for it. His tears stopped when he felt the cold metal of a Maglite. It was even heavier in his hand than normal.

For a moment, Alex considered driving away.

He had climbed down the well on his own before. He was the only one to come to this place without his teammates. But when he thought about having to look into that hideous, vacant eye of a hole again, his body became wrapped in a blanket that somehow made him feel colder. It felt like—

The presence hugging him. Heavy against him, then light. Floating like there was nothing inside them but helium.

He slapped himself. The pain in his swollen eye came back with a vengeance but at least the torture was hot and fast. It broke him from his cold temptation.

It was easy enough to go down there when you had a wish to make, but now that you have the chance to save your brother, you're too chicken shit, huh? Suck it up, dude. Be a man!

He thought the last sentence in his father's voice, of course, then secured the flashlight and went back inside the house. He clicked on the light as soon as he was in the front room even though this was the one room where he could see without it.

The blood from his scratches had stopped. His swollen eye seeped a goopy substance, and he yearned so badly to rub it. His jaw buzzed achingly. A metallic taste filled his mouth, his tongue vibrating like he had licked a battery. A part of him longed to float again. That would take away the pain.

He dropped the rope by the side of the well and stared into the void inside and imagined that breezy echo from the half-moon opening.

Then he heard a car rolling down the path between the trees. He swung the Maglite around as if someone would have already exited the moving car and was standing right behind him, ready to push him down the well. But that was insane. The thought of someone who still had a lingering presence standing behind him all day, and Alex no longer did, and a part of him missed the presence.

He moved back into the front room and peered through the broken screen door. He didn't recognize the car as it moved down the old driveway, long overgrown with weeds and clumps of dirt. It was a maroon Chevy Malibu, making a whistling sound, like the engine was about to start smoking.

Alex stepped outside.

The driver's face was silhouetted by shadow until he got out. It was Kelvin. He appeared his normal self. Then he closed the car door and stepped toward Alex without limping, despite the white cast on his lower leg.

Oh, goddamn. Not you too.

Kelvin's confident, crooked grin haunted Alex. His eyes were like the eternally black ring of the well. Alex stood and took up the Maglite, wringing it like a weapon.

"Don't be scared, Alex."

"I'm not—I'm going to get my brother."

"Dude. He's as safe as can be. You should be jealous. You won't get to make the descent for some time. At least you're not supposed to. Things change. I can change them if you want."

"It's controlling you, man. Just like Mikey. And-and Letty."

Kelvin chortled. "I can't believe you hit that, bro."

The metal handle of the Maglite was cold in Alex's palm, its heft making his shoulder ache. He wondered if he could follow through with swinging it if he had to. Kelvin was right about him except he hadn't gone far enough. Alex wasn't just scared, he was a coward. The difference there being scared people could still act when they needed to. Cowards avoided what had to be done.

Kelvin put up his hands in defense. "No offense. She's cute. But she's Allen Prospect's sister. They're trash, man."

"Is that why it killed Allen?"

"Oh, even trash make the descent. We all do."

"Neither you nor I are making any descent today. Don't-don't you want to see the boys? Logan? Big game today."

"Oh, I'll see him. But you..." Kelvin shook his head. "I'm not sure anymore. I knew you were jealous of me, but I didn't know you were *that* jealous of me."

"I'm not jealous of you, you arrogant prick."

"You should be. You really should be." Kelvin kicked the dirt and shoved his hands into his pockets, like he was thinking about what to do. His grin widened, and his dark eyes glistened. "You know what? Fuck it. You helped bring Mikey here. Your own brother, man. That's pretty damn cold. You also made a wish and followed through—for a couple of games, at least. It's still pissed you didn't play more. Use that wish of yours. And it wants you to, Alex. You could leave now and be back in time for the championship game. It wants you to, Alex. Don't you get it? You're supposed to be stuck *here*—" He motioned all around him. "—living out your miserable life. Marrying some girl just like Letty Prospect and having trashy little shits, working at Wrangler's until your dad dies, then moving to Virginia. But you know what? Nothing controls me, man. Nothing tells me what I can and can't do."

Kelvin tapped his finger against his mouth, then sucked on his teeth and simply said, "Yeah…"

He rushed Alex. He moved quicker than a guy with a broken leg should have. Alex raised the Maglite, but before he could bring it down, Kelvin slammed into his midsection and carried him through the screen door, breaking it from its hinges. His back slapped against the mesh screen and hardwood floor beneath it.

The Maglite skittered across the floor toward the slew of bloody letters Alex had always ignored when he came to the house. It was the last thing Alex saw for a while. He and Kelvin wrestled across the front room. He felt fists and kicks, the hardness of the cast catching him in the shin—Alex imagined his leg snapping like Kelvin's—and a knee in his ribs, scratching, pulling.

All the wounds inflicted by Mikey yesterday—*two days ago?*—radiated like he had been set on fire. But his adrenaline pushed all pain to the back of his mind where it was there but also not there. Finally, Alex pinned Kelvin against the threshold of the hallway. To the left was the kitchen, to the right the rooms and bathroom and—

Letty.

He held his knees against Kelvin's arms and hit him hard across the face. Kelvin was dazed for a moment.

Breathing hard, Alex said, "Get a-fucking-hold of yourself, man!"

"You'll see, dude...I'm doing you a favor." His wooziness and his dead eyes fixed on Alex. "Oh, that's right. You don't want to see...You want to be seen."

Alex hesitated, and Kelvin slid an arm free, gripping him by the throat and slamming him backward against the hardwood. Two hands wrapped around Alex, cutting off his air, his throat burning like hot grease. He slapped at Kelvin's face but had no reach.

In his peripheral, he saw the black shine of the Maglite reflecting sunrays through the broken window. He reached for it, tapping the end of his finger against the cold steel. It was just out of reach.

Alex gave up on it and squirmed desperately until his leg found purchase. Bending his knee toward his shoulder, he reared back and kicked Kelvin as hard as he could in the ribs. His old teammate collapsed to the floor, gasping for breath.

Alex stood upright for the first time in the fight. He coughed hoarsely and stepped toward Kelvin, who curled into himself, struggling.

"I'm taking you out of here," Alex croaked, with whatever voice he had left. "You'll feel better when we get away from here."

He reached down to grab him, and Kelvin swung around, the handle of the Maglite cracking against Alex's temple.

Floating in darkness. How nice it felt.

Alex came to but didn't really. Barely aware he was being dragged out of the front room and into the kitchen.

Blackness again. Staring into a face of nothing. A black hole.

He came to a second time when warm blood ran down his broken, swollen cheek into his mouth. And then—

Floating again, swimming through an endless black stream.

Something rough was pulled across his neck. He thought it was Kelvin's hands again, but its callousness was much coarser than skin. Kelvin's legs wrapped around him from behind, as cold and heavy as the shadow figure. Alex reached for the noose around his neck, but his arms were held down by Kelvin's legs.

One hand gripped Kelvin's cast. The other, a hairy leg. The noose was pulled tight, and Alex was fully conscious now, aware of what was happening.

He choked on his blood. Already, he wished he had let Kelvin go to the well. Alex could have made it to the city in time for the championship, just like Kelvin. Alex could have won STATE.

Could have been a hero.

"Don't worry," Kelvin said softly. "You'll be seen."

Alex tried to speak, but only a gurgle of blood came out.

"The others will come. Doug, Marshal, Emily. In a couple of hours, they'll walk through the entryway and see you lying here. Who knows, they might even cry. And you'll get an open casket, which is more than the rest get. A little blood, a little popping eyes, a little ring around your neck. Maxwell will fix you right up. He'll see you too. And then your funeral...Man, oh man. So many people will show up. Your parents will *weep* over your perfectly still body. They will see you, maybe for the first time ever. Don't worry, Alex. You'll get what you've always wished for."

7

Emily kept wiping her palms on her pants when Marshal drove them toward the line of tall pines that served as an entry gate to Nowhere. She felt no emotion, so the sweat on her palms was the only reminder of her nervousness.

Her stability had been shattered. It had started cracking long before Marshal told her about the kitchen well. She had seen Allen in her rearview mirror; she had seen the black cloud in the road; she had woken from a coma when she shouldn't have and felt this comforting warmth on the surface she knew was false from the small tinge of dread beneath it, warning her.

Cheering on the team was only a distraction until the boys from West Archer began screaming. She had never seen full body cramps like that. Lumps of hard muscle beneath their skin shifted to places they didn't belong. In the story her mom told her about Green River's miraculous run, nothing like that had happened.

A numb despair gripped Emily at the sight of them, a feeling that reminded her of when she first learned her aunt was dead. She was two when it happened, much too young to remember, yet sometimes, when she looked at Aunt Jocelyn's picture, she had a faint memory of her aunt holding her and talking to her in a jabbery baby voice.

But the despair she felt really started long before West Archer. It started when she watched Kelvin break his leg.

"Almost there," Marshal said, although the others already knew. It was as if he couldn't handle how quiet they had been the past three hours.

The pines were less inviting than before, looming over Snakeback Road. Her mom's car corkscrewed around the dirt road, fish-tailing wildly. Dust misted the air around the car. Finally, they turned off the road onto the hidden path leading to the house, what used to be someone's driveway. She wondered who had lived here and if they had known what their well would become when they built it in the kitchen.

"What's Macy's car doing here?" Jessica said, panicked, pointing from the backseat.

"Was she at the game yesterday?" Marshal asked.

"Yeah…she and Reba arrived after us, so we weren't standing together. Do you remember, Em?"

Emily nodded. "Mal was with them too. Macy seemed flustered. She—oh shit."

"What?" Marshal breathed out.

"Letty wasn't with them."

"You're right," Jessica said. "Oh god…Letty."

Emily felt tears welling up. They were only prevented because there was an even more immediate concern. "Um, Marsh?"

"Yeah," he said, staring ahead as they pulled closer to Macy's car and the house and two other—

"Whose cars are those?"

"I don't recognize either one."

"The blue truck is Maxwell White's," Jessica said. "He always gives a good tip with a slip of paper like a fortune in a fortune cookie, only it's a Bible verse. Melinda says he used to put them in her cereal box when she was a kid, and she'd get pissed, thinking it might be a toy." She rattled off the whole thing like she'd taken a shot of adrenaline.

"What's the preacher doing here?" Marshal asked.

"He's not," Emily said, putting it together. "It's Doug."

"What about the Malibu?"

"Kelvin. It has to be him." Her heart skipped its little warning at her.

"They didn't come together when it…*called* them?"

Now, a tear did fall down her cheek. She sniffled the rest away and said to herself, "He's actually here."

Emily had never been to the kitchen well. The house looked like it could collapse at any moment. The roof even bowed in above the front room. There was no door—only an unwelcome opening. A jolt of fear made her hesitate before it. She wished Logan had gotten here before her.

She was tempted to let Marshal go inside first but knowing Kelvin was here gave her an inexplicably optimistic feeling. It was possible he had not been brought to the house to hang himself the way her aunt had. It was possible the ones whose bodies had never been found were different than the others. Savable. Maybe even meant to be saved if you were brave enough to find them.

She passed through the doorway.

Enough light illuminated the front room for her to immediately notice long streaks of blood across the fallen screen door and hardwood floor.

Whatever optimism she'd had disappeared. Fear surged through her, and she went cold. To her right, open letters were scattered around, dried blood staining the pages and the couch. But the long smear of blood on the floor was fresh.

A pungent shit smell with an acidic hint filled the room.

Marshal bumped into her as she abruptly stopped.

"Holy shit," he said. Then he yelled, "Alex! Kelvin!" He ran past her, around the corner into the hallway.

She followed slowly.

"Oh *God*!" Marshal's voice, almost comically unlike him, echoed.

The sheer volume of it made Emily jump. Her skin buzzed and she froze. Jessica put her arm around her and propelled them forward.

It was dark in the kitchen, but Emily could see enough to

realize Doug was leaning down in prayer, faced away from them, in front of a black lump.

Jessica clicked on the Maglite she had picked up. She and Emily screamed, and Doug finally stood to face them.

The white spotlight illuminated Alex's body, leaning against the side of the well. A noose was around his neck, his face purple and swollen, eyes protruding and bloodshot, staring into the middle distance where nothing existed. Blood reddened his cheeks, jaw, and neck, one arm splattered with blood. There had been a fight, and Alex had lost. Choked to death by the rope they had used to climb down and make a wish.

Emily's mind shut down while it tried to comprehend the scene. The more her eyes focused on Alex's body, the less she understood it. In the absence of thought, her mind conjured an image of Allen in the backseat of her Kia, his face rising above the dark into the moonlight, his skin pulled up and away from the rest of him.

"He's not one of them," Doug said.

"What, Dougie?" Marshal asked, surprisingly calm.

"Alex isn't like the others. He wasn't killed by the wish. He was murdered."

"We thought it took you too, man."

"No, I...I had to come here, so I took Brother Maxwell's truck. Do you think he'll forgive me? Will God?"

"I don't know, man." Marshal shook his head and looked up at Emily, as if he wanted her to understand the next thing he said. "I think Kelvin killed Alex."

"Where's Logan?" was all Emily could say. She wanted her big brother to be here, to comfort her like he had in the hospital.

"We don't know it was Kelvin." Jessica approached the well.

Emily envied how in control of her body she was.

"We don't know anything." Jessica shined the flashlight into the well. "Damn. That's deep."

Emily relaxed now that the light wasn't pointed at Alex's body. She was happy to stand in the dark and forget what she had seen.

Her feet felt less heavy. She might even be able to move in a minute.

"Kelvin!" Jessica called to the empty house. "I'm gonna check the other rooms."

"I'll come with you," Marshal offered. "Just in case he's waiting to murder us too."

"Please don't," Doug said. "It's not a pretty sight."

"Dude...what's back there?" Marshal almost seemed excited.

"Letty. She was killed too."

"We need to get to a phone," Jessica said. "We need to call the police."

"We have to wait for Logan," Emily objected.

"We'll give him five minutes," Marshal said, "then we get the hell away from here until the cops come. We can go to my house and call." When he and Jessica passed by her to check the rest of the house, Marshal put his hand on the small of Emily's back with too much lightness, too much familiarity. "I'm sorry, Em. I can't believe he'd do this," he said as if Kelvin had *chosen* to kill anyone.

She shrugged him off.

Doug watched Marshal and Jessica move to the other rooms from the opening to the kitchen, where a bit of light hit him. Emily remained in the dark half of the kitchen, knowing Alex's body continued to stare at her.

Emily caught a glimpse of what Doug was clutching tightly in his hand.

"Is that a cross?" she asked.

"It's a symbol," Doug said, "in case I need the reminder."

"Reminder for what?"

"That we're in a spiritual battle."

"You think Kelvin did it too, don't you?"

Doug sighed. "Kelvin isn't Kelvin…He's possessed by the Devil, Emily. If we can find him, I can save him."

Jessica's flashlight waved about distantly, shining here and there against the hallway walls in random, hypnotic twirls of light. Behind Emily, Alex's presence felt palpable. She slowly began to feel a presence on her neck, imagining Alex rising and standing behind her, a zombie ready to clamp down.

She shivered and moved closer to Doug until she saw something new had entered the house. She paused.

"Doug…"

"What?"

She pointed at his feet.

"What the—"

A black fog crawled from the front room, through the hallway, and over Doug's feet. It drifted further into the kitchen, disappearing in the darkness, no doubt hovering around Emily now too. She pulled up one of her jean legs and felt a cool mist against her bare ankle.

She dropped her jean leg and stood rooted again. She wanted to run to Doug, get away from Alex's body, but hoped to avoid the source of the fog.

She wondered where it had come from. Was it the front room? Outside?

The well?

She slowly turned to face the kitchen well. Her eyes had adjusted enough to make out Alex's outline, still lying there against the brick, like a soldier neglecting his duty.

Somewhere in the distance, Doug called out Marshal's

name and she whipped back around to find he wasn't a few feet away anymore.

Emily was alone.

She wished her brother was here. Logan should have been here by now. Her mind's eye conjured another image: Kelvin climbing out of the well and standing before her on his broken leg.

"Where are you, Logan?"

8

Will sat in the stands watching the Class A girls' team from Seiling finish off their opponent and win yet another championship for the small town. After the game, each player received a medal and took a picture with the director from the Oklahoma Secondary Schools Athletic Association. Then the team posed together with the gold ball trophy between them.

It was something the Nowhere Devils would never experience. Will often denied his support for the team. He enjoyed hating on them. But his disappointment had been there since Kelvin's injury—the abrupt end to their undefeated, dominant season.

Logan's wish had delayed it, taking the boys all the way to the championship game. Now they would have to lose on purpose. No matter what any of the players thought, the Devils were not good enough to beat the Olney Mustangs without Kelvin, without Alex, and without magic. The only question was whether Logan would do what he should have done yesterday.

Will still couldn't believe Logan had made the game-winning shot. Maybe he had been trying to knock the ball out of bounds, but he should have known better than to even go for it. The crowd's pleas had gotten to him.

Every Nowhere fan near Will had cried out, "Hustle! Play harder! Get the rebound! Find the open man!"

Like every other game, there were fans who had to be heard. They thought they were an extension of Coach Park. But at the Big House, Will doubted the players on the court could even hear the crowd from this far back, so the fans had no impact on Logan.

No, it was only Logan who had decided to tap the ball up, the magic propelling it through the hoop.

After yesterday's game, Will was disappointed to realize he had been right about Logan ever since they stopped hanging out because Logan wanted to be a basketball player. Logan was no different than the rest of them. Pretend good guys. Someone so desperate to win a game, he didn't care who got hurt in the process.

Logan hadn't even told Will that Alex and Mikey Spruce went missing after the King-Marlow game on Thursday. Will had to find out with the rest of the crowd against West Archer. The big man was being careless and irresponsible, acting like they had never gone to Green River and spoken to Betty Bromide.

If Logan had seen what Will had seen, he would have known what was at stake.

The frightened corpses of the Beaumonts were never far from Will's mind. He hated his curiosity and wished he had never followed Ryan Holbrook into that house.

He couldn't sleep on the uncomfortable hotel bed last night. He preferred the wooden bleachers to that bed and got here early because of it. Now, he waited eagerly for the Nowhere-versus-Olney game to start. It was the number-one ranked team against the number-two ranked team.

Since their lone loss came in Districts, Nowhere remained ranked number one. If any fans weren't aware of Kelvin Harris or his injury, they thought they were going to get a great game.

It will be something...

Despite the fact it should be an Olney blowout, the magic would pull out all the stops to tempt Logan and the others. The West Archer cramps were like nothing Will had ever seen before. It had looked like four guys on the team bench were having simultaneous seizures. Like they were being abducted by a UFO.

All that was missing was their stiffened bodies being beamed up. The sight of West Archer cramping like that made Will ache all over. If the well did that to get Nowhere to win the semifinals, he had no clue what it would do in the final game to fulfill the wish.

More and more Nowhere fans began to show up. Will mentally noted everyone who sat around him—those who took the nicer, closer seats, and the students filling the lively standing-room-only section. In his mind, he checked off attendees who should be here but weren't.

Someone had died last night. He had no doubt Logan's putback game-winning basket had sealed someone's fate, the same way Bolan Grimes's arrest had sealed Red Springer's and the phantom calls against Colesville had sealed Mr. Tune's. Not to mention Ethan Crist getting food poisoning and killing Will's elderly neighbors...*Or how your grandma's healing sealed Bird's...*

Will's life had changed because Logan played a prank on him. That was how all this started. His trip to Dallas to see his grandma had been an awe-inspiring week of celebration. She had looked at him clearly for the first time ever. He almost cried every time they made eye contact. Will also wanted to tell her why she was suddenly healed.

She spent the week thanking God for her blessing, and he

had to stop himself from interjecting, "If this is God's doing, well, you're looking at his instrument."

Will wasn't sure if he believed in God, but after that magical week in Texas, he was inclined to think an almighty creator put the wishing well in that kitchen just for him. Then he went back out there with Logan and Alex.

Already, he was taking a backseat to the basketball team. Some things never changed. Still, he had been just as excited as Logan to see the magic work during the Regional finals. For the first time, he could root for the team because he rooted for the well.

Will began dreaming of other wishes he would make when the season was over. He wasn't a great student but aspired to be a screenwriter in Hollywood. He loved movies and stories, had read a hundred screenplays to figure out the format, and worked on his own during free time. He had to get into a university that would look good on paper for film school, and he would need a scholarship to pay for it.

It was the perfect second wish. But now there would be no second wish. It turned out the well wasn't a miracle from God, but more likely from the Devil.

The Olney Mustangs took the court. Twelve players of similar height and build, led by the Mosely brothers, who were only a tad more athletic than the rest of the team but a lot smarter. They formed layup lines and attacked the basket with force and energy, as though the game had already started.

Four of the Nowhere Devils came out shortly after, each with a ball, taking shots from all over the court. There was no purpose or strategy to their shots—like Jack Ward would ever get an opportunity to shoot a three or fadeaway jumper from midrange.

Logan focused on gathering rebounds for his teammates, clasping each one in his thick paws.

Will shifted in his seat when his butt went numb. He was tempted to sit closer, where the seats were cushioned, but he was committed to his observations. It was his role in all this. He had gotten Logan to go to Green River, where they had learned once and for all it wasn't a coincidence—that there were consequences for the wishes.

He continued scanning the crowd for anyone missing and realized he hadn't seen Logan's sister Emily or Jessica Fromm. They had been in the student section for each previous game. The girls weren't there—or anywhere else he could see.

The scoreboard above center court counted down to tipoff. Less than five minutes now. No sign of Superintendent Walker, who always arrived early.

Will's heart sped up.

He imagined the kitchen well taking several sacrifices after the semifinals. There was no rule that it was limited to one per magic result. The Beaumonts were two.

Although they looked like one, didn't they? Lying in their marriage bed, horrified to die together, their tortured faces leaning toward each other like conjoined twins.

The scoreboard clock continued ticking down. Under three minutes now until the national anthem and starting lineup announcements, then the tipoff between the tallest guy on the court, Logan Tramer, and the highest leaper of the three Mosely brothers—Will couldn't remember which one.

He continued scanning the crowd until his attention returned to the court. Dylan Lovegood looked afraid; he kept gazing up like his brother would dive from the rafters like Sting in WCW.

Will had been so distracted by the crowd that he hadn't realized there were still only four Devils shooting around. No Marshal. No Doug. No Kelvin by the bench. He hadn't seen Coach Park either.

Two minutes until tipoff.

What the hell is going on?

Sweat bubbled on his fever-hot forehead. He leaned forward and tapped Principal Jacobs's shoulder. "Any idea what's happening, Ms. Jacobs?"

"What do you mean, Mr. Roebuck?"

"Where's Coach? Where's Doug and Marshal?"

The white-haired principal squinted her eyes toward the court. "Well, I'll be...I don't know." She stood, her red Devils t-shirt wrinkled in the back. No matter how many games he noticed it, it was still strange to see his principal in jeans.

"I'll see if I can find Hewitt."

Will tapped his leg unconsciously. He only realized he was doing so when his seat began to shake. He wondered if he made a mistake asking her. *You won't find Hewitt, Ms. Jacobs. Superintendent Walker is dead. He has that same look the Beaumonts had. So do the others...Coach Park, Mooreland, Lovegood, Emily, Jessica. They're all dead, lying there in a bed, staring at me.*

"Goddammit," he muttered aloud, and other spectators glanced his way.

They appeared just as confused. In fact, the whole Nowhere crowd had noticed the on-court absences. Doug and Marshal's families were seated in the closer seats. They began to stand, then sit, then stand, or nervously pace on the open concrete space next to the seats. He thought Marshal's mom might do something erratic after the incident he witnessed before the semifinal.

Less than a minute until tipoff.

Coach Park emerged from one of the tunnels. Will gathered himself quickly, recalibrating.

The referees were with Coach. He seemed to be arguing with them while they shook their heads dismissively and scampered toward the scorer's table. Coach Park was desperate and furious. The refs were determined to dismiss him.

Will realized what was happening.

Whether Doug and Marshal were dead or not, they weren't coming, leaving Nowhere with only four players. Coach Park could argue all he wanted, but you couldn't play a game four on five, certainly not a championship game. Will recalled seeing a four-on-five situation once or twice. It was always after too many players fouled out. That was different than starting a game with four players.

And yet, Logan continued rebounding calmly under the basket.

A buzzer sounded. It was time for some high school student from some small Oklahoma school to sing the national anthem. Only that student might not get the chance. The lead referee finally held up his hand to stop Coach Park's argument and leaned over to the scorer's table, no doubt telling the announcer to get on the intercom and announce Nowhere had forfeited due to too few players.

Superintendent Walker sprinted from the other side of the court, the OSSAA director powerwalking to keep up with him, holding a thick spiralbound booklet. His finger, an impromptu bookmark, was jabbed between two pages. Principal Jacobs walked a few feet behind them—an observer just like Will.

Wasn't that all he was these past few weeks? He had no responsibility for what had happened to the Beaumonts. Will was here to witness Logan's madness.

Superintendent Walker shouted to interrupt the lead ref. It worked. He and the director approached and dropped the booklet onto the scorer's table, opening it to the marked page.

Jacobs remained a few feet back, shaking her head in disbelief.

Walker pointed to a line on the page. The lead ref nearly

touched his nose to the booklet to read it. He motioned for Walker to step aside. The other referees came forward and read the booklet.

No way, Will thought, his eyes on Logan again.

The big man paid no attention to the adults at the scorer's table. He already knew the answer. The wish wouldn't let him down.

Don't do this, Tramer.

The refs called over both coaches, and the OSSAA director remained in the huddle too. They discussed the situation. Olney's coach nearly burst out laughing, slapping his hand over his mouth. He apologized, then shook hands with Coach Park. The huddle dispersed, and the announcer proceeded as if this were any other championship game.

While Will stood for the national anthem, he awaited the starting lineup announcements with dread. There was no longer any plan to lose on purpose.

Logan had decided to finish what he had started.

9

The black fog thickened and rose to Doug's waist in the front room. He had moved into the room when he saw the daylight shift into an unnatural red through the broken windows and open doorway. The red tint window-paned the room like stained glass.

His arm took on the same translucent redness when he stretched it in front of him, holding his tiny cross. The Devil had come, and only Doug could stop him.

"Doug—"

"Stay back!"

Marshal and Jessica stood in the hallway. She beamed the Maglite forward, but it couldn't pierce the thickening fog.

Smoke billowed upward from the front doorway like exhaust from Tim's truck. A putrid stench—like swampy standing water at the bottom of a well—filled the room, mixing with the death smell they had whiffed before.

The higher the smoke rose, the more resolute Doug became. He had a new superpower—something greater than Pity. This was why Mal had come to him in his dream last night and told him to go to Nowhere, why he had been tempted on Monday and Tuesday nights.

He recalled Brother Maxwell's words: *If you find yourself afraid, clutch this cross and trust in the Lord. He will give you strength.*

Doug had been forgiven for his shameful acts, the sins he couldn't resist. Forgiveness washed over him like the warm water of his baptism. He was part of God's army. The Lord's strength was his superpower now. No demon, nor the Devil himself, could stand against God Almighty.

"Begone, Satan!" he shouted, stepping toward the wall of smoke.

It plumed before him.

"The Lord is in control here. This is His house!"

"What the fuck are you doing, Dougie?" Marshal called. "Get away from there!"

"Shut up!" Doug clutched the cross until tiny splinters of wood pierced his palm.

The black wall took shape, a demonic figure near Doug's size but slighter in shoulders. The feathery smoke quickly solidified into a dark silhouette—a mere absence of color, like the fog that lingered at Doug's waist. The red light framed the silhouette.

"Our Father who art in Heaven, hallowed be Thy name!" Doug recited the Lord's Prayer like a chant, spittle glazing his bottom lip. The cross soaked up the sweat in his palm.

A figure began to emerge from the silhouette. The darkness rolled away, melting like foam from the bottom up. Shapely white legs came first. When he saw pubic hair, Doug lost his concentration. He forgot the words and the cross slipped from his grip.

The body continued to emerge—past breasts and slight shoulders—until it stopped at her neck, hiding her face in shadow. Not that it needed to. He knew Mal had come to confront him one last time.

Doug dropped to the floor, completely covered by the fog. He searched for the cross at his feet. Cold hardwood against his fingertips, then something warm and wet. He swallowed hard. Alex's blood.

His hand brushed wooden corners. He couldn't resist looking at the body when he rose to his feet, clutching his bloody cross. She had a mole on one breast.

He felt deeply cold.

This wasn't Mal Turner.

He stared into the cloudy nothingness of her face and continued his prayer: "Lead us not into temptation, but deliver us from—"

"Why did you do this to me, Doug?" The voice was familiar but muffled like her mouth was full.

He froze but managed to keep his cross between him and her. She had not spoken in his nightmare.

A face finally revealed from the cloud. It was Coach Reed, her face wide in terror, her eyes strained and red, her nose pulled toward her chin. Her entire face stretched into a crescent moon. Her tongue swelled thickly from a slack mouth.

"Why did you have to do it, Doug?"

He stared down, unable to look at her twisted face. Her nude body was no reprieve. His mind took him back to the morgue as if he was actually there.

He pulled each corpse from the refrigerated cabinet deliberately. First, the old Beaumonts, then Allen with his crushed head, but this time there was another body: Coach Reed. He couldn't help but pull the sheet off her and stare at her blue skin. His eyes were drawn to her face. He wanted to cover her with the sheet again, but it slipped from his hand and floated out the open doorway, into the red sky.

"I'm sorry," he cried. "Forgive me."

He dropped the cross again, this time on purpose, leaving his open palm slack next to his jeans, a cross-shaped smear of blood on it.

10

Marshal waited in the hallway, watching things unfold, irrationally hopeful that the most faithful person he knew could defeat this devil. He had no idea what this supernatural force truly was but wondered if the reason faith existed was to fight monsters. Perhaps it had been necessary for survival.

Whether God was real or not, maybe human evolution required a belief in something beyond yourself.

Then the nude girls' coach stabbed her claws into Doug's face and peeled his skin away.

Marshal screamed until he couldn't. His entire body convulsed. A cocoon of smoke wrapped around both Doug and Julia Reed.

Jessica dropped the Maglite, and Marshal yanked her toward the kitchen, where Emily stood, catatonic. He couldn't see anything in the back of the house, his eyes having adjusted to the red light. Marshal felt around until he found Emily's hand.

"We have to get out of here," he said.

She squeezed his hand, and they turned, inexplicably, back

toward the nothing-shape. Marshal already knew there was no backdoor in this house, and running felt better than standing still.

He ran in the dark of the kitchen and slammed into a wall, his shoulder burning with heat, then slid into the hallway. The red light blinded him for a moment.

When his vision cleared, the black fog had rolled up the walls and crawled across the ceiling in the front room. A small tornado swirled nearby. Marshal knew it would form another silhouette—another person brought back from the dead to haunt and kill them.

The Maglite rolled beneath his foot. He tripped, pulling Jessica and Emily down with him, twisting his ankle in the process. They turned to help him up.

"*Go!*" he shouted. "Get out of *here!*"

His voice was so menacing, both girls flinched. Was that what he was to women—a danger? Was that why Emily didn't want to be with him?

Then the girls listened to him and ran.

The tornado paused, and Marshal waited for it to take him. But the figure quickly formed its three-dimensional silhouette, cutting off the girls' path to the front opening where the screen door had once been. The silhouette rose as high as the ceiling, blocking Jessica's way and pushing Emily back toward Marshal at the hallway entryway.

Marshal pulled himself up by the entryway threshold and limped past Emily toward Jessica, but she was already being swept upward.

He dove for her hand, grasping it and pulling with all his strength. The figure was stronger, flipping Jessica upside down and yanking her higher. Emily wrapped both arms around Marshal's waist, adding resistance. Jessica, stretched out, was lowering toward the floor again.

She slapped at the silhouetted arm, but her hand passed right through it, a spritz of mist wafting away before the arm solidified again.

"Hold on," Marshal said, gritting his teeth. Sweat rolled down his face. He pulled harder.

The shape cleared like smoke, revealing a giant-sized Allen Prospect. His head was caved in, black blood spilling from the wound, down his loose-skinned face.

Jessica screamed.

"Hold on," Marshal said again, his resolve slipping. His grip started to falter. "Hold...on..."

He lost her, falling into Emily.

Jessica was pulled face-to-face with Allen. His vacant stare betrayed no recognition of the time she had tried to help him in the backseat of Emily's Kia. His mouth opened impossibly wide, a smoky pit inside, and swallowed her face first.

As soon as her body was inside the unreal mouth, Allen became smoke again. No face, no mouth—only a curling black hole covering the entire front room, plunging it into darkness like the back half of the house.

Marshal rolled atop Emily, feeling his way to her hand. He grabbed it and pressed the car keys into her palm.

"You gotta get out," he said.

"Marsh—"

"However you can. Get out of here."

He stood, hoping the figure would come for him next—still, improbably, madly, even, thinking if he showed Emily he was her hero, then they would be together.

Emily's steps pattered away until he was certain he was alone in the dark. He backed up as far as he could, willing it to follow him into the house and clear a path for Emily.

All he had left was futile hope.

He stumbled backward until he hit the wall, then side-stepped into the hallway, backing into the kitchen until his back met the well's brick.

"C'mon, asshole," he said. "Come and fucking get me."

The smoke cleared before him, its own red light haloing behind the silhouette.

"Oh, you like to be seen, don't you?" He laughed, his mind unraveling. "You vain fuck."

The figure transformed.

Emily stood there.

A pang gripped his heart.

The figure made no attempt to trick him. It wasn't dressed as Emily had been today. Its hair was down, its face bright with color, and she wore a summer dress he had never seen before that clung to all the right places on her body. She was barefoot, floating elegantly toward him.

"Em..." he whispered.

She finally wanted him. For two months, ever since seeing her holding hands with Kelvin in the hallway, he had wanted this so badly.

And this Emily certainly wanted him to. She placed a hand against his cheek and smiled.

Slowly, she slid her hands behind his neck and hugged him. Her cheek brushed against his.

Hadn't he imagined this?

It was the night after Bolan's arrest. He convinced Emily to go to the party at Turner's barn instead of Kelvin's house. They had a toke from Reba Jacobs' joint but were mostly riding the high of saving Ryan Holbrook from getting his skull crushed in by Uncle Thomas—Marshal's distant relative.

They found themselves outside of the barn, standing close to each other unconsciously because of how cold it was. Emily told him how much he meant to her, how loyal of a friend he had been all these years. How *patient* he had been.

She looked up at him with more than friendship and pulled him into a hug, her cheek brushing against his. He was no longer cold because her body pressed against his. Marshal held the hug a little longer. She seemed okay with it.

Finally, they pulled ever so slightly away, her face an inch from his. So close he could feel her breath against his lips. Before he could kiss her, she kissed him. Her tongue slid inside his mouth, and the warmth of her mouth intoxicated him.

Her hands slid across his scalp. He ran his hands along her back, feeling her body against his. She wore nothing beneath the dress, and Marshal began to get hard.

But then she bit down on his tongue with gritty teeth. Hard rocks grinding against his flesh.

Marshal couldn't scream, only gurgle helplessly from the back of his throat.

She yanked on his tongue, sending a searing pain in his mouth. Her hands massaged his scalp until they stretched over his entire head and squeezed.

11

Emily closed her eyes to stop the burning sensation as the front room filled with smoke. The stench was unbearable. She would have vomited if she could, but instead, she swallowed hot acid and felt her way forward. On the inside of her eyelids, a bright red interrupted the darkness.

She opened her eyes just enough to see the faint red rectangle of the front doorframe. The smoke cleared while she ran from the house, her adrenaline pushing her forward until she reached her mom's car and climbed inside.

Emily fumbled with the keys, desperate to leave this place —leave *Nowhere* entirely. Maybe that was all it took to escape it

—but she knew that wasn't true because Aunt Joss hadn't escaped it.

The inside of the car glowed red, like the rest of the world. She finally got the key into her trembling hand, shoved it into the ignition, and started the engine.

Then the car was lifted. Her stomach dropped like she was on a rollercoaster.

A moment later, the entire vehicle tilted onto its side, the ground growing further away.

The nothing-face appeared through the passenger's side door, stretching toward her. She reached for the handle and pulled it. The driver's side door flung open, and gravity yanked Emily to the ground. Instinctively, she tried to catch herself, and her wrist snapped.

She didn't see it, but the pain was immediate—a sharp, cold, and burning agony that followed a brief shock. Emily screamed in an unrecognizable voice. Hadn't she screamed like this before?

The car hovered above her before it dropped. She rolled to avoid it, dragging her broken wrist across the dirt.

When the car slammed down five feet away, she screamed again.

Yes, she had screamed like this before—when Kelvin's leg split apart. Emily had been sitting just behind the team bench, watching him because she always watched Kelvin. Even before they started dating, she'd had a crush on her brother's best friend.

Kelvin had known—he said he could always tell.

That night, she had watched him closely while he destroyed the Mutton Rams. He didn't even need to be in the game anymore, but Kelvin loved playing basketball. You could hardly get him off the court. Logan set a damn good screen, and Kelvin curled around for an open shot near the free-throw line. The defender was nowhere near him.

Untouched, Kelvin came down on one leg—an awkward landing, but one he'd had a hundred times before. This time, it was different.

That was immediately clear when his leg landed like a bird's, straight and certain, then his shin folded backward like a drawing compass, and Emily screamed. Just like now, she screamed.

At least, that was how she remembered it.

Perhaps it wasn't true. Maybe she gasped and braced herself for a sigh of relief like the crowd who hadn't seen the injury. Or maybe she couldn't release the scream, like everyone else who had witnessed it.

Had she misremembered? Had she given herself a more dramatic memory of her reaction?

Her wrist burned, and she fixed her blurry gaze on the sky— no clouds, no sun, just a blank sheet of unreal redness. She was already dead because no way the sky could look like this in the living world.

The red tint made the silhouette even darker. It crawled toward her on all fours and raked its body over hers. It was too heavy to be just smoke. Its nothing-face filled her vision, an inch away. A tickling mist brushed her lips.

It stared into her eyes, though it had no eyes—no face, no features, just a solid, empty oval.

Emily waited for it to transform into Allen Prospect, as it had with Jessica. After all, she had been the one driving. She was as responsible as anyone for his death.

Instead, she saw nothing but darkness.

The figure didn't transform. It hesitated.

She had no other thought while it remained above her for who knew how long. Time didn't seem to pass in this red world.

Finally, the weight lifted, and the figure dissipated into a cloud, merging with the black fog before creeping away. The sky returned to light blue, the high-noon sun bearing down on her.

Emily breathed for the first time in an eternity and let out another yelp of pain. She grabbed her wrist, and another agonizing shot of pain wrecked her. She climbed to her feet awkwardly, keeping her left arm loose to stop the throbbing. She started toward the other vehicles, hoping Macy's car or the random Malibu had their keys.

Macy's car was closest, but there were no keys in the ignition. She shivered at the thought of searching Alex's corpse for them. She tried the Malibu and sighed with relief when she found the keys in the ignition. Through all this, her eyes kept darting around, expecting the smoke to return for her.

Emily was surprised she could move with any purpose, but her body and mind were numb, and her intuition took over. Inaction was no longer an option. She had to leave. She had to get help. She started the Malibu and gripped the steering wheel with her good hand.

Then she paused.

Her eyes fixed on the abandoned house. It felt like another part of her—perhaps her subconscious—was pushing through her instincts to survive, attempting to send a thought into her mind. But nothing came to mind except *leave, leave, leave*. She put the car in reverse and eased her foot off the brake. The Malibu began to roll back when she started turning the wheel.

Then she squeezed the brake pedal.

The car stopped abruptly. Her head whipped back. Her left wrist shot with pain again. She bit her lip and screamed, "Fuck you!"

Emily was tired of moaning in pain. Her voice echoed back to her, jarring loose an epiphany her subconscious had been desperate to deliver:

Make a wish.

What?

Bring them back.

Emily put the car in park.

Is that possible?

You never know until you try.

She climbed out of the car.

"Be brave," she said. Her voice was breathy and unconvincing. "Be goddamn brave," she said more assuredly.

Emily marched toward the house before she could change her mind. In the front room, she regretted it.

Doug and Jessica wore matching grins. It was hard to think of their mouths as anything else. Their smiles pulled so far to the sides, their teeth protruded like horse teeth, and their tongues hung out like fat slugs against the hardwood. The expressions were lurid and devilish. The bulging eyes didn't help—they seemed to follow her when she passed.

You're okay. You're okay.

She picked up Jessica's flashlight near the hallway and clicked it on.

They'll be fixed before you know it. Just like Marshal fixed you.

Marshal.

Her former best friend lay in a fetal position next to Alex's corpse, which still leaned against the well. Fortunately, Marshal's head was turned to the side, his face pressed downward into the kitchen linoleum so she couldn't see it. She imagined him slowly turning to face her, and her body shook violently.

Emily let out an involuntary sound before moving toward Alex's body. She almost changed her mind when she pulled the noose from around his stiff neck. It caught on the back of his skull. She yanked it free, hearing the back of his head make an awful thud against the brick.

Emily looped the rope around the railroad spike, hoping it would hold her weight. It had held Logan, hadn't it? She laughed, thinking she was losing her mind. Maybe she would need to check herself into Willow Lane after all this.

The climb down to the bottom of the well was treacherous. The rope groaned, and her wrist screamed with pain. She kept the Maglite in her hand, aiming at the rope and her arms, but it only made the climb more dangerous. Emily had to wrap her arms around the rope, her soft skin burning each time she slid down, carrying her weight.

Somehow, she managed to reach the bottom, though she wouldn't dare shine the flashlight on her raw forearm. She suspected it looked like hamburger meat.

Ignoring the pain, she searched the standing water for the opening she had heard about. Dropping to her knees, she got a closer look. The smell and sliminess of the water didn't matter after what she had seen in the house.

They're dead.

How can they be dead?

It was the same as Allen—alive one minute and nothing but an unrecognizable corpse the next. Dying was too easy.

They'll be fixed before you know it, she repeated. *Just like Marshal fixed you.*

A soothing breeze hit her face. She directed the light at the half-moon hole.

Marshal had said it felt like a breeze, but it hadn't made sense until now, when she saw the opening herself. It was wide enough for someone to pass through.

Emily wondered where the air was coming from but told herself to focus on the wish. She inhaled deeply, the warmth of the breeze soothing her dry throat.

"I wish for Doug, Jessica, Marshal, Letty and Alex to come back to life."

Part of her regretted the wish immediately, fearful of its consequences.

Who cared, she told herself. She had to bring them back. Emily couldn't leave them lying there in the house.

A rotting smell escaped the hole with her echoing wish. She rolled over and vomited into the standing water, then found the rope.

Pulling herself up was impossible with her broken wrist. She had to wait for Logan. But he should have been here by now.

He should have been here...

On one hand, she was thankful he hadn't experienced what they had. On the other, she knew what it meant.

Logan wasn't coming. All she could do was hope her wish would come true. She imagined Marshal and Alex peeking over the side of the well, smiling happily.

"Guys?" she yelled.

Emily waited but heard no movement. She called out a few more times.

No answer.

Finally, she shone the Maglite onto the half-moon opening again—the hole within a hole.

Where is the air coming from?

Once again, she dropped into the standing water, feeling the breeze against her face. She directed the flashlight into the hole but saw only darkness.

"Kelvin?" she said.

Her voice echoed back to her without the uninviting stench.

Savable...if you're brave enough.

She took a deep breath, ignoring the burning sensation on her soft skin and the pain in her broken wrist. Then she began to crawl into the hole.

2004 CLASS B BOYS STATE CHAMPIONSHIP

NOWHERE DEVILS ROSTER

Logan Tramer

Sam Turner

Dylan Lovegood

Jack Ward

NINETEEN
CHAMPIONS

1

OLNEY, Oklahoma, was a dusty southwestern town near the Texas panhandle border. Logan imagined cattle drives like those in *Lonesome Dove* going through Olney. His dad loved the Larry McMurtry novel, but its length was too intimidating for Logan, so he stuck to the TV miniseries starring Robert Duvall and Tommy Lee Jones.

They had watched it at least half a dozen times together. Each time, Logan dreamed of being a cowboy, testing himself on the open range. But they didn't make cross-country cattle drives anymore like they had a hundred years ago. Logan would never be a cowboy.

He could be a STATE CHAMPION, though. His final test. This was what it meant to be a man: set a goal and achieve it, knowing there might be sacrifices along the way.

He felt at peace with his decision—better, in fact, since his sister and Jessica wouldn't be in the crowd. Since Kelvin disappeared, he realized it wasn't enough to be an accomplice. Knowing about the wish didn't make you safe.

But now, his sister and Jessica were in Nowhere, far away from witnessing what the magic would do to help the Devils win the game.

Logan had lied to everyone. He had no intention of telling Will that Kelvin was gone, just as he had no intention of meeting them in Nowhere. The Devils had unfinished business at the Big House, although Logan barely recognized his team anymore, surrounded by two freshmen and one sophomore.

Instead of seeking out Will, Logan went to his room to get ready for the game. It was legal to play with only four players—a random fact he had come across last summer during a bored afternoon at the Holdendecker Public Library, when he had found himself reading through pages of OSSAA rules.

Four on five against the second-ranked Olney was impossible odds, so Logan knew exactly what he was accepting by not forfeiting. The magic, the Basketball Gods, the well, the wish, Fate—whatever *it* was would save the Nowhere Devils and deliver them a championship.

Then, there would be a sacrifice.

Logan clung to his denial: perhaps four deaths and a couple of disappearances were enough already; or if it had to take someone, at least it would be someone already destined to die soon. *Kelvin wasn't old, sick, or suicidal,* he had argued with himself. *Yes, but Kelvin left* willingly. *He wasn't killed.*

"Everything is all right," his best friend had said last night. "It's not your fault. It's Fate."

The magic would do what it did, but the Devils still had to do their part. Only Logan could get them over the finish line. He controlled what he could.

He won the tip-off.

He snatched every available defensive rebound and stole some offensive boards over two guys attempting to box him out.

He covered the paint as the four Devils played a zone defense.

He gave up no easy layups, leaving opponents open to shoot three-pointers, knowing the magic would make them miss.

He watched Olney's players become increasingly frustrated at how poorly they scored despite their five-on-four advantage.

He made Olney pay when they drove to the hoop, blocking shots and landing hard fouls.

He demanded the ball in the post on offense, scoring over double teams.

He set the best screens of his life, getting Sam open shots, who gained confidence with every made basket.

He called out mismatches and leak-outs, demanding more hustle from his teammates.

He encouraged the young guys, slapped their bony asses, and lifted them up when they hung their heads after a turnover or missed shot.

He picked his teammates off the floor when they took charges.

He pleaded for the crowd to show them love, even when it looked like Olney might make a run to win the game in the second half.

He listened as the crowd chanted "Defense!" and then chanted his name when Nowhere took a ten-point lead with less than a minute remaining.

He gazed into the crowd, watching classmates, middle schoolers, and kids from Holdendecker scream and jump up and down.

He saw his parents point at him, his dad mouthing "You're the man!" and then his mom kissing his dad on the mouth.

He peered at the bleachers farther back, where his superintendent, principal, and other older folks from Nowhere sat, and knew one of those old-timers would be the final sacrifice.

He spotted Will Roebuck back there too, the only person on the Nowhere side of the court not cheering.

He wanted to flip off his judgmental ass but refrained.

He watched the seconds tick away, then pointed his large finger toward center court, signaling to his young teammates what was about to happen.

He slid to center court when the final buzzer sounded, and his three teammates jumped on top of him.

He smelled sweat and felt their energy, no vicarious feelings—the *real deal* this time.

He basked in the overwhelming happiness of accomplishing what he had dreamed about for years, the only thing he had ever wanted so badly.

Best feeling in the world.

2

How does someone describe something so few experience? One could speak of Logan's elation, the permanent smile on his face, the holy lights from above—fluorescent yellow—illuminating him in the center of his teammates while they posed with the championship trophy. They could also mention the way eyes dwelled on him, like he was more than just a kid from Nowhere. One could describe the coldness of his sweaty jersey now that he had stopped running, how it felt soothing after a win and miserable after a loss—but somehow both after this win.

And the crowd? The Nowhere folks who came down to the court to celebrate with their neighbors: Ryan's dad, the shop teacher Mr. Holbrook, holding his wife whose concerned look was finally turning to a smile, or Superintendent Walker removing his tie for the first time ever at a school event, tossing it into the bleachers with no intention of ever retrieving it, shaking a hundred hands without complaining about the numbness from so many squeezes, planning to take the trophy to the Nowhere gym himself, knowing it would be the last trophy ever added to the case and that someday soon there would be no custodian to wipe down the trophies. They would collect dust until the Amish, or a metals manufacturer, or a local farmer bought the land and insisted the trophies be taken to storage before the gym—and everything that resembled a school—was torn down.

How about Mal Turner, who felt like she was waking from a daze when the buzzer sounded, unable to remember how she had broken her arm? She no longer felt hatred toward Doug, unsure why she ever had. Mal peered around as if looking for him—*she really did like him*—before realizing he wasn't there. Had he not played? She grabbed her little brother instead, the happiest she had ever seen him, the proudest she had ever been of him. The two of them jumped and howled like wolves, like when they went camping.

Or Jack Ward's family—his parents, three siblings, and cousins from Miner—who came to the Big House, not expecting to see him play, which only made them more excited by how well he had done. How he had helped his team win the championship with only four players. A miracle from God, his Methodist family proclaimed, and Jack could only agree. What else could it be?

While Doug's family had left when they saw he wasn't there, Marshal's family remained to watch Dylan play, his dad clapping him on the back celebratorily, his mom interrogating him about Marshal's whereabouts. He ignored them while the ceremony continued. Parents were invited to take a picture with their son and the championship trophy. Dylan, Jack, and Sam took turns.

Logan stepped up last, his parents on either side.

A month ago, on Senior Night, when Logan had posed with

his mom and handed her a rose, he would have never expected to be here tonight with both parents. His dad squeezed his shoulder and said how proud he was. Even now, it was difficult not to feel resentment, but being a champion had a way of burying it, letting it rest beneath his happiness.

Who cared? he could tell himself. *Be in the moment. Your dad just watched you lead your team to the championship.*

Everyone had.

He would be royalty in Nowhere, talked about beyond the little country community. Logan would get free food in Holden-decker and girls throwing themselves at him, and Logan wasn't sure he would turn them down since Jessica had been so against him during the discussion about forfeiting. Other boys would glare at him with envy, old-timers would too.

His new life would begin with a picture. What a feeling. He thought of the way he only ever imagined his aunt by her basketball portrait. Her life had ended with a picture, he thought, then shook away the thought and focused on the perfect moment. He always felt awkward taking pictures but not in this moment. The photographer didn't even have to ask him to smile.

Yes, what a wonderful feeling.

Then his mom paused the photographer. "Wait, wait, wait," she repeated. "Where's Emily? We need to get her in the picture."

"I haven't seen her," his dad replied. "Maybe she's with her boyfriend. He wasn't here either."

"It's all right," Logan said. "They're okay. Let's just take the picture."

His mom turned to him, confused. "Your sister isn't here?"

"Don't worry about it, Mom. We won STATE. We have to celebrate."

He tried to pull her in beside him, now forcing a smile at the photographer, who hesitated.

Just take the goddamn picture.

Janice Horn wiggled free from Logan's grip around her shoulder and stepped in front of him. She pulled his face down to look her in the eye. "Logan. Where's Emily?"

"Janice—"

"Shut up, Bill. Tell me, Logan. Where is she?"

He huffed stubbornly, an unconscious action from the part of him still a child. "She left town with the others."

"What?"

"They took your car."

"Excuse me?"

"It's fine, Mom. Dad can give us a ride home."

"Sure, I can—"

"Why wouldn't they stay for your game?"

"It was all Marshal. He was being dramatic, so he boycotted the game."

His mom started to leave the court, pushing through a crowd of Nowhere folks celebrating around them.

"Do you still want a picture?" asked the photographer.

Bill, feeling awkward, made a corny joke and asked her to give them a minute.

Logan had already started following his mom, yelling for her to stop. Finally, she leaned over a bleacher, like she was crying.

"Mom? I'm telling you, everyone's fine. It was just a disagreement. They all left. Marshal, Em, Jessica." He could feel his shifty eyes and forced them to stay on his mom. "Kelvin and Doug too," he lied. "They went home, back to Nowhere."

Janice turned toward him, as upset as he'd ever seen her. She had been so strong when Emily was in the hospital, only allowing herself to cry when her daughter woke up—those had been joyful tears. The crying face before him was accompanied by fear.

"Mom...we should be celebrating."

"I don't like this, Logan...You shouldn't have won."

His guilt returned, tearing through him. She stared, like she knew what he had done. But that was impossible. No one had told her.

"There were only four of you," she said. "It was only you and the three most inexperienced players on your team."

It hit him. He understood now what upset her. Green River was on her mind.

Logan had gone too far. Winning with four players wasn't possible. He finally realized that someone didn't have to know about wishes and wells to understand how closely fortune and misfortune were connected.

His mom understood. She had ever since watching Green River win the title and then finding her sister hanging in her bedroom from the ceiling fan. Logan had never thought he looked much like his aunt, but the same could never be said about Emily. His sister looked just like Jocelyn Horn.

Too much like her.

"Where's my daughter?" his mom said.

"She went home, Mom," he pleaded. "You'll see. She'll be at the house when you get there."

Bill Tramer came over, his cell phone in hand, the other hand in his pocket. His shoulders were hunched like he wanted to be invisible.

Logan saw the look on his face. His dad was a man attempting to be supportive during a trying time but wanting to escape.

"I called the house," he said. "No one picked up."

TWENTY
NOWHERE

1

LOGAN WAS the only one of his teammates to take the bus home. He hadn't planned on it, but he didn't want to be near his mom right now. Earlier, he had escaped to the locker room to avoid her questions. What did she want him to say?

He had essentially told her the truth. A disagreement had led to Marshal forfeiting the game, who then went with Emily and Jessica to Nowhere. What he left out fueled further speculation.

Where were Kelvin and Doug? Why had Alex and Mikey missed both the semifinals and today? And, apparently, Letty Prospect had left when Alex and Mikey did. Macy Goode had told anyone who would listen that Letty borrowed her car and never brought it back. The celebration had turned chaotic, led by Marshal's mom, and the Nowhere crowd didn't want to leave the court when it was time for the Class A boys' teams to warm up.

Logan had to get away. Coach Park was shocked when Logan told him he was taking the bus.

"I'm just picking up McDonald's," Coach had said.

"I could go for some Chicken Selects," Logan had replied.

When they reached the school grounds, Superintendent Walker was waiting with the trophy in hand. His face wasn't as gleeful as it had been after the win. He was speaking to Coach Park quietly in the office when Logan slipped away.

He didn't dare go home. Over three hours had passed since his dad had called and no one answered. It was likely Emily was home now, everything resolved. They had found Kelvin and the others, woken them from the spell they were under, and everyone had met at the abandoned house to celebrate that no more sacrifices were needed. Then they all went home.

Still, when Logan turned down Snakeback Road, his heart pounded like a drumbeat. The clouds had overtaken the spring sun since he left the city. The evening sky shifted from blue to soft yellow. Spring didn't feel as pleasant now as it had this morning.

Why are you even going to the house? he asked himself. *You'll see that no one is there. Everything is fine.*

When the abandoned house emerged from behind the trees, he slammed on the brakes. His blood turned cold. His mom's car was crushed on its side. The image of Emily lying in the hospital bed, comatose with tubes down her throat, flashed to mind.

He jumped out of his truck and ran to the car, tunnel vision narrowing everything around him, blackening his peripheral vision. His friends could have been nearby, waving, and he wouldn't have noticed. All he cared about was getting Emily out of the car.

But the car was empty.

A breath of relief escaped him before he saw the damage. His surroundings came into focus: other vehicles, two familiar, one not; the open doorway, with chipped wood where the screen door had broken off; disturbed dirt where a struggle had taken place.

His eyes glazed over, and he ran to the house.

Logan didn't find his worst-case scenario, but it wasn't far off. Crimson smeared the hardwood floor. Letters were torn from their envelopes in the den, some pages lying on the dirty couch, new dents in the walls and around the threshold of the opening to the back of the house. Everything that had been eternally still during his previous visits was disrupted by some event that took place here until it settled in a slightly different way, like shaking a snow globe.

He clicked on his keychain flashlight and ventured into the back of the house. The rear bedrooms looked untouched: a busted mattress in one room with spring coils stabbing through the fabric; stained sheets thrown across a bed in the other with an off-kilter ceiling fan above it; grime on the windows, closets with no doors. The pitiful bathroom was also undisturbed.

He saved the kitchen for last, fearing what he would find. The blood in the front room had been a warning. His whole body shuddered when he approached.

But there were no bodies, only more of the same terrible aftermath he had found earlier: a pool of blood next to the well. He shined his light down the hole and began hollering names.

"Emily? Jessica? Kelvin? Alex? Doug? Marshal? Anyone here?"

No answer.

They left, he told himself. *They escaped. They went to Clearwater Creek or Turner's barn.*

But all the vehicles were still outside, and his mom's car had been thrashed.

He returned to the front room, saw the smeared blood in what remained of the natural light again, and his knees buckled. Logan collapsed to the floor and began to cry.

What have you done?

A thought echoed in his mind: *Check the well.*

But they weren't at the bottom of the well. Alex, Doug, or Marshal would have seen Mr. Tune when they made their wish, if he had thrown himself down there. A pile of bodies would have gathered high enough for him to see, even with his small keychain light, when he had pointed it down.

Logan used the grimy couch to pull himself to his feet, not caring that his hands picked up any dirt. It reminded him of the night Will had read the letter after Logan had pranked him, picking it up despite the blood thumbprints. Logan had picked it up too—

He scanned the mess of letters on the floor, then dropped to the floor among them and began reading quickly.

He wiped his bleary eyes, the dried tears still on his face. His hazy vision made it hard to read, not to mention the small cursive handwriting, the fading ink, or the spots of fresh blood from the floor mingling with old thumbprints.

A mad hope gripped him with each letter. In them, a woman was writing to a man who refused to leave the house. Logan wondered how many wishes the man had made. He wondered if everyone who had ever died in Nowhere had been the result of a wish.

Finally, Logan snatched the bloodiest letter. He found the revealing sentence:

I know you've been tempted to crawl inside, but you can't. If powerful wishes are delivered from that hole with a sinister cost, then what must be at the end of the tunnel? Evil itself?

Logan dropped the letter. Even from the short height where

he sat on the floor, the letter floated slowly, as though someone had set it down delicately.

He stood, knowing the truth but fearing what it meant for him.

Then a voice startled him from the front doorway.

"I knew it."

It took him a moment to recognize the voice, but deep down, he already knew who it was.

Of course, Will had come.

He stood in the doorway, staring at Logan with those annoyingly judgmental eyes.

"You fucking asshole," Will said. "Back for more, are you?"

2

Logan tried to explain hastily. "I know where the missing people are. Inside the well. Through the tunnel."

But Will was stubborn in his superiority, ignoring anything that didn't fit his narrative. He marched toward Logan like he wanted to fight him.

"You had the audacity to play that game today and then come right back here for more wishes." He shoved Logan.

The shock of it caused Logan to stumble back a few steps. It angered him that little Will Roebuck had knocked him off-balance.

"Listen to me, asshole." Logan's head grew hot, and his eyes glazed over.

"Why would I? You're a lying piece of shit, and now everyone's dead because of you."

Everything is all right. It's not your fault. It's Fate.

"I didn't kill anyone. Do you see any bodies here?"

"Wake up, Tramer. There's fucking blood right over there."

It's not your fault. It's Fate.

"I know where they went—"

"What're you gonna wish for now, huh? A new girlfriend? A car as nice as mine? Another championship? You want to be the best basketball player in the world, Tramer?"

It's not your fault.

"Fuck you!" Logan shoved Will then, knocking him to the floor.

Will's face contorted, turning bright red. He had a crazed look in his eye. He jumped up and swung a fist at Logan.

Once again, Logan hadn't expected Will to escalate things. His coworker's fist connected with his jaw. It hurt like a wasp's sting. Logan held his ground this time and let his anger go. Heat coursed through him, and his mind went blank.

He punched Will, knocking him to the floor. Then he jumped on top of him and hit him again.

After everything they had been through together, Will was still the same shit-talking, jealous worm he had always been. He had always deserved a beating.

Another large fist went into Will's face, followed by another. Logan started to black out.

Another voice cried from a distance. It echoed around the room.

No, not an echo.

Instead, the words were being repeated: *Get off him, Tramer! Get off, Tramer!*

"Get off him, Tramer!"

Coming out of his fog, Logan noticed Ryan Holbrook in his peripheral. He realized he was panting like a mountain lion. He slowly uncorked his fist. His knuckles gave a painful retort. His vision cleared. Ryan was pointing his gun right at him.

"Stand and back away slowly."

"Ryan—"

"Do it now, Tramer."

Logan glanced down at Will's pulpy face and felt sick. His knees scraped across the hardwood floor when he rose onto his feet.

"Hands up."

His feet were so heavy he had to backpedal slowly, moving away from Will.

Poor, pathetic Will Roebuck.

"That's enough."

"Ryan…You don't understand—"

"Whose blood is that?"

Logan stood over the smeared patch of blood, wishing he knew.

"Alex? Mikey? What did you do to them?"

Logan laughed wetly. Warm snot shot out of his nose. "Why does everyone keep blaming me?"

"Because it's your fault," Will mumbled. He stood up between Ryan and Logan and spat blood. Will faced Logan and spread his hands out. One eye was already nearly swollen shut, his lips bulbous and purpling. "It's mine too."

Will's admission cut through Logan, and he found himself accepting the ugly truth. The blood beneath his feet was slippery. His planted foot slid involuntarily.

"Step aside, Will," Ryan said. "I'm placing you under arrest, Tramer."

Will's back was to Ryan, which flustered the deputy. He seemed hesitant to approach the two boys, perhaps shaken by a memory of the voice on the radio or the terrible expressions on the corpses he had seen.

"The well, huh?" Will said, opening his one good eye to peek at Logan. A look of skepticism faded. Will's optimism made Logan nervous. "I guess it's your turn, then."

"What?" Logan didn't understand until he asked himself, *My turn to do what?*

Will took a wide step with one leg stretching out further between Ryan and Logan, then stated what Logan had already figured out. "Head start?"

Ryan shouted, "Roebuck, move—"

Logan turned and ran into the dark. He was immediately blinded in the void, but he knew the way. He rounded the hallway corner into the kitchen, bumping his shoulder against the wall but mostly making it through the entryway without trouble. He only slowed down when he neared where he projected the well was in the dark.

Still, he banged into the brick wall harder than he expected, losing his balance and tumbling over the side. Even in the dark —or perhaps *especially* in the dark—he knew he was spinning. Disoriented and lightheaded, he grasped outward, hoping his hand would find the rope.

It finally did.

The rope tore the soft flesh of his palms when he gripped it desperately and slammed into the inside wall, stopping his fall.

Only for a moment.

The momentum of his fall and the sudden weight straining against the rope must have caused the rusty spike to break loose from the brick exterior. Logan was suddenly holding a slack rope, and he was falling again.

He hit the standing water on the side of his right leg first. The back of his head had banged against the wall at some point, leaving it warm and wet. But the greater pain came from his leg. It hadn't snapped in two like Kelvin's, but it was fitting enough that it was at least fractured after taking the brunt of the fall.

A part of him wished the bone had folded like Kelvin's because he deserved it and much worse. He reached for his leg near his shin, where the bone had no doubt chipped or cracked, and he squeezed it. The agony made him scream.

"You alive?" Will called from above. His voice was still muffled by a bloody and swollen mouth.

"What the fuck, Tramer?" Ryan shined his flashlight down, but all Logan could see was a bright light filling the top of the ring above him. "Can you see him, Roebuck?"

"It's too deep."

"It's so damn dark in there," Ryan said.

"It's the magic," Logan called up. "It doesn't end with the wishes."

"What the hell are you talking about?"

"I'm going inside to get them. I'll be back." He wasn't sure the last part was true.

Logan took his keys from his pocket, but his little flashlight had been crushed on impact. He dropped to his knees. The water was slimy and cold. He felt the rope coiled in a heap. Then he searched along the circular wall with his hands until he felt nothing but air. The breeze warmed him.

"Tramer!"

Ryan could yell as much as he wanted. Logan would no longer answer until he had returned with his friends and his sister. Then they would find a way up.

His shoulders grazed each side of the half-moon hole, but he shimmied forward anyway. He had to see where the missing went.

3

Will had trouble concentrating. How could his face feel so numb and so painful at the same time? He wanted to touch it, but each time he did, it *yakked* painfully. It freaked him out too, when his fingers came away covered in blood, smooth and thick like finger paint.

"What the hell is he doing down there?" Ryan asked. His

uniform was wrinkled, like he hadn't washed it in weeks. His hair was disheveled and face unwashed. Ryan hardly looked like the confident deputy who had arrived in the Nowhere gym to arrest Bolan Grimes.

That man was someone Will had envied. He had daydreamed about being a cop almost as much as he daydreamed about being a screenwriter. Eventually, he had figured he would split the difference and write a cop movie. But it hardly seemed like an admirable occupation right now.

Staring at Ryan through his one good eye, Will had to turn his head to see to his right. The blind spot made him feel like there was a constant presence beside him.

"Tramer!" Ryan hollered again.

"He can't hear you," Will said. "He's in the tunnel."

"The what?"

"He's going to save them."

"This is fucking crazy. I'm calling this in."

"Wait—"

"There's blood all over the place, Roebuck, and the Spruce brothers are just the latest missing people I've been searching for." Ryan laughed to himself and swiped at his face. "I should've known to check this place. I've been all over Nowhere since Thursday morning—Clearwater Creek, Turner's barn, hiking through the woods—then I remembered this fucking house, where me and the boys would drink and throw shit down the well and make stupid wishes. Goddamn. What are y'all doing out here?"

"The wishes are real, man."

A frightened realization seemed to slide across Ryan's face. "You're as crazy as Tramer is."

Ryan walked away, back into the light of the front room, clicking off his flashlight and leaving Will in the dark. Will didn't want to move away from the well in case Logan and the others returned. He desperately wanted Logan to be right—that the missing people were hidden on the other side of the tunnel.

Was that what the letters said? The one Will had read weeks ago talked about a woman's regret bringing someone out here. At the time, he had dismissed it as a sappy romance gone wrong. Now he wished he had read all the letters. Maybe the Beaumonts didn't have to die. Maybe Bird didn't either.

You couldn't have changed anything. The Beaumonts died because of Logan's selfish desire to win state. And Bird died because you wanted your grandma to see again.

And boy, did she.

He couldn't bring himself to regret his wish. Will loved his grandma more than anyone in this world. He would never take away the gift he had given her.

Rather than his eyes adjusting to the dark, the darkness seemed to grow more absolute, leaving Will with only his mind's eye. All he could see was the huge wooden bedframe, the vase of flowers on the nightstand, and the black-and-white photograph above the bed of two attractive young people getting married. So many pillows. The Beaumonts loved their comfort.

Their quilt had been pulled up to their chins. If only it had been pulled a little higher. Will had stood in the doorway to their bedroom, but when he looked into their bulging eyes, he felt pulled closer and closer, until he was nose to nose with the corpses.

Quickly, he left the kitchen and followed Ryan into the front room.

Ryan was already on his radio asking for a fire truck. Will supposed it didn't matter if more people showed up at this point, as long as he had time to tell Ryan the truth. They would need a way to get Logan and the others out of the well anyway since the rope was now at the bottom.

"Holbrook," he said.

Ryan turned to face him, his back to the open entrance where the screen door used to be. Now the screen door crunched beneath Will's feet. He stood on it, like the rest of the floor was covered by blood. The screen door was plenty tainted itself, though.

"I'm not crazy. Neither is Logan. Well, he might be a little bit. But my point is, this place is the real deal. It's—" Will lost his train of thought immediately when a figure flashed by the front doorway. "Alex?"

Ryan spun to face the door, snapping his sidearm from its holster like a gunfighter.

"Easy!" Will said.

"Did you see him? For real?"

"For real, for real...I mean, I think so. I can't see very well right now, man."

"Stay here."

Ryan stepped toward the orange evening haze.

Will kept wiping his good eye, which was constantly wet with thick discharge. The other side of his face burned every time he tried to open the swollen eye or speak.

He turned ninety degrees to his right, feeling a presence in his blind spot. At least he wasn't in pitch-black anymore. The front room was now reddish-orange, shadowy while time passed outside.

Will followed Ryan outside. The deputy was at the front corner of the house, arms outstretched, aiming his gun around the corner.

"Alex Spruce?" Ryan called, as if he had never met his old teammate before.

"I definitely saw someone," Will said.

Ryan jumped. "I told you to stay inside. I don't want to shoot you in the face, dude."

"Maybe don't be so trigger-happy, then. Why do you even have your gun out? Are you gonna shoot Alex when you find him?"

"Why would he be hiding from us? Are you sure you saw—"

Something rustled near the cars.

Will couldn't immediately see what distracted Ryan since the cars were in his blind spot to the right, but the expression on the deputy's sickly face said enough. Ryan took two steps forward, then paused, letting out an involuntary, shuddering breath. Will turned his whole body and saw three figures rising from behind Macy Goode's car.

At first, the nightmare was too much to comprehend.

It was exactly that: a nightmare. Something Will had conjured in his worst dreams after seeing the Beaumonts.

And sure, Will had woken up in a sweat in the middle of the night several times since then, the lasting image of Bird or the Beaumonts marching toward him. But the image always faded.

These figures were not fading.

Marshal was out front, the top of his head crushed inward, his mouth an oval black hole, his eyes dangling from their sockets. He tried to speak but could only croak an aggressive drone.

Doug was over his shoulder, his face twisted into a half-moon shape, chin pointed one direction, his nose the opposite. His tongue swung back and forth from a bottom lip stretched loose, while the rest of his mouth spread wide, almost reaching his earlobes. Frothy saliva caked his swollen tongue, and a line of drool descended to the ground.

Jessica stood a couple of feet back from Doug. She was no longer his attractive coworker, but an undead thing with a face as disgusting as Doug's.

Like Marshal, Doug attempted to speak too, but his words came out muffled, a frightening moan.

"What the fuck!" Ryan raised his gun higher.

Doug stuck his arm out, moaning louder.

"Don't," came another voice from behind Ryan—a voice able to form words, but wheezy and mechanical, like someone with throat cancer.

At the sound of the voice, Ryan's gun went off. The shot blasted through Doug's shoulder, skidding into the grass behind them. Doug was knocked back but rose again, moaning angrily.

Alex and Letty ran from around the side of the house. They looked almost normal, except for their matching purple faces, with matching rings around their necks of broken capillaries. They jumped on Ryan from behind. Marshal tumbled forward to wrestle with Ryan from the front.

Doug and Jessica seemed to notice Will for the first time. Their unblinking, bulging eyes glared with maniacal fury.

Will ran away from the house, toward the tree line. It didn't even cross his mind to make a run for his Camaro, even though his keys jabbed into his thigh from inside his front pocket when he high-kicked into the pines.

More gunshots went off, along with the groans of his old classmates. Will screamed and tumbled, smacking his shoulder into more than one tree thanks to his blind eye. He stumbled, righted himself, crawled if he had to.

All the while, his mind was far away from the woods, back in his neighbor's house, gazing down at the Beaumonts in their death bed.

4

There were times during Logan's crawl when the tunnel widened enough for his shoulders to clear each side completely. He breathed regularly during these moments.

But the rest of the time, his broad shoulders scraped against dirt and cement, rubbing his arms raw. The pain was bearable compared to the constant shocks from his fractured leg. He had just enough space above his head to keep himself up on his hands and knees, attempting to keep his injured side off the ground, but every twist or turn was a direct stab to his shin.

Logan had no idea how far the tunnel went. His eyes never adjusted to the dark, leaving him blind and reliant on the feel of his hands, knees, and shoulders. Strangely, the putrid smell which had emanated from the opening during his wish lessened the farther he went.

Or maybe you're just getting used to it.

The thought panicked him, like it was a sign he would never leave this place.

The tunnel narrowed, forcing him onto his belly. He dragged himself forward, the walls tightening on either side. *Don't get stuck. Don't get stuck.* His breathing shortened, and he was sure he was running out of air.

Then, something ahead caught his attention. It wasn't an object or silhouette, but a shift in color—from absolute darkness to a hazy gray. He moved toward it and felt mist wet on his face.

The mist cooled his lungs. The walls widened again, and his back no longer scraped the tunnel's ceiling. Soon, he could rise onto his knees, then his feet, and move forward.

When the mist cleared, a bright red light blinded him, piercing through his eyes. He had never thought colors could feel like this—this was what "red" felt like. A debilitating migraine.

Finally, his vision cleared, and he nearly collapsed. Fear, confusion, and something overwhelming inside him made his brain shut off before he could comprehend what he saw.

In the center of the room stood a tall, blood-red cylinder

with a brilliant red light ascending from below. The cylinder glistened wetly, like fresh blood. It towered over the room, which seemed to be at least fifty feet high. Surrounding it were dozens, maybe hundreds, of people kneeling with their heads bowed, hunching forward. Their dirty rags, once clothing, draped over their bodies.

The smell hit him next, making his eyes water—a foul, sulfuric stench worse than the sour bottom of the well, even worse than his echo from when he made his wish.

At least, you aren't used to this yet.

Part of him wished he was as he dry-heaved and stared blearily at the kneeling crowd.

There was as much standing water on the floor as there was in the well—ankle-high. The worshippers didn't seem to care that the water covered their legs, many of them up to their thighs.

Clarity didn't hit Logan until he spotted Larry Tune near the front of the crowd, close to the pillar and red light.

Seeing what had become of the missing made no sense to him. He imagined the crowd during the championship game. What if they had stormed the court and kneeled before him and the team? It might have looked something like this.

The image of the crowd at the Big House was the only way he could comprehend the sheer number of worshippers. He was terrified but couldn't turn and run.

Logan had crawled through the tunnel for a reason.

He scanned the area near Mr. Tune for any other familiar faces. Directly to the history teacher's right was an Amish kid with a tall hat, and on his left, Logan recognized Mikey's long, floppy hair. Next to him—

"Dr. Warren?"

Logan stopped short, surprised by how loudly his voice echoed across the space.

No one moved. They remained statuesque, heads bowed in prayer.

Why is Dr. Warren here? His mind couldn't reconcile the wishes and their consequences. The crowd blended together, and Logan felt responsible for them all. He wondered where the others were, if not with these four. His entire group of friends gone. Not to mention his sister, and the girl he liked. They were supposed to have a date tomorrow...he would have started crying again if he was still in the house but here his face was dry, his eyes bloodshot, unable to blink, unable to understand. He was overwhelmed which strangely made him calm.

Reluctantly, he stepped forward, looking down at the worshippers. Their clasped hands shook from how tightly they gripped them, the only part of them that wasn't eerily still. Their arms stretched out in front of their bowed heads.

"I knew you'd come."

The voice echoed, distant yet close, as if it was behind him. He spun around, but all he saw was darkness the farther from the red light he looked. The gray rectangle in the wall—the tunnel opening he had crawled out of—reminded him of his escape from above and his fractured shin pulsated angrily. He noticed other gray openings, one every few feet.

"Kelvin?"

He flinched, expecting the worshippers near his legs to reach for him. They remained still.

"Hey, buddy."

Logan sloshed through the water, following the voice, unsure of where it had come from in the vast chamber. "I came to save you," he said.

"I've got good news for you, Logan. You don't have to worry about that anymore. You see, everyone's already been saved."

"I doubt that, dude."

Kelvin's loud guffaw gave Logan a better sense of his location. Reluctantly, he turned toward the cylinder and limped past it, heading for the opposite side of the room.

"It's really happy with you, man," Kelvin said. "You really came through for it. Hell of a wish, Logan. Hell of a wish."

"And it's what? A god? A devil?"

"It's not that simple, dude."

"Looks simple enough to me. Just another insecure piece of shit that needs to be worshipped."

"Logan...you hurt me with your words."

The blood-red cylinder loomed to Logan's left, even more imposing the closer he got. He had to crane his neck to see the top of it, which appeared to reach the rocky ceiling, though he couldn't be sure. The bright red light didn't reach that high, and the ceiling was lost in shadow. Light seeped from cracks in the ground and around the sides of the cylinder, which seemed to be plunged into the earth like a stopper.

"Why would you be hurt by that?" Logan said. "You're clearly not like the rest of these people."

"I am and I'm not. Thanks to you."

"Thanks to me?"

Kelvin chuckled. "Oh, you like hearing that, don't you? You should. You deserve it, Logan. How did it feel winning state? Was it everything we dreamed it would be?"

"And more..." Logan admitted. "Until I got here. Where are they, Kelvin?"

"Well, they were dead."

Logan paused. "You're lying," he said, though his doubt was less certain.

"Sorry, bro. Everyone but your sister anyway. They *were* dead," Kelvin said. "But she brought them back. That's why you didn't find their bodies in the house."

"Emily made a wish?"

"Yeah…At the end of the day, man, people always make a wish."

"You didn't."

Kelvin said nothing to this.

Logan moved away from the cylinder, stepping to the far side of the room. The darkness beyond the crowd began to come into focus.

"And this is where the wishes are granted, huh? The source?"

"It's much more than that. We all make the descent, Logan. Some are lucky enough to do it sooner in life. Like me…Like you."

"I just crawled through a tunnel. Nothing to it."

"That's not what I'm talking about. Your sister crawled through the tunnel too, but she's got a long way to go before she makes the descent. Thanks to Marshal."

"So, I haven't descended yet? Well, it sure feels like hell."

Kelvin laughed again, his voice closer now. Logan picked up his pace, his shin yakking at him. He moved toward the back row of worshippers. Squinted into the dark and saw a silhouette near the far wall.

Along with all the gray openings, something else was there.

"You're someone who gets more confident when you're scared, you know that?" Kelvin said. "I was never like that. Before my first state game, I shit myself. I never told you that, but it's true. Rushed to the bathroom, didn't make it. And you should have seen me the other night, when it came to me in our hotel room."

"I did see you. You woke me up."

"No, I mean when I was still lying next to you in bed. I opened my eyes and saw it coming for me. Couldn't move. Couldn't scream. I thought I was gonna shit myself then too. But when it reached me, I realized it wasn't there to hurt me. It was there to show me that this little life is nothing compared to eternity. And eternity is so much better."

Logan extended his arms. "Yeah, it looks better."

Kelvin's final guffaw echoed through the chamber before Logan saw him clearly. His best friend stood ten feet behind the crowd. Logan stopped, about five feet away from him, just out of reach.

Kelvin still wore a cast on his leg but was putting weight on it like it had healed. Maybe it had. Perhaps the well had granted him a wish without him saying a word. Logan felt an almost overwhelming sense of guilt for not wishing to heal Kelvin instead of winning state. If he had, they could have won on their own with next to no consequences. The sudden guilt almost broke apart his confident exterior.

"Did they really all die up there?" Logan asked.

Kelvin nodded slowly, as though ashamed.

"And it was because of my wish, wasn't it? Because I won state?"

"Four on five, Logan. It takes a lot of energy to make a team miss that many shots."

Logan laughed bitterly. "All my friends for a few missed shots. But not Emily?"

"It can't kill her. A wish is a wish. It has to be fulfilled and honored. Those are the rules."

Whose rules?

"Then where the fuck is my sister?"

Kelvin's eyes widened. Logan saw it—Kelvin's laughter was a mask for nerves. He hadn't expected Logan to be so confident. Logan wasn't sure where his courage came from, but perhaps he had the magic to thank.

Winning bred confidence.

Kelvin tilted his head, eyeing him with curiosity. Then he pointed, his thumb jabbing up to the right. Logan turned his head to see his sister floating near the far wall, surrounded by black smoke. Her eyes were all white, her mouth open while the smoke sifted in and out.

"What the fuck?"

"She's all right, Logan. I already said it can't kill her."

"What's it doing to her?"

"Just holding her, wishing it could do more." Kelvin laughed again. "Isn't that funny? It wishes it could make wishes like the rest of us. But it just does our bidding. Kind of fucked up, huh?"

"Let her down."

"You think I'm in control of that thing?"

"It can't keep her here. You said yourself it has to abide by Marshal's wish. He wished to save her, and this isn't saving her."

"It's not?"

"No, it fucking isn't."

"You'll have to take that up with it, not me."

Or whatever sets the rules...

Logan glanced at the erect blood-red haze in his peripheral. "Can it hear us?"

"If it can hear you from the bottom of the well, it sure as hell can hear you in here. Why do you think everything we say echoes?" Kelvin cupped his hands around his mouth and hollered, "Echo!" His voice bounced around the room.

"Stop fucking around, Kelvin. Let her go."

"Don't worry, man. It's just been holding her until you got here. She has to be awake for what happens next. Well, she doesn't have to be, but it's more fun for her to see what she caused."

Emily's body floated to the ground. The black smoke cleared from around her, and she gasped, collapsing to her knees, coughing. Logan ran to her side as best he could with the gritty pain in his leg and put his arm around her. She was favoring her left arm. The wrist was swollen.

"You're all right, Em. You're all right."

"Logan...Oh God...this place..."

"I know. I know."

She crawled away in the dark, as if desperately searching for her glasses.

"Em—" Logan followed, pain shooting up his shin with every step.

Emily stopped and grabbed the Maglite she had dropped when the smoke had taken her. She rose, aiming the flashlight at Kelvin.

"Dude—" He covered his eyes.

Logan was shocked by the well-lit view of his best friend. Black veins slithered through Kelvin's arms and neck. A line of saliva pasted along his chin. Circles around his eyes were so black they gave the illusion his eyes were solid black too. Seeing him put weight on his leg cast in full light was such an off-putting sight it almost made Logan bark with crazy laughter. He *was* going crazy in real time with pity and guilt and grief. What had he done to his Kelvin?

Emily didn't stop aiming the flashlight. "We're leaving," she said.

"Sure," Kelvin said, his tone casual. "But you should know something first."

"What?" Logan asked, though he already knew what was coming.

Kelvin had already told him.

"There's a consequence to every wish. A sacrifice is needed."

Logan felt it immediately—a tingling on his neck. A presence stood behind him. He shoved Emily away.

"Get out," he ordered.

"Logan—"

"It's me, Em."

She turned her light toward him and screamed.

Logan stared at the three-dimensional silhouette behind him. The same darkness Bird, Red Springer, Ed and Pauline Beaumont, and Allen Prospect had seen.

And Jessica, Doug, and Marshal...they saw it too. What about Alex? He wished he knew. He wished they had solved this together.

Was it the same thing the missing had encountered? Mikey, Mr. Tune, Dr. Warren, Kelvin...? Logan wasn't sure. What he was certain of was, the figure wasn't here to make him worship it.

It would tear him apart, like it had done to Allen Prospect in Emily's Kia. After that, he would descend into the darkness beyond the blood-red cylinder. The descent beyond the descent.

"Emily, go!"

"Screw that." She grabbed his arm and pulled him forward.

Despite the pain in his leg, he kept moving, following his sister and the spotlight. Logan was dizzy with fear, but he managed to stay upright.

The crowd began to move, their brittle bones snapping. Logan heard arms break, fingers crack, and felt skin tearing against his jeans.

Soon, they passed the cylinder.

Mr. Tune tackled Emily.

Mikey, Dr. Warren, and the Amish kid grabbed Logan.

Brother and sister fought against their attackers. Logan punched, clawed, and threw bodies aside, ignoring the pain. Emily clocked Mr. Tune with the Maglite, and he collapsed. Logan helped his sister up.

They ran again. The crowd remained on their knees, reaching for them but too weak to stand.

Logan and Emily emerged into the darkness beyond the red light. Now, with the flashlight, they could see the opening from which they had come.

Then, Logan was snatched from behind. It felt like a knife digging into his skin, gripping his fractured leg. The bone snapped with a sickening crack. He screamed in agony, saliva spilling from his mouth while he was spun around to face his killer.

An insane thought struck him: *A leg isn't supposed to bend like that.*

"Been there, man," Kelvin called.

Logan saw Kelvin running from the side, not caring about his own leg. Logan was pulled off his feet, floating toward the nothing-face.

"Run," he yelled to his sister. "Please, Em."

She stood frozen, sobbing helplessly. "I'm sorry, Logan," she cried.

Logan couldn't believe his life was ending with his sister apologizing to *him*. The world was fucked up.

He stared into the nothing-face. The smoke dissipated, revealing a terrifying image: Logan's own face. Not a reflection, but his flesh, right in front of him. His eyes, his hair, his mouth. The shock of seeing his own face staring back at him was beyond comprehension.

But instead of letting fear take over, he found a small place inside himself to hide—some tiny compartment of comfort to help him get to the end.

He just wanted it to be over.

"I wish this place didn't exist," Logan said, staring into his own brown eyes, "that no more wishes could be made."

5

Will collapsed next to the largest pecan tree he had ever seen. He crushed pecans beneath his feet and leaned his back against the rough bark, hoping the tree was wide enough to keep him hidden.

He wanted to keep running but struggled to breathe, taking it cold breaths. A sharp pain in his chest made him think he was about to have a heart attack. The blind spot on the right side of his face unnerved him. He just knew they would come from that direction, so he kept craning his head to check, but all he saw were budding trees and evergreens.

Resting here gave him a moment to think. His face had gone numb, the pain replaced by an unsettling sensitivity. It gave him time to remember the keys in his front pocket, the Camaro parked nearby—able to haul ass faster than any other car in Nowhere, ready to get him far away from here.

It also gave him time to imagine what Logan would see at the end of the tunnel—more uncanny faces, like those of the zombies who had once been his classmates. And it gave him time to accept the truth.

Logan wasn't going to save anyone. He would be torn apart, like the zombies must have done to Ryan—or worse, Logan would save himself.

"Every man for himself, Tramer," he recalled saying to Logan after being shot at in Green River. "No offense, but if it's between you and me, I'm choosing me. And I expect you to do the same."

"None taken," he said aloud to himself in his pathetic acceptance that the Camaro was too far for a frightened little boy to reach.

The leaves crunched and pecan shells popped. He whipped his head to the right.

Nothing in his blind spot.

Will scanned to his left and behind him.

All was clear.

He almost exhaled before figures emerged ahead of him. They made no effort to sneak up on him.

Will wriggled his legs and shuddered. A weird, animalistic sound rumbled up from his gut—frighteningly natural.

"Help us, Will," Alex said. *"I'm so cold."*

Will knew why. Alex's paleness told him he had no blood left in his body. But Alex and Letty weren't in as bad of shape as the other three. They moaned, desperate, and reached for him with bloody hands.

"Wh-What did you do to Ryan?" Will asked, his voice shaking.

"He wouldn't put the gun down," Letty said. *"He wouldn't just let it go."*

"Guys—"

"Will!" Alex dropped before him. *"I feel...wrong."*

Alex grasped at Will's pants. Will kicked him off. The others fell before him now too, all five of them reaching for him, as if clinging to his body heat. Their faces drew closer. Their terrible grins made him scream.

"You have it, Will. Please share it."

"A-Alex—"

"Please give it to us!" Letty cried.

Cold, bloody hands pulled at Will's shirt, climbing his body, until all five of them covered him like a dogpile after winning the championship game. Hands clawed at his neck, yanking at his face.

This was it—what Bird had experienced. What the Beaumonts had felt. What Ryan had gone through. It was Will's turn now—

A sudden booming sound reverberated through the woods.

Instantly, the squirming bodies atop him went still. Their gripping fingers slackened.

Will wiggled free and rolled away, peering at the five bodies lying still in the leaves.

"You're dead?" he asked, his voice barely a whisper.

They didn't answer. Their moaning had stopped. They were corpses on the verge of rigor mortis, like their death process had paused, and now resumed where they left off. That was exactly what they had done.

He wondered how long rigor mortis would last. Would their faces loosen when the rest of their muscles loosened—or would they remain twisted? Will was too scared to move, too afraid he might stare at them long enough to find out, long enough to see them blink.

6

Logan hadn't expected words to come out with any clarity in his final moments. But the wish was clear and confident. It echoed toward him immediately.

The smile on the other face—the one that would kill him any moment now—disappeared. Instead, it tilted its head, furrowing the eyebrows that looked so much like Logan's own, and peered at him curiously, listening to the wish reverberate toward it.

I wish this place didn't exist, that no more wishes could be made.

I wish this place didn't exist, that no more wishes could be made.

I wish this place didn't exist, that no more wishes could be made.

I wish...I wish...

A loud boom vibrated from the center of the cylinder. Pressure stabbed at Logan's ears, the ringing growing louder. The face he stared into—his own—whiplashed back. Its brown eyes rolled into the back of its head. Then the face was gone, and Logan was falling through the smoke.

The earth shook, and voices screamed out. A red light sliced upward from below, cutting through the black smoke and making it dissipate. It was replaced by a thick, choking dust cloud into which Logan fell.

Rocks smacked against his back. The ground trembled beneath him. By the time he stood and oriented himself, he realized the walls were crumbling. The entire place was coming down. Darkness was nearly replaced by the red light, which burst upward everywhere as the ground split apart.

Behind him, the worshippers screamed and crawled away from the cylinder. What had been small cracks beneath it spread outward like they were fueled by fire, slithering across the entire room. Red cracks were already widening beneath his feet.

"Logan!"

Through the rubble, he saw his sister, but the gap between them was too wide for him to reach her. Her Maglite waved wildly while she struggled to stay balanced.

"Get out of here, Em! I'll find another way!"

Kelvin appeared beside Emily, and she screamed at his presence.

Logan imagined him wrapping his hands around her throat and choking her to death. They would fall into the cracked earth long before she suffocated—a small comfort when the options were so bad. But Kelvin raised his hands. No black veins to speak of.

"Em, what the hell is happening!" He struggled to stay upright, keeping his weight off his casted leg.

"Y'all have to leave now!" Logan yelled, and Emily understood.

Kelvin was himself again.

"I'll find another way!" he repeated, as if trying to convince himself.

Emily grabbed Kelvin's hand and led him toward the tunnel, back to the kitchen well and home. Logan's best friend looked back at him, and Logan couldn't help but feel it might be the last time they would see each other. Kelvin wore the guiltiest look imaginable, and Logan wished he could cross the room, grab him, pull him close, and tell him he wasn't responsible for what happened.

It wasn't Fate either that had snapped Kelvin's leg on Senior Night. It was worse—random misfortune. It wasn't Fate, misfortune, or Kelvin's late-night talks with Logan at the hotel that had killed their friends. It was a choice, one Logan Tramer had made alone.

He would say this, with Kelvin's face held in his hands, so convincingly, that Kelvin would have to believe it. But Logan didn't get to do any of that, and Kelvin's guilty look remained. All Logan could do was give him a head nod.

Then dust billowed between them, and he couldn't see either Kelvin or his sister. All he could do was hope they reached the tunnel before the ground split entirely.

Logan raced for the nearest opening. Red blades of light shot up from the earth, and crumbling rocks fell from above, threatening to block the exit. He squeezed through just before larger rocks finished sealing him inside the cavern. He passed through the gray mist, its cooling effect soothing his pain for a moment.

The pain returned, zapping through his whole body once he was out of the mist and into the void. Soon, he was ducking, then down on his knees, and eventually crawling on his belly when the tunnel narrowed, just like the one leading to and from the kitchen well.

It was very quiet.

No more rocks crushing together. No quaking beneath him. No red light consuming former worshippers who had now become confused innocents. He crawled forward in the dark, picturing the skeletal old folks—bones brittle and hair white—falling into the light. Descending one way or another. Then he pictured Mr. Tune, Mikey, Dr. Warren, and that poor Amish boy. They must have fallen too.

And what of his friends?

If Alex, Doug, Marshal, and Jessica had come back to life, what were they now? He wanted to hold onto hope, but it wasn't possible. Because Logan was alive. And there could be no wish without a consequence.

He wondered what they had looked like when they lay dead in the old house. When Tim found his father, he had seen something so horrendous that he had to leave town. Logan remembered sitting in the back pew of Red Springer's funeral, imagining the dead man breaking free of his closed casket.

After everything that happened, Logan still hadn't seen any bodies himself. Hell, even Doug had snuck into the morgue to take a look. Will had followed Ryan Holbrook into the Beaumonts' house to see them. Even Emily. His sister's life had been spared in the abandoned house so she must have walked past the bodies to climb down the well. Part of Logan felt left out, but another part of him felt spared.

He didn't deserve to be spared.

When he had climbed into his truck in the school parking lot after returning from the city a champion, Logan pulled off his medal because it began to irritate his skin, like he was allergic to the fabric. So much for the championship medal being better than the runner-up, he had thought then. Now he knew why his skin didn't want him to wear it.

Even his body was protesting his decision.

He crawled, letting his snapped leg drag behind him. Each

time he slid forward, pulling himself along with his arms, a new wave of pain tore up his leg and spine to his neck and face. Logan cried, hoping that not fighting the tears might bring some relief. He wondered how Kelvin had stayed so quiet while lying there at the free-throw line.

The pain became so repetitive that it felt as though Logan had come out the other side of it and could feel nothing. His mind was still protecting him, not fully realizing the predicament he was in.

Hope. Stupid, laughable, painful, irritating hope.

After everything he had done, Logan still wanted to save himself.

He followed the darkness, the standing water sloshing beneath his arms and belly. The walls scraped both shoulders, and the rocky top raked across his back.

Finally, he reached forward to drag himself, his hand catching on a half-moon entryway to the tunnel. He pulled himself through, grimacing and swallowing dirty water. Logan spit it out and grimaced again until he was out of the hole and into the well.

It was pitch-black except for a tiny sliver of light at the top. The light was blue, like it was reflecting from a full moon, not the sun.

It's already night, he thought, unsure of how time worked at the other end of the tunnel. He figured the gray mist was some kind of veil, but it didn't matter now. That place didn't exist anymore. Logan had wished it away.

He felt along the mossy brick and circled the well, hopping on one leg. The broken one was useless, limp. Even if he wanted to fight through the pain and use it, he couldn't. It was far beyond the manageable fracture it had been.

His good foot caught on something, and he reached down to feel something leathery and gooey. He traced his fingers along it until his fingernail tapped something tiny and hard inside a small hole. Logan dug further, pressing against something cushiony and dry. Then he reached down with his other hand and felt the hardness of a skull.

Logan backed away from the corpse, forgetting to hop. He landed on his broken leg. When he accidentally put the smallest amount of weight on it, he felt the shin bone bend further, the broken halves grinding together. He howled, white light flashing through his dark vision.

Logan didn't know how long he rested there, crying and yelling, waiting for the leg to go numb again. Eventually, his throat grew raw, and he couldn't cry anymore. He kept moving along the wall.

Then he came to cold, rusty metal.

A ladder.

Someone had been smart enough to install a ladder down this well. Much better than a rope looped around a spike, as if the noose at the kitchen well had been there to remind Logan of his aunt's death.

He took the ladder without hesitation. Relying heavily on his arms, he carefully hopped up each step with his good foot. Before long, he reached the top, and his fear was realized.

He knew where he was and cackled for only a moment but long enough to feel like he wasn't alone because of how unrecognizable the sound had been.

A thick board blocked the top of the well. He shoved at it, but it wouldn't budge. Logan peeked through the crack, seeing a sliver of the bright moon above but nothing else.

He screamed for help until his voice went out. He banged on the board until his knuckles bled. Soon, he had no fight left. He wrapped his arms around the ladder and rested his head on the top step. The coolness was a welcome reprieve from the fever he was no doubt running. His body shook. His broken leg dangled above the open air.

This well was even deeper than the kitchen well. A fall from this height would kill him. He would be just another corpse at the bottom.

Hope dragged out the inevitable.

Perhaps Will would figure out where Logan was after rescuing Emily and Kelvin from the kitchen well. But hope could only drag on for so long.

Night turned to day, and day turned back to night, with only a sliver of light through the wood to indicate the change. Eventually, Logan climbed back into the deepest dark to rest at the bottom of the well.

He didn't want to. He wanted Will to find him.

But where was he, exactly?

As his hope waned, Logan questioned himself. In this permanent dark, was here anywhere?

Thank you for reading

ABOUT THE AUTHOR

Michael Hallows is a left-handed shooting guard who never won STATE. This is his first novel.

instagram.com/mikehallowseve
facebook.com/mikehallowseve
threads.com/@mikehallowseve